Praise for

WILBUR SMITH

'A thundering good read is virtually the only way of describing
Wilbur Smith's books'
THE IRISH TIMES

'Wilbur Smith . . . writes as forcefully as his tough
characters act'
EVENING STANDARD

'Wilbur has arguably the best sense of place of any adventure
writer since John Buchan'
THE GUARDIAN

'Wilbur Smith is one of those benchmarks against whom
others are compared'
THE TIMES

'Best Historical Novelist – I say Wilbur Smith, with his
swashbuckling novels of Africa. The bodices rip and
the blood flows. You can get lost in Wilbur Smith and
misplace all of August'
STEPHEN KING

'Action is the name of Wilbur Smith's game and
he is the master'
THE WASHINGTOI

'A master story
THE SUNDAY 1

D0191193

Wilbur Smith is a global phenomenon: a distinguished author with a large and established readership built up over fifty-five years of writing, with sales of over 130 million novels worldwide.

Born in Central Africa in 1933, Wilbur became a full-time writer in 1964 following the success of *When the Lion Feeds*, and has since published over forty global bestsellers, including the Courtney Series, the Ballantyne Series, the Egyptian Series, the Hector Cross Series and many successful standalone novels, all meticulously researched on his numerous expeditions worldwide. His books have now been translated into twenty-six languages.

The establishment of the Wilbur & Niso Smith Foundation in 2015 cemented Wilbur's passion for empowering writers, promoting literacy and advancing adventure writing as a genre. The foundation's flagship programme is the Wilbur Smith Adventure Writing Prize.

For all the latest information on Wilbur, visit: www.wilbursmith books.com or facebook.com/WilburSmith

Imogen Robertson studied languages at Cambridge and was a TV director before her first novel *Instruments of Darkness* was published in 2009. She is the author of The Crowther and Westerman crime series and *The Paris Winter*. Her novels have been shortlisted for the CWA Historical Dagger three times. You can find her online at www.imogenrobertson.com or on twitter @RobertsonImogen

WILBUR SMITH

WITH
IMOGEN ROBERTSON

KING OF KINGS

ZAFFRE

First published in Great Britain in 2019 by

ZAFFRE
80–81 Wimpole St, London W1G 9RE

Copyright © Orion Mintaka (UK) Ltd, 2019
Author image © Hendre Louw

A CIP catalogue record for this book is
available from the British Library.

Paperback ISBN: 978-1-78576-847-7
Export ISBN: 978-1-78576-848-4

Also available as an ebook

1 3 5 7 9 10 8 6 4 2

Typeset by IDSUK (Data Connection) Ltd
Printed and bound in Great Britain by Clays Ltd, Elcograf S.p.A.

Zaffre is an imprint of Bonnier Books UK
www.bonnierbooks.co.uk

I dedicate this book to the gal I love, my Nisojon.
You keep my mind and heart ablaze,
with you beside me I fear nothing.

Part I
January 1887

Amber Benbrook was dazzled for a moment as she stepped out from the shadowy cool of the Gheziera Club into the Cairo sun. She lost her footing on the shallow steps that led down to the gravelled driveway, and instinctively clutched the arm of her fiancé, Major Penrod Ballantyne. He steadied her and looked down fondly into her lovely eyes. She smiled back up at him.

'I don't think I'm quite used to these new boots yet, Penny. The shop-girl said they are quite the latest thing and they were terribly expensive, but it seems they aren't really made to be walking about in.' She sighed and poked one foot out from under the long folds of her striped skirt, turning her ankle a little to examine her neat suede boots with their delicate low heel and elaborate fastenings of hooks, eyes and ribbons. 'In the harem I used to go about barefoot most days.'

Penrod clenched his jaw. Captain Burnett and Lieutenant Butcher of Her Majesty's Coldstream Guards were standing behind them in the shade of the portico. They would have certainly heard Amber's little speech, and her remark about the harem would be spread around the club before dinner.

Penrod admired Amber, loved her, even, but he would have to explain to her again that the fiancée of a senior officer should not speak of certain things in public, and her time living in the harem of Osman Atalan, numbered among the greatest enemies of the British Empire, was most certainly one of them.

In the fortnight since their engagement, Penrod had discovered that being linked to such a famous young lady had its disadvantages as well as its pleasures. Amber was in many ways a gemstone of the first water. She was beautiful, stunningly so. Her old nurse in the Sudan had called her al-Zahra, the Flower, and the name suited her. At sixteen, her figure was youthfully slim yet womanly, and although she had lived most of her life in Africa, her skin was the colour of cream and she had the blonde hair and blue eyes of an angel on a Christmas postcard. She also had an innocent charm, was clever without being opinionated and friendly without being forward. Thus far, she was an ideal choice for a man such as Penrod. He was an ambitious officer already decorated for his bravery, but he had a tendency to clash with his superiors from time to time and had a temper he could not always control. Such a charming and lovely wife should have been a perfect political asset, smoothing his ascent through the ranks to high command.

However it was not just Amber's beauty that made her famous: her history also made her an object of fascination. She was one of the few survivors of the siege of Khartoum, that terrible stain on British imperial pride. For ten months General Gordon, hero of British campaigns in China, had defended the city from the rebel warriors of Sudan and their spiritual leader, hailed as the Prophet reborn by his followers but called the 'Mad Mahdi' by the horrified reporters of the British newspapers. As Members of Parliament in Westminster and the leader writers of the London press demanded Gordon be saved, the ministers of state hesitated and the city was left to starve. Penrod had been the only intelligence officer able to slip across enemy lines and bring the messages and orders of their government to Gordon, and the British consul in the city, David Benbrook. Then Penrod had met the beautiful Benbrook girls, the eldest, Rebecca, acting as hostess over her father's table of scraps, and the twin sisters, Amber and Saffron, who spent most of their days grinding riverweed to feed the people. Penrod had fought on the walls of the city to fend off the repeated assaults of the Mahdi's warriors, and then led the government's troops through the treacherous desert to lift the siege, but relief came too late. Before the British forces could reach Khartoum, the dervishes launched one final attack across the river. Through a daze of hunger and fever, Amber Benbrook saw Gordon killed and her own father beheaded in the street as he tried to lead his family to safety.

Amber's twin, Saffron, had escaped with a trader who had also been caught up in the siege, a man called Ryder Courtney, whom she had since married, but Amber and her elder sister Rebecca were taken as spoils of war and held first by the Mahdi himself, then by his most powerful warlord, Osman Atalan. Penrod refused to desert the sisters but was betrayed as he infiltrated Osman's camp, then held as Osman's slave and tortured for many months.

Rebecca chose to make herself Osman's favourite concubine, convincing him Amber was still too young for his bed and instead making herself mistress of his appetites. For a time it seemed they had been forgotten, but Saffron, Ryder Courtney and Penrod's friends among the Arabs staged a daring rescue by river just as Amber's maturing beauty was provoking Osman's attentions. Rebecca, however, refused to leave. She was already pregnant with Osman's child. Certain it would be a son, she chose to raise him under his Islamic father's protection rather than to expose him to the scorn of her own people as a half-breed.

Amber spent the weeks after her rescue writing down everything she could remember about what had happened, and discovered in herself a talent for storytelling. The resulting book, *Slaves of the Mahdi*, become an international sensation. Everyone had read it, from the prime minister of Britain to the lowest paid, most ink-stained and incompetent clerk in government service in Cairo. Amber had been in England for the publication, but she could not leave Africa for long. She returned to Cairo and to Penrod in time for her sixteenth birthday, celebrated in Shepheard's Hotel with her twin. Amber and Penrod's engagement seemed a fitting end to the fairy tale.

At first Cairo society had welcomed Amber, but Penrod was increasingly aware that his fiancée did not act as a young English woman should, and her failure to do so was drawing comment. She did not tremble or faint at any mention of Khartoum, she described shooting a crocodile or a kudu with relish, and rather than refusing to speak of the terrible fate of her elder sister, Amber said openly that she was very sorry not to know her nephew, and she hoped that her elder sister Rebecca was happy with their friends in the harem. She had added that the baby would probably be much prettier than most, as Rebecca was beautiful and Osman Atalan very handsome. Every white mother in Cairo was deeply insulted by her remarks. The whispered commentary on her behaviour distressed and embarrassed Penrod. Unless Amber learned to follow the unwritten codes of the club and the army, she might not be such an asset to him in his career as he had expected. Then he considered her unfortunate association with Ryder Courtney. Penrod was the younger son of a baronet, and had a large private income from the family trust as well as his army pay. He had been educated at Harrow and discovered his talent for languages travelling through Europe before joining the army. He was an officer and a gentleman, born to command and loyal to Queen and Empire. Courtney was a trader, a self-made man who had fought for every penny he owned, and who was openly contemptuous of all forms of soldiering. It was true he had fought the dervish with great personal bravery, and played a key role in their escape from Osman Atalan, but Penrod would rather that his fiancée's sister had married a gamekeeper.

As Amber examined her boot, Penrod glanced upwards and noticed Lady Agatha Woodforde watching them from the balcony above, a slight smile on her lips. He felt a tug in his loins. She caught his eye and made a small moue of disdain. At once Penrod found himself recalling her naked body in a tangle of fine cotton sheets in his bedroom at Shepheard's Hotel. However, he dismissed the image from his mind. For now, at least, he would be faithful to his rather difficult young bride-to-be.

'Ballantyne! Watch your pockets!'

It was a shout from one of the officers still smirking at Amber's remark about the harem. Penrod twisted around and stared into the face of a dark-skinned boy of perhaps ten years old. The boy already had his slim hand in Penrod's coat pocket. He danced away a few steps as Penrod made a grab for him and opened his fist to show Penrod's 18-carat half-hunter pocket watch in his palm, then he turned and ran. The drivers and servants who were crowded in front of the club lunged after him, but he ducked and twisted and slipped through their fingers like an eel. Penrod glanced at Amber.

'Don't worry about me, Penny,' Amber said, slipping her arm from his. 'But do get your watch back.'

Penrod winked at her, then set off at a sprint in pursuit of the young pickpocket.

Amber watched him go and felt her skin flush. He was so handsome; watching him made her mouth go dry and her heart flutter in a way that was both delicious and frightening. Though her sister's subtle subterfuge meant Amber had left the harem untouched, she had heard enough while living there to know what she might expect on her wedding night. The idea of it, of doing such things with her beloved Penrod, made her both afraid and desperate to be married as soon as possible.

'Miss Benbrook?' Captain Burnett approached her from the shade of the veranda. 'Perhaps I can be of assistance. Do you require a carriage back to your hotel?'

She blinked at him. 'Why would I require your assistance for that? My Arabic is much better than yours.' Behind her, in the shadows of the entrance hall, Amber heard a rich female laugh. She turned to see a rather beautiful blonde woman walking towards them across the chequerboard floor of the lobby with the light, animal grace of a cat. Amber thought she recognised her, but knew they had never been introduced.

'That's you put in your place, Burnett!' the woman said, holding out her hand to Amber. 'My dear, I am Lady Agatha Woodforde and I am *so* delighted to meet you. I am a very old friend of Major Ballantyne's, you know. Do let me treat you to some tea while he is out chasing criminals.'

Amber thought rather longingly of her suite of rooms at Shepheard's Hotel. She wanted to change out of these horrible boots.

'I want to hear everything about your romance, my dear,' Lady Agatha continued smoothly, 'and I shall tell you all the dramatic details of Major Ballantyne's former service.'

Amber remembered when she had seen her before. On occasion, when Amber had walked by a group of ladies and gentlemen on the club grounds, she had felt their gaze on her, then heard a burst of laughter just after she had passed. It had made her uncomfortable, exposed. More than once she had turned back and seen Lady Agatha at the centre of the group, watching her. Though now she seemed friendly enough.

'Do join me! Though it is too bad of Penrod to dash off and leave you like that for the sake of a pocket watch.'

'I gave him that watch,' Amber said simply. 'It's engraved.'

Lady Agatha laughed again, showing her even white teeth. 'That explains it! He had to go, of course, if it was a present from *you*.'

She smiled and touched Amber's sleeve. It was too tempting. Amber could never tire of talking about Penrod, and even Saffron, who was an indulgent sister most of the time, had started rolling her eyes when Amber talked about him and their wedding plans. A suspicion flitted across Amber's mind and she looked at Agatha narrowly. She was beautiful, but she was quite old, Amber decided. She must be at least twenty-five. Comforted, she gave Lady Agatha her hand and allowed herself to be led away.

. . .

The boy had a good start on him, but Penrod felt that he was not really putting his full effort into his escape. Penrod was almost insulted. As they raced across the bridge and into the city, dodging between the water-sellers in their sky-blue *galabiyyas* with swollen waterskins over their shoulders, and the carriages of the Europeans going from club to office to home, the boy paused and looked back, and when he saw that Penrod was still pursuing him at speed, he grinned before running on again. As soon as they were off the bridge, Penrod expected the boy to turn into the maze of twisting narrow lanes that formed the Arab quarter, but instead he continued down the main open boulevard, past the handsome frontage of the Opera House and the Esbekeeyah Gardens. The boy danced through the crowds of Abyssinians and Turks, European tourists balanced awkwardly on patient donkeys, Albanians with their multicoloured sashes, and the proud, aloof-looking Bedouins.

'What are you playing at, my boy?' Penrod wondered aloud and increased his speed. The boy was cursed in a dozen languages as, with a graceful bound, he leaped a low ornamental box hedge like a champion hurdler and tore across the grass, then sprang back on to the roadway, ducked under the nose of an affronted camel, and headed into the narrow shadows of the buildings opposite. Penrod drew the hot, spiced air of the city deeper into his lungs and felt the prick of sweat under his collar. The pleasure of the chase fired his blood and he lengthened his stride.

The boy looked back over his shoulder. His small face showed shock and concern as he realised Penrod was gaining on him. He dropped his head and lifted his knees, quickening his pace, then swung suddenly right into the silk bazaar. Penrod swore and forced himself to go faster, knowing the twisting labyrinth of alleyways would make a perfect hiding place for the thief. He must not let him out of his sight even for a moment; the watch had special value to him. As the road narrowed, two men carrying a large wicker cage full of live turkeys and slung on a pole between them started to cross in front of the speeding boy. He dropped into a crouch and skidded below the swinging cage on the heels of his leather sandals. Bemused, the two men set down their load to stare after him. Penrod shouted a warning as he leaped over the cage, touching his hand to the dusty pavement as he landed, then springing up and after the boy again.

They raced down the long line of shallow shopfronts hung with woven silks in golds and purples, the shopkeepers quickly sweeping their goods out of the way of the charging pair. Penrod was gaining on the boy as he turned sharply right into a narrow courtyard and a sudden shaft of light struck Penrod like a blow after the deep shade of the main bazaar. The boy grabbed hold of the central fountain and used his momentum to swing around and hard left. The change in direction almost worked, but Penrod let his instincts, honed by years of triumph on the polo ground and battlefield, guide him and he pushed off from the fountain base with his left foot, throwing himself sideways and after the child. The boy was nervous now, looking back to check the progress of his pursuer too often. Old Arab men in white and green turbans raised their delicate coffee cups, shielded them with long fingers and began placing bets on the outcome of the race. The boy looked back again and stumbled into the wares of a tinsmith, scattering his goods to the ground with a crash, but before the stallholder could get his fingers on the boy's trailing rags he was up and off again. Penrod hung to the right wall, climbing a precarious pile of thin tea chests to avoid the scattered metalwork, then hurled himself towards the boy like an eagle swooping on a rabbit. His quarry turned once more and it seemed that at last the boy's luck had run out. This was a dead end, a gap between houses filled with rubbish and burst barrels. The boy darted left through a wooden gateway left half ajar under a sandstone arch. Penrod followed just in time to see the boy race up the stone stairs from the courtyard to a studded cedar door that led to the interior of the house. He plunged after him into the sudden darkness of the old house and followed the sound of the boy's feet upwards. A woman stepped out onto a landing and screamed, covering her face as Penrod dashed by. The stairs became more rough and unfinished as they climbed, small children and curious cats watched them from narrow doorways, then suddenly Penrod was out into the light and heat of the afternoon sun once more, on a flat rooftop dotted with storage bins and washing lines. He caught sight of the boy through the shifting cotton sheets and ran once more over the twisted and irregular jigsaw of the roof. The boy came to a sudden stop in front of him, his arms windmilling. He was at the edge of the roof, staring over the low parapet at the fatal drop back into one of the twisting alleyways. He had nowhere left to run. Between the boy and the next rooftop was a chasm some eight feet across. Penrod felt a moment of satisfaction, then he saw the boy take a step back and crouch down.

'Don't do it, boy!' Penrod shouted, but the boy had already launched himself forward and into the air, his limbs flailing.

Penrod skidded to a halt at the edge of the roof, prepared for the sickening sight of the boy's small body broken below him. But no, the boy had almost made it across the gap. He was hanging by one hand from a slight overhang of the opposite roof. But there was no balcony or awning beneath him to break his fall, no place for his thrashing feet to find a grip. A man shouted from below and suddenly the pit of the alley was full of faces looking upwards. None of them were laughing now; they were mesmerised by the imminence of death. For a moment Penrod was tempted to leave the boy, let him fall and collect his watch from the corpse. The child obviously did not have the strength to pull himself up again; it would be only a matter of seconds until he lost his grip and fell. Plaster crumbled under the boy's hand and he slipped an inch with a small frightened yelp. Penrod thought of Amber. How would he tell her he'd done nothing to try and save this child? He could lie, of course, but he was keeping enough secrets as it was. He sighed, turned and retreated a dozen strides from the edge of the roof, then lowered his shoulders and sprinted back. At the edge of the roof he pushed off with all his strength and speed. He heard a scream, a gabbled prayer below him, then he landed hard but cleanly on the opposite roof. The boy cried out again; the jolt of Penrod's landing had jarred him and he lost his last desperate fingerhold. He began to fall, then a strong hand gripped his wrist and Penrod hauled him up onto the rooftop. The boy would have tried to run even then, but Penrod kept a firm hold of him, lifting him up by his thin shoulders.

The boy recovered quickly. As Penrod held him suspended in mid-air, he let out a stream of insults and complaints in Arabic. He could talk as well as he could run. But he wasted no words thanking Penrod for his rescue; instead he called on Allah to witness the cruelty of the *ferengi*, and then he begged every *djinn* now resident in Cairo to pity him and come to his aid, and defend him against the monstrous accusation of thievery that was such an insult to his honour, the honour of his forefathers and the honour of the city itself. Penrod grinned as he listened, setting the boy down halfway through this tirade and, while keeping him from escaping with a firm grip, brushing the dust from his trousers and smoothing his hair with his spare hand. Then when it seemed the boy would never run out of breath, he said, in the same language: 'Empty your pockets, honoured son of Cairo, or I swear by the Prophet, peace be upon him, I shall put you back where I found you, hanging off the end of the roof gables.'

The boy was suddenly silent. He looked into Penrod's eyes and whatever he saw in them convinced him it would be better to obey rather than argue any longer. He dug his hand into his robe, retrieved the watch and presented it to Penrod on his open palm.

Penrod took it and restored it to his own pocket, but did not let the boy go.

'And the rest.'

This brought another wail of protest, but Penrod lifted the boy on to his toes so his robe pressed against his throat and began dragging him back towards the edge of the roof. The boy squealed, dug into the folds again and produced a handful of silver coins, which he flung at Penrod's feet. Then he began to weep.

The tears of women or children did not have much effect on Penrod, but he was surprised. He would have expected a thief like this one to have a collection of small items: purses, jewellery, not a handful of freshly minted English shillings such as these. He frowned at them as they glinted in the dust among the flickering shadows of the drying cottons hanging on the wash lines above them.

The boy saw his tears were having no effect. He sniffed then began to talk again. This time he spoke of his poverty, his mother's sickness, of how he was trying to take care of her by guiding an honoured *effendi* like himself around Cairo. Of course, he could see that Penrod was no ordinary tourist, but he, Adnan, son of Mohammed, knew all the secret places in Cairo where a rich man might be entertained: gambling, women, drink and opium-soaked scenes of delight straight from the pages of *The Arabian Nights*.

Penrod shook him until he was quiet again. He thought of the way the boy showed him the watch just after he had stolen it, how at first he had run more slowly and down the wide boulevards where Penrod could follow him easily, the expression on his face early in the race as he looked back to check if Penrod was still following him.

Penrod spun around and used two hands to lift Adnan off the ground and brought his face close to the boy's. 'Who paid you to steal from me, Adnan?'

• • •

The Ladies' Veranda of the Gheziera Club was a triumph of elegant design, bringing the best of European and Egyptian architecture together to create a cool and tranquil Eden in the heat of the afternoon. Servants in pristine white kaftans, sewn with gold thread at the throat and wrists, each wearing a dull scarlet fez, moved between the low tables carrying trays of bitter black coffee, silver teapots and mounds of delicate patisserie that would be the envy of the best Parisian hotels. For the officers and men they carried mixed drinks, beaded with moisture and crackling with ice. For the ladies, lemonade that tasted both sweet and sour and was as refreshing as bathing in pure spring water.

Lady Agatha led Amber to a pair of low sofas in a corner, shielded by the delicate fronds of growing palms. At the far end of the room a string quartet was playing something soothing and gentle, and under the hum of general conversation Amber could hear the trickling music of the central fountain, where a stone goddess poured the water of the Nile eternally into a shallow pool lined in sparkling turquoise mosaic.

As Lady Agatha ordered for them, Amber held her little reticule on her knee and observed her. Amber did not know a great deal about clothes other than she liked them, and though she had learned to dress hair in the most elaborate styles in the harem, they were not the styles approved of in Cairo. She knew enough though to tell that Lady Agatha was marvellously well dressed. The cut of her tight satin jacket suggested both sophistication and modesty while emphasising the curves and swells of her body. Her skirts were full and long and a startling white, but their scarlet satin stripe and lace fringing gave them an original dash. What was most remarkable about her clothes, however, was the way Lady Agatha seemed to take no notice of them. Amber could not stop herself fidgeting and itching. Her corset pinched her, the lace around her neck scratched. She was forever trying to loosen one thing or tighten something else but whatever she did, she could never get comfortable. Her twin, Saffron, was of little or no help. She wore breeches and long shirts she borrowed from her husband when they were on the trail in the wilds of East Africa, and for formal occasions would produce from her trunk some elaborate evening dress of her own design. These dresses drew gasps of wonder and envy from every woman in the room, but Saffron seemed as easy in them as she did in her travelling gear. The style, however, did not suit Amber at all. She had once tried one on, but when she'd emerged from the dressing room in the hotel, Saffron had laughed so hard at her she had given herself hiccups. So Amber was condemned to the dressmakers of Bond Street and Parisian-trained guardians of couture plying their needles in the European quarter of Cairo.

'Now we may have our talk,' Lady Agatha said as the waiter brought them their lemonade, cakes and tea, served in the English manner.

For a while Amber listened happily. Lady Agatha knew all sorts of interesting details from Penrod's early career and Amber was fascinated by her account of his fighting retreat from the disaster at El Obeid, and of the reception he'd received when he returned to Cairo. Amber forgot about her awkward clothes, and the suspicious laughter of Lady Agatha's friends, and told her stories about Khartoum, Penrod's time as a captive of Osman Atalan and the humiliating privations he endured.

'And now we are to be married. I don't think anyone has ever been happier than I am.'

Lady Agatha put her head on one side. 'My dear girl! How romantic!' She seemed to hesitate. 'Should I say nothing? Oh, I wish I could stay silent and let you enjoy this happiness.'

Amber thought suddenly of the cobra she had once stumbled upon in the scrub just outside Khartoum, how it raised itself and stared at her, swaying its beautiful head from side to side. She felt the same instinctive, sickly fear she had felt then, the same sense of being frozen and helpless.

'Amber – I do hope I may call you Amber, my dear – I must ask you: are you sure you know Major Ballantyne *quite* as well as you think you do?'

'Of c-course I am,' Amber replied faintly.

Lady Agatha's voice became a soft purr. 'I *am* glad. Then you will not be surprised by anything he has said and done. You must know it all already! You see, he told me everything in confidence while you were in England seeing to the publication of your *thrilling* little book. *Of course* nothing I could say about Penrod would surprise you, dear, but for the sake of my conscience I must make sure you are aware of what he said to me about your family, and about your beautiful, tragic older sister in particular. Rebecca is her name, is it not?'

For the next twenty minutes Agatha talked in her lovely, lilting voice while Amber's world collapsed around her. Each word she spoke pierced Amber's naive heart like a dagger forged of the finest Damascene steel. When Agatha finally stopped speaking and let go of her hands, Amber stood up at once. Agatha looked like a pretty cat on the sofa with her cakes and cream, her ease and elegance.

'I . . . I must go,' Amber said.

'I think that's best,' Lady Agatha replied without even bothering to look up, instead admiring her manicured fingernails. Her voice was cold.

Amber turned and hurried blindly towards the door, unable to comprehend what she had just heard, but at the same time believing every word. She had to get away before she burst into tears in front of all these people. She almost succeeded, but her fashionable little boots betrayed her again and she slipped on the marble tiles near the threshold of the lobby. One of the waiters reached out an arm for her, but he was late and clumsy and they fell together, the tray of empty glasses he was carrying in his other hand crashing to the floor. Even the string quartet stopped playing to turn and look at them as Amber struggled to her feet.

'I'm sorry, I'm sorry . . . ' She pushed away the hands that reached out to help her, then ran down the steps, out into the bright sunlight and into the first waiting carriage. She managed to ask for Shepheard's Hotel, then fell back against the upholstery.

From the veranda of the Gheziera Club the cream of Anglo-Egyptian society watched her go, followed by the low, musical laughter of Lady Agatha.

. . .

When Penrod heard that a beautiful blonde English lady had paid Adnan to steal his watch and lead him on a good long chase, his heart went cold.

He let the boy go and headed for the dark well of the staircase, which would lead him back to the street. Adnan scooped the coins from the dust, then followed him.

'She said it was for a joke! You British like jokes?' Adnan was trying out his English now. His voice echoed surprisingly as they descended into the shadows. It was strangely quiet after the noise of the street.

'Get away from me!' Penrod snapped at him, but the boy stuck close, skipping down the steps behind him. Penrod reached the bottom of the stairs and let himself out into the main courtyard.

'You will not have me arrested? Perhaps you think it was a good joke, too?'

The crowd who had watched the chase and rescue from below now crowded around them. Adnan received a series of gentle cuffs around the top of his head and Penrod was praised and congratulated in Arabic, English and French. He heard himself called a warrior, a miracle, unseen hands brushed dust from his uniform, people grasped his wrists, patted his back, blessed him. Penrod kept moving forward until the crowd parted and he turned into the main bazaar. He saw nothing, heard nothing until another hand grabbed his sleeve. His impatience overwhelmed him and he lifted his fist to strike the offender.

'Hey, master, be good to Yakub!'

Penrod lowered his arm. His vision cleared a little and he realised he was looking into the face of an old friend and ally.

Yakub had guided him across the desert to Khartoum, and risked his life to help Penrod escape the slavery of Osman Atalan. Penrod managed to nod a greeting. Yakub examined his face and frowned, then he turned his attention to Adnan, who still jogged along at Penrod's side. It seemed news of the chase had already reached Yakub's ears.

'You stole from *Ababdan Riji*? Are you mad, you little frog? Why do you think we name him "One who never turns back"?'

'I was not told his name,' Adnan said sulkily.

'What shall I do with him, master?' Yakub asked. 'Throw him in the river? Have him shut up in the gaol? If the other thieves don't eat him, the cockroaches will.'

'Give him honest work, if he can do it,' Penrod told him. His voice sounded cracked and hollow. 'But leave me alone now, both of you.'

The shopkeepers along the narrow way raised their coffee cups to him, but Penrod ignored them all. He pushed aside the offered bolts of silk and thought back instead to the last night he had spent with Lady Agatha. It was only a month ago, while Amber was still in England. Agatha had suggested they smoke opium together, and he, languorous after the heat of their love-making, had agreed. It had been beautiful to watch her, her heavy white breasts swinging free under her silk dressing gown as she carefully prepared the drug; a little brown bubbling ball in the cup of the pipe. He had thought the drug overrated, although it had induced a pleasant haze and introduced a slower, more sensual note to their caresses. It was easier to be slow, to savour her full, ripe body under its influence. But then . . . What had happened then? They had lain together in the cool shadows drinking a fine old brandy and he had told her about his adventures in Khartoum, how he had seduced the eldest daughter of David Benbrook, Rebecca, taking her virginity as easily as one might pluck a ripe fig from a wayside tree. He had told Agatha that when he realised Rebecca had also made love to Ryder Courtney, he had decided he was under no obligation to her. Since then, of course, Rebecca had become whore to the Mahdi himself, then after his death, to Penrod's blood enemy, Osman Atalan. Had he used that word, 'whore'? Yes, he had.

He walked back along the boulevard towards Zamalek Island and the Gheziera Club, but the sights and sounds were lost to him. He could think only of that night, talking to Lady Agatha, telling her everything. What a fool he had been! He knew Lady Agatha was a jealous snake, but the drug had fatally loosened his tongue. Penrod understood Rebecca had performed the office of concubine to save her sister's and her own lives, but he had not explained that to Lady Agatha. No, instead he had said: 'Osman Atalan can have the whore, and I will take the virgin bride.' His mouth went dry. Had Lady Agatha flinched when he said that? Perhaps. It was possible that Agatha had still expected to be Penrod's wife herself until he had uttered that fatal remark. Shortly afterwards Amber had arrived back in Cairo to celebrate her birthday with her twin. She was flushed with the success of her book, suddenly wealthy in her own right and so obviously in love with him. They had announced their engagement. Penrod had not made any effort to warn Agatha.

He was nearly at the club. His hand closed around his rescued watch. The gold was cool to the touch. He knew the inscription without looking at it: *To Penrod, Always, Amber.* A shy and simple declaration. Perhaps Lady Agatha did not mean to say anything offensive to Amber, perhaps she was only curious. Perhaps he would find them both talking fashions and wedding arrangements and his only punishment for his indiscretions would be that sly, sensual look from his former lover. He began to walk more quickly, and that small flame of hope tried to flicker into life, even though he knew it was false.

S affron Courtney, née Benbrook, was already tired of Cairo. It had taken them two weeks to reach the city, travelling through the Ethiopian highlands on ill-tempered donkeys, then by steamer from Djibouti up the Red Sea to Suez and then here. After the first excitement of seeing Amber was over, Saffron had felt listless and bored. If she had had a studio here, a home, it would have been more bearable, but stuck in the hotel in the middle of the city she had nothing to fill her days. Ryder was out from morning until evening, and Penrod kept taking Amber to the stupid Gheziera Club. Ryder Courtney was not deemed worthy to be a member, so Saffron refused to go anywhere near the place. Penrod, who of course played polo at the club, was always taking Amber on to the little island on which the club-house stood. Saffron snorted. They had even made the gardens look like an English estate. Idiots. Why come to Africa at all if you wanted to pretend you were still living in Chelsea?

Saffron liked the bazaars and narrow streets of Cairo, how the light was softened by the balconies of the old houses, which hung so close together in places the women could pass each other sweetmeats across the alleyways, and the great stacks of glinting metal goods, mounds of dates and almonds, and open sacks of red and yellow spice. She went out to paint what she saw, but found herself surrounded and harassed. Once she dressed as a boy and wandered around with her sketchbook. She was thrilled with the drawings she made that day, but even Ryder's friends had been horrified at the idea of a European woman going about dressed in men's clothing and they had made her promise not to do it again. In her luxurious suite in the Shepheard's Hotel, all she could do was paint still lifes: bowls of fruit and flowers, which irritated her so much that when Ryder said he thought her work in progress 'very pretty', she had pelted him with oranges.

She was also profoundly bored with being pregnant and feeling sick made her cross. When Ryder told her they might have to be in the city several months longer while he made his arrangements for his next enterprise, she had burst into tears. She was not a woman who cried often, and the incident had surprised her as much as it had Ryder. He had said something about taking a house, something small and not in the European Quarter, so she might feel less confined, but she had been so sick and miserable by that point, she couldn't tell if he really meant it. The people at the Gheziera Club might not approve of the Courtneys setting up in such a place, but Saffron thought they could go hang. In her own house she'd be able to entertain her husband's Arab friends and get their children to pose for her. She bit her fingernails and hoped very hard that Ryder *had* meant it. However, he had a great deal on his mind at the moment.

While hunting mountain nyala in the mountains east of Adrigat some years ago, Ryder had discovered signs of what might be a large deposit of silver-bearing ore. He had sent the sample to the assay office of the Cape Colony and when they escaped from Khartoum and made their way to the court of Emperor John in Abyssinia, they found the report waiting for them. It confirmed the ore was rich with the precious metal. She and Ryder were both favoured in the Abyssinian court. Ryder had brought the emperor news of the dervish activities on his borders, and the empress had made a pet of Saffron, proudly wearing dresses of her design. They had acquired all the proper permits, agreed what percentage of the silver mined would go to the emperor's treasury and sent agents to purchase the land and negotiate with the local chiefs. Since then, Saffron knew her husband's every second thought had been of the strike and how to exploit it. Now they were in Cairo he was spending all his time with mining engineers and experts in metallurgy.

Saffron knew Ryder loved the highlands of Tigray. The landscape was an astonishing series of high plains and steep valleys studded with ancient churches cut into the rocks and monasteries perched on the highest peaks, only accessible by rickety rope ladders. Like the desert it was burning hot in the day and cold at night, but its beauty was more striking than the austere grandeur of the Sahara. Lush after the rains, its meadows would fill with game, exotic birds and strange purple and white blooms. In the dry season, when the landscape turned to the colour of a lion's pelt, the villages would stand out as vivid patches of emerald green. The people were farmers who measured their wealth in friends and livestock, but they were also storytellers and singers of wit and grace, inheritors of a culture rich with myth and mystery. The site of the prospective mine was in an isolated and uninhabited valley three miles from the nearest village, and Saffron longed to be there with her husband. Every night after they made love she asked Ryder to describe it all to her again and explain every detail of how the camp would be laid out, where they would grow their food and keep the animals, the workers' huts, the buildings they would need to process the ore. After years of trading across Africa, Ryder wanted to build something permanent. He believed the mine could make him very wealthy, but he also wanted to bring wealth to the people of Tigray. He talked of training engineers and metalworkers from the local population, of how the profits of the mine might protect them all from the vicissitudes of famine or war. Saffron could imagine no higher happiness than helping him, bringing up their children as the mine grew, and she desperately wanted this exciting future to start at once. However, such an undertaking needed a huge amount of planning. Ryder wanted to recruit a handful of American and European mining experts. He needed men experienced in working in isolated locations, so began looking for veterans of the great Comstock silver strike in Western Utah. He also needed time to gather the equipment required to process the ore. Saffron was not very interested in the details of the machinery. When Ryder began talking about quicksilver, amalgamating pans, feeders and stamps, she stopped listening. It all seemed very expensive, and very heavy, so difficult to transport into the mountains, but she had complete faith in her husband's ability to arrange everything to perfection. She only wished it wasn't taking so long.

In the meantime she gazed dreamily out of the window. So it was she who saw Amber return to the hotel from Zamalek Island. Even from this angle Saffron could tell something was wrong with her sister. She felt it in her chest, a sudden sick squeeze of the heart. She jumped up from her seat, her own troubles forgotten, and hurried to Amber's rooms.

• • •

Penrod asked after his fiancée at the club gates. The servants all knew Miss Benbrook – an English girl who looked like a flower grown from the first rains, who could also speak a fluent, classical Arabic that made them feel as if they were all poets, was not quickly forgotten. Penrod could also tell from their narrowed eyes and short replies that Amber had not looked happy when she left, and they, her champions, blamed him. Let them think what they liked. While he was asking his questions, Captain Burnett sauntered past. The captain stopped by Penrod and paused to light a cigarette. The flame swayed slightly.

'Miss Benbrook's run off again, Ballantyne,' he said in a drawl. 'Was taking tea with Lady A, then dashed off in the most peculiar manner.' He blew a lungful of blue-grey smoke into the afternoon air and chuckled to himself. 'Tried to throw herself into the arms of one of the Arab servants on her way out. I suppose you can take the girl out of the harem, but old habits die hard!'

Penrod's hand went to the hilt of his sabre, but Burnett was swept out of the way by Lieutenant Butcher.

'Shut up, you idiot,' he hissed at his friend before turning to Penrod. 'Apologies, Major. Man's had too much sun.' He hustled Burnett in the direction of the shade, while still bowing and smiling slavishly towards Penrod.

Penrod watched them go, then stepped into the carriage waiting at the top of the line. He gave his orders for the Shepheard's Hotel brusquely. The driver set off with a sharp jerk, which Penrod was sure was deliberate.

．　．　．

When Penrod was shown into the private sitting room of Amber's suite, his fiancée was alone. Her small face was very pale, but her manner was calm. Too calm. Amber was a girl of quick smiles, a keen, witty observer of the world around her. Not until he saw her as she was now, her expression so blank she might have been carved from marble, did he realise how much he loved that liveliness, that enthusiasm for life she wore like some women wear jewels. Jewels. A sparkle of diamonds caught his eye: it was the engagement ring he had given her so recently, a simple circlet of small but perfectly cut diamonds lying on the small rosewood table in front of the empty fireplace. He had sent Yakub to buy it and barely glanced at it himself, but he remembered the look in her eyes when he gave it to her – she had shone with happiness.

'Major Ballantyne, please take the ring. Our engagement is over.' Now she spoke quietly, with no inflection or emphasis in her voice.

Penrod forced an indulgent, affectionate laugh and held out his hands. 'My darling girl, I have no idea what poisonous rubbish that woman has told you, but please ignore it. Agatha arranged for that little pickpocket to steal from me to get the chance to speak to you alone and slander me. She is jealous, that is all.'

Amber stepped swiftly away from him so the low coffee table was between them. 'I know that, Penrod. She was your lover, wasn't she?'

He did not reply, but let his hands fall to his sides.

'I thought so,' Amber continued. 'Whether she said it out of jealousy or not, I still think everything she told me was true.

She wouldn't have enjoyed saying it so much if she were lying.
So I cannot marry you.'

Penrod had felt fear very rarely in his life, but he felt it now.
He pushed it down.

'That's ridiculous.'

Amber turned towards him. He saw in her eyes a flash of sudden rage and her cheeks were flushed.

'Ridiculous? Did you or did you not seduce my sister Rebecca?'

Her anger awoke his own, and he held on to it like a friend.
'I did. Your sister, my dear girl, was rather easy to seduce. Ryder Courtney had her too before she was bundled into a harem. A place for which she has a natural talent, I can assure you.'

'You monster! She saved my *life*! If she had not protected me . . .' She rested one hand on the mantelpiece, looking away from him. He could see her thin shoulders shaking as she struggled to control herself. 'I know about my sister and Mr Courtney, so you can't throw that at me. Ryder Courtney is a better man than you are. *He* told Saffron all about it. *He* felt that Saffron should know everything before they married. *He* asked Rebecca to marry him but she hoped that you were coming back, so she refused him. Ryder told Saffron everything because he is a good man, not like you and your stupid friends at that stupid club who think you are all so superior. Officers and gentlemen? The morals were better in the harem.'

Penrod's voice was icy. 'I did come back. I came back for both of you.'

'But you'd already decided you could never marry her by then, hadn't you, Penrod? That she would be an embarrassment to you? I bet you were relieved when you found that she was staying there, choosing to remain in the hands of that monster Osman Atalan to protect her baby. She did everything to save me. To save *me*, Penrod. Then you go to that viper Lady Agatha's bed and dare to call my sister Rebecca a whore.' She made no attempt to hide her disgust.

He tried to soften his voice. 'Rebecca gave herself to me. Very willingly. Was I supposed to be pleased to find myself tied to a concubine? I know you are just a child and can't possibly understand such things, Amber, but yes, I am glad she stayed. If I'd been forced to marry her, my career would have been ruined. Now be sensible, my silly girl, and put your ring back on.'

He had turned away slightly as he spoke, wanting to hide his own rising emotion from her. When he turned back he was gazing into the muzzle of a Webley revolver. Amber's hand was steady now, and her finger was on the trigger.

'You, Major Ballantyne, were never fit to touch a hair on my sister's head. You are not worthy of licking the dust from her feet. And you are not worthy of me either. Was I a silly girl when I washed your filth off you while you were dying, tortured by Osman Atalan? Was I a silly girl when I killed the dervish who was about to split you in half by the river in Khartoum? Do you think I am silly now?' She cocked the hammer of the revolver with her thumb. David Benbrook had taught all his daughters to be experts with firearms.

'Get out of this room, Major Ballantyne, or I swear to God, for Rebecca's sake, I will shoot you dead where you stand.' She was staring at him with an expression of utter contempt. She was brave, beautiful, and implacable.

Penrod drew in one deep breath, then bowed to her. 'I see you have made up your mind and nothing I can say will change it. I will leave you then with my warmest wishes for your every happiness.' He walked out of the room, closing the door calmly behind him as he left.

Amber lowered the gun, carefully uncocked it and removed the bullets, like her father had taught her, before laying it down in its box on the mantelpiece. Then her strength finally gave way and she fell to her knees and wept quietly.

P enrod descended the wide mahogany staircase to the hotel lobby in a sort of stupor. She didn't mean it, he told himself. She was upset. Agatha had shocked her, but once Amber had been given time to think, she would come back to him. No one need know anything about it. A note would be waiting for him at the club or at his house before nightfall.

As his polished boot hit the tile of the lobby he heard his name called. It was Ryder Courtney, leaning up against the bar with his mining cronies. Ryder was a tall man, broad-shouldered with thick, black, tousled hair and deeply tanned skin. While every other Englishman in the city was either in uniform, or wearing a high starched collar and tie, Ryder was dressed with his usual casual disregard for custom or fashion. He wore a scarf as a loose cravat and a long leather travelling coat. He looked as if he still had the dust of the Abyssinian highlands on his boots.

'Ballantyne, come and raise a glass with us! Saffy and I have a house here. Our wives will be able to fuss over weddings and babies, then when they start fighting, Saffy and I will head to Axum. We are going to mine silver and these fine gentlemen will find me the expertise and the materials. Come have a drink to the latest Courtney enterprise.'

Penrod crossed the space between them in three short strides. He grabbed Courtney by the collar and brought his face close to his.

'Couldn't keep your mouth shut about the sister, could you?'

Ryder stopped smiling, set his tumbler carefully down on the bar and looked at Penrod calmly. 'I told my wife the truth about what happened between me and Rebecca, if that's what you mean. Saffy deserved to hear it. If you've lied to Amber and have been found out, that's your problem, soldier-boy.'

The men either side of them could hear the low growl of threat in Ryder's voice. They picked up their drinks and moved quietly to a discreet distance.

Penrod felt his rage blossom in him like a dark flower. 'You're a disgrace, Courtney. You make me ashamed to be an Englishman. Spilling your guts out to a woman. Well, you've done it now. Amber has decided she doesn't want to marry me any more, so I suppose you are saddled with her.'

Ryder moved fast, bringing his hands up and through the hold Penrod had on his collar and bursting it apart with the explosive force of his broad, muscled forearms. Penrod staggered back and Ryder hunched his shoulders and bent his knees a little, ready to move. One of the waiters had stopped in the middle of polishing the glasses and was staring at them open-mouthed. His colleague, obviously better at spotting the signs of trouble, was swiftly removing the better bottles of champagne from the cut-glass shelving behind the bar and securing them under the mahogany countertop.

'Amber's a good girl, better than you deserve, and she will always have a home with me and Saffy if she wants one. She'll breathe cleaner air in the highlands rather than in that swamp of a club with you.'

Penrod charged at him. Ryder was waiting for him to move and was the larger man, but he recognised a murderous rage in Penrod's eyes that startled him. Penrod delivered an explosive uppercut to Ryder's jaw. Ryder felt the pain burst in a white blast through his skull, and realised with amazement that Penrod was going to try and kill him with his bare hands. He blocked Penrod's following left and concentrated his own power into a punch into Penrod's kidneys. It was a blow that would have slowed a bull elephant; it lifted Penrod off his feet and slammed him back into a pyramid of champagne glasses. They exploded into a storm of shards and scattered across the marble floor. Penrod didn't even seem to feel it. He grabbed on to the brass rail that ran along the upper edge of the bar and used it to launch himself into a flying kick at Ryder's chest. It forced all the air from Ryder's lungs and he staggered back. Penrod grabbed a solid soda syphon behind him and lifted himself up to smash it across Ryder's temple. Somewhere a woman screamed. Ryder dodged the blow, twisting sideways, but it caught him on his forehead. The skin split and blood ran into his eyes, but he trusted his gut and his answering left hook connected. The syphon was knocked from Penrod's hand and spun across the floor, but Penrod leaped forward like a lion attacking a buffalo. Ryder went down heavily on his back, with Penrod on top of him, and felt Penrod's hands close around his throat. Ryder got his left hand free and struck Penrod again and again in the ribs. He felt the bone crack under his fist, but the grip on his throat never weakened. Ryder looked into Penrod's eyes and saw in them the killing fury of a carnivorous animal. For the first time in his life, Ryder was afraid he was taking his last breaths. Black spots appeared in his vision and he felt the strength draining from his limbs.

Suddenly the world seemed to explode about them. The crystal chandelier that had been hanging on the high ceiling above them was now hurtling down on them both. The barmen leaped for cover. Penrod released his grip, and both men wrapped their arms around their heads and rolled out of the way. The glittering mass exploded on the black and white tiles, and Ryder found himself covered in shards of glass. He twisted around and saw his wife, the shotgun she had just fired into the ceiling already broken and hanging over the crook of her arm. She was watching Penrod, her mouth set in a firm line and her honey eyes glittering as if they were reflecting every shattered remnant of the Shepheard's chandelier. The complete silence was broken only by the crackle of glass as one of the barmen stood up from his hiding place to see what had happened, his drying cloth still held in his left hand.

Ryder got carefully to his feet and coughed, rubbing his bruised throat. He could taste his own blood in his mouth, sweet and metallic, and the air stank of spilled alcohol. He pulled off his scarf and pressed it to the wound on his scalp.

'I'm sorry to interrupt, Major Ballantyne, gentlemen,' Saffron said crisply. Ryder's cronies smiled at her weakly. 'But I would like to have a word with my husband in private. Would you mind excusing us for a moment?'

Penrod got to his feet and brushed the glass from his coat, then smoothed his thick blond hair back into place. His hand shook a little as he did, but that look of animal frenzy in his eyes had faded.

'Of course, Mrs Courtney. Good day to you.' He bowed to her, receiving a microscopic nod in return, then turned and left the hotel.

A door at the end of the bar, marked *Manager*, opened, and a slight, middle-aged European man emerged. He pointed at the chandelier and his mouth worked as if he were trying to say something, but nothing came out.

'Sorry about the mess, Mr Simpson!' Saffron said brightly. 'Do add it to our bill.' She looked at her husband as one of his friends handed him back his glass and tilted her head to one side. 'Ryder, now I think of it, I had better have a quick word with Amber. Might you have time to speak with me after that?'

'Of course, my dear.'

'Thank you.' She walked away, the shotgun still slung through the crook of her arm. He watched her, admiring the sway of her hips in her long brown skirt. He couldn't resist.

'I take it the wedding is off between Penrod and Amber, then?' he called.

She had reached the bottom of the stairs before she replied. 'That seems a reasonable assumption.'

'I found us a house, Saffy.'

She turned and looked at him over her slim shoulder, her gaze flickering over the wreckage of the hotel bar.

'Perfect timing, I should say, my love.'

The upper caste of Anglo-Egyptian society saw nothing of Miss Benbrook or Mrs Courtney after that. Everyone knew they were still in the city, and that the engagement between Miss Benbrook and Major Ballantyne was at an end, but Amber was no longer a presence at polo matches or the parade ground. Some of them missed her, others thought that Major Ballantyne was better off out of it, and although the way he flaunted his renewed affair with Lady Agatha was perhaps not in the best possible taste, well, Lady Agatha was beautiful, rich and a genuine aristocrat, so was approved of whatever she did.

Meanwhile, Mr Simpson of Shepheard's Hotel presented a bill for the chandelier, which made Ryder whistle between his teeth, but he paid it without argument.

Courtney House, in the wrong part of town, became a lively and cheerful home. The air was full of the voices of women chattering in English, Arabic and, from time to time, Tigrean and Amharic. Saffron and Amber had employed language teachers from the shifting population of Cairo to teach them. Saffron painted happily in her studio and seemed to bloom as her morning sickness passed and her belly swelled. Amber threw herself into the study of the new languages and care of her sister. Twice Saffron parcelled up her work and sent it to the family solicitor, Sebastian Hardy, in London. He sent back compliments and later clippings from various newspapers praising a small show he had put on of her works in Cork Street, London. All the canvases were sold within a week. He also told Amber that he had allowed a stage adaptation of *Slaves of the Mahdi* to be performed by the company at the Haymarket Theatre. It was the sensation of the season, and the Benbrook Trust bank balance continued to swell.

The twins hardly ever saw Ryder. He was either at the docks while his orders from various European foundries came in or was writing letters in his office. By the summer of 1887, Ryder had recruited the men he needed and amassed a huge cargo of mining equipment in Suez, ready to ship to Massowah, the nearest port to Tigray. The British had let the Italians take control of Massowah to prevent the French influence spreading too far along the coast of the Red Sea, a decision that had irritated the Abyssinian Emperor. In January, one of the emperor's most trusted deputies, Ras Alula, had slaughtered five hundred Italian troops at Dogali when he felt they had strayed too far into Abyssinian lands, but now an uneasy peace existed in the region and Ryder was sure that with a little diplomacy he would be able to transport his gear through Italian territory and into the mountains where he intended to mine. Now he waited only for the birth of his child, and the end of the rains in early September to depart.

On 9 August, Saffron delivered a healthy baby boy, and they named him Leon. Amber was the baby's godmother, of course, and Sebastian Hardy accepted the honour of becoming the little boy's godfather. He sent a handsome silver christening mug from London. Saffron recovered quickly from the birth and by the end of the month they were at last ready to leave Cairo.

• • •

The three men playing cards in the saloon of the steamer *Iona*, as it made its steady progress down the Red Sea from Suez to Massowah, looked like brothers. They were all dressed in worn but well-repaired travelling clothes, leathers and dull tweeds that showed signs of days under hot suns and nights in the open. Each man also had the solid muscled shape of men who laboured hard for a living. None of them was clean-shaven, and their occasional curses from their luck – or lack of it – with the cards suggested they were not used to polite company. Most of the other first-class passengers on the steamer, who were a mix of army wives, diplomats and the occasional businessman, avoided them and this corner of the saloon was acknowledged theirs for the duration of the voyage.

If you took the time to examine them, though, they were not as alike as they appeared at first glance. One was some years older than the rest. His short beard and black hair were strongly woven with white, and the lines on his tanned face were deep and plentiful. Still, his was the broadest back, and the other two treated him with a friendly deference. Of the two other men, one was slimmer, with pale hazel eyes and a thick head of red hair visible under his wide-brimmed slouch hat. He would, from time to time, interrupt their game to pull a beaten leather-bound journal from his pocket and make notes with the stub of a pencil. The other, a blond man whose skin had been burned almost scarlet over years of outside work, growled whenever the game was broken off. He would have been handsome, but the heavy scarring on the right side of his face made him look almost monstrous and he wore a patch over one eye.

'What are you making notes for now anyway, Rusty?' he said. 'If it's a shopping list you're making, forget it. Anything you haven't got now you'll have to do without. Nothing but donkeys and women in Massowah. Courtney's bought up all the donkeys already, and the women you can't afford.'

The slimmer man, Matt 'Rusty' Tompkins, finished his note and slipped his journal back into his coat pocket. He spoke with the swinging lilt of the American Irish.

'It's ideas, is all, Patch. Things to talk over with Mr Courtney. If we're going to be processing the silver in those savage lands with no trained help and half the water I'd want, it all needs thinking on. And I do my best thinking when I write things down.' He picked up his cards again and scratched his nose. 'I'll raise you two.'

'Call,' the man with the grizzled beard said, 'and you, Rusty, make your notes if you want but don't feel so free to name the nature of our enterprise in public.'

Rusty glanced around the empty saloon, then shrugged. 'This isn't Utah, Dan. No one here is going to grab a pickaxe and follow us. It took Courtney months to get the permits sorted and he speaks them savage languages. Any fool who tries to follow us will get a spear in the belly before he's within a hundred miles of the strike.'

'Fold,' Patch said, then leaned back in his chair and struck a light for his half-smoked cigar. 'You may be right, that you may, Rusty. Still, Dan's right also. I see no good in jabbering. While it's quiet up here, I don't mind saying, gentlemen, it feels like a queer set-up out in the hills on our own. Courtney learns quick, fair play to him, but he knows little enough about mining as yet, and he's the only one to have seen the strike.'

'He's put his money in it.' Rusty shrugged and stared at his cards. 'Raise you two more, Dan. I'd swear he's sunk every cent of it into this enterprise and I like a man who bets big.'

Dan didn't answer at once; he was distracted by a movement outside. All three men turned to watch as Saffron Courtney and Amber Benbrook passed by beyond the large saloon windows. They were talking with their heads close together. Saffron's tawny mane of hair and Amber's blonder tresses seemed to mingle together as they were caught by the sea breeze. All three men sighed.

'I told him to leave the women in Cairo, and the baby,' Patch said. 'What the hell are they going to be but a problem a thousand miles from civilisation?' He blew out a cloud of smoke with the satisfaction of a connoisseur. 'Not that they aren't a pleasure to look upon.'

'Raise you five.'

'Call,' Rusty said. 'I told him the same. He laughed in my face and said his wife would follow him no matter what he said. And I for one wouldn't argue with that little girl, not after seeing how she rearranged the decoration in Shepheard's.' Dan laid down his cards.

'Full house, aces over tens.'

Rusty threw down his cards. 'Damn, do you never bluff, Dan?'

'Not when you scratch your nose, I don't, Mr Tompkins.' Dan gathered in the ragged pile of Egyptian currency they were playing with. 'Guess this will be as much use as play money where we're going. Still, warms my heart to win it. Anyone know what happened to that soldier who wanted a piece of Courtney?'

Patch yawned. 'I heard his superiors smoothed things over in Cairo, but he went straight back to that Lady Agatha's bed and started treating her like a whore.' He looked out of the window again where Amber and Saffron had passed. 'Poor kid. Did you read her book? Seems like she's suffered enough.'

Rusty scratched his nose, then looked at his hands as if they had betrayed him, and nodded his head. '*Slaves of the Mahdi*? I read it on the boat out from San Francisco, along with everyone else. Seeing the Mahdi's men kill her father like that at Khartoum . . . Swear those fellows are worse than Indians . . .' He whistled between his teeth. 'And their sister still in the harem? I'd have thought the Brits would have gone out and taught them a lesson or two. Taking white women . . .'

Dan finished counting his money and folded it neatly away in his pocket. 'Brits are busy enough elsewhere and the Mahdi's fellows are kings of nothing but sand. Hey, you know if they are Christians or heathens where we're going?'

'What difference would it make to you? When you come into town, Dan Matthews, it isn't the church you head for,' Rusty said and began to shuffle the ragged pack. 'They're heathen Christians in Abyssinia, I'm told. But the men have strong backs and the women . . . Oh, I've heard stories about the women.' He began to deal.

Patch picked up his greasy cards with suspicion. 'They better have more than donkeys for sale in Massowah. If we're going to be stuck up in the mountains digging year in and year out, we're going to need another pack of cards.'

• • •

Ryder Courtney was in his cabin while his mining experts gossiped over their game. He was in his shirtsleeves, with a cheroot clamped between his teeth and surrounded on all sides by books and papers, diagrams and journals. They would dock in Massowah tomorrow and he needed to be ready. He had the best part of three tons of mining and processing equipment in the hold of the steamer and he had to shift all of it inland up into the highlands, a hundred miles west of the ancient capital of Axum. For anyone else such an enterprise would have been financial suicide, but Ryder had advantages as well as his brains and his broad back. For one thing, he had travelled through Abyssinia many times, one of the few white men to have done so, and spoke Amharic and the local Tigrean language with the same fluency he spoke Arabic or English. Emperor John, King of Kings and ruler of Abyssinia, had been the guest of honour at his wedding to Saffron a little more than a year ago. Ryder also knew and respected the local ruler and general of John's northern army, Ras Alula, and had cultivated the friendship of the priests who held great influence over the local people.

Ryder laced his fingers together behind his head and leaned back in his chair. Next to him the baby in his rocking basket yawned widely and blinked up at the patterns of light cast over the ceiling of the cabin. Ryder gently set the basket in motion with the edge of his boot and the baby snorted and closed his eyes again. It was time to build something, make a mark on the empty maps. Ryder had traded in ivory, dhurra corn and gum arabic across East Africa since he was little more than a boy. He had amassed a fortune, but kept his reputation as an honest man. Now was the time to put some of the accumulated wealth to work. It might take years before the mine produced the profits he hoped for, but Ryder was willing to invest time as well as money to create something lasting.

He remembered coming into Saffron's room just after Leon's birth and seeing his child for the first time, feeling the grip of his tiny fingers and wondering at the miracle of his fluttering breaths. He grinned to himself. He had thought himself a man before the siege of Khartoum, but marriage and fatherhood had matured him. He had worried that the love he felt for Saffron would weaken him, but he knew now it had made him stronger. It bound him to the world, to life, to the future.

Ryder had also been careful enough to hire the three best men available in the western world for the work ahead. Dan Matthews had made and lost a fortune in California in 1849, when he was hardly more than a boy himself, and then made another fortune working the massive wealth of the Comstock silver lode in the wilds of Utah after that. Dan's wife and child had died in a cholera outbreak in the city of Virginia, the sprawling boom town that grew up near the strike, and he'd disappeared for a while. When he returned, he claimed to have nothing but the clothes he stood up in and his pick. The man could read rock, though – see its strengths and its failings, feel where tunnels would collapse and where they would hold. They said he saved twenty lives in 1880 because he sniffed the air and knew the water was coming, and coming hard. Ryder listened to the stories, made his enquiries and decided he was the best man for the job, so had written as soon as he had his permits in his hand, sent sketch maps of where he hoped to mine and offered Dan his passage and a fat fee to come and help him. Dan must have boarded a boat the same day and was waiting in Cairo in a flea-ridden dosshouse when Ryder arrived. It turned out he could have stayed in Shepheard's if he'd wanted to. He said he preferred the company at the dosshouse and fleas had stopped trying to get through his hide in 1876.

Matt 'Rusty' Tompkins was their smelting and processing expert. He too was a Comstock veteran, hauled into the wilderness as a boy by his father – one of the thousands whom bad luck and strong drink made a failure even when he was living on a once-in-a-lifetime strike. The boy's mother left with the first man who would take her, and his father was killed in a hunting accident before Rusty was twelve years old. Rusty found work in the mills watching the ore being ground to the consistency of sand, then forced to give up its treasures in the amalgamating rooms and furnaces. He had a sharp mind and was fascinated by the processes that made and unmade stone. Before he was twenty, men twice his age were paying top dollar for his advice. He seemed to have little interest in the money, though. It was the challenge of the rock that Rusty loved. His fellow miners thought him a bit simple for all his cleverness, but the women of the camp liked him. On Dan's recommendation, Ryder had written to the owner of the Homestead Hotel in Virginia, looking for a man with Rusty's skills. She wrote back with his name and said he was one of those men always looking up at the hills as if he wanted to know what was on the other side of them, and as he seemed to crave neither women nor drink, a new place in the wilds might appeal to him. Ryder wrote to him and two months later went and collected him off the boat in Alexandria. His notebook was already full of questions and ideas.

Finally there was Tom 'Patch' Western, another veteran of the Comstock Lode. He'd not stayed in Utah long, though, instead leaving America for work in the Transvaal. Ryder wrote to his own nephew Sean, who had made a fortune on the Witwatersrand goldfields, and asked for the name of a trustworthy man who could lead a team of natives without becoming a tyrant or an embarrassment, and who knew about explosives and engineering underground. Sean had told him to take Patch and no one else. The raw scar on his face was a souvenir of when he was last drunk and let his assistant supervise a blast. The assistant had died, squeezed to a pulp under the rockfall, and Patch had lost his eye and his looks in the explosion. Sean wrote to his uncle that Patch hadn't taken a drink since, was fierce but loyal to the men who worked in his crew, and happy to damn his superiors to hell and back if they pushed too hard.

Now the baby was sleeping again, Ryder picked up a sheaf of documents and ran through the columns of figures, calculating swiftly in his head. The three miners in the saloon were wrong: he had not sunk every penny of his fortune into this mining venture. Back in Cairo and under the guard of his trusted Arab lieutenant, Bacheet, Ryder had left a reserve in trade goods and gold, but the hunger to make something of this mine had meant he had invested more heavily than he had first intended. He had not heard from the men he had sent to buy the land and begin establishing the camp since before the rains. That was to be expected, of course – nothing moved during the period of those fierce daily storms – but what would the sun shine on when they were over? Ryder had heard rumours in Cairo that the Italians were supplying John's southern rival, Menelik, King of Shoa, with modern rifles and quantities of ammunition. Ryder believed the Italians were playing a dangerous game. Menelik was a shrewd man with expanding territories and an Ethiopian patriotism. If the Italians thought they could use him to control Abyssinia, they were wrong. Would the Italian appetite for Abyssinia be sharpened by rumours of large silver deposits in the mountains of Tigray, so temptingly close to their base at Massowah? Possibly.

The penalties if Ryder failed in this venture were clear: he would lose fifteen years of profit and have to start building his fortune all over again, only now he had a wife and child to support. But if they succeeded in working the lode . . . In that moment the thought crossed his mind, like a bird of prey crossing a high blue sky between distant peaks: what might be the penalties of success?

· · ·

On deck, watching the shore drift by, Saffron was testing her sister's Amharic.

'The translators at Emperor John's court are nice enough, but they never bother to translate things precisely,' Saffron said with a shrug. 'Ryder says he learned years ago that shaking hands on a deal made through them was a recipe for disaster.'

Her sister didn't reply and Saffy looked at her sideways. She knew she talked about Ryder too much, but she couldn't help it. She had fallen in love with him under the walls of besieged Khartoum with the unquestioning, wholehearted devotion of a child. That love had deepened and matured as she grew up, but it was still the absolute centre of her existence. When she thought of his hands on her, on her waist, in her hair, she shivered and flushed. When she was pregnant, she was afraid that she would have no love left in her for the baby, but then Leon was born and she realised love was not something one ran out of, like fuel for a lamp. She had plenty for her son too, and though she knew she'd never be the sort of mother who devoted every breath and word to her child, she knew that her heart had room enough for him. In fact, having his child had made her love Ryder even more, and she had never believed such a thing was possible.

Amber had felt the same way about Penrod, Saffron knew that. She knew every fibre of her twin's being so she never tried to fool herself that Amber's devotion to Penrod had been less intense than what she felt for Ryder. When she tried to imagine what it would be to lose faith in her husband, her heart almost stopped in her chest and she was terrified by her own good luck.

Saffron lived her life by running at it, throwing herself into every endeavour and adventure with abandon. As soon as she was bored or unhappy, she quickly found the next challenge and embraced it. From learning to shoot to learning how to ride, from feeding starving crowds in Khartoum to learning to paint or designing her own elaborate evening dresses, she had excelled in everything she had done. She felt she excelled in being a wife too. Amber had never failed at anything either. She could shoot just as well as Saffron could and the first time she had tried to write a book, it had become an international bestseller. But then she had broken off her engagement with Penrod. Not that Amber had failed – it was Penrod who had ruined everything – but a small voice in Saffron's head told her that it might feel like a failure to Amber.

They had fallen silent, staring at the rocky coastline, while the handsome, dashing soldier Amber loved was in both their thoughts. He got everywhere, Saffron thought, like sand in the desert wind.

'What exactly did Ryder tell you?' Amber asked, her blue eyes still gazing unseeingly at the coastline.

Saffron understood what she meant. The twins had not spoken the name of Penrod Ballantyne since that day in Shepheard's Hotel. They didn't need to, and Saffron knew that any mention of him while they were still in the same city as him would have been a knife in Amber's heart. She had been so brave, the way she bore those months before Leon was born.

'No more than what I told you after Agatha spoke to you. That it happened only a few days before Osman Atalan led the attack on Khartoum and they took you and Rebecca. Ryder and Rebecca made love in his office at the compound and he asked her to marry him. She wouldn't give him an answer because she hoped that Penrod would come back for her.' Even saying the words made Saffron feel a little sick. 'Ryder told me the day after I told him we should get married. He said I had to know.'

'Did Ryder think Rebecca was a whore?'

Saffron turned and leaned against the ship's rail. 'Ryder said he tried to think bad things about her after he realised she'd been with Penrod, but it didn't work. He said he thought she was very brave and very beautiful and if he could have rescued her, he would still have married her and thought himself a lucky man.'

Amber hung her head, leaning over the rail and staring into the churning waters of the Red Sea as the steamer cut through them. The steady beat of the engine made the teak planks of the deck throb under her feet. 'What did you say?'

Saffron did not reply at once. 'I did a lot of shouting. And hitting. Then he got hold of my wrists, so I tried to kick him instead. He'd locked my revolver and hunting knife in the money chest before he told me, and hidden the key.' She considered this for a moment. 'Which was probably a good idea.'

Amber smiled reluctantly. 'Then what happened?'

'After the kicking and shouting? He kept hold of my wrists so I couldn't scratch his eyes out, until I was too tired to fight any more, then he let me go. I suppose I cried myself to sleep in the end. I didn't speak to him for three days. Wouldn't even look at him, even when I put his evening whisky in front of him.' Her voice took on a rather satisfied note. 'It made him feel *terrible*. I think he found out then how much he loved me.' She turned back out towards the water and put her arm through her sister's. 'When the three days were up, I went to him and said I realised that I had been too young for him to love in that way before, and Rebecca *is* brave and beautiful, so I understood why he might like her. I said it was good he had told me, and if he could promise that he loved me more now than he had ever loved Rebecca then I would still marry him.'

Amber moved closer to her. 'And he did promise you that?'

'Oh yes. He was so relieved he fell on his knees and made me a proper proposal. That was nice because the first time around I proposed to him. Well, actually I said I was going to follow him around until I died so he might as well marry me, which is almost the same thing. I'm glad he ended up asking me too and looking like he meant it, otherwise I might always have thought he just married me because he didn't know how to make me go away.' She sighed. 'I'm still glad the compound where they made love was burned to the ground, though.'

Amber put her head on Saffron's shoulder. 'And you still love Rebecca?'

Saffron stared out across at the eastern shores of the Red Sea. Rebecca was somewhere in the Sudan in the harem of Osman Atalan, caring for his children, going everywhere with her eyes cast down.

'Yes. Though I think perhaps she is not the Rebecca we knew any more, if she is still alive.'

'Do you think we will ever see her again?'

Saffron kissed her twin's head quickly. She could feel Amber was crying, and hoped it was doing her some good. 'No, darling, I don't think we shall. Alive or dead, our sister belongs to the desert now.'

• • •

The weather was being kind to them, warm but not savagely hot with a steady breeze to cool them, but no sudden squalls. The ship made steady progress through the calm waters. That night, Ryder stared up into the darkness, still considering how to move the machinery he needed out of Massowah. Saffron lay across his broad chest, one slim leg lying across his own. He could see the line of her collarbone in the moonlight as it shone across her from the brass-rimmed porthole. He could feel the weight of her breasts against his chest and his desire for her began to grow. She would not mind being woken by him, to emerge from her dreams to find his hand making its way up her smooth thigh. He could already hear her answering moan of lust when she felt him hard against her. No. He fought temptation. His wife needed to rest. Saffron had nightmares too often. The horrors she had seen in Khartoum, the starving men and women killed as they stormed Ryder's compound, her father's head held high by the dervish executioners, often returned to her in the darkness. Three or four nights in every seven, Ryder would wake to find her sweating and trembling beside him. She never cried out, and never spoke about her nightmares during the day. Ryder knew and understood, though. Tonight Saffron was smiling in her dreams, her fingers resting feather-light on his chest. No matter how he wanted her, he would not wake her. He carefully slipped out from under her and she made a soft keening sound then turned towards the cabin wall, still lost in her dreams.

Ryder dressed and took his leather wallet of documents and calculations on to the private area of deck outside their stateroom. The moon was full and the stars so bright and numerous in the heavens he could read by their light. He began going through the papers once more. The risk and challenge of the enterprise excited him and he realised he was smiling as he worked. After half an hour he struck a match to light his cheroot, then flicked it, still smoking, over the rail. Nearby on the deck someone coughed.

'Who's there?' he said quietly.

A small white face leaned forward out of the shadows. 'Only me, Ryder,' Amber said. 'I didn't want to disturb you and I like the smell of cheroots. The smell of matches always makes me cough, though. Silly, isn't it?'

'Have you been there all this time, al-Zahra?' He spoke quietly and fondly in Arabic, which flowed from his tongue as easily as it did from hers.

'I was out here thinking; I didn't want to disturb you.'

The door behind them opened and Saffron emerged onto the deck, her feet bare, her shift covered only by Ryder's long leather travelling coat. It hung down below her knees and the sleeves hid her hands completely. She yawned and stretched.

'What are you both doing up? Lord, what a beautiful night. Ryder, do you need anything?'

Ryder took her hand and kissed her palm. 'All is well, Filfil.' The twins' nurse had named Saffron 'pepper' in Arabic. 'Go back to sleep.'

'Oh, all right, but it seems a shame when the stars are so lovely.' The last word was almost lost in another yawn. She turned to shuffle off to bed, when suddenly below and behind them there came a dull, smothered boom, then another. The ship gave a shuddering groan and lurched hard. Ryder leaped to his feet and caught Saffron before she fell. She clutched his arm.

'Ryder! What in God's name—?'

'I've no idea. I'm going to see. Get ready. Don't go below and if they lower the boats move fast. Take Leon. Promise not to wait.'

She had gone pale in the moonlight, but his wife was not the sort of woman to panic. He could see her mind working already, figuring out what to save and what to leave. He put his hand to her warm cheek for a moment.

'I promise, Ryder. Go. Remember to come back.'

• • •

Ryder had run a steamboat up and down the Nile before the fall of Khartoum. He had taken his turn stoking the furnace, watching the pressure in the boilers and learning how to squeeze vital extra power from the engine when he needed to outrun or outmanoeuvre an enemy on a swift-flowing and capricious river. He had learned the power and danger of steam in those years. The ship on which he found himself now was on a very different scale to the *Intrepid Ibis*. The *Iona* was nearly four hundred feet long, and could carry up to three hundred passengers as well as cargo. She was brigantine rigged, but powered her way through the waters with a compound steam engine that could put out five hundred horsepower. Ryder and his companions had been given the tour by the chief engineer while they were waiting to leave Suez. The engineer was a young Australian, whom Ryder liked. He had shown Ryder around the engine room like a bride showing off her new marital home. The stokers who fed the furnaces were teams of lascars, Indian sailors valued for their hard work and skill at wielding a shovel in the suffocating temperatures. The boilers were over sixty tons each, made of riveted steel plates thick enough to contain the pressurised steam, which drove the labouring engines. Ryder had seen that the crew understood their business and treated the power they controlled with respect, but he also knew from his own experience that accidents happened even to good crews, and when dealing with such explosive forces, accidents could swiftly become disasters.

Ryder tore down the narrow companionway to the lower levels. The second-class passengers, clouded with sleep and confusion, were standing at the doors of their cabins. They looked like lambs in their cotton shifts and shirts. The small faces of children peered around their parents' knees, eyes wide. A young Indian, dressed in a grey European-style suit, called after him as he ran by.

'Sir, what's happening? Sir?'

Ryder half turned, trying to decide if he should send them back to bed, reassure them and prevent panic, but he remembered his instructions to his own wife.

'Get them all up on deck. Dressed, no baggage. It might be nothing, but . . .'

The young man was already clapping his hands, urging the passengers into their clothes and up the companionway. 'I understand, sir. Come on, everyone, quick and calm . . . No, ma'am, leave that! Just you and the little ones . . .'

Ryder ran back and slid down the next companionway into the bowels of the ship.

• • •

Saffron pulled on her travelling skirt, belt, socks and her boots, then lifted Leon from his cot. He grizzled and stretched. If she had to get into a lifeboat, she'd need her hands free. She laid the baby back down again, took her hunting knife from its sheath at her waist and sliced one of the snowy cotton sheets into thick bands. Then she settled Leon across her chest and bound him securely and comfortably to her, tying the strips over her hip. Next she belted Ryder's heavy coat around her and folded back the sleeves. Then she glanced around the cabin. Ryder's box of cigars she thrust into her coat, then she flung open one of the trunks and plucked out their money-bag, packed with their supply of Maria Theresa silver dollars. They were the only currency that was worth carrying in Abyssinia, but God, they were heavy. If she ended up in the water they would drag her and Leon into the depths in moments. She hesitated and felt a touch on her shoulder. Amber was beside her, dressed and ready with a leather satchel slung securely across her back.

'Split them with me, Saffy. You have your knife?'

Saffron nodded. They divided the silver, took half each and tied the heavy leather pouches that held them under their skirts. They left the thongs that secured them exposed at the waist so they could be cut quickly if they needed to lose the weight. They could hear voices in the corridor outside, a wondering exchange of questions and answers, a masculine laugh.

'What else?' Amber said quickly. 'Ryder has his document folder, I saw him tuck it into his waistcoat.'

'Good. Father's revolver?'

'I have that.' Amber patted her leather bag.

'This, then.' Saffron picked up Ryder's large silver hip flask and filled it from the decanter on the desk. She was glad to see her hand was steady.

Amber made her own choices. She grabbed Saffron's sketch-book and pencil box from the unused upper bunk, wrapped them in oiled cloth and thrust the package into the satchel.

'The Star of Solomon,' Saffron said suddenly. She yanked open another leather-bound trunk and for a minute the air was full of lace and linen as she threw her shifts and petticoats over her shoulder. 'Here!' She drew out an ornately carved wooden case and opened it. Inside was a decoration, a sort of silver emblem set in an elaborate network of chains and covered with ribbons. She plucked it out, opened her coat and began to try to fasten it to the inside.

'Let me help.' Saffron lifted her chin and Amber helped fasten the decoration securely, then she smoothed down the coat again over her sleeping nephew. A fine silk shawl lay on the bed, green and gold and still smelling faintly of the spiced air of the Cairo bazaars. Amber wrapped it around her sister's neck and tucked in the ends. The tassels brushed Leon's nose and he sneezed, then slept on.

From the deck they heard a great rattle and bang, then a new chorus of shouting.

'Amber, they're lowering the boats. We have to go. Ryder said.'

Amber looked around her at the comfortable, quiet cabin. The gas lamps still burned steadily in their etched glass shades, warming the shadows away. 'What if it's nothing, Saffy? We could wait and see.'

'If it's nothing they'll pick us up again.'

Amber nodded sharply. One final glance around the cabin and they left it. In the corridor they saw the wife of a colonel, a large lady wrapped in a white, quilted dressing gown making her look like an expensive cream cake.

'Where are you hurrying to, my dear girls?' She yawned.

'On deck to the boats, Mrs Cobbett, and you should come too,' Saffron said.

'Oh, nonsense, my dear. Just a little engine trouble.'

Amber put her hand on the woman's arm. She smelled of lavender soap. 'Mr Courtney has gone to see what is happening, Mrs Cobbett. But he said we should go to the boats. Do come with us.' She looked into Mrs Cobbett's face with urgent appeal. Saffron was dragging at her wrist, pulling her away.

The older woman chuckled. 'After reading *Slaves of the Mahdi*, my dear, I can understand why you see disaster in every little thing, but you'll feel foolish in the morning, Miss Benbrook, I promise you.'

Amber tried again. 'Please do come, Mrs Cobbett!' Saffron gave a hard yank on Amber's wrist. Mrs Cobbett only waved and turned back into her stateroom.

Amber allowed herself to be dragged through the saloon and out into the chill night air. Several of the male first-class passengers were on deck, taking the opportunity for a smoke and a little conversation. The scene seemed so at odds with the sense of rising urgency in her own blood. None of the gentlemen appeared alarmed, but Amber was watching the faces of the crew as they moved around them. They looked serious.

'Look!' Saffron said, and pointed. One of the double-ended lifeboats on the starboard side was almost ready to be lowered. The canvas cover had been removed and stowed, supplies from the lock-box on the deck were being handed in and, as they watched, four of the lascar crew climbed in, while four others manned the ropes, ready to lower it into the water from its cast-iron davits.

Even in this dark corner of the deck, they could see the lifeboat was half empty, but the crew was already preparing to swing it free. One of the officers saw the two girls hurrying towards them.

'Hold!' he shouted to the crewmen on the ropes, then offered his hand to Amber and Saffron as if he were helping them into their carriage in St James's Park.

'It isn't full!' Saffron said.

The officer spoke quickly. 'If the boiler blows, the ship could go down in minutes, Mrs Courtney. Best to get some boats in the water as fast as possible. If you need to pick up survivors you can. Ready!'

The crewmen on deck started working cranking handles at the base of the davits from which the lifeboat was hanging. The boat swayed as the metal arms clanked and rattled into position until the lifeboat was over the water.

A shadow passed over the full moon and Saffron's knuckles whitened as she clung to the swaying sides of the boat. For a moment it was strangely quiet, but the night did not seem so beautiful any more.

'That's enough!' the officer on deck shouted. 'Lower away!'

· · ·

Ryder reached the boiler room within minutes of the initial explosions. One of the crew tried to hold him at the door but he shouldered his way forward without even slowing down. The bells on the telegraph were still ringing. As Ryder pushed his way in, one of the engineers shoved the wooden handle into position and shouted the 'Stop Engines' order. From above Ryder heard the clatter of boots on the metal gangway, and the chief engineer, his uniform jacket half on and his face still creased with sleep, slid down the companionway.

'What in hell's name?' he shouted before he had even hit the deck.

'Explosion in fireboxes of boilers three and four, sir.'

Ryder looked around him. It was hot and dark as hell. The door of the middle firebox on the stern side had been ripped open, and the narrow opening through which the beast of the ship was fed with coal had been torn wide. The explosion had been enough to rip the metal back and apart. The floor on which he stood was slippery with blood and the air stank of coal dust and hot metal.

The chief engineer grabbed the man who had spoken by his collar. 'What the fuck do you mean, "explosions"?'

Someone was screaming. A metal fragment flung from the door of the firebox had sliced through the arm of one of the stokers at the elbow. Senseless with pain and shock, the man was sitting in a lake of his own blood and staring at his severed limb that lay, its fingers gently curled upwards, a yard to his left. He wailed and babbled. One of his crewmates in a sky-blue turban was trying to tie up the gushing stump with an oily rag, but he was already soaked in gore.

'They exploded!' the man said into the engineer's furious scowl. 'Trimmer Khan brought in a load from the bunker and tipped it between boxes three and four, where it was wanted, then two minutes later, *boom boom!*'

One of the crew shouted over from the speaking tube. 'Boss, Captain wants to know what's happening!'

'Tell him I want to know that too.' Ryder felt a tug at his sleeve and looked down into the face of a boy of about twelve years old. His skin was much darker than the lascars; he could be Zulu, Ryder thought.

'Sir,' he whispered in English. 'Sir, look . . .'

'Where's bloody trimmer Khan, then?' the engineer bellowed. 'What did he shovel into my fireboxes?' The man who had lost his arm screamed again. 'And get him out of here!'

'That's trimmer Khan,' the man answered, nodding towards a body on the floor. The face had been blasted by red-hot coals. You could hardly tell the smoking flesh had once been a man.

'Please, sir!' The boy pulled on Ryder's arm again and he glanced in the direction the boy was pointing. It was the water gauge on the side of the second boiler and the arrow was sinking fast.

'Chief!' Ryder yelled. 'Check the gauge!'

The engineer flung the man he had been questioning away from him, and he stumbled to his knees near the trimmer's smoking corpse. He began to retch. The chief saw the gauge and his face went stone white.

'Christ save us, the shell must be cracked. Open the valves! Flood the boilers now.'

'It's too late, man!' Ryder shouted. 'It's going to blow whatever you do. You have to run.'

'I said open the valves. We have to try. You can do nothing here, Courtney! Get out, save as many as you can. The rest of you too! Get out!'

The surviving stokers began to crowd up the companionway. The man in the blue turban was trying to lift the stoker with the severed arm. Ryder ran the few strides towards him and felt for the injured man's pulse. Nothing, and his eyes were fixed and staring.

'He's dead – save yourself.'

The man mumbled something, it might have been thanks or a word of prayer in his own language, then ran for the companionway.

Ryder lowered his head and squared his shoulders, then he remembered the boy. He was frozen where Ryder had left him, among the blood and cinders, the hissing of steam and the ghastly light pouring from the torn fireboxes, the last angel in hell.

'Come here!' The boy blinked at him, startled, then obeyed. Ryder crouched down. 'Get on my back, kid.'

The boy had instincts enough left to wrap his arms around Ryder's neck and legs around his waist. Ryder stood, the boy feather-light, and ran up the cast-iron stairs. Behind him he heard the engineer still shouting orders, then a great clang and rattle as the valve wheel was forced, a groan from the boiler, as well as the sucking roar of the flames. He could picture the arrow and the gauge in front of him. One minute, two at the most. The men remaining below would be killed instantly, but the explosion would do more than that – it would rip the ship apart. He didn't look back.

When he reached the lower passenger decks on the starboard side of the ship, he yelled the order to abandon ship as he ran along the narrow passageway. The sound bounced off the plain whitewashed walls. Nervous families of all colours and creeds stared at him and the fleeing stokers with blank-eyed confusion. He shouted the order in every language he knew and flung himself up the next ladder-like stairs. He was smothered in the stink of blood and coal, but he caught the scent of the night air. He was counting the seconds, imagining that arrow juddering lower as each one passed. His muscles burned and cramped but he only pushed harder, as if trying to outrun the devil himself. Under him the ship shuddered and shook. He hauled himself up the last steps. Ahead he could see the first-class saloon, its doors standing open, and beyond that the moonlit forward deck.

• • •

Saffron was twisting around trying to catch sight of Ryder in the darkness and confusion on deck. The lifeboat swung wildly as the ship shuddered and the engines stopped. She shot out a hand to save herself, then she felt a strong grip holding her shoulder, stopping her full weight being flung forward.

'Steady, Mrs Courtney.'

'Dan!' She peered into the swaying shadows. 'Are Patch and Rusty with you?'

'Sure are. We were playing cards in the saloon. Thought we'd take a little jaunt.'

'You don't think we're in any danger then?'

She watched him shake his head. 'Think the danger is how these boys handle getting this thing in the water. Certainly ain't nothing but a blown pipe in the engine. Can you swim, Mrs C?'

Saffron half nodded. She had swum for her life when escaping Khartoum, but that was more splashing around, keeping her head above water and hoping Ryder would pluck her out before the Nile crocodiles or the rifle shots of the dervish got her first.

'Well, I was built to sink like a stone, so if we go into the drink, don't hang on to me.'

Someone shouted on deck and the prow of the lifeboat suddenly dropped down heavily. Saffron gasped and found herself staring straight into the darkness of the midnight waters. Her stomach twisted sickly and her head swam. Amber screamed. She was slipping away from her. Saffron took a hard hold of a grab rope hanging from the gunwale, at the same moment shooting out her right hand to her twin. Amber seized her forearm, and Saffron gasped as her shoulder took her sister's weight. Amber scrambled for a footing and found it pushing against the brass-rimmed ribs of the lifeboat. The Gladstone bag of one of the other passengers tumbled towards them. Amber swung to the right as it plummeted by, an inch from her head, then plunged the last thirty feet into the water and disappeared with a heavy splash.

Above them orders were being shouted, sharp and rapid. The boat was righted and immediately lowered again in one, two, three lurches, dropping them with a hard percussive smack onto the gently rolling waters of the sea. Saffron felt baby Leon stir against her chest. She put her arm around him and tried to control the sick fear rising in her head and brain. Her attention sharpened to a knife-like brilliance. The crewmen who had boarded the lifeboat were unshipping the oars – four lascars, wearing royal blue turbans, and a European in the white uniform of a deck officer. The lascars fitted the rowlocks into place. Saffron noticed they were of polished brass and shone in the moonlight. The lascars slid the oars into place and looked to the deck officer for orders.

'Pull away!'

It took all of Saffron's self-control to stop herself shouting at them not to, that she needed to be near to Ryder. She looked over her shoulder at the ship. It looked perfect and unharmed, four yards away, six, ten. With the ship engines stopped, the night was silent apart from the chatter and creak of the rowlocks as the lascars pulled in easy, perfectly co-ordinated strokes. The air was salty and chill. She pulled the thick leather coat around Leon to keep the damp away from him, then twisted around again to look at the ship. She could see more passengers coming out on deck and strained to see if Ryder was among them. Another boat had been lowered; the sound of it hitting the water carried over to them clearly. It followed their line away from the ship. Saffron's heart was beating fast, the dread running through her veins making it difficult to breathe. She tried to calm herself before the baby sensed her fear.

Why are we going away? Saffron thought in confusion. They are waving at us. We should go back. I might have dropped all our money in the sea, or Amber might have been hurt, and all because we did not stay on the ship with the sensible people like Mrs Cobbett. She breathed as slowly as she could, but her mind felt heavy. Perhaps I have been in danger too much, she thought. Now I see it everywhere. She heard Amber gasp.

'What is it?'

Amber pointed back towards the ship. Saffron could just make out shapes falling from the side. People. People were jumping into the water.

Saffron felt dizzy. 'Why are they doing that?' she said. 'That must be terribly dangerous.'

A deep ear-splitting blast tore through the air and the rear of the ship exploded. The force half lifted their boat out of the water and for a moment it seemed she would flounder. Saffron heard wreckage crashing into the sea around them and the salt spray soaked her hair and skin. She felt a sharp pain and nausea that seemed to come from within and without her at the same time.

'Ryder!' she gasped, then the world went dark.

• • •

Amber felt the blast rather than heard it, and her first instinct was to shield Saffron and baby Leon, wrapping her arms around her twin and pulling her sideways, trying to put her own body between them and the ship. The explosion blinded her. The lifeboat crashed back into the waves, rocking so violently the starboard gunwale dipped under the water. The passengers shrieked and scrambled to port, and it seemed the boat would overturn.

'Hold hard!' the deck officer roared as a burst of cold salt water washed down Amber's back.

The lascars shoved the panicked passengers back into place and lowered their oars into the water to steady the craft.

'Balers!' the officer said. 'Buckets under the thwarts!'

Amber heard Patch, Dan and Rusty exchanging grunts as they untied the shallow wooden buckets and began scooping the cold water out of the boat and back into the sea where it belonged. They worked fast.

Amber held her sister close. She was heavy in her arms. She must have fainted, Amber thought, and she was glad of it. It was better, much better, for Saffron not to see the catastrophe and chaos behind them.

The ship's stern was on fire and the first great blast had been followed by other, smaller explosions. The flames climbed thirty feet into the air, and the moon and stars seemed to disappear, wiped out of the sky by the sudden light. The prow of the ship began to lift. Bodies were falling from the decks; some figures were leaping, others tumbled. In the confusion of flames at the stern, Amber saw people moving, their clothes and hair on fire as they stumbled and spiralled into the water. Their terrible screams carried across to them only too clearly. In the lifeboat one of the passengers began to pray out loud, while another turned and vomited into the water as the smell of burning flesh and timber reached them.

'We must go back!' Amber shouted at the officer. 'The people!'

She could see his face, made horrible by the light of the inferno on the ship casting shadows on his drawn features.

'We can't. She's going down and if we don't get further away we'll go down with her.'

'But . . .'

'God, you think I don't want to?' His voice was almost a wail. 'It won't be long now and we'll go and pick up survivors as soon as we can.' He took off his cap and ran his hand through his shaggy blond hair. Amber realised he was probably only a year or two older than she was. The mask of the English officer slipped for a moment and he looked very young. 'I have friends on that ship.'

Amber felt tears sting her eyes and wiped them away with the back of her hand. Behind them Rusty cursed as a corpse floated by them in the water, the face smashed into a grinning pulp. Amber gasped but she managed not to cry out. 'Oh, Ryder,' she whispered. 'Please be alive.'

She squeezed Saffron's unconscious body to her, feeling Leon kick his little limbs between them. The shoulders of the coat Saffron was wearing were soaked. Amber felt the water seeping through her fingers. A cold dread washed over her; something about the feel of the liquid wasn't quite right. She shook her sister's shoulder.

'Saffy? Saffy, open your eyes!' Behind her came another dull explosion and a burst of light. Amber looked down at her palm. It was covered in blood.

'Saffy! Saffron! Oh God, Rusty! Something has hit her, she's bleeding.'

A match flared.

'Hold her, Miss Benbrook. I see it, top of her arm. Damn!' The flame was shaken out as it burned his fingers. 'I need a light. Get a lantern, someone. You in the back, break open that locker. Look for a lantern and something for bandages. Come on, folks, stop staring and move your arses!' Amber felt his hand close around her own. 'Now, Miss B. You press down here, and hard.'

Amber squeezed where Rusty had laid her hand on her sister's upper arm and felt the blood bubble up between her fingers. A bustle of activity took place in the shadows as someone found and lit the boat's lanterns. The passenger praying in the darkness lapsed into silence. Amber almost wished the praying would start again, for now she could hear the screams and cries coming from the darkness around them all the more distinctly. Rusty leaned forward again, holding the light over his head. Amber looked away towards the ship. The prow was rearing high out of the water, the final lights on the deck flickered out and she was lit only by the flaming wreckage that surrounded her. Figures were in the water, bodies, others who seemed to be swimming away from the floundering steamer. With a thunderous roar of water, the stern sank completely into the darkness. The rest of the ship was dragged down behind it in seconds with such sudden violence it seemed some sea monster had reached up and pulled it down into the depths. The waves foamed around Amber in a great sucking rush and the lifeboat rocked hard. Helplessly she watched as the floating bodies, the wreckage, the swimmers nearest the ship were dragged back towards her. They lifted their arms, calling out, crying for help, then disappeared like the damned into hell. Amber lowered her head and began to cry.

She heard the sound of ripping fabric and blinked as a lantern, now held by Patch, half standing, half crouching behind Rusty, stung her eyes.

'Miss B, you need to take your hand away now, and we'll get her arm out of the sleeve so we can see what's happening,' he said calmly, ignoring her sobs. 'Let's move quickly. She's losing a lot of blood. Count of three. One, two, three.'

Amber lifted away her hand and pushed the heavy sleeve of Ryder's leather coat down, lifting Saffron's arm free. Saffron yelped, but did not seem to wake. Leon began to cry and Amber put her hand across his head to shield and comfort him. Rusty leaned in close. The shirt Saffron was wearing was scarlet. Rusty ripped it away at the shoulder seam. Amber supported her sister against her chest. She could feel the silk scarf around Saffron's neck soaked and stiffening as the blood began to thicken in the cold air.

Rusty scooped water out of the sea with his hands and used it to clean the wound. A deep jagged gash running down Saffron's arm appeared out of the gore. At once it refilled with blood. Rusty reached into his jacket and produced a stoppered half-pint bottle. He pulled the cork with his teeth and Amber caught the rough tang of whisky. He poured it liberally over the wound. Saffron twisted and keened, and the boat rocked.

'Bandage,' Rusty said, and from somewhere in the shadows a bundle of clean strips was handed up to him. He quickly folded three into a pad and began to bind them around the wound. He drew the ties hard, the muscles in his jaw standing out as he did.

'That should have woken her. Can you get the light closer, Patch?'

'We have to get to the survivors,' the deck officer said. 'Now.'

'One more minute, fella,' Rusty said through clenched teeth. He touched Saffron's scalp on the side of her head above the foul tear in her arm. 'Whatever caught her arm hit her here too.'

'Broken?' Patch said quietly.

'Can't tell. No fresh blood, though.' He looked up at Amber. 'Miss B, that's all we can do now. You hold her still as you can and quiet.'

'I shall,' Amber said. 'Thank you.' Over her sister's shoulder she looked out on to the flickering nightmare. Yells and cries punctuated the darkness, the sound of men and women thrashing in water, glimpses of desperate faces lit by patches of flaming debris, bodies floating quietly by on the dark waters like autumn leaves fallen into a boating lake.

· · ·

The force of the explosion had flung Ryder out onto the deck. For a moment he lay sprawled on the polished teak boards, stunned. He shook his head hard in an attempt to reorder his senses. The boy had been blown from his shoulders. He reached for the child, who grabbed on to his forearm and looked up at him, wide-eyed with terror.

Ryder felt the deck beginning to tilt under him almost at once. He scrambled into a crouch and launched himself forward, clinging on to the cold metal rail at the bow before it was out of reach, swinging the child's entire weight upwards in an arc that seemed to wrench his shoulder from its socket. The boy was frightened, but he was also quick and clever enough to see what he had to do. He hooked his leg and one arm over the same railing that Ryder was clinging to, pulling himself up and over it as the ship's prow begin to climb into the air. Ryder dragged himself up next to him.

'What's your name, son?'

'Tadesse,' the boy panted, staring behind him as passengers and crew who had not found a grip tumbled, shrieking, into the darkness and flames below.

'Tadesse, we have to jump into the water now, and swim as far away as we can. Can you swim?'

The boy nodded. 'Yes, sir. I grew up by Lake Tana.'

'We go now.' Ryder took the boy's hand and, not giving either of them time to think about the fall or what waited for them below, Ryder pushed off hard from the railing and leaped into the darkness. They landed feet first, bent at the knee, breaking through the wall of the water's surface and plunging down. Already Ryder could feel the pull of the great ship behind them. For a moment he was too stunned by the fall and the cold grasp of the sea to move his limbs. The darkness above him seemed unending. Then something struck him on his side. A hand gripped his ankle and he felt desperate fingers trying to climb his body, the weight dragging him down. He kicked out hard in the water and felt his foot connect. The grip was released. The pressure in his lungs was agony and lights burst behind his eyes but another force heaved him upwards. He pushed hard, fighting the awful desire to open his mouth and suck down the water into his screaming lungs. One more kick and his head broke the surface. He gasped and spat, only then realising he was still holding hands with the boy. Tadesse choked and coughed, pulling his hand out of Ryder's so he could keep himself afloat. For a moment the world seemed to swing left and right as Ryder struggled to understand he was still alive. He spat out more seawater and looked about him, then pointed out into the darkness, at an angle away from the ship. The boy nodded and began to swim with strong, confident strokes. Ryder thanked his stars the boy could manage alone, then struck out after him. Behind him he heard a great groan of steel and splintering wood, then a roar as the ship finally pointed her bow to the stars and then plummeted downwards. Ryder felt its weight hauling him back, and pushed hard. The muscles in his broad shoulders were burning as if they had caught fire, and his thighs felt cold and heavy as lead. He clamped his jaw and forced himself away from the drag of the ship. Then he felt the release; the ship had lost its hold on him.

He trod water and looked around him again. 'Tadesse!' he croaked. It was a calm night, the sea became quickly still, yet he got a mouthful of salt water and darkness nevertheless. The chill clamped its fingers around his chest. 'Tadesse!'

'Here.'

The boy appeared out of the moonlight next to him.

'Can you see a boat?'

To the left and right of them debris blown from the ship was flaming, blinding them in the darkness.

'Sir, move!' Tadesse was pointing.

Just in time Ryder saw a lifeboat scything fast towards them across the water. It was ablaze; great gouts of dirty fire were all it carried. Ryder and Tadesse swam one, two, three strokes to get out of its path. It went by them, still driven by some devilish momentum from the explosion and sinking of the ship. Half hung over the side were a pair of burning bodies, already nothing but black, twisted silhouettes in the flames. Ryder caught the stench of burning flesh and felt the sickness rise in his throat. The heat singed his eyes, turning the night white, then it carried on past them, bearing its grotesque crew remorselessly on. Ryder blinked and swiped the seawater from his eyes. Behind was a light – not raging fire, but a lantern held high, and he heard a voice. Not a scream of pain or fear, but someone calling for survivors. Some of the lifeboats had got away then, and now were coming back.

'Sir?' Tadesse called him.

Ryder willed his limbs to move once more and he began to swim alongside the boy towards the lantern and voice.

Arms reached for them.

'The boy first.'

Once Tadesse had been swung onboard, Ryder took the grip offered him and was hauled out of the water. The lifeboat was full and low in the water, but no one panicked. Someone put a blanket over his shoulders, someone else offered him a bottle and he felt the rough caress of cheap brandy. He wiped the water from his eyes and looked towards the lantern. It was being held aloft by the Indian man he had last seen in the corridor urging passengers out onto the deck. How long ago was that? Twenty minutes at most. He was scanning the water looking for the living, and when he spotted someone still moving in the water, he told the men at the oars which way to pull. God bless the Indian civil service, Ryder thought, and he yanked the blanket around him again as a fit of shivering ran through his body.

• • •

It was still pitch black when the *Romeo*, a steamer out of Aden, came upon the site of the explosion. She seemed to materialise out of the night like a ghost. Within minutes the air was full of the rattle of oars and the calls of rescuers as she let down her own lifeboats to gather survivors from the waters. Rope ladders unfurled down her side and soon her decks were filling up with those reclaimed from the sea.

As they came under her lee, Ryder began to strain his eyes into the pre-dawn dark looking for any sign of his wife. Two other lifeboats reached the bottom of the ladder at the same time as theirs. Both were half empty, and neither contained his wife. He felt his chest growing tight with fear. Above them, a net was lowered to lift those too injured to climb. Tadesse clambered up the ladder ahead of Ryder. He was halfway up, following the boy, when he heard a cry and looked up into Amber's face, peering over the rail.

'Oh, Ryder! Thank God! Come quickly.'

He scrambled through the crowds on the deck until he reached the small party of his friends. They had found a spot by the great funnel. His wife lay between them on a bed of blankets, with his employees' coats over her. She was white as snow, even through her tanned skin. Rusty handed the baby awkwardly to Amber, who bounced him against her shoulder.

He was fractious and crying. Ryder dropped to his knees by his wife, a terror he had never known before turning his thoughts thick and heavy. He put his hand to her throat and felt her pulse, weak and rapid, but he could feel it, and he thanked God as it fluttered under his fingertip.

'What happened?' he said.

'Something from the explosion struck her. Shoulder and head,' Rusty said quietly. 'We've stopped the bleeding, but she hasn't woken.'

Ryder had not even noticed Tadesse had followed him. The boy dropped to his knees and began gently to touch Saffron's skull with his long, delicate fingers.

'What are you doing, son?' Ryder whispered.

'My family were healers,' he replied. 'I can help.' He looked up. 'Does anyone have a needle?'

A middle-aged woman with an infant on her lap, who was watching from a foot or two away, put her hand in her coat and brought out a felt needle-holder. She passed it over to them without a word. Ryder noticed it was embroidered in green letters: *With happy memories of Ireland*.

Tadesse opened it carefully, then pulled out the thinnest of the steel needles it contained. He examined it in the dawn light, then put it between his lips, sucking it carefully. Then he bent over Saffron again.

'You had better know what you're doing,' Ryder growled.

'I do.' Tadesse didn't look up, but probed carefully with his fingers behind Saffron's right ear at the edge of her skull. He nodded to himself and pushed her hair away, then very gently at first, then with a little more pressure, pushed the needle into the spot he had found. He shifted its position slightly, then Ryder saw the muscles around his neck and shoulders relax, and he pulled the needle out. A trickle of watery blood ran across Saffron's neck and chin. Tadesse patted away the liquid with his sleeve, then cleaned the needle and returned it to the case. 'She'll wake now.' He touched her cheek with his knuckles and, as if in answer, her eyes fluttered open.

'Tadesse, I owe you my life,' Ryder said.

'Ryder? You are here at last,' Saffron murmured. 'Where is Leon?'

'He's here, Saffy. Amber too. We are all safe.' He stroked her forehead with infinite care.

'Good. What happened, Ryder? Why did the ship blow up?'

'I don't know, my darling.' She seemed content, and her eyes closed again. Ryder looked quickly at Tadesse.

'Better you let her sleep, sir,' the boy said. 'She must stay quiet for a while, to let her head heal. But she may sleep now. I shall watch.'

Ryder settled himself on the deck and closed his eyes as exhaustion washed over him. He looked at the boy again, studying him more carefully. His skin was very dark, but his features were almost European. He was perhaps older than Ryder had thought at first, but he couldn't be more than twelve years old. He shivered slightly as the dawn air chilled his damp cotton shirt and knee-length trousers. Ryder took the blanket from his own shoulders and put it over the boy's. Tadesse thanked him without looking away from his patient.

Amber was having trouble with her nephew. He stretched his limbs out and yelled at the breaking dawn. Saffron stirred in her sleep and Tadesse frowned at the baby. Ryder reached up to take him from his sister-in-law, but though Leon stopped crying for long enough to peer at his father for a moment, he soon started up again.

'He's hungry,' the woman who had given them the needle said. Tadesse offered her back the green felt case. 'Don't think I fancy having the one you stuck in that wee girl's head, son,' she said, eyeing it suspiciously.

Tadesse removed the needle and threaded it into his shirt, then closed the case and handed it to her.

'Thank you.' She turned to Ryder. 'And while I'm doing your family favours, how about you hand that baby over? I'm still nursing my youngest, and that little devil could do with learning to share.'

Ryder laid his son in her arms, and she turned away slightly and began fiddling with the buttons at her breast. The engineers coughed and looked out to sea, and the woman rearranged her shawl over her shoulder and baby Leon.

'That's the idea, treasure,' she said to him. The crying stopped at once and the woman began to sing a lullaby to him, very softly. Ryder put his hand over that of his sleeping wife and saw that she was smiling again.

Rusty risked glancing back and, seeing all was decent, pulled his pack of cards from his pocket and started dealing cards to Patch and Dan. Amber was sitting cross-legged on the deck, staring out as the sun began to climb. Ryder looked around him. It was a strange moment of peace. For a second he thought of what he had lost, the fortune in equipment and goods that had gone down with the ship, then he stopped himself. Time enough for a reckoning later. At least, he thought wryly, he no longer needed to work out how to get all that heavy mining gear to the mountains. Rusty paused in his dealing to hand Ryder a cheroot and his matches. Ryder lit up and drew deep. The Abyssinian boy settled himself in the shade where he could also watch over Saffron's sleep.

'Tadesse,' Ryder said, 'do you speak the languages of Tigray?'

'Yes. It is my mother's country.'

'We are travelling that way. Would you like to join my family?'

The boy stared slowly around the group, then squinted at Ryder sideways.

'What is your name?'

'Ryder Courtney. You just saved my wife, Saffron.' He named the other members of their party, pointing them out with the glowing end of his cheroot. 'Well?'

Tadesse shook his head. 'I went to Cairo in service of a white man, Mr Ryder. He lost his money at cards and left me there. I thank you for carrying me from the ship, but I shall serve my own people now.'

'As you wish,' Ryder said. 'I shall be in Massowah for some days if you change your mind.'

At first Penrod thought the rapping on the door was part of his dream of distant gunfire. Then he thought it was simply Lady Agatha's servants, keen to make sure they did not catch their mistress on her hands and knees, her delicious pink buttocks lifted and trembling while Penrod took her hard from behind. Once they were sure of that, they would clear the debris of last night's debauchery and then be gone again in silence. But the rapping didn't stop and he opened his eyes. Of course, they had returned to his own house last night. Penrod had suffered deprivation without complaint when travelling across the desert. He could sleep on rock as soundly as on silk and dine off flatbread and gruel as well as pheasant from his brother's estate in Scotland and foie gras imported directly from Paris. When luxury was available, however, Penrod had the means and the taste to enjoy the best, and his own servants were as discreet and efficient as Agatha's.

'Go away,' he called out. At first he thought he'd been obeyed, but instead the door squeaked as it was inched open and a small face peered around at him. The eyes widened as they took in the sleeping form of Agatha. She was quite naked, lying on her back, arms thrown wide. The swell of her large milk-white breasts would have made Rubens choke with eagerness. Penrod made no attempt to cover her.

'What do you want, Adnan?' He had seen the boy once or twice in the months since their encounter in the bazaar. Yakub had obviously found work for him of one sort or another – the boy looked better dressed and better fed than he had before. He stepped into the room and with a visible wrench tore his eyes away from Lady Agatha and looked at Penrod instead. Luckily for him, Agatha snorted in her sleep and turned away. Perhaps not so lucky, as now Adnan had to resist the temptation to stare at her peach of an arse.

'Speak, boy, or get out of here.' Penrod's head throbbed. He had never had a hangover before in his life, but since Agatha had introduced him to opium, his mornings were becoming heavier and more clouded.

The boy stepped forward. He held out a newspaper, which Penrod snatched from him. The front-page story described the arrival in Massowah of the steamer *Romeo*, carrying the survivors of a terrible maritime disaster. The editor was sorry to tell his readers that the boilers of the steamship *Iona* had exploded in the dead of night, and the resulting loss of life had been terrible. Penrod knew perfectly well this was the ship that Amber was taking into Abyssinia with that tradesman Courtney. Not that he had made any enquires himself, but his fellow officers at the club always seemed to find a way to let him know any news of Amber and those associated with her. He had been informed of the success of the stage version of *Slaves of the Mahdi*, the outrageous praise lavished on Saffron's paintings and the birth of Leon Courtney. It did not matter that he had seen none of them since that day in Shepheard's; each fragment of gossip had eaten into his soul like acid.

He did not move or breathe. Adnan began talking.

'My master, the wise and brave Yakub, your loyal companion through many adventures, sends you greetings, and wishes to let you know that out of the great love he bears for you, he lowered himself so far as to speak with the mercenary and untrustworthy oaf Bacheet, slave and follower of Ryder Courtney, and enquire of the fate of al-Zahra, who was once dear to you. Although this Bacheet offered my master grievous insults, my master insisted on knowing all that the perfidious monster had to tell. Bacheet has received a telegram from Massowah. Al-Zahra is well and survived the disaster uninjured. Her sister was wounded but will, *inshallah*, recover swiftly, and Mr Courtney and his son escaped without injury. Your loyal Yakub has no wish to trouble you, or suggest you may still have any love for al-Zahra, but out of his love for you he offers this crumb of news in case it may be of any interest to you.'

All this came tumbling out in one fluid, rehearsed speech and at a great rate. Penrod could imagine Yakub making the boy practise and repeat it. He could even imagine Yakub's stately address to Bacheet in the coffee shop they both frequented, and where for the most part they took great pleasure in refusing to acknowledge each other's existence.

Breathe, Penrod told himself. Breathe. He lifted his head and looked at the boy.

'My greetings to my honoured friend, your master, and with them my thanks. While I have no particular interest in the fate of Ryder Courtney or his hangers-on, it is always an advantage to have the best information and I thank him for the trouble taken in procuring it.' Penrod spoke in the same courtly style of the little speech the boy had given. 'Now get out,' he added.

Adnan needed no more encouragement. He turned and ran, and Penrod heard his sandals slapping on the stone floor of the corridor outside.

Beside him Agatha turned back towards him and yawned. 'Who was that?'

'No one,' Penrod replied, throwing the newspaper to the floor. He ran his hand firmly down her side, along the curve of her body. Was it in his own mind or did her body stiffen at his touch? The thought excited him. He pulled her towards him, under him, then leaned down and took one of her large pink nipples into his mouth, sucked it, then as it hardened, bit just a little too sharply. She groaned then yelped. Her hands gripped his upper arms, and he neither knew nor cared if she was pulling him to her or holding him off. He took a handful of her thick blonde hair, still tousled and matted from their love making of the previous night. She closed her eyes and gave a little moan. He thought of the glimmer of pleasure he had seen in her eyes the day Amber had broken off their engagement, how eagerly she had returned to his bed, hung off his arm, thought herself victorious.

He lowered his face so his moustache just brushed the pretty pink lobe of her ear. 'Be careful what you wish for, my dear,' he whispered, then thrust into her.

. . .

'Mr Ryder!' The voice cut through the pandemonium on the dockside like a church bell. 'Mr Ryder!'

Ryder turned, keeping his arm around Saffron as the man who had called out strode towards them through the crowd of passengers, officials, porters and the wrecked and wondering survivors of the *Iona*. He was a very tall Abyssinian, dressed in snow-white robes that fell in soft folds to his knees, and he carried an ebony walking stick with a silver head. Not that he seemed to need it to walk, as his stride was easy and fluid, but it added to his air of authority. The crowd seemed to part miraculously in front of him.

Lord, Amber thought, we are being greeted by Moses himself.

Ryder put out his hand and the Abyssinian gentleman took it in his own. They both bowed low until their shoulders touched.

'Ato Bru!' Ryder said. 'Are you well?'

'Thanks be to God, I am well. And you?'

Amber had learned about the proper manner to exchange greetings with a native of Abyssinia. This gentleman undoubtedly knew that Ryder had lost everything during the disaster of the *Iona* and he could see with his own eyes that the party was exhausted and threadbare, but for the next few minutes, as Ryder and Bru kept their hands clasped, they asked after each other's families, harvest and business, each time thanking God for his kindness, they reported only health, wealth and well-being. Amber listened carefully, hearing Amharic spoken by a new voice. It had a rhythm and flow to it which reminded her of Arabic, but it had a weight to it too. A fine and subtle language for telling of epic adventures around a campfire, she thought.

Dan leaned forward and whispered to her, 'What's the news, Miss B? Can you understand anything they are saying?'

'I can,' she whispered back. 'And no news yet. They are still saying hello.'

'Lordy, lordy!' Dan said and began to stare around him, shielding his eyes as he did from the brilliant sun. The heat was astounding. They had docked on the island that provided Massowah with the best deep-water port between Suakin and

Djibouti. A town had grown up to serve and exploit it, connected to the mainland by causeways made of huge slabs of pale yellow stone. In the distance, smudged in a lavender haze, rose the foothills and the long, almost invisible climb to the highlands of Abyssinia and the kingdom of Emperor John. The steep slopes seemed to trap the heat around them. The waters in the port were a startling blue and the sands of the shore bone white. Above the fort, which watched over the port, the Italian flag hung limply, as if exhausted by the heat. The stone minaret of the mosque rose imperiously over the town, which seemed to be mostly made up of wicker huts arranged along the shore.

'What sort of place is this?' Rusty asked quietly.

'Massowah itself is a coral island,' Amber answered, happy to be the guide now. 'They have no fresh water here. Rainwater is gathered in cisterns, and the rest is brought over from the mainland.'

'And is it always this hot?'

Amber nodded. 'Oh yes, that's why the houses are all wicker. You can't breathe in a stone house.' She saw his puzzled look as he glanced at the scattered stone buildings dotted among the wicker. 'Those are for stores. In case of fire.'

Ryder and Ato Bru seemed to have finished their conversation.

'We have a house,' Ryder told them. 'On Talud.'

'But damn all to put in it,' said Rusty under his breath.

• • •

Ato Bru had procured two local servants for them as well as a house. The house was in fact a large courtyard with a stone storehouse at one end and four thatched wicker huts close to the shore, positioned to catch any shade or breeze. Saffron had refused any offers of a donkey to carry them the short distance from the port to their new home, but now she looked exhausted. The men Bru had hired both spoke Arabic and for the first time since she had broken off her engagement, Amber thought she might be of use. She discussed with the senior servant, a very correct middle-aged man who appeared from his dress to be a Mohammedan, where the different members of the party would sleep. He listened to her with his eyes cast down, surprised at first to hear her speak his language so well, then he began to nod at her suggestions and make some of his own. These Amber greeted with enthusiasm, and before they had spent ten minutes together, it was clear they approved of each other mightily.

Amber then persuaded Saffron into the hut she would share with her husband and child. Saffron looked in danger of arguing; her jealously guarded role as bringer of all domestic comfort was being usurped. Amber ordered her to sit on the woven couch that was the only furniture, and by way of settling the matter, handed Saffron baby Leon. Then she sat down beside her.

'Let me help, Saffy! I'll consult with you about everything, of course I shall, but you are injured and you have to get well as quickly as you can.' Saffron still looked sulky and suspicious. 'After all, I might just be able to manage here, where everyone speaks at least some Arabic, but I shan't be of any use at all for ages once we get to the interior, so you have to be fit for that.'

Saffron appeared mollified. She gave a quick nod, then lifted Leon's tiny hand to her mouth, blowing on his palm till the baby beamed and giggled.

'Now, Mr Ibrahim is preparing something for us to eat, but what shall we dress in, Saffy? We have nothing but what we are wearing now. Shall we wear native dress?'

'Certainly not,' Saffron said in a singsong voice, so the baby would carry on gurgling happily. 'The Abyssinians have quite strong ideas about Europeans who turn up looking as if they are going to a fancy dress party, don't they, Leon?' She yawned. 'Perhaps Leon and I might just sleep for a little. Ryder said it was hot here, but I don't think he explained the half of it.'

A shadow moved across the doorway. Amber twisted around and saw Tadesse was waiting for them to notice him. He had a bowl of water at his feet and a cotton bag slung over his shoulder.

'The wound, Miss Amber, in Mrs Saffron's shoulder – it should be washed and . . .' He made a sewing gesture with his hands, then patted the cotton bag. 'I have brought everything I need.'

Amber looked slightly doubtful. 'Of course it must be taken care of, but Saffy, would you not like me to fetch an Italian doctor? We must be able to find one, surely.'

Saffron snorted and handed Leon back to Amber before she carefully withdrew her bandaged arm from Ryder's coat.

'Any Italian doctor here is bound to be a drunk. No, I'm better off with Mr Tadesse, I think.' The boy looked pleased. 'You can leave me with him, Amber.'

Amber moved so Saffron could settle more comfortably on the woven couch and laid the baby down next to her. Leon's large eyes searched the patterns of light and shade above them, and he reached out his small fists as if trying to catch the heavy air. The heat didn't seem to be bothering him at all and he blew neat little bubbles. Amber stroked his soft scalp and felt a twist of envy and longing in her loins. Then she sighed. She had no memory of her mother – she had died when the twins were very small – but she did know the reputation her mother had enjoyed for making do and managing in whatever far-flung corner of the empire her husband was sent to. Amber hoped she had some of that spirit of enterprise in her own blood.

Tadesse began to lay out bandages and a pair of small clay pots from his cotton sack, and Amber left the hut to discuss female tailoring with Mr Ibrahim.

• • •

Once Ryder saw that Amber was taking control of the domestic arrangements and looking after Saffron, he said his farewells for the day to Ato Bru, then returned to the dockside to speak to the local shipping agent. He was owed some insurance money by the shipping company, though it would in no way be enough to compensate him for his losses. He signed a vast number of papers and the agent agreed to hold any funds for him until he called for them.

Someone waved from a patch of shade a few yards to his left, and he saw the Indian gentleman who had helped pull him and Tadesse from the sea. He was seated on a shaded bench and drinking tea. He was still wearing the grey suit he had been wearing on the *Iona* and had somehow managed to keep his dress immaculate despite the shipwreck and rescue. He could have just stepped out of a government office in Cairo.

Ryder went to shake his hand and accepted his offer of a seat in the relative cool of the eaves of the teahouse, and a glass of what tasted like dusty warm water. It was still welcome. The man introduced himself as Sanjay Guptor and told Ryder he had been studying law in England, and was now returning to his own country.

'Though without my books!' He threw up his hands, then winked and tapped his forehead. 'I must hope some of the learning has stuck. Now, when I saw you first, Mr Courtney, you were dashing to the engine room, I think. Tell me, what did you see?'

It was strange, he seemed to have emerged quite cheerfully from the disaster. Ryder was impressed, so described what he had seen and heard in the engine room without reservation.

Mr Guptor looked thoughtful. 'Explosions in the fireboxes? Coal does not usually explode, does it, Mr Courtney?'

Ryder sipped his tea and stared out across the bustling docks. Some of the injured were still being taken off the rescue ship. 'It does not, Mr Guptor.' A number of men in Italian army uniforms were arranging transport to the military hospital for the most severely hurt, reuniting families, organising help for the rest. 'I once read about a thing called a coal torpedo used during the civil wars in America,' Ryder continued.

Guptor pursed his lips briefly. 'I have heard of such things also. One drills a hole in a lump of coal, or many lumps if one has patience and time enough, then fills the holes with gunpowder. A little wax and coal dust and it is a bomb just waiting for its moment. But who would want to destroy the *Iona*? Do you think some rival shipping line would do such a thing?'

Ryder shook his head. 'No.'

They were both silent for a while. 'You lost a great deal more than books when the *Iona* sank, did you not, Mr Courtney?' Guptor asked.

'I did.'

'Tell me, when you were preparing for this adventure, did you perhaps experience unusual delays, more confusions and difficulties than you might have expected?'

Ryder frowned. 'I have been doing business in Africa for many years, Mr Guptor. I am used to delays and confusions.' Even as he spoke he ran through the events of the last few weeks in his mind. A lost order now and again, another incident when the specifications in his letter had apparently been misread, Rusty's anger at a botched delivery of chemicals from London. Had he also said something about an Englishman asking rather too many questions in Lamb's Hotel? In the fury of preparation and the excitement of Leon's birth, Ryder had dismissed each incident, but now, in the light of the explosion at sea, they seemed to form a pattern.

He cleared his throat. 'I am sorry about your books, Mr Guptor.'

The Indian shrugged. 'I can buy more. I shall sit here and wait for the next ship home, and think how to tell my thrilling tales of adventure to my family when I arrive. London was rather dull, nothing but work and fog, so I am glad to have a story worth repeating.' He set his glass down on the bench beside him. 'I have spoken to many people from the *Iona* in the last few hours, Mr Courtney. I can give you my thoughts, if you would like to hear them?'

'Please do.'

'The only unusual cargo being carried on that ship was yours. The shipments otherwise were the usual luxuries and trade goods that pass along the Red Sea twenty times a month. Thus I conclude if the ship was not sabotaged by a rival shipping line, it must have been your cargo someone wanted to sink to the seabed. Now I consider it, and I think if I were a man who wanted to destroy or delay an unusual cargo, and not be close by when this destruction occurred, then I might use this coal torpedo.' He sipped his tea again and kept his eyes fixed on the activity of the dock. 'And I think a person ready to sink a ship to stop you might try again to do so, unless you cease in this endeavour.'

Ryder breathed deeply, letting the hot air fill his lungs. 'They might. My thanks for the tea, Mr Guptor, and your thoughts.'

He shrugged. 'You are welcome to them. Perhaps it was just some strange accident and you have nothing to worry about at all, but be careful, Mr Courtney. If this was an act of sabotage against your enterprise, then you have an enemy who is willing to slaughter many innocent men, women and children just to frustrate you.' Ryder felt the hairs on the back of his neck prickle. 'I would not have such an enemy. I shall pray for you when I return home, Mr Courtney.'

'My thanks again.'

Mr Guptor put out his hand and Ryder shook it warmly, and then strode off into the blazing light.

● ● ●

Tadesse had cleaned Saffron's wound and applied some oil from one of his clay pots. Now he was threading his needle. The scent of the oil was sharp and medicinal. The smell made Saffron think of vivid greens. The ache of the wound had been replaced by a sensation of cold and she felt a pleasant tiredness.

She asked Tadesse, 'It's not my brain going soft, is it?'

'No, Mrs Saffron, I think your head will heal nicely if you rest for a few days. The oil numbs the pain and makes us a little quiet and dreaming.' He sucked the needle, then rubbed more of the oil over it and along the thread until it glistened. 'But I must draw the wound together now, and it will still sting as I do so. Are you prepared?'

She nodded and stretched out her arm.

'You can turn away, if you wish.'

'I want to be sure you sew straight.'

He laughed quietly. 'You will have a scar, I think.'

'I don't mind. Scars show we've lived. Now do get on with it.'

She couldn't help hissing with the pain as the needle went through her flesh, but she did not flinch or turn away. Tadesse tied and cut the first stitch and began the next.

'Straight enough, Mrs Saffron?' he said, without taking his eyes from his work.

'Straight enough, my friend.'

Saffron wished she had her sketchbook to hand. The way the fierce light made its way through the wicker walls, highlighting the shadows of the boy's face, would have made a beautiful study. She wondered if she'd be able to get that shading in oils. Almost all of her supplies were at the bottom of the Red Sea now, all the beautiful colours she had ordered from London – Cadmium Yellow and Rose Madder, Prussian Blue and Viridian. She had a vision of the elegant tubes floating down through the water. Tadesse had already finished another stitch. The pain became distant, just another colour in the day.

'What is your story, Tadesse? How did you end up on the ship?'

He snipped the thread with a pair of small steel scissors. 'Perhaps I am a lost prince, Mrs Saffron.'

'I am sure you are a prince, but you don't look lost.'

He shifted the position of her arm slightly so the light fell across the part of the wound he was now drawing closed. 'I was born by Lake Tana. My father was from those parts, my mother from Tigray. It was my father and aunties who taught me medicine. Then, when I was ten, some Englishmen came to the lake. I liked them. But they brought a disease with them. Smallpox. My mother, father, aunties were all killed by it.'

'I am sorry, Tadesse.'

He shrugged and smoothed a little more oil on the needle and thread before beginning his final stitch. 'One of the Englishmen, Jones, felt sorry for me. I went as his servant as far as Suez, but then he lost his money in a card game and he had to sell his watch to pay for his passage to London. He got me work on the steamer so I might find my way home. Very good, Mrs Saffron, it is done.'

Saffron looked at the row of neat stitches running down her arm. The edges of the wound were pink and clean. She could almost feel the flesh knitting together again.

'Now, I shall bandage it again, so the little baby does not pull them out.' Leon gurgled next to them as if he had heard and they both smiled. Tadesse picked up the prepared strips of clean cloth.

'Where did you gather all these supplies, Tadesse?'

He shrugged his thin shoulders. 'I met a man of my people in the market. He has heard the name Ryder Courtney and gifted me these things to treat you.'

Saffron looked at him closely. She had heard her husband's offer of work to the boy and his refusal, yet here he was now, tending to her.

'Have you changed your mind, Tadesse? Will you come with us?'

He shot a glance at her, but seemed embarrassed to meet her eye. Saffron wondered if his friend in the market had also told him he had little chance of working for anyone else.

'Yes, I shall work for you and Mr Ryder. Though perhaps you are going back to Cairo?'

The wound was beginning to ache again. He carefully laid pads of cloth over his handiwork, then began to bind them loosely around her arm.

Saffron frowned. 'Why do you say that?'

'I heard the men of Mr Ryder talking. They say you have no reason to go to Tigray now.' He finished, helping her put Ryder's coat over her shoulder again.

Saffron narrowed her eyes. 'We'll see about that.'

• • •

Having made his way back to the house on Tàlud, Ryder walked slowly across the yard to the hut where his mining crew had been billeted. Now his wife was recovering and his son safe, it was time to calculate his resources and decide what he should do next. He thought with wry nostalgia of his compound in Khartoum, the place where, before the dervishes of the Mahdi had brought chaos and destruction, he had laid up a store of treasures. Ivory and gold, trade goods gathered from the richest and most unexplored territories of East Africa, a leather-bound library on the flora and fauna of this continent he loved, a menagerie of exotic beasts calling to him from the compound and his own river steamer, *Intrepid Ibis*, waiting at the dock, ready to carry it all to Cairo. That was before General Gordon commandeered her, of course, and before the victories of the Mahdists had made it impossible for him to carry on his business on the broad reach of the Nile.

Now almost all of what he had salvaged and saved for was at the bottom of the Red Sea. On the other hand Amber had told him that she and Saffron had rescued their supply of fat Maria Theresa dollars, and that Saffron still had his Star of Judea pinned to the inside of her coat. It had no great value in itself, but it was a sign of the regard in which he was held at the Abyssinian court and as such was worth more than diamonds. In his own wallet of papers, protected by their oiled leather case, he still had the letters of introduction from Emperor John, requesting Mr Ryder be given every assistance and even noting the daily pay due to any subject of the emperor's whom he might employ. The folder also now contained permissions to mine and the deeds to the land in the mountains above Adrigat procured by Ato Bru. These pieces of parchment, heavy with seals and each written in four

languages, had cost him dear, but what were they worth without
the equipment he needed? Might he have to return to trading
until he could afford to replace what was lost and rusting on the
seabed? Could he risk continuing further in the enterprise if, as
Mr Guptor had suggested, someone was trying to sabotage him?
He had no fear for himself, but the idea of any harm coming to
his wife and son laid a heavy weight on his heart. The sisters were
rich from the sales of Amber's book. For a moment he considered sending them away to England, ordering them to live on
their own in respectable comfort until he got back on his feet
again. He shook his head. Saffron would never go to England
without him. She didn't even remember the place, staying with
him in Abyssinia when Amber went to visit the land of her birth.
Home was wherever they were together.

He looked up at the hills beyond the port. Beyond them lay
Abyssinia, the roof of Africa. He could almost taste the air and
he realised his hands had clenched into fists. He refused to go
crawling back to Cairo defeated. He would find a way.

He stooped to enter the hut. Rusty, Dan and Patch were loung-
ing on rugs laid across the beaten earth floor. One of the servants had brought them coffee and flatbread, and the local version
of beer. It tasted thin and acidic, but it was safer than unboiled
water. Ryder sat down between them and a beaker of the stuff was
poured and handed to him. Today the beer tasted like nectar, far
better than the dusty tea he'd enjoyed with Guptor, and he sensed
a new energy flowing through his tired muscles.

'Mr Courtney, a boat heading for Suez is due to stop off here
in three days' time,' Dan said. 'I guess I'll be on it.'

'Me too,' Patch said, scratching his stubble with his fingernails. 'It was a bold venture, Courtney, but the gods are against
you. If we could have got that kit up into those hills, and the
strike was as good as you hoped, we might have had a throw
of the dice. But now it's gone and your money with it, well, we
haven't even got dice to throw with.'

Ryder did not reply, just looked around at Rusty and raised
his eyebrow. The engineer's leg was bouncing up and down.

'I'm not so sure,' he said at last. The two older men groaned. Ryder guessed they'd been talking this through without him.

'Now listen, fellas—' Rusty tried to continue.

Patch waved his hand dismissively. 'Enough, Rusty! It took six months and all Courtney's money to get that kit together when we were in Cairo. You're never going to get replacements here in a year, even if Courtney can afford it. And even if you did, I'm not rotting in this oven waiting while you do.'

'I know, I know,' Rusty said, leaning forward. 'But these people have been digging treasure out of hills higher than these since Solomon was king. If they could do it, why can't we?' He scratched his head. 'Sure, it'll be hard going and low yields at first, scavenging what we can until we can get the gear together to process the ore properly. But Mr Courtney here has paid me for a year, and I don't want to pay him back.' Rusty folded his arms. 'So I reckon that means I'm staying and making myself useful until that year is done.'

Ryder looked at Patch. He shrugged. 'It's a crazy idea, but if you're going . . . I already spent your money paying off my debts in the Transvaal, so I guess I belong to you.'

Dan drank his beer in silence for a full minute. 'It's my opinion you'll be sending good money after bad, Courtney. Now that's said, if you want to take your family up into the wilds, I'll come with you and show you where to dig.'

Ryder drew breath to speak, but before he had the chance Saffron had ducked under the door.

'We are *not* going home!' she said and stamped her foot. The men snatched their beakers of beer from the floor before they spilled. 'Ryder, don't you dare tell me you are thinking of it for even a minute.'

'Saffy . . .'

Her scarf was still matted with blood. It made her look like a warrior wild with the spirit of battle. 'No, Ryder, listen. They've been mining here for hundreds of years. We can buy shovels, can't we?'

'My dear, you'll open up your wound,' he said quietly.

'Oh, Tadesse arrived and sewed me up. He's changed his mind and he's coming with us, by the way, and stop laughing at me . . . If these boys are too cowardly to go up to the mountains . . .'

The three men groaned and protested, and before Saffron had stopped telling them to shush and let her finish, Amber had appeared in the doorway with bolts of blue and green cloth over her shoulder. 'What's happening? I could hear you shouting from the market,' she said.

'Amber, these idiots think we should go crawling back to Cairo, just because they lost their silly equipment!'

'Why would we do that?' Amber said, her blue eyes sparkling in the gloom of the hut. 'Half the Italian army is in Massowah! They'll have gunpowder to blast the rock, and all the camping and building equipment we need to set ourselves up. Did Tadesse sew up your wound, Saffy?'

'Yes, neatly, too. Oh, what lovely fabric!' she replied with a grin, then spun back towards the men. 'See! That's exactly what I said! Well, almost. Ryder, you won't make us go home, will you? As soon as my arm is healed, I can dig and—'

Ryder stood up and in one swift movement caught his wife around the waist and kissed her hard. She struggled away. 'Ryder, I'm still talking—' He kissed her again, harder, and she yielded. Then he released her and kissed her forehead more gently.

'No, child-wife of mine, we are not going home. We are going to Axum and then on into the hills, and I swear we're not coming down until we have enough silver to build you a house of it.'

'Oh, Ryder, I am glad!' Saffron said. She put her good arm around his neck and stood on her tiptoes to kiss his cheek.

'Thank goodness for that,' Amber said brightly. 'I shall go and see about dinner.'

When Major Penrod Ballantyne arrived on the second floor of the British Consulate in Cairo to see Colonel Sam Adams, the adjutant asked him to wait for a few minutes in the anteroom.

Penrod frowned. 'I recognise you,' he said. 'You were with Evelyn Baring in 1884.'

'I was, sir,' the young man said, his surprise showing on his smooth pink face. 'But we met so briefly, and it was three years ago. You have a remarkable memory.'

Penrod did not reply at once, just turned to look through the tall windows at the mass of human activity along the banks of the Nile. The water was studded with the sails of small boats. Women laughed over their washing at the shore, trading jests with the water-sellers and fishermen. Penrod was an exceptional intelligence officer, so of course he had a remarkable memory. For many years it had been a huge asset to him in his work. He could be trusted with the most confidential and complex information, the most subtle of diplomatic messages, and carry them in his mind across deserts and over mountain ranges. But his memory also had its disadvantages. For example, he could recall with perfect clarity every moment he had spent in the company of Amber Benbrook. He could recite every word she had ever spoken to him, see every smile and, with a precision that would not fade, recall the exact expression of disgust on her face when she told him that the morals of the harem were superior to those of the Gheziera Club. Only opium dulled those memories. They remained his constant companions, but when he smoked they became tinged with a sweet nostalgia, rather than causing him immeasurable pain.

In the Sudan, Penrod had been tortured by Osman Atalan and lashed to a device called a *shebba*, designed to punish disobedient slaves. The *shebba*, simple and terrible in its design, was cut from the fork of an acacia tree, and Osman's men lashed his arms to it so the base of the fork pressed hard against his throat. Only by lifting its full weight with outstretched arms could Penrod ease the pressure on his windpipe, or by kneeling in a stupor of agony, with the trunk resting at an angle on the ground until one of Osman's henchmen kicked it aside and sent Penrod sprawling and choking into the dust. It was crucifixion without the final relief of death. He had been unable to eat or drink, or clean himself of his bodily waste. Six days tied to it had nearly killed him, but if wearing it again for a month could cure Penrod of the pain he had experienced since his engagement to Amber had come to an end, he would embrace it as a friend.

'Much has happened since then,' Penrod said to the young man at last, still looking out of the window.

'Indeed, sir.' Something in the man's tone made Penrod turn to look at him again. The adjutant blushed and hurried out of the room. The heavy door closed softly behind him, and Penrod could hear his footsteps snapping away along the marble hall.

A portrait of the young Queen Victoria, and a matching study of her handsome consort, hung in every room of importance in this building. Penrod remembered studying the one of the late Prince Albert in 1884 while waiting to be sent to the besieged city of Khartoum. Back then Penrod believed he looked rather like the handsome prince. While waiting for Baring, he had stood very straight so as not to mar his uniform of the 7th Hussars with ugly creases, his bearskin busby under his arm and his dolman slung over his shoulder. Everything about him had been perfect, from the precisely trimmed mustachios to the glossy sheen on his riding boots. He glanced up now at the portrait of Prince Albert, ageless in death. Penrod looked leaner than he had in 1884, harder, and his body was scarred with souvenirs from the months he spent with Osman Atalan. He no longer wore the magnificent uniform of the Hussars, either. While he had been a captive, Sir Charles Wilson, an intelligence officer left in command of the Khartoum relief column after Sir Herbert Stewart was mortally injured, had made Penrod a convenient scapegoat for his own incompetence. After the victory of Abu Klea, it was Penrod who had delayed their progress to Khartoum, Wilson claimed. On his return to

Cairo with the rescued Amber Benbrook, Penrod discovered the betrayal. He was disgusted, but Colonel Sam Adams persuaded him into a compromise to avoid a scandalous court martial. The senior brass were desperate to avoid dragging the whole sorry business of General Gordon and Khartoum back into the newspapers. Sir Charles was hurried off into a comfortable civil service job and Penrod, his heroic reputation garnished by his appearances in *Slaves of the Mahdi*, was asked to put together a brigade of desert fighters for the Egyptian army, a prestigious role that his fellow officers saw as yet another sign he was fortune's favoured son. Penrod had agreed, but found the work no challenge at all.

Now, as he waited for Sam Adams to summon him to his presence, Penrod did not try to stand straight. His grey serge frock coat and fawn breeches were beautifully tailored, and his servants made sure the leather of his field boots and Sam Browne belt were polished to a smooth sheen, but he no longer cared for these things as much as his tailor or servants did. For one moment he wondered if his habitual use of opium over the last few months was part of the reason for this indifference, but he dismissed the thought at once. He could stop taking opium any time he wished. He had already twice stopped using the drug for a week or two simply to demonstrate to Lady Agatha that he had a control she did not. He had suffered very little – some flu-like symptoms – but they passed quickly. When he put the pipe aside, however, the memories of Amber tortured him. Opium, like Agatha, was available, so why not make use of it? Cairo was full of quiet establishments of luxury and ease where one might enjoy its gentle pleasures if the sight of one's own walls became dull. He could almost feel the silk under his fingers, hear the soft music played in the courtyard to lull and lift the rich dreamers in the richly appointed private rooms above.

The inner door swung open and Sam Adams leaned out.

'Ballantyne! Do come in. Sorry to have kept you waiting.'

Penrod followed him into his office. It was another tall-ceilinged, elegant room – a reflection of the high esteem all the officials and central command of the army had for Sam. Penrod had won the VC that was now pinned to his chest, saving Sam from the disaster of El Obeid in 1883. The wounds Sam had received then troubled him a little even now and he walked stiffly, but he still projected the calm physical force of a natural soldier, both in the saddle or returning to his place behind his polished oak desk. It was empty of any clutter; only one sheet of paper lay in front of Sam on the green leather inlay. Penrod could see, even upside down and at this distance, that it was his own, most recent, report.

Sam settled in his chair and picked up the sheet. 'You seem to be making good progress, Ballantyne. Your superiors are impressed with the fighters you've found and the system of training you've arranged for them.'

'Thank you, sir.'

Sam continued to stare at the paper as he spoke. 'I myself have even been up to see them going through their paces once or twice. As has the commander-in-chief. We were impressed, as I say.' He looked up finally. 'But I was surprised you were not present to take them through their manoeuvres yourself.'

'I am often prevented from being with them as much as I would like because of business in the city, sir,' Penrod said smoothly. 'And I think it is important my officers have the opportunity to get acquainted with the men without me breathing down their necks.'

Sam's face suddenly flushed red. 'Business in town? Yes, we all know what that business is. I have no idea why you ended your engagement with the lovely Miss Benbrook, but the way you paraded Lady Agatha around on your arm only days later was distasteful. And what are you doing to that woman? She's aged ten years since you took her up again.'

'Are you speaking to me now as my friend, or as my superior officer?'

'As a friend, of course.'

'Then mind your own damn business.'

Sam slammed a clenched fist down on the table. Penrod did not flinch. 'Then now I'm speaking as your superior. You are an officer in Her Majesty's British Army, a representative of the empire and you do damage to our interests haunting the opium dens of Cairo with that woman on your arm. God damn it, Ballantyne, you don't even bother to hide the fact you are treating her like a whore. They are laying bets in the club that you are already selling her to Arabs in those squalid hovels for your own amusement. God, man! She is the daughter of the Duke of Kendal!'

Penrod felt a delicious, icy calm descend on him. 'And an ornament to any establishment she graces. And Sam, we never smoke in the squalid hovels. The places Lady Agatha prefers make the Gheziera Club look like a farmhouse.'

'Do not sneer at me, Major Ballantyne. I am the one friend you have left in Cairo, and even you need friends from time to time. It's bloody typical of your arrogance that you don't understand that. Heed my warning. Miss Benbrook has gone. The latest telegrams from our contacts in Massowah tell me that even after the disaster of the *Iona*, the Courtneys will not be returning to Cairo any time soon. I have cut you all the slack I can since your engagement ended, but as I say, Miss Benbrook is gone now and it is time you forgot about her. Put down the pipe, throw yourself into your duties and leave Lady Agatha alone. You've made her suffer enough.'

Penrod did not speak or move.

'At least that nonsense will be taken care of soon. Her father has heard the rumours. He's coming out to fetch her, and I would advise you to stay out of his way when he does.'

Penrod's face showed no reaction. He felt neither sorrow nor relief at the idea of Lady Agatha leaving Cairo. She had done him a great wrong and he had avenged that wrong by taking her love and turning it on her like a poison. If she stayed in Egypt he would continue his game. If she left, he would find another lover. Most women were much the same to him now.

'So be it,' he said. 'Sam, please do not concern yourself. As you said yourself, the brass are impressed with the work we've been doing and I can stop making use of the pipe any time I wish.'

Sam sighed deeply, then waved at the chair opposite him.

'Sit down for a moment.'

Penrod did so and crossed his long legs, brushing some invisible speck of dust from his breeches.

'Ballantyne, you are a fine officer and your achievements and adventures over the last few years have been nothing less than astonishing.'

'Sam, are you proposing?'

'Shut up. But you have also suffered a great deal. I read about what happened to you in Atalan's camp and though I may not be an imaginative man, I can imagine enough. Then you returned, only to be confronted with the selfish lies of an officer like Charles Wilson, then were left practically at the altar by the woman you love.'

For the first time in the conversation Penrod flinched, and Sam noticed.

'I know you enough to be sure that you were very much in love with that remarkable little girl. You show no sign of suffering – of course you don't – but I know you must suffer.'

Penrod did not reply or look at him. Sam's voice dropped as he continued to speak.

'But do not underestimate the power of opium. I saw a man die of it once. It was in India, oh, almost twenty years ago now. He was working in the stores, but he was a slippery fellow. Of course, one expects a few things to disappear, but his thievery became an embarrassment. I was ordered to lock him up until he decided to confess as to where he'd been selling the goods. It turned out later, he'd been selling them to the man who supplied him with the drug and he was so dependent on it by then, his opium-dealer was the last person in the world he'd give up to us.'

'Sam,' Penrod sighed. 'I've already told you, I'm not—'

'Oh, just sit still and listen. At the end of the first day he was groaning and shivering. We knew he wanted the drug, of course, but keeping him locked up seemed like the best way to get the information we wanted. The next day the worst of it began. Vomiting and shitting himself, then within a couple of hours he was too weak to make it to the bucket. It was around then he began screaming. God knows how he had the strength to make such an awful sound, but he did. I asked my commander every hour, on the hour, for permission to send for the doctor, but the commander always answered: "Has he given us names yet?" And each time I said he hadn't, and each time the commander said: "No doctor, then."'

Sam rubbed his chin. He seemed so lost in the memory that Penrod wondered if he even knew he was still speaking out loud.

'At dawn the following morning I had the cell swilled out and gave him fresh blankets. By Christ, the stench . . . It made a three-day-old battlefield smell like a rose garden. Two of my men threw buckets of warm water over him and his cell until most of the filth was gone, but still it came – liquid shit and bile, and the screaming . . . That was how we knew he was finally dead, when the screaming stopped. Something in his intestines must have ruptured. We wrapped his corpse in a blanket and buried it in an unmarked grave in a corner of the regimental graveyard. His body was so light. He was my height, and thin before he went in. These opium fiends always turn into living ghosts, but still. Almost nothing of him was left to bury. He was hollowed out. My commander simply said: "It will serve as a lesson to others," and carried on with his paperwork. I requested a transfer that afternoon. But I still hear his screaming some nights. I would rather face a thousand dervishes on my own than spend another hour listening to that man scream and shit himself to death.'

Penrod lifted his head. Sam Adams, the man whom he had carried from the battlefield, was comparing him to some opium-crazed servant. He felt a cold breeze of anger run through him.

'Is that all, sir?'

Sam gazed back at him. He had a look of profound sadness in his eyes, which made Penrod want to kick him.

'That's the way it is, then, is it? Yes, Ballantyne. You may go.'

• • •

A week later, Penrod recalled this conversation and was amused rather than angered by it. The contrast between himself and Agatha, and the screaming demon of Sam's nightmares, could not be more marked. They were presently occupying a room set aside and maintained purely for them in a handsome house not far from the Esbekeeyah Gardens. The sun was softened and filtered by ornately carved latticework covering the unglazed windows, leaving them in a perpetual twilight. Both Agatha and Penrod wore loose robes of the softest, snow-white brushed cotton, delicately embroidered with patterns of leaves and flowers. The floor where they reclined was thickly furnished with coloured rugs and soft silk pillows. Agatha was cooking another opium pill for him. He regarded her steadily as she worked. Her great blonde mane of hair was tumbled around her slim shoulders. He felt the twitch and pull of arousal. Savoured it. He savoured everything when he was smoking. With delicious pleasure he ran his fingers through his hair, scratching his scalp. Had Agatha lost some of her curves? Perhaps. But her leanness suited her. He laughed softly. He and the opium were harrowing the sin out of her. She used to be such a fiery little thing, the central star of Cairo high society, but now she hardly bothered with the receptions, concerts, dinners at the club and the card parties that had once been so important to her. She only wanted to be here. He had pulled her claws, right enough.

When she had called at his house in her carriage to request his company – was that this morning or the day before? – he had told her he knew her father was coming shortly, adding, 'Then this charming little liaison of ours must end.'

She had been forced to stifle a sob, putting her hand to her mouth and turning away from him. Her distress gave him a stab of satisfaction.

'What? Still hoping for marriage, Agatha? Or are you just afraid your father won't be pleased with what you've been up to on your travels?'

Her sob had turned into a sort of choking laugh. 'You used to like me, Penrod. I know you did. Then *she* came.'

Penrod turned away from her, his satisfaction spoiled. But she went on speaking.

'You liked it when I gossiped and said cruel things. It excited you. But she'd been through hell and was still such a sweet, trusting little soul, and I was enraged, more in love with you than ever, dropped and forgotten. Of course I did what I did. It's in my nature.'

Outside the carriage Penrod heard the beginning of the call to prayer, taken up and spread across the city, the great god asking his people to show him their love.

'And I knew when she broke off the engagement you'd come back to me just to punish me for wanting you,' Lady Agatha continued. 'And you have. You do. Perhaps I hoped – perhaps I still hope – that one day you will grow weary of torturing me, of torturing all that passion and cruelty out of me, and then maybe you might grow tired or bored enough to marry me.' She brushed away the tears that had gathered in the corners of her eyes. 'But you haven't forgiven me, and you aren't tired of torturing me yet, are you?'

He stared at her, a slight sneer marring his handsome face. 'No. Not yet, Lady Agatha.'

She shook her head. 'Strange – the opium makes it almost bearable, a little bit of pleasure refined out of the pain of it. And it makes the torture more delicious for you, doesn't it? Perhaps you will whore me out to your Arab friends, like they say you do in the club.'

Penrod had a sudden vision of his former fiancée standing on the steps as he'd left her that bright day outside the club. The last time Amber Benbrook had looked at him with her face glowing with love and trust.

'I would not insult my Arab friends with your touch, Lady Agatha.'

Again she gave that half laugh, half sob.

'Oh, very good, Penrod. You are a great swordsman; you always know where the blade will strike deepest, do most damage.' She bit her lip. 'I used to be frightened of my father. He is the coldest, cruellest man alive. The most unforgiving, the most ruthless. I suppose it makes some sense, then, that I fell in love with you.'

Penrod said nothing.

'And Father is here already, I think. His man – his creature – Wilson Carruthers has been here for weeks. I have seen him in the distance from time to time.' The carriage came to a gentle halt outside the house where the drug and its peace waited for them. She peered out of the shuttered window. 'Thank God we are here.'

• • •

Agatha did not speak of her father's presence, or his imminent arrival in Cairo, again, so Penrod ceased to think of it. When he was smoking he was wrapped in a soft, dark-grey cloud of indifference and pleasure. When he stayed away from the drug and saw the emptiness of his life without Amber clearly, he only punished Agatha to distract himself from the pain. Penrod had lived a charmed life until he lost Amber. He had been born into a family of wealth and prestige, and from his earliest days had been blessed with looks, courage, intelligence and a physical prowess that made him a prodigy both at his school and in the army. The world had presented him with laurels again and again, and he had accepted them as his due. Women fell into his outstretched hand and he had enjoyed their favours without ever feeling the pangs of love. Until now. Now Amber had disappeared into Abyssinia, with that adventurer Courtney, and left him here. He did not understand the feelings that assailed him, so he reacted with the rage of a wounded, cornered beast – unless the pipe was ready to calm him.

Not until the door to their sanctuary splintered open did Penrod pull himself far enough out of his opium dream to realise something was wrong. Looking back on it there must have been sounds of the men arriving, arguments in the house, but dulled and soothed, Penrod heard nothing until that moment. Framed in the light coming from the corridor Penrod saw four men. Three looked like natives of Cairo and the last was dressed in European clothing, but the light was too dim to make out his features. They hesitated, trying to see who was in the room and where. The European gave sharp orders in basic Arabic. One of the men crossed the room towards Lady Agatha, where she lay dreaming across a mess of silk pillows. He kicked aside the opium lamp as he went, and it spluttered and went out. His sandaled foot cracked the slim stem of the pipe with a harsh snap. He reached down, grabbing Agatha under the arms and hauling her to her feet. She began to fight and call out, struggling hard through the haze of the drug, but the man wrapped his thick hands around her wrists and began to drag her out of the room. She fell to her knees and tried to pull against him, but he twisted and picked her up around her waist, handling her as if she were nothing more than a doll. The two other men had been ordered to prevent Penrod interfering. They approached cautiously, unsure if he was awake or asleep. He let them come, then reached out his right hand and closed his fingers into the half-basket hilt of his cavalry sabre and drew it free of its scabbard as he leaped to his feet. The younger of the two men approaching him pulled a revolver from the folds of his *galabiyya*.

Idiot, Penrod thought. His mind felt as clear and cool as a mountain spring. He turned, raising his blade. 'You've got far too close to me for that to help.'

He swayed his own weight forward a little and the blade flashed down in a perfect arc, severing the man's wrist. For a second Penrod's assailant was too shocked to do anything but stare at his own hand, still holding the revolver but no longer any part of him, lying among the royal blue cushions at his feet.

Then he began to scream, staggering backwards as the wound began to spurt an arterial flow of blood across the embroidered hangings on the walls.

The second man had his knife in his hand and was coming in fast, the committed attack of a real warrior. Penrod caught the glimmer of the blade and brought up his sword, catching the razor edge of his opponent's dagger at the hilt, half an inch from his throat. Penrod saw the man smile slightly as he let the momentum of Penrod's block carry him to his right. He ducked under Penrod's sword arm as he threw his knife from his right hand to his left and aimed for Penrod's exposed right side. This man was an expert.

Penrod brought the dagger down with his sabre, again almost at the hilt, and launched a left hook with his closed fist against the man's right jaw. His opponent's head snapped back, but he tossed the knife back into his right hand and went low, aiming to come under and behind Penrod's sword, reaching for Penrod's femoral artery. He had found the killing blow, but in reaching for it, he had left his neck undefended for a split second and the swell of his Adam's apple was in line with Penrod's sword.

Penrod swung up fast and hard against the man's throat, and the blade went through flesh with the same ease as it sang through the perfumed air. He felt the tiny snick and pause as the sword sliced upwards through the vertebrae, while the dagger grazed his thigh. The knifeman's head was separated from his body and Penrod felt the hot, salty blood hit his face and eyes as the body fell back into the cushions.

Penrod looked around him. The man who had pulled the revolver was unconscious, if not already dead, but otherwise the room was empty. Lady Agatha, the European and his remaining Arab henchman were all gone. His sword held pointing down and slightly in front of him, Penrod raced out onto the internal balcony that ran around the central courtyard and went down the stairs. The arched doorway to the street was blocked with women and men, confused, weeping, shouting. When they saw him, the women screamed and he remembered the warmth of the knifeman's blood on his face. He threw himself into the crowd and pushed his way through the gate with the hilt of his sword. The street outside was deserted and quiet. Then he saw a carriage at the south end, just now turning into the boulevard and moving quickly. Could he reach it? He had a momentary, flashing image of himself dressed in his robe and barefoot, soaked head to foot in blood, running through the centre of Cairo.

'I shouldn't think that would be a very good idea, do you?' A voice, male and unmistakably aristocratic, drawled out of the shadows.

A match flared and Penrod winced at the sudden light. The man stepped into the small halo cast by the torches above the gates to the house. He was wearing evening dress but was bareheaded. His chestnut hair was slicked back away from his face and though both it and his moustache were lightly salted with grey, he was certainly under fifty. He was slim, but the cut of his coat showed strong muscles across his shoulders. A physique much like Penrod's own, that of a horseman and polo player.

'The sight of Major Ballantyne soaked in gore, racing through Esbekeeyah, would quite put the ladies on the veranda of Shepheard's off their champagne.'

'And you are?' Penrod said.

'Oh, I think you know who I am. And I know all about you.'

'You do?'

'Now, Major, mind your manners. When addressing a duke it is customary to do so as "Your Grace".' He exhaled. The scent of a truly magnificent cigar bloomed in the darkness. Then his gaze flicked slightly to the left and he gave a microscopic nod. Penrod did not have time to parry the blow. Something hard, a club or cosh, hit him from behind and everything went black.

· · ·

Penrod woke in his own house. He swung himself out of bed and crossed to the shaving mirror that was part of the mahogany washstand in the corner of the room. The morning breeze stirred the thin cotton drapes around the window and he could hear the clatter of carriages outside and the cries of the water-sellers. One of his servants must have tried to wash him before putting him to bed, for the worst of the gore that had covered him was gone, but his face was still smeared with blood. His head was pounding, but when he felt with his fingertips the place he'd been struck, he found no open wound or any indication his skull had been cracked. It just felt as if it had. He was naked – presumably his stained robes were being washed or burned. His uniform, freshly pressed, was hanging on the door of his wardrobe, and his sword, in its scabbard, was slung from its usual brass hook on the whitewashed wall. He opened the door and called for a hot bath and, after it was fetched and filled, he sank himself into the waters with a sigh before beginning to scrub the rest of the knifeman's blood off his skin and out from under his fingernails. The servant stood by the door, towels over his arm, ready to provide him with whatever he required.

'Who brought me home?' Penrod asked in Arabic.

The servant looked straight ahead. 'Two gentlemen: one a local, the other a European, sir.'

'Did the European wear evening dress? An Englishman in his forties?'

The servant shook his head. 'No, *effendi*. The European was younger than that.'

Penrod remembered the 'creature' Agatha had mentioned – surely the European in the doorway giving orders.

'And did they do or say anything to explain . . .' Penrod thought of how he must have appeared, unconscious and soaked in blood. '. . . my situation?'

'They said you had defeated a band of robbers, *effendi*, who had set upon them in the street, but you had been overcome by one of them in the very moment of your victory. We were told where to go and collect your uniform and sword.'

'Were you indeed?' Penrod murmured.

His headache was getting worse and his eyes felt sore and sand-blown. A slight opium cold. Well, if Agatha had been reclaimed by her father, perhaps now was the time to abandon the pipe and search out some other amusement.

'Anything else?'

'The European left a letter of thanks from his master for you.'

That would be interesting.

'Very well, I shall read it over breakfast.'

The servant looked startled. 'You wish to have breakfast, sir?'

Had it been so long since he'd eaten regular meals? Certainly time to lay down the pipe, then.

'I do,' he said calmly, then put his hand out for the towel.

. . .

The letter was interesting but brief. It informed Penrod that the disturbance at the opium house had been tidied up and Penrod was not to have any further communication with Lady Agatha. It was astonishing how condescending and insulting the duke managed to make those few lines. Penrod had never intended to see Agatha again, but now he questioned that decision. Why should she be allowed to return to the privileges of her father's protection? It amused him to think of that suave gentleman's frustration when he discovered that Agatha would climb out of the window of whatever residence he had taken if Penrod crooked his little finger. He gave a few orders and dressed, then took his charger to visit the parade ground where his troops were being trained. The day passed pleasantly enough and his headache faded. The effects of the opium cold he could conceal without much difficulty. The evening he passed in his own rooms with Sir Colin Campbell's *Narrative of the Indian Revolt*, which he had been meaning to read for some time, and a bottle of excellent scotch. He made a number of marginal notes and slept soundly.

. . .

The following morning Penrod ate a breakfast of figs and honey with genuine pleasure, and after he had drunk two thimble-sized cups of black coffee, made in the proper Egyptian manner, he stepped out into the street and prepared to mount his horse. As he was taking the reins from his servant, a slight Arab girl spoke his name. He recognised her – Akila, Lady Agatha's maid. Penrod had never spoken to her directly; he had noticed her flitting nervously through Agatha's rooms, always disappearing off into the shadows whenever he was in the house, a pretty ghost. She was shaking now. Penrod thought at first she had come for money. It was likely the duke had dismissed all Agatha's servants. She told him her name and he waited for the inevitable open palm. After a moment or two of silence he grew bored.

'What do you want?'

'They are torturing my lady,' the girl said in a rush. She looked up at him. Penrod could see her large brown eyes were wet with tears.

'Don't be foolish, child.' He began to turn away and she shot out a small hand to grab hold of his sleeve. He raised his eyebrows and she removed her hand, glancing nervously up and down the street to see if anyone had noticed her commit this immodest act of touching a man.

'No, stop,' she hissed. 'They will not give her the drug, *Af-yun*, and now she is sick. She is very sick. Please.'

'You may speak in Arabic, my dear.' He continued in that language. 'Her father will see no harm comes to her and my lady was too fond of the pipe.'

Akila shook her head hard. 'They have brought an English doctor, but he knows nothing of this sickness. The cousin of my good friend works in the house. My lady is sick and crying out. The doctor only tries to feed her English soups.'

Penrod recalled Sam's vivid description of the effects of opium withdrawal. Agatha had been smoking daily for a long time now.

'You must go,' Akila said. 'They will not listen to me. Tell them to give her the drug before want of it kills her, please, for the love of Allah who sees all and knows all.'

Penrod hesitated. His horse, irritated at the delay, whinnied, and Penrod stroked its broad shoulder.

'I cannot.'

Again that little hand shot out and grabbed him, but this time, she did not let go of his sleeve.

'You must. It is *your* fault. Yours. Before you brought your little English girl to the city, she had smoked perhaps once, twice. She thought it might amuse you. Then when the English child came, my lady began to smoke more, too much more. When you sent the little girl away, I thought now my lady will be happy and will stop, but it was a thousand times worse. You! You brought her to this. She cries out, like a soul in hell, and it is your fault. They will not let me see her! Strangers attend her! Wash her poor body! You must help.'

Penrod felt his conscience stir stiffly in his chest, like an animal that has been asleep a long time.

'I will write to the duke, her father, my child.'

The girl let out a great sob of relief and he reached out a hand to touch her shoulder, to offer some comfort, but she turned and ran away up the road, and his fingers only touched the warm air where she had been.

'Walk my horse,' he said to the servant and handed back the reins. 'I shall be a few minutes more.' He went back into the house, stripping off his riding gauntlets, and called for paper and ink.

. . .

When Penrod returned home in the early evening, he was not surprised to see an envelope waiting for him on the silver tray by the door. He opened it. It contained his own letter to the duke, and a note on a visiting card.

His Grace the Duke of Kendal declines any correspondence with Major Ballantyne, it read, and was signed in an oddly neat, almost schoolboyish handwriting: *Carruthers*. Penrod flung it back onto the tray, then went out into the courtyard.

Yakub was waiting for him. They greeted each other with the warmth of old friends and settled in the courtyard under the flowering jasmine to drink tea. When the leisurely unfolding of mutual enquiries as to the health of each, their families and Yakub's trade was completed, they came to the matter at hand.

'Who is this man, *effendi*?' Yakub asked, as he curled his long, gnarled fingers around his glass and lifted it to his lips, sighing with elaborate pleasure as he sipped the delicately perfumed brew.

'The Duke of Kendal, James Woodforde,' Penrod replied. 'His family is an ancient one that has long enjoyed much power politically in my country. He also made a great deal of money when coal was discovered on one of his estates in the north. Since then he has invested in gold and diamond-mining in South Africa, and is exploring the mineral wealth of North and East Africa.'

Yakub nodded slowly. 'He has taken a house on the west bank. It is a very fine house with gardens of its own. The house a king would be proud of. He keeps many servants. One or two Europeans. One who is a snake and does everything for him, this Carruthers. He has been in Cairo for some time. The other is called Doctor – a trembling leaf of a man.'

'What manner of local servants has he hired?'

Yakub twisted his lip and spat richly on the ground. 'He has hired mercenaries and put them in the uniform of houseboys. All his daughter's servants have been paid off. She has one woman to tend her now. An old, cruel, stupid woman I would not let tend to the most flea-bitten pig-headed curse of an ass in my yard.' He sipped his tea with great delicacy. 'The lady's maid – Akila – she waits at the gates of the house and will not leave, such is the love she has for her mistress.'

Penrod had never thought of Agatha as someone who might inspire loyalty in her servants.

'When does the duke mean to leave for England?'

Yakub shrugged. 'I think he does not mean to leave for some time. The house is taken for three months.' He paused, and Penrod waited for him to go on.

It was a perfect evening now. The heavy and languorous heat of the day was gone. The scents in the garden were sweet without being cloying, and in the centre of the little garden the fountain sang, low and cheerful. Yakub looked unhappy, though, his ugly but friendly face folded into creases of thought and worry.

'What else, my old friend?'

'I sent the boy Adnan to talk with some of the servants who work in the garden. They know nothing of Lady Agatha, but they told him to run away quick because the duke has a *djinn* trapped in the house who screams all day and night to be released.'

Penrod felt his mouth go dry. 'Very well. Yakub, I thank you, and I ask that you and Adnan keep away from that house and those men from now on.'

'Whatever your wish, *effendi*. My only desire is to serve you.'

Yakub was a Jaalin Arab, driven out of his own tribe after a blood feud, and with a limp from an old wound that meant neither Queen nor Khedive would take his service. He had guided Penrod through the Sudanese desert many times, and the bravery, endurance and military skill Yakub saw his master display had won a devotion from him bordering on reverence. Penrod had thought nothing of risking death by torture to help Amber escape from the harem, and without him they might never have broken free of the grip of Osman Atalan. Since that triumph,

Yakub had taken his reward, bought a boarding house in the city and made a number of other shrewd investments, from coffee houses to the luxurious *dhows* adapted to carry tourists rather than cargo up and down the lower reaches of the Nile. Whatever his recent successes, his devotion to Penrod had never wavered. Except for a moment in that garden, Penrod saw another expression cross his face, swift as a bird's shadow on the desert sand. It was pity.

• • •

Penrod found Sam Adams at the Gheziera Club, of course. Penrod responded to none of the greetings offered by his fellow officers or the local dignitaries who used the club as a second office, only acknowledged the beribboned generals with whom Sam was dining with a quick nod.

'I must speak to you. Now,' Penrod said, and he said it in such a way that Sam excused himself at once and followed Penrod out of the dining room and into a quiet corner of the lobby.

'Well?' he asked sharply.

Penrod explained as quickly and concisely as he could.

'And what exactly do you expect me to do about it?' Sam said and hunched his shoulders.

'Whatever needs to be done!' Penrod replied. 'Talk to him, and if you can't make him see sense, send in the police.'

Sam's face flushed a dark red. 'You hated that woman a week ago and now you want me to tell the Duke of Kendal how to care for his own daughter? And on what charge exactly would you send in the police? Keeping his daughter away from opium?'

Penrod leaned in close to him. 'Sam, you know what might happen to her if you do nothing.'

'The process of withdrawal doesn't kill every opium fiend.'

'That's not good enough.'

Sam Adams raised his voice. His words echoed across the black and white tiles of the lobby and reverberated off the marble columns. Passing men in uniform flinched and hurried past.

'You dare tell me what's good enough? You?'

Penrod did not move and held Sam's gaze. Sam's voice dropped again.

'Damn you. The duke dines here tonight. I shall speak to him. You get out and stay away from me, Ballantyne. I can't stand to look at you.'

He strode back into the dining room, leaving Penrod on his own in the chill shadows of the lobby. He took a long, slow breath. Sam would speak to the duke, Penrod was certain of that, but could the duke be persuaded to be reasonable in time to save Agatha? Penrod had no idea how long Agatha might be able to survive in her current state. Every hour was precious. If Sam could not be stirred into immediate action, Penrod had to do something himself.

Within two hours he had changed his uniform for a filthy turban and stained *galabiyya*, and his riding boots for rough camel-hide sandals. Now that he could pass through the streets of the city without attracting a second glance, he made his way to the duke's temporary palace. It did not take him long to find Akila. She was keeping vigil at the gate that led to the servants' entrance on the north wall of the house's elegant garden. He whistled to her softly out of the darkness and she approached warily, coming to a stop some ten feet from him and showing in the light of one of the torches that lined the walls the glimmer of a knife in her hand.

'If you are a robber, I have nothing. If you come to mock the grief of a loyal woman, I shall cut the laugh from your belly.'

'Peace, my child. I come neither to mock nor to steal.' Penrod stepped forward and lifted his head.

She gasped. 'You?'

'The duke will not listen to me. Have you more news?'

She sheathed her knife and shrank back into the shadows. 'I have bribed the guards to send me word. They have taken every coin I have, and tell me only she grows weaker and continues to cry out. The old woman, who says she is looking after her, leaves her in her filth, my poor, beautiful lady.'

Penrod followed her out of the light, then reached into the leather bag hidden in the folds of his dirty robe and brought out a small glass bottle.

'You must get this to her. It is the drug in its liquid form. A drop or two under her tongue and the pains will leave her.'

The girl grabbed it from him with a cry of delight, then looked up at the high walls. 'But how?'

Penrod handed her a purse; the weight of it startled her.

'You must bribe the guards to let you in. The duke is dining at the club, so now is your best chance.'

Akila nodded and turned to go, then hesitated. 'Do you have any message for my lady, if I succeed?'

Penrod thought of the last conversation he had had with Agatha, before they made love in the sweet smoke, before the henchmen of the duke arrived and bundled her away.

'Tell her Penrod Ballantyne forgives her, and that he prays for her.'

She nodded and left him in the shadows.

• • •

Penrod waited until just before dawn. He saw the duke's carriage arrive soon after midnight, but Akila did not come out of the side gate. Finally Penrod returned to his own house, washed and dressed carefully in his uniform, before presenting himself at Sam's office.

Sam arrived only minutes after he did. He did not look pleased to see Penrod, but nodded to him.

'The duke would not listen to me,' Sam said without preamble. 'He's a cool character and no mistake. I should not want to be any child of his.' He rapped his knuckles on the edge of his polished desk. 'I wish to God I'd never told you that story, and the woman is nothing but trouble, but I have to tell you, Penrod, thinking of the state she might be in robbed me of my sleep last night. It did indeed. Well, we'd better be going. I have the best doctor I know in Cairo for this sort of thing coming to join us and half a dozen of my best men downstairs, so let us go rescue the maiden.'

'Thank you, Sam.'

'It will mean a nasty scandal if we have to force our way in. We'll be thrown in gaol if we're lucky, but I can't do nothing.' He looked straight into Ballantyne's eyes. 'But do not fool yourself; I'm not doing this for you, Penrod.'

• • •

When they reached the house, the doctor, an Egyptian in European dress, was waiting for them. He was a young man, dark-skinned and with a soft handshake. Penrod took no great notice of him and he asked no questions. Sam ordered his men to stay at the gate and approached the main entrance with Penrod and the doctor.

Before they reached it, the great polished door was pulled open and they were greeted by a young, sandy-haired Englishman, who welcomed them with solemn politeness, introduced himself as Carruthers, and told them that the duke would receive them in his study. If Sam was disconcerted by this he didn't show it, and so they followed Carruthers into a high, elegant chamber. It was lined with leather-bound volumes on three sides; the fourth was made of glass doors leading to a shaded porch and giving views over the gardens. The effect was an oddly pleasing combination of gentleman's club and country house veranda.

The duke was standing in front of the desk, which stood at an angle in one corner. The floor was scattered with Persian rugs and dotted with leather armchairs. The duke had his hands clasped behind his back, and he did not invite his visitors to sit.

He looked well rested, and as elegantly arranged as the room in which he stood.

'Good morning, Colonel Adams and . . .' His hazel eyes moved over Penrod and the doctor. '. . . friends.'

Sam took a step forward but the duke held up his hand.

'One moment, Colonel. You are here to continue the discussion we had regarding Lady Agatha last night, I assume. There is no point. My daughter died a little over an hour ago.'

Penrod did not wait to hear anything more. He turned and left the room with long strides, calling Agatha's name, the echo bouncing off the white walls. He took the stairs two at a time, then began flinging open the doors on the first floor. One or two servants, as pristine and dignified as the house, watched him with mild curiosity, but did nothing to hinder him. Finding each light and elegant chamber empty he ran further up to the second floor and recommenced his search.

He found Agatha's body behind the door of the second chamber, a cramped narrow room tucked under the eaves. It had bare boards, plain walls and was oppressively hot. The stench hit him like a physical force. The room had been stripped of most of its furniture, except for a narrow bed and a bucket that stood in the corner, overflowing with bodily filth. The floor was streaked with what seemed to be vomit, flecked with blood. Bars were fastened across the open window. The one spot of cleanliness was the white sheet draped over whatever lay on the single bed. As Penrod stepped through the doorway, his handkerchief over his mouth and nose, he saw a heavy chain padlocked to the bed frame. It snaked under the white linen. He lifted up the corner of the sheet where it disappeared and saw the delicate curved arch of Lady Agatha's foot. The chain was threaded through a leather restraint attached to her ankle, and though the restraint was padded, the skin around it was bruised, mottled purple, red and yellow. Her toenails were painted crimson. Penrod had a sudden vision of Agatha bending to paint them, a fashion, she said, she'd picked up from some of the most daring Parisian courtesans. In his mind's eye she turned and looked up at him, a sad, twisted smile on her pretty face.

Penrod went to the other end of the bed and folded down the sheet so he might look at her face. Poor Agatha, her skin grey and waxy. He touched her cheek, and the flesh felt cold and dead, inhuman already. Her lips were pulled back in a horrid grimace, and the flesh around her mouth was crusted with spittle and dried blood. Her blue eyes were still open and staring, the white sclera thickly threaded with red, and the skin around the sockets looked bruised. Her beautiful hair was lank and filthy. Penrod gently closed her eyes, his fingers shaking a little. Her monstrous father had taken the time to dress in mourning, but no one had yet come to tend to poor Agatha's corpse. He stroked her cold cheek. He had hated her, but it was a hatred born out of passion, desire and pain, and what were those feelings but the dark elements of love? Agatha had been right, it was in her nature to say what she had said to Amber, and standing in the silence of that filthy room, Penrod realised he had been punishing Agatha for his own failings. It had been he, Penrod, who seduced the oldest Benbrook girl then called her a whore. It was he who had made love to Agatha when it suited him and ignored her when it did not. It was he who had allowed Amber, that brave, beautiful child, to believe he was a hero and he had accepted her faith and devotion as his due.

'O Allah, forgive our living and our dead,' he recited softly in Arabic, quoting one of the prayers from the Hadith. Then he covered her face again and walked downstairs.

The closer he came to the duke the more he felt a dark anger building in his blood. By the time he had reached the ground floor and thrown open the door to the study, his hand was on the hilt of his cavalry sabre.

'You murderous dog!' He strode across the polished tiles towards the duke. 'I shall kill you where you stand.'

The duke did not flinch. A flash of steel to his left, and Penrod found himself stopped by the flat of Sam Adams's sword across his chest.

'Stay where you are, Major Ballantyne,' Sam said calmly. 'That's an order.'

Penrod continued to stare at the sleek duke in his spotless black suit.

'He murdered her, Sam. He let her die and they have left her in her filth.'

The blade remained across his chest, but Penrod felt the tremor of Sam's shock.

The duke looked slightly bored. 'The body will be dealt with in due course.'

'Body?' Penrod said. 'That was your daughter.'

The duke raised his eyebrows. 'Yes, Major. *My* daughter. My charge and my responsibility, and you are a guest in my house.' He turned towards Sam. 'I will try and forgive this gross and officious intrusion, Colonel Adams, from you and your friend.' The duke glanced at the Egyptian doctor. 'You did leave your band of uniformed apes at the gate, at least. Well, all but one of them.'

Penrod pushed forward, but Sam pressed back against him with the flat of his blade.

'But you, Major Ballantyne,' the duke continued, 'you I will not forgive.'

'I do not want your forgiveness.'

Penrod rocked his weight back a fraction. It was a promise to Sam he would not attack. Sam lowered his sabre and sheathed it.

'Major Ballantyne has only acted out of a justified concern for Lady Agatha, and in coming to me—'

'But he didn't just come to you, did he, Colonel Adams?' the duke interrupted. He nodded to one of the servants before continuing. 'Major Ballantyne, as well as harassing both you and myself, bribed a former servant of my daughter's to steal into my home and supply my unfortunate child with the very drug that was killing her.'

'A good idea,' someone said quietly.

Penrod realised it was the Egyptian doctor who had spoken. He wore an expression of sorrow and sympathy, and as Penrod met his gaze, nodded slightly to him. The other Europeans in the room ignored him entirely.

Sam had gone white. 'Is this true?' he said to Penrod.

Before Penrod could reply, the sound of a woman crying was heard in the corridor outside. The doors were opened again and two of the thuggish servants dragged Akila into the room. Her headscarf had been torn away and her black hair hung below her shoulders. They held her by her wrists, twisting her arms back so she was forced on to her knees. She managed to lift her head and Penrod saw her face. Her lip was cut and her right eye swollen closed.

'I was so close, *effendi*!' she gasped. 'I got into the room, I touched her but before I could give her the drug, they found me.' Then she dropped her head again. Penrod found he could not move.

'I gave her your message, *effendi*. She died with your words in her ear and her heart.'

'May Allah bless you, sister,' Penrod said, his voice husky.

Akila began weeping quietly.

'Get her out of here,' the duke said.

Sam stepped forward. 'Your Grace—'

The duke held up his hand. 'But do not harm her,' he added wearily.

Akila was dragged to her feet and hustled from the room. The duke picked up a small sheaf of papers from his desk.

'I'm sure you will implement the proper steps to discipline Major Ballantyne, Adams. Now, if you'll excuse me, I have quite a busy day ahead of me.'

• • •

The words exchanged between Colonel Adams and Major Ballantyne outside the duke's residence were brutal and unforgiving on both sides. Sam was undoubtedly shocked by the behaviour of the duke, but he felt betrayed and humiliated by Penrod's covert actions. Penrod, seized by a toxic mixture of rage and guilt, accused his friend of cowardice. They parted with extreme bitterness on both sides. Sam declared his intention to reduce Penrod to the ranks and have him sent to Suakin, a miserable outpost on the Red Sea, until he could learn to treat his superiors with respect and behave like a gentleman in society. Penrod, who had thought of little but service to his queen and country since childhood, took this as further evidence of Sam's unworthy kowtowing to a man little better than a murderer and said so. He rode back to his own house at a reckless speed, and wrote at once resigning his commission. He then dressed in civilian clothes and plunged into the narrow alleys of the old city in search of the drug he suddenly craved beyond anything else, taking his black and wounded heart with him.

• • •

Lady Agatha was buried quietly at a private ceremony. The duke remained in the city, apparently continuing to pursue a number of investment opportunities. He was often seen at the club with his secretary always nearby and a constant supply of cold champagne on his table. Penrod Ballantyne had disappeared, it seemed. His house was shuttered and his servants dispersed. His fellow officers, tired of being outplayed, out-fought and out-thought, were glad to be rid of him. A number of rumours drifted in on the breeze. He had been spotted in Bombay, or seen lunching in his club in London. He had gone to the desert and turned mystic. He had been executed during a raid on the camp of Osman Atalan.

Bacheet, Ryder Courtney's partner and guardian of that adventurer's remaining wealth, knew different. He watched and listened. Yakub was seen often in strange parts of town. The boy Adnan and a gang of street rats in his pay seemed to be everywhere. Letters and parcels arrived from England, from South Africa, addressed to unknown names. Bacheet knew that Penrod Ballantyne was somewhere in the city, in the never-ending twilight of an opium house, and that from that place he was spinning plans across Victoria's Empire with a patience built of cold rage.

Part II
January 1888

Horatio Gardner did not seem to be enjoying his stay in Egypt; the climate did not suit him. He was a large man, red-faced with thinning hair and an expression of constant surprise. As he stepped off the train in Cairo in the first days of 1888 he looked startled, alarmed when he reached Shepheard's Hotel and mildly bemused as he took dinner that evening and was introduced to the several guests who had asked particularly to meet him.

Gardner was a man of reputation, and the better informed of the citizens of Cairo knew that behind his blinking green eyes was an exceptional mind. He had made his reputation excavating ancient sites in Palestine and on the Balkan coast, and had acquired, along with his reputation as an expert in Greek and Roman artefacts, a considerable personal fortune. Exactly where this fortune had come from was unclear, but it was noted that the collections of various European monarchs, bankers and industrial magnates now included articles of rare beauty and value that could only have come from his digs and through his hands.

His arrival in the city could only mean he was on the trail of something interesting, but no one could extract any hint from him as to what that might be. The gossip hounds brought him glass after glass of champagne. He blinked at them, drank what he was offered and told them nothing. He stayed only one night at Shepheard's, then disappeared for a week. When he returned, he looked more startled and sweaty than ever, and a close observer might have seen a pulse in the thick veins of his temple and recognised the nervousness of a man who had closed his fingers around a great prize but now feared it might burn him.

Carruthers, secretary to the Duke of Kendal, was one such careful observer. He made a number of discreet enquiries, and as a result was able to ensure that when Horatio finished his appointment with the director of the Museum of Antiquities, the duke happened to be at the museum and saw him as he left the director's offices.

The duke turned away from the cabinet he was admiring and greeted Horatio warmly. Horatio looked alarmed. Kendal spoke to him soothingly.

'I am glad to see you, Horatio,' he said. 'I feel you have been neglecting me. I am eager to expand my collection, and yet you never write to me.'

Horatio flushed a deep scarlet. 'Your Grace, it was only last year I helped you acquire the Sirmium vases. They are worthy of a museum of their own.'

Kendal opened a silver cigarette case and offered one of the black and gold cigarettes, emblazoned with his family crest, to Horatio. He took it and bent forward as the duke struck a match for him, studying his pink and sweaty features.

'I think them very fine, but I am, like you, Horatio, a treasure hunter. I hunger for the new.' He took a cigarette himself and fitted it between his pale lips, then snapped the case shut, and the sound echoed around the high ceilings and marble floors.

Horatio blinked and coughed. 'I was sorry to hear about the death of your daughter,' he said, when he had recovered.

'Yes, poor Agatha,' Kendal replied casually and lit his own cigarette. 'But tell me, Horatio. What can I do for you?'

Horatio glanced around nervously. The museum was empty apart from the duke and one or two Egyptian guards, but it seemed to Horatio that the green-glaze statuettes in their glass cases were watching him carefully.

'Do for me, Your Grace?'

'Yes, Horatio,' the duke said. 'I would like very much for you to owe me a favour so that next time you come into the possession of something very beautiful and very rare you will think of me first.'

The duke wandered away from him towards a display of bronze amulets and bent forward to examine them. Horatio trotted along behind him.

'I have a home here in Cairo, you know,' the duke continued. 'A very well guarded home and an excellent system of security. I had Mr William Pinkerton himself make all the arrangements. If, Horatio, you acquired something on your recent trip up the Nile that you would rather not carry on your person, or trust to that rather quaint safe at Shepheard's, perhaps I could be of assistance.'

Horatio went white, which with his florid complexion gave him the colouring of pale rose.

'How did you know, Your Grace?'

'A simple conjecture,' the duke replied, moving from the case of amulets to one of bronze spearheads, which was a little closer to the door. Horatio followed, his pink face as hopeful as a child before Christmas.

'Your arrangements were made by Pinkerton himself? Of the Pinkerton Detective Agency? I know their reputation, of course.' He chewed his upper lip thoughtfully, then spoke with sudden resolution. 'I do have something,' he said, 'something rather special from a trader I know who works in Mahdist territory, and it is a treasure indeed. I cannot sell it to you. It is already promised to . . . to another gentleman and I am waiting for his agent to arrive in Cairo to take delivery of it. But if you could keep it for me, I swear on my honour the next item of such beauty I come by, I will deliver to you.'

The duke led the way out of the lobby and into the honey-coloured sunshine. 'Then it is agreed.'

'Your Grace, I apologise, but such is the value of the item I would have to see the arrangements myself,' Horatio added nervously.

Kendal made a slight bow. 'Naturally, Horatio. Come, my carriage is waiting outside. Let me give you lunch and I shall tell you anything you wish to know.'

• • •

Horatio was given the full tour of the duke's house in Cairo and the particulars of the security arrangements before they sat down to lunch. With each sentence the duke spoke, with each carefully worked out detail he showed Horatio, the large man looked easier. The gardens were walled and the top of the wall lined with embedded shards of glass. Guards patrolled the grounds both day and night, and a man was always on watch seated directly outside the duke's study. The study itself might have appeared vulnerable at first glance, given its wall of glass overlooking the gardens, but the individual panes were too small for anything larger than a mouse to crawl through, and the panes were divided by painted iron. After they had lunched on salmon and minted new potatoes, the duke led Horatio into the study and invited him to sit. The duke walked behind the desk and he felt under the edge of one of the bookshelves in that corner of the room, reaching his slim fingers past a fine-looking edition of Gibbon's *Decline and Fall*. The volumes were all bound in green leather and stamped on the spine with the duke's coat of arms.

Horatio heard a soft click, and a section of the bookshelf, some five feet square, swung softly outwards. The duke opened it fully to reveal a black iron safe with a tumbler lock.

'It is a Herring and Company model,' he said. 'Fireproof, naturally.' He patted it as if it were a well-behaved gun dog.

Horatio cleared his throat. 'Your Grace, how ...? May I ask why you have such measures installed in a temporary residence? I am delighted, for my own sake, that you have done so. It must be the most secure place in Cairo, and I do not wish to be crude, but these arrangements must have cost a great deal of money.'

The duke nodded. 'So they did. I place a very high premium on security, Horatio. I have many business interests across the world, and certain documents I must have with me at all times. Arranging their security is both time-consuming and expensive, but it's time and money well spent. And if I can do you a favour as a result, so much the better. Now, will you make use of me?'

Horatio reached awkwardly into his breast pocket and removed a bundle of cotton wraps about the size of his fist and laid it on the desk. The duke watched his movements as a cat watches a bird hopping innocently across the lawn in front of it.

'I must repeat, Your Grace, that I cannot sell this to you. Not at any price, but given your kindness in this matter, and knowing you are a connoisseur of the ancient and beautiful, I feel justified in showing it to you.'

Horatio was unfolding the soft white wrappings as he spoke. At last he shifted the final veil aside. It was an ivory carving of a man's face. The duke made no sound, but his attention seemed to focus and intensify. Horatio turned the carving towards him and pushed it on its bed of wrappings across the leather inlay of the desk.

'You may examine it, though I beg you to be careful.'

The duke stood away from the safe and sat down at the desk, supporting his chin in his hands and staring at the carving, his lips slightly parted. It was roughly eight inches high and six across, and thin as if designed as a miniature mask. The face was of a man of mature years and the sculptor had marked the fine lines around his eyes and mouth, but the face, with its tight curls, high cheekbones and long aquiline nose was handsome. Such was the detail of the carving, it gave almost the impression of a photograph.

It had suffered some slight damage to the top right edge, but otherwise seemed perfect and intact. Traces of colouring were still visible on the fine surface, a suggestion of darkness on the hair, and a reddish tint on the cheeks. The duke picked it up and lifted it into the light, cupping it with both hands the way a bishop holds the communion chalice. He shifted it right and left to see how the light fell across it, then lowered it and turned it over. Slight marks were visible on the underside. Kendal reached into his desk and took out a jeweller's loop, which he fitted to his right eye, and brought the carving towards him.

Outside Horatio could hear the soft footsteps of a servant in the hall. At last the duke sighed, set the carving and loop down, and rested the small masterpiece on its wrappings again.

'It is a miracle, Horatio,' he said at last.

'You could read the inscription on the back?'

'I did, but it seems impossible.'

'A likeness of Caesar given as a gift to Cleopatra herself.' Horatio blinked rapidly. 'I thought it unlikely myself, but the director of the Museum of Antiquities and I examined it again this morning. We could find nothing that might indicate that the inscription was added at a later date, and we compared the carving with other busts of Caesar that were made during his lifetime. The likeness is striking.'

The duke still stared. 'It should go without saying, Horatio, that I will pay anything you ask. Anything.'

Horatio looked solemn. 'I understand that, but I have promised it elsewhere.'

'To whom?'

'I cannot say. I hope you will not object, Your Grace, to giving me a note in your hand confirming that I have put this item into your hands for safe keeping.'

'I will pay double the agreed sum. You could live out your days in luxury, Horatio, if you let me have this.'

Horatio shook his head. He leaned forward and pulled the carving back towards him, then began to wrap it again.

'Very well,' the duke said. 'You will not tell me who the buyer is either?' Horatio did not reply and Kendal took a piece of paper from his desk drawer and began to write. 'Of course you will not. But I think I already know. For one thing, few people in the world could afford this, and for another, you, Horatio, are a snob.'

'Your Grace!' Horatio protested, looking up quickly.

'It is not an insult, Horatio – you pick your friends wisely. I think if you were selling to some banker or American tycoon, you would not be so resolved to honour your original bargain, so you must be selling to someone who outranks me. That rather narrows the field. And it purports to be a like-ness of Caesar, that great hero of Rome. I conclude then, my dear Horatio, that your buyer is a member of the Italian roy-alty. Most likely the king himself. He is the collector in the family.'

Horatio's mouth opened and closed like a fish, and a fresh layer of sweat broke out on his forehead. 'I . . . I could not pos-sibly confirm or deny . . .'

The duke looked pleased. He leaned back in his chair. 'Give me forty-eight hours, Horatio. I have had dealings with the Italian royal family in the past – some of the younger members, at any rate. If, before those forty-eight hours are over, I can give you a letter from the Italian consul here in Cairo, confirming that King Umberto is happy for you to sell this treasure to me instead of him . . .?'

He signed his note with a flourish and handed it to Horatio. Horatio read it, nodded briefly, then folded it and slipped it into his pocket.

'If you can show me such a letter, then of course, Your Grace, the carving is yours. But forgive me, it is a vain hope.'

'Perhaps, perhaps not. Now I shall put this wonder into my safe, and you may spend a day or two in Cairo without worry-ing about it further. Perhaps you would be so good as to turn your back.'

The duke picked up the wrapped carving and waited while Horatio stood and turned to face the door. He heard the ticks of the combination wheel, the bolt being released and turned back in time to see the duke placing the carving on a thick pile of card folders in the red plush interior. The duke then shut the steel door and closed the section of bookshelf over it. Horatio marvelled at the design. If he had not seen it open, he would never have spotted it.

'Thank you, thank you, Your Grace.'

• • •

Two days later, when Horatio returned to the house, he still had the countenance of a happy man. When he saw the letter from the Italian consulate, however, he looked startled again.

'I would never have believed . . . And yet here it is! The king agrees that I sell the carving to you, Your Grace. Yet I was assured the purchase was of great personal interest to him.'

The duke made no attempt to explain.

'The price you agreed with the king was, I understand, twenty thousand pounds. I shall happily write you a cheque for forty, as agreed, but as we are both men of business, I wonder if you might take twenty thousand in paper money and a further ten in diamonds. It is a little unorthodox, I know, but I believe the arrangement might suit you better. I have both the diamonds and the notes on hand.'

Horatio went scarlet. He would lose ten thousand, but the remaining fortune would be his in currency more discreet and immediate. 'Indeed, Your Grace.'

'Then take your money.' The duke lifted a briefcase from the floor beside him, placed it on the desk, opened it and turned it around to face Horatio. Horatio picked up the small velvet pouch that lay on top of the neat bundles of notes, pulled at the drawstring, then tipped the diamonds into his hand. They sparkled on his palm, each a cluster of rainbows.

'Would you like to have their value assessed, Horatio?' the duke asked with a glimmer of amusement.

Horatio swallowed and tipped them back into the pouch. It went into his breast pocket and he closed the case and set it down next to him.

'That will not be necessary, Your Grace. I am content. But may I beg one last favour? When I placed that carving into your care, I did not know it would be my last chance to see it. May I look on that face once more before I go? I think a man of your understanding will know what it would mean to me to have a chance to bid it farewell.'

The duke looked at him sideways, then laughed. 'Of course, Horatio. It is your love of such beautiful things that has made you such a useful man to know. If you would be so kind as to turn your back again.'

Horatio did, and on the duke's command turned back to look once more on the face of Caesar. He touched the carving with his forefinger.

'Thank you, Your Grace.'

He blinked rapidly and bent down to pick up the case of money, then turned and walked out of the room without looking back.

• • •

Horatio left Cairo four hours later. The first-class compartment on the train to Alexandria was wonderfully cool, but he was still shiny with sweat and chewed the skin around his fingernails like a nervous schoolgirl. The train ticket had been waiting for him in a thick envelope at the reception of Shepheard's Hotel, along with the news that a passage had been booked for him on the next sailing back to London from Alexandria. The envelope also contained a short note, written in a flowing masculine script. It told him that his most pressing gambling debts in London had been paid and was signed only with the initials: P.B.

The men who guarded the gates of the Duke of Kendal's home in Cairo had grown used to Abdul, a local beggar and comic drunkard, over the last few weeks. He would appear in the late evening and tell dirty jokes and stories for the price of a drink. Occasionally he had a pack of grubby cards showing buxom ladies in various states of undress, which he would sell for a similar price. Sometimes the guards took the cards without paying, and beat Abdul for the whining old sinner he was. Still he amused them. Tonight he staggered up the road towards them singing, and the two men on the gate grinned at each other as he approached. He stumbled against them.

'My friends, my brothers! Have you got the price of a drink for your good friend Abdul?'

'You've had enough already, you heathen,' the larger of the two men said. 'Get away, or I'll crack your ribs for you again.'

Abdul mewled and shrank away. 'Oh, you lion, I'm still carrying those bruises, they have bloomed all over me like roses.' He wet his lips and leaned forward again. 'But I have a secret to tell you! You know Asha, the little beauty who works in the kitchens? Would you like to know a juicy bit about that lovely minx?'

The guard looked unsure, but could not resist and he nodded.

'I shall whisper it to you.' Abdul crept close to him and laid a filthy palm on the guard's shoulder. He bent down a little so Abdul could put his mouth close to his ear. 'She thinks you are a bully and coward, and beater of old men and women. I told her I would send you to hell, and such was her joy she kissed my hand.'

'Wha–?' The guard began to pull away. The blade Abdul used on his throat was so sharp, he didn't even know his windpipe had been severed until he tried to call out. The other guard turned as he crumpled to the ground and let out a curse. Before the second guard could draw his sword, Abdul had used his knife again. The second guard clasped desperately at his throat, as if he could seal the wound with his fingers, and fell by his friend in the dust, spluttering on his own blood. Abdul waited until he was dead, then gave a low whistle as he plucked the gate key from the corpse's belt. From the far side of the roadway two other men appeared. They wore dark brown tunics and loose trousers very similar to those worn by the dead guards. Together they dragged the corpses into the shadow on the inside of the wall and then the new arrivals took their positions.

One of the men handed a leather satchel and a roll of cloth to Abdul. '*Effendi*, may Allah the Merciful go with you.'

'Thank you, Yakub,' the beggar said, handing him the key. 'I will signal when I am clear.'

Yakub watched him disappear into the shadows and in the moments before he was lost to sight, Abdul transformed like a *djinn*. The drunken beggar had disappeared, replaced by a young man, six feet tall and quick and lithe as a leopard. The cringing posture vanished. Just before he disappeared around the corner of the house, he turned back and Yakub could swear he caught a flash of those ice-blue eyes. Yakub looked out into the road as a good guard should, glad he had chosen to serve a man like Penrod Ballantyne.

• • •

Penrod had been watching the arrangements of the house very carefully while he had been playing the role of Abdul. He knew he had between twelve and fifteen minutes before the guards on patrol would pass this way again. He unrolled the cloth bundle and lifted a short bow from its wrappings, strung it, then from the shadows shot an arrow up and over the upper branch of a sycamore that shaded the pathways around the house from the heat of the day.

Its lower branches had been pruned away, on Pinkerton's advice, no doubt, but the arrow Penrod fired had a long coil of fishing line attached to it. The arrow arched over a solid branch about twenty feet from the ground and fell silently to earth again on the other side, burying its head deep into the soil.

Penrod retrieved it and used the fishing line to pull a manila climbing rope over the branch so it hung to the ground on either side. He grasped it just above head height and twisted the two lengths between his feet, forming a brake, then hauled himself upwards, gathering the rope up behind him when he reached the branch.

He had selected an unoccupied room on the first floor as his point of entry. A young maid in the house had been encouraged to take a romantic interest in one of Yakub's servants, the same man now pretending to guard the main gate. Through her, Penrod had learned who was in the house and where they slept. The only rooms occupied on the first floor were those of the duke and his secretary Carruthers. The duke spent his evenings at the club, leaving to dine at eight, and rarely returning before three o'clock in the morning. Carruthers would take a light supper on his own and extinguish his reading lamp before midnight. This chamber, halfway down the eastern flank of the house, was empty, and below the window was the sloping roof of one of the bay windows on the ground floor.

It was a distance of some ten feet from the end of the branch to the smooth roof, but Penrod had the advantage of height. He landed lightly and waited for a moment to see if he had been heard. The house remained quiet.

The window was latched. Penrod worked one of the small glass panes free, teasing away the putty with his penknife, and caught it carefully by its edges as it came loose. Then he lifted the sash and slipped inside, shutting the window carefully behind him in case any of the patrolling guards thought to look up.

The next stage of his plan was the most dangerous. The duke's office was always kept locked, and only two people had the key: Carruthers and the duke himself. Yakub had wanted to persuade the maid to take a copy of the key, or steal it while Carruthers slept, but Penrod would not risk it, not after seeing the beating Agatha's maid had received. When he slept,

Carruthers placed it on the table by his bed with his watch and wireframe glasses.

Penrod let himself into Carruthers' room on the other side of the landing. The secretary appeared to be sleeping peacefully in his canopied bed and the thin sickle of the moon cast only the barest of lights across the room. In the landing and hallway the gas was kept lit until the duke himself had retired to bed, so Penrod waited for his eyes to adjust.

He moved silently to the side table by the sleeping man's head. Carruthers stirred and Penrod felt his feathery breath on his fingertips as he took up the key. It clicked on the walnut veneer.

'Is someone there?' His voice was heavy with sleep. Penrod did not move, letting himself disappear into the warm silence of the room like a *fakir*. Carruthers turned over and soon his breathing resumed the gentle rhythms of sleep.

• • •

The guard outside the office sat with his back to the study door, giving him an unobstructed view of the entrance hall and passage leading to the back of the house. It would be impossible to reach him with a knife. A gunshot would wake the household. Penrod crouched at the top of the stairs, took the bow from his back and nocked an arrow. The man who crafted these arrows was an artist. The haft was of straight-grained cedar, half an inch in diameter with a narrow bodkin head, and the goose feather fletching was bound to the haft with a tight spiral of silk. The bow was of English ash, and for a fleeting moment as Penrod drew the arrow, he had a vision of woodland, mossed banks, running streams and dark fairy tales. He released and the arrow flew through the wrought iron banisters with a low hiss and buried its iron point deep in the man's throat. He gasped, choking on his own blood, but hardly had time to lift his hands to the shaft before his eyes glazed, his hands dropped and his body slumped forward.

Penrod put the bow across his shoulder, ran lightly down the stairs, unlocked and entered the study without glancing at the guard, then closed the door behind him. He felt over the row of green leather volumes for the *Decline and Fall* and the catch, which would reveal the safe. The fake section of the bookshelf swung away.

It had taken a lot of time and trouble to find Horatio, an expert who knew the duke but who had both the intelligence to play the role Penrod had in mind for him, and a weakness for gambling, which meant Penrod could bribe him into compliance. Once Penrod had discovered the make and model of the duke's safe from a careless assistant, keen to make a sale, in Pinkerton's Cairo office, Horatio was contacted and then confined to a room above a sweatshop in Limehouse with a London safecracker for five hours a day listening to the dials spinning on a matching model. When the safecracker reported that Horatio could give an accurate estimate of how far the dial was turned between numbers during the combination sequence, Penrod sent the curio dealer further instructions, and a ticket for Cairo. The mask of Caesar had been procured by Penrod's former lover, Bakhita. Once the wife of a grain trader, she had become a trader of antiquities along the upper reaches of the Nile and as her reputation grew, desert travellers shared their news with her, as well as the small artefacts they found lost among the desert sands. This news she shared with Penrod and he had learned to trust her skill and her discretion. The carving was quite genuine. Penrod knew he needed something to provoke the duke's lust, and nothing less would be certain of doing so.

After his first meeting with the duke, Horatio had gone wandering in the spice bazaar, as instructed. As soon as Yakub was sure he was not being followed, he had scooped him up and questioned him closely. Horatio was quietly confident. The pattering clicks of the combination dial had become a very familiar music to him during his weeks of training and he could share what it told him about the distance between the two-digit numbers that formed the sequence of the combination, even if he could not supply any of the numbers themselves. The partial information Horatio provided created an elegant problem for Penrod and he had wagered everything on his ability to solve it. He lay among the opium fumes in his room at one of Yakub's boarding houses and let the numbers play in his head. He was sure they would not have been chosen at random. After all, the duke was a man of monogrammed silk handkerchiefs and books and cigarettes stamped with his coat of arms. The numbers of the combination would be personal and contain some hint of vanity. When at last the solution flashed across his mind, Penrod was proved right. 13 48 18 75. The pairs of numbers gave the year of the creation of the dukedom and that of the current Duke's own succession. Horatio's second visit provided a confirmation, and then Penrod released him, confused by his adventure, but rich and swearing never to gamble again. Horatio and Penrod had never met, and never would. The only direct communication between them had been the final note of dismissal Horatio had read on the train taking him to Alexandria.

The tumblers clicked obediently into place and Penrod opened the steel door. The interior was just as Horatio had described to Yakub and Adnan. The mask, still in its snowy wrappings, was resting on a stack of folders and three black ledgers.

Penrod had learned swiftly that the duke's international mining and processing enterprises were sustained and supported by the systematic use of bribery, blackmail and coercion. For months Penrod moved discreetly through the duke's past, finding fear and silence, but just occasionally he would meet a man or woman with nothing left to lose who would share what they knew about the duke's networks and activities. Kendal had discovered early that investments in high-class brothels and gambling dens yielded more than financial rewards. Men of power and influence, or members of their families, were seduced into the duke's establishments and their worst excesses documented and photographed, then when the duke needed permits and permissions, favourable customs deals, or to have his rivals undercut, Carruthers would make a polite visit to the gentleman making the decision with his dossier of depravity under his arm and explain to his trembling interlocutor what was to be done. Attacks on workers who tried to unionise went uninvestigated, murders of rivals were hushed up, reports on accidents attached no blame to the company, governments across Europe paid over the odds for the raw materials they were sold, and each detail of every corrupt deal was neatly documented in the ledgers Penrod now held in his hands. The duke had built an empire on the blood and foolishness of others. Penrod set the ledgers and folders on the desk, then, with a grim smile, placed the wrapped mask in the open safe again. Penrod slipped the ledgers and folders into his satchel, closed the safe and spun the dial, then closed the false bookcase over it.

Somewhere upstairs a bell rang. Penrod heard a footstep outside in the corridor, then a shout. The body outside the office door had been seen. Sounds of alarm began to spread through the house. It was pointless to attempt an escape through the window – thanks to Horatio he knew about the iron window fittings. He had only one exit, and that was the way he had come.

He opened the door. Wilson Carruthers was standing at the top of the stairs in his striped silk dressing gown, still confused with sleep. One of the house servants was bending over the body slumped in its chair, two more were by the main door, calling into the darkness for help from the patrolling guards. Penrod darted left, heading through the back of the house towards the kitchens. One of the servants sleeping on the floor made a brave grab at his ankle, but Penrod kicked up with his heel and felt the crunch of the man's nose breaking. The doors to the gardens would be locked, but the windows here were not reinforced. He sprinted into the back kitchen, leaped from the floor to the table, then across to the dresser, which reached to the high ceiling. He clambered up, kicked out the glass of the high narrow windows and dived through the opening, rolling forward to break his fall on the other side. He crossed the garden and followed the perimeter wall around to the guardhouse, then whistled to Yakub, who quietly opened the gate, even while he yelled to the guards at the house he'd seen a shadow racing towards the rear of the garden. Then he and his man dropped their weapons and followed Penrod silently out into the road, closing the gate behind them.

It took ten minutes for the other guards to realise no one was at the main gate, and another ten to find the bodies of their comrades.

• • •

The duke was summoned from the Gheziera Club at once. He arrived just after the search of both the house and grounds had been completed and the servants and guards were offering their stuttered reports to Carruthers. Kendal ignored the cluster of servants in the hall and went immediately into the study, with Carruthers at his heel.

'The two men on the main gate were killed, Your Grace. Whoever did this replaced them with his own men. The bodies were cold, but the guards in the grounds had seen two men at their post only a moment before the alarm was raised. Nothing in the house is missing, nothing has been disturbed. I saw a man in Arab clothing fleeing from here, but as you see,' he gestured around the peaceful-looking study, 'it seems nothing has been taken.'

'Have you checked the safe?' Kendal asked quietly.

Carruthers shook his head with a puzzled smile. 'I can see no sign the thief even discovered it, and only you have the combination.'

Kendal reached for the concealed catch and the secret door on the bookshelf swung open. Carruthers turned his back automatically as the duke spun the dial. Silence. He turned back and saw that, apart from a bundle of cotton wrappings, the safe was empty.

'But that's impossible,' Carruthers spluttered.

'Apparently not, Carruthers,' the duke replied.

'How could anyone . . .?' Carruthers managed to stop himself. 'Sir, I do not know precisely what was in the safe. Only that they were materials of vital importance.'

'It contained enough to ruin me a dozen times over.' The duke took his silver cigarette case from his jacket, removed one of his black cigarettes and lit it before continuing. 'I fear, Carruthers, I underestimated Penrod Ballantyne.'

'But the man is an addict, a fop,' Carruthers protested. 'He has not been seen for months. Why do you think it was him, sir?'

The duke laughed softly. 'Oh, just something in his eyes when we last met. Something I recognised from the mirror. I had thought he might attempt to assassinate me, and I took precautions, but I had not thought he would do this.' The duke's tone was admiring. 'And this is a great deal better than simply killing me.'

'We shall turn Cairo upside down, find him and the missing documents before any harm can be done.'

'You will not find him in time, Carruthers,' the duke said. 'I would imagine the contents of the safe will find its way into the newspapers very quickly. No hope exists. It is over.'

'I feel I have failed you, sir,' Carruthers said, his voice strangled.

The duke turned away from the safe at last. 'You have served me faithfully for many years, Carruthers. I do not blame you for this. I was outplayed. But perhaps you might do one last thing for me tonight.'

'Anything.'

'Thank you. Could you perhaps fetch my Batchelor shotgun from the gunroom?' The duke smiled and ground out his cigarette in his crystal ashtray.

• • •

The contents of the safe kept Penrod, Yakub and Adnan occupied until the middle of the next day. As evening fell, a number of Adnan's young friends went through the city with packages under their arms. One went to the British consulate building and refused to hand over his package to anyone but Sam Adams himself. Another went to the Sheridan Hotel, where a Venetian businessman and known intimate of the Italian royal family was staying. Another went to the telegraph office and sent two identical but lengthy messages to the editors of the *New York Times* and the *Pall Mall Gazette*. Extracts from the black ledgers were made into parcels and posted after them. The operators blinked as they tapped out the messages to the newspapers detailing the crimes and corruption of the duke, and whispered to each other about a crop of telegrams brought in by a liveried servant that morning to be sent to addresses across Europe and America. All had been signed Kendal and carried the same message: *Burn everything and get out*.

More than a thousand miles away, Ryder Courtney watched as the kudu lifted his head, sniffing at the morning air, and the white chevron on his forehead flashed for a moment in the shadows. His corkscrew horns seemed a part of the curling network of acacia branches behind him and his soft grey pelt, with its darker slashed markings down his flanks, made him almost invisible. He was some sixty inches at the shoulder and five hundred pounds in weight, yet at the first breath of alarm he would be able to run faster than a stallion and leap for cover among the scrub as if he had wings.

Two hundred yards from him Ryder breathed softly, letting the great beast settle to his feeding again. The rifle he held was relatively new to him, an Italian Vetterli bought in Massowah. It had a tendency to pull right, which he was certain his own rifle, now rusting at the bottom of the Red Sea, would never had done, but today he felt as if he and this new model had reached an understanding. He breathed out once more and let his body relax, then squeezed the trigger. The sharp crack echoed through the valley, and the other kudu barked out their warnings and scattered into cover, but the great beast in Ryder's sights only lifted its head to the sky one final time then collapsed. The boys who had come with Ryder to help carry his spoils let out great whoops of admiration and delight. Ato Asfaw, the *chiqa shum*, district headman and former soldier in the army of the emperor and Ryder's friend, spoke to them sharply and cuffed the one closest to him.

'What, children! Will you frighten the rest back to Adrigat? Will one beast feed all the mouths at Courtney Mine?'

The boys were silenced, but could not help grinning at Ryder. He winked at them, then got to his feet and began walking across the meadow to where the kudu had fallen. The short rains had painted the plateau and valleys emerald green, and now, as the dew began to lift from the grasses, the wild flowers spread open their purple and yellow blossoms towards the sun.

They found the kudu's body in the broken shade. Ryder knelt beside it, pleased to see his shot had been exactly on target, hitting the flank cleanly in line with the animal's heart. It had been dead before it hit the ground. In truth it was a large enough beast to have formed the centrepiece of the evening's feast, but Ryder was enjoying the freedom and challenge of the hunt. He patted the still warm flank of the animal and smiled up at Ato Asfaw.

'What say you, my friend? Shall we follow them a little further into the next gorge and see if we can get another?'

Asfaw looked around the horizon, the crazy peaks and valleys of the landscape crimping the edge of the pale blue and cloudless sky.

'Naturally,' he said. 'The next shot is mine.'

• • •

Five hours later they reached the top of the ridge and stopped for a moment to drink in the view of the camp. Asfaw put his hand on Ryder's shoulder.

'You have made progress, my friend.'

'Some,' Ryder replied.

The Courtney Mine and Camp were built on the lower slopes of a wide, steep-sided valley, which twisted and jackknifed through the mountains of east Tigray. The camp and mine were separated by the towering height of the Mother, the great outcrop of sedimentary and igneous rock that forced the river to move out of her way and where the silver strike had been discovered. If asked, Courtney would say the Mother was a local name, and so it was, but his few local workers had named it the day Dan first saw the size of the vein of ore and had thrown his weather-beaten slouch hat in the air, letting forth a stream of fluid American curses that had echoed around the valley. The one word the workers had picked out was 'mother' and so the outcrop was named.

From where Ryder watched, the workings of the mine were hidden. He looked down instead at the camp where his workers and their families lived. The traditional round, wattle and mud huts of the area, with their coned roofs of thatched reeds, still had a gleam of freshness to them, but they were few and scattered and half were still empty. Around them, struggling up the hillside and on the far side of the river were the terraced fields where they grew their food: teff, beans and rye to the south, and on the eastern escarpments, Amber's new fruit gardens. A thinly planted orchard was waiting to mature, with occasional straw beehives dotted between the saplings and clusters of fast-growing berries, gesho and nut bushes.

Ryder's sister-in-law had dragged the gardens into being by sheer force of will, bribing, cajoling and begging the wives of the mineworkers into helping her, then labouring alongside them. They took the water supply from a tributary of the main river, diverting and damming it in such a way it would neither be overwhelmed by flash floods in the sudden violent rains, nor starved in the long dry seasons. It had been a gruelling process of trial and error, but at last it seemed as if her workings would hold and her weak saplings and thin bushes were beginning to thicken, take root and reach into the still blue air.

Saffron had supervised the building of the huts and barracks. She, Ryder and Leon had one; Dan, Patch and Rusty bunked together; and Amber and Tadesse had a two-room hut close to Ryder's family. Each evening, when Ryder returned from the mine along the river, he would find his wife covered in mud and pale with the work. She'd offer him a glass from their precious store of whisky and talk about construction methods, where materials should be fetched from and how the local people arranged their homes, until he fell asleep to the low music of her talk. At some point, it seemed, he'd agreed to have a small church built in the camp and a priest appointed to it. The first he knew of it was when he came home at dusk to discover Saffron had managed to acquire soap, and made him use it. An hour later he was presiding over a modest welcome feast for their new priest, offering roast kid and the fiery honey wine, *tej*, to a young man who seemed as bemused as Ryder was. Saffron, though, was convinced. A priest at the camp would bring luck, and the local people who regarded mine-working as beneath them or, worse, tainted with bad luck and the suspicion of witch-craft would change their minds.

Traders were occasionally persuaded to journey out from Adrigat to bring seed, leather, nails and needles, and Amber and Saffron gave each one a princely welcome, hoping they would tell favourable stories of Courtney Mine in the surrounding villages and slowly infuse into the women and children a fierce independent pride. The men worked harder and more willingly. Ato Asfaw was right, they had made progress, but it was slow and hard-fought-for, and the memory of the fortune in equipment sunk to the bottom of the Red Sea made Ryder grit his teeth in rage and regret.

Looking down on the camp, Ryder could see preparations for this evening's celebrations were advancing and his wife was at the centre of them. A bonfire was being built in the centre of the square and woven straw mats laid around it. Amber was stand-ing behind one of the worker's wives, helping her plait her thick black hair into a series of intricate braids, while Saffron was car-rying firewood to the pit. He saw her turn and say something to one of the women grinding outside her house and heard an answering laugh. One of the oldest girls was looking after the youngest children by the river. They were building towers from pebbles. Ryder could see his chubby-limbed son among them, reaching forward to grab at the stones and laughing as they clat-tered and fell. Saffron had spotted Ryder and was waving, then pointing towards the fire pit. As she did the rest of the hunting party joined Ryder and Asfaw on the crest of the escarpment. The boys were in pairs and each pair carried a long pole across their shoulders from which was slung the cooling body of a fat dik-dik, the small deer-like creatures who foraged in the mountains. The oldest boys had the honour of carrying the kudu. Saffron lifted her hands and applauded when she saw it. Ryder bowed.

'Will you come and eat with us, Asfaw?' Ryder asked.

The older man hesitated, then shook his head. They made their farewells and Ryder watched him stride off, swinging his walking stick, and felt a familiar sting of resentment. The farmers dotted around the district would still not come to Courtney Mine. They were a conservative, deeply traditional people, convinced that those who worked with metal were infected with the evil eye. Anyone who worked at the mine was regarded with the same suspicion. Ryder was forced to travel from market to market, cajoling and bargaining for his workers. Eventually news of the camp and the strange work available in it brought curious families from across the region. Some were workers in metal or earthenware, some had inherited only poor land, others had to hand over most of their crops to the church, so when they heard the stories, they came from their scattered compounds to investigate and many stayed. They liked Ryder and though the work in the mine was hard, the promised pay was good and the village comfortable. The metalworkers built small furnaces. The men who had been farmers took up pickaxes, shovels and wheelbarrows.

Ryder was proud of the work so far, but one problem remained. Though Courtney Camp was now slowly, painfully establishing itself on the high slopes, Courtney Mine produced only the thinnest trickle of saleable ore. The wealth locked up in the slopes was beyond question, but they needed quicksilver to release it, and quicksilver they did not have. Until today.

• • •

Amber was happy that the preparations for the party were well underway, so she decided to take the path down to the riverbank and spend some time with her nephew.

The party to be held this evening was an important celebration. Yesterday Rusty had returned from the coast, waving his cap above his head and yelling out his news like a schoolboy. Against all the odds he had arranged for a fresh supply of quicksilver to be delivered to Massowah in iron flasks, then managed to get that precious cargo from the port up into the highlands by mule. Ryder had told him flat out that it would be impossible, that they must content themselves with roasting and smelting the ore for a year at least, but Rusty could not be dissuaded. He knew – he could tell by the feel of the ore in his hands – that if he only had quicksilver and copper sulphate, he could draw a steady stream of silver from the mountain. He continued to plan, drawing designs and labelled diagrams in his notebook. Dan supervised the roasting and smelting of the best grade ore, but produced little. Ryder spent hours with the metalworkers he had recruited, with Dan and Patch bent over kilns and furnaces, but again and again their efforts failed. Quicksilver, Rusty insisted. They must have quicksilver and that was it.

The men argued. Dan thought Rusty was being pig-headed, and said so. Ryder said he did not have more capital to risk. Patch settled the fight. It turned out he had yet to spend a penny of the joining fee and advance wages Ryder had given him. He threw down the leather pouch at the feet of his friends.

'How much quicksilver can you get for that?'

So began Rusty's great quest. He spent weeks kicking his heels in Massowah, and became such a fixture in the telegraphist's office, finding suppliers and arranging delivery, that they gave him his own stool. Tensions between Emperor John and the Italian government meant that the wires mostly hummed with diplomatic cables, but any time the operator had a moment to pause and look up, Rusty would pounce on him, all dogged enthusiasm, with a fist full of messages in one hand and a box of the operator's favourite cigars in the other.

Ryder had greeted him like a brother on his return and declared a feast for the following day. Together they stacked the flasks of quicksilver in the store, and eager to see what they'd brought, filled the storage tank. The iron flasks were sent to the metalworkers on the hill to be turned into a dozen other necessities.

Amber was about to cross the pebbled shore to where the toddlers were being entertained when she noticed Dan sitting in the shade of a fig tree. It was strange to see him unoccupied. Like the rest of the men, he worked, ate and slept, nothing more. She had thought he would be with Patch. Now Rusty had returned in triumph they would begin building the processing works, and that needed careful planning and intense study of Rusty's designs. Then all the ore they had struggled to dig out of the earth over the past months would at last start paying them back for their efforts.

Dan was clutching what looked like a letter and staring out at the children playing among the pebbles. Amber would have called out to him, made some comment about Ryder's success on the hunt and the quality of the feast to come, but something about the way he sat staring at the children made her hesitate.

He noticed her anyway and stood up quickly. After giving her the briefest of nods, he walked away from her towards the mine. He was already around the bend in the river before Amber noticed he had dropped something. She went to retrieve it. It was a photograph of a woman and child, done up into a sort of postcard. The woman was handsome, perhaps in her thirties, and the boy, a pretty lad looking stiff and uncomfortable in a little suit with a tight collar, was around ten years old.

Amber turned it over in her hands. The studio had printed their own name on the back, Hamiltons of San Francisco, and the names of the sitters. Mrs Gloria Martin and her son James. Then, in a rather shaky hand, someone had written 'we depend on you'.

Amber's first impulse was to run after Dan and return it, but he had never in all their months together mentioned this woman or child. She decided it must be a private matter, so called out to the older girl watching the infants on the shore.

'Arsema!' She turned, smiled and came to Amber's side. 'Ato Dan dropped this on the shore. Will you run after him and give it to him?'

She took it with a nod and set off after the American at a steady lope, while Amber went to take her place among the children. Her nephew gurgled with pleasure at the sight of her and held up his arms to her.

• • •

Late that night Rusty stumbled along the shallows of the river with his torch held high, cursing when he missed a step, then grinning into the shadows again. Mr Ryder Courtney, a man he had come to respect greatly, had made a speech in his honour at the feast and proclaimed him the saviour of Courtney Mine. He was prouder of himself than he had ever been in his life, and happier. A job of work lay ahead, no doubt, but he knew now, knew as sure as his own name was Rusty Tompkins, he would succeed and the mine would make them all rich.

It had been a wonderful feast, then to cap it all, one of the minstrels who wandered along the trails of Tigray had joined them and sung for his supper. He was the first minstrel who had made the journey to the camp and they all, westerners and Abyssinians alike, took it as a good omen.

Rusty chuckled. Amber Benbrook had been fascinated by the minstrel's explanation of 'wax and gold' poems, those little verses with clever double meanings so popular among the people here. The musician told her firmly it took years of study to master their forms and rhythms, but no way was that going to stop her. She was trying to invent her own within an hour and she chose him, Rusty, and his quest to fetch quicksilver as her subject. However beautiful she'd looked in the firelight, calling out her clever rhymes, Rusty never lusted after her. He had never felt that passion for a woman, or a man. He knew this was a lack, somehow, but it did not distress him much. His pale cheeks only flushed with blood at the idea of the work ahead. They would soon begin to use their precious store of quicksilver to draw the silver out of the ore. Ryder Courtney would be building his silver houses in a matter of months. Rusty chortled again, thinking of Ryder sitting in the square of the camp on a silver throne, with a silver crown on his head. He imagined Saffron fitting all the goats with silver bells, all thanks to him, and laughed out loud.

He knew he should be asleep now like the rest, full of kudu stew, *injera* bread and the glowing honey burn of *tej*. His feet were sore from dancing and he had no pressing need to visit the tank where the quicksilver was stored, only he wanted to. He wanted a moment to stand over that glittering liquid with his torch held high and see it. It was like a church to him, that storehouse. Dan had shown the men how to make and fit the square timber frames that would support the workings, Patch had shown them how to blow open the rocks with a minimum of risk and designed the wheelbarrows they used to haul the ore to the surface. Bringing the mercury here was Rusty's great contribution, and he could not help indulging in a moment of private pride. He would offer it his prayers for success in the weeks to come, then go back to bed and sleep. He almost fell again. Hell, he would just sleep in the mouth of the main dig on a bed of ore and be ready in the morning.

He turned the corner and watched his feet carefully as he climbed the bank to the quicksilver store. It was a steep climb. No flash flood of the river would reach his precious mercury here. Then he heard something. Not the calls of the owls or jays, or crackle and chirp of insects, but a human sound. He looked up from his feet, puzzled. Someone was in the storehouse. He could just see the light of a hurricane lamp in the window. Perhaps Ryder had decided to come and stare at the mercury too, though given the way he had been looking at his wife over the fire it seemed unlikely.

Rusty sniffed, a little sorry he wouldn't be able to be alone with his beautiful quicksilver, but still too flush with drink and imminent success to be anything but happy. He pushed open the wooden door. A man was bending over at the base of the quicksilver tank. At first Rusty couldn't quite understand what he was looking at. The man was fiddling with the tap at the bottom of the stone tank.

'Hey! Don't do that! It'll run off.' The man looked up and Rusty grinned at the familiar face. He relaxed. 'You had me worried for a moment.' He hiccuped. 'Why ain't you in bed?'

The man moved fast. Before Rusty could react, he had sprung to his feet and charged at him. Rusty was knocked backwards and the air went out of his lungs. He dropped his torch and the darkness pressed in hard. All he could see was the glimmer of the quicksilver, illuminated by the swinging hurricane lamp. Rusty started laughing. The whole thing was ridiculous.

'What you playing at?'

Strong arms lifted him by the collar and he realised he was being dragged towards the tank.

'What you doing?' he panted. Then he felt himself being lifted up. The knowledge of what was happening suddenly crashed through his befuddled consciousness.

'No! For the love of God, man! No!'

He was thrown backwards over the high edge and the metal swam up around him. He floundered his way up, every nerve screaming with white terror now.

'No! Please! Get me out! Get me out!' He grabbed at the side of the tank with his right hand, then screamed in agony and let go as something heavy and iron smashed into his fingers. He fell back and felt the metal slip into his mouth. He spat and cried out again. The metal did not want him, it punched him upwards. He slipped and flailed and fell backwards. He managed to scream. A hand closed around his ankles and dragged them upwards. Rusty thrashed left and right but his head was forced down into the mercury. He could feel it, cold and knowing, finding its way under his clothes, into the shell of his ears, clutching the skin of his chest, forcing its way past his eyelids and freezing the soft wet matter of his eyes. He could get no grip, no hold on the sides of the tank. He had a memory of watching the walls being made, of instructing the workers to grind them smooth so none of the precious mercury would be trapped. He remembered the heat of the Abyssinian sun, the scrape of stone tools, the stir of the breeze in the grasses by the river, the sound of the picks coming from higher up the slope and his name being called. He felt himself turn and smile as Ryder walked towards him along the riverbank, bringing water for him and his workers. He put the beaker into his hand and smiled at him. Rusty took it and drank. His mouth opened and the mercury poured into him and through him. In those final moments of indescribable pain, another Rusty existed, it seemed, observing, a little sadly, with the fresh water in his hand, and Ryder Courtney's arm resting across his shoulders, how this other mortal man was being unmade by the metal, split apart like the ore he had worked on for so many years into its base and precious elements.

Rusty heard, like a dream, his killer, weeping and saying again and again, 'I'm sorry, I'm sorry'.

His body stopped thrashing. In his fading vision he looked up into the African sky and his last thought was of its implacable beauty.

Amber had gone to sleep dreaming of her wax and gold lesson with the singer. To have earned that wandering man's soft applause gave her a burst of pride that warmed her as the night grew cold.

When she woke with a start in the darkness, her first thought was: why am I afraid? She swung her legs down off the sleeping platform and wrapped a shawl around her shoulders and went to the door of the hut. She saw Ryder in the centre of the camp by the warm remains of the fire. He held a torch above his head. The flames wavered and shrunk as if they did not want to face the cold night breezes.

'Did you hear that?' he said.

'Something woke me.' She pointed towards the bend in the river. 'From the mine.'

Ryder nodded. 'Stay here, al-Zahra.'

'Should I not wake some of the men?'

'It might be nothing. Stay here and listen for me. I'll shout if I need help.' He left at once, walking with long, confident strides. Amber watched him go. Only a couple of hours before he had been singing and storytelling, laughing with his men until Saffron had wagged her finger at him. He had picked her up and carried her to their bed, still laughing and pretending he might drop her, as Saffron started shrieking and giggling too. Now he moved like a man who had never touched strong drink in his life. He disappeared into the darkness around the bend of the river, and Amber walked slowly to the place where the path dropped steeply towards the water. A half dozen tree stumps and logs were set here, dug up when they were making and remaking the gardens, or pilfered from the mine workings. It had become an unofficial meeting place for the women of the camp, a corner to rest and gossip between chores. She found her way to one of the logs by memory and pulled her knees close to her body, wrapping her shawl around them too. The days were hot here, but the nights were cold. She could sense morning coming, though the night was still pitch black. Soon the sudden African dawn would spill into the valley and the cooking fires would be lit.

The river sang softly over the stones and a sudden dread squeezed her heart. She knew that something had gone terribly wrong.

She heard the splashing of Ryder's boots in the shallows.

'Tadesse!' he shouted as he appeared around the corner. She could see Ryder was carrying someone over his shoulders. Amber jumped to her feet and ran towards him. Behind her she heard the sound of people coming from their houses, cries and sudden prayers. Ryder strode by her, and she moaned and put her hand out as she recognised Rusty's red hair and narrow frame.

Ryder set him down by the ashes of the fire. Dawn was brightening by the second and Amber saw the first light of the sun catch the shimmering mercury beading across Rusty's clothes, in his hair, around his nose. As Ryder set him down, tiny pools of it slithered down his cheeks like silver tears. Tadesse came at a run, his feet and chest bare, and skidded to a halt beside Rusty, falling into a crouch. Ryder said something quick and low to him in Amharic, too fast for Amber to catch. Tadesse felt for a pulse and shook his head. He bent down and breathed into Rusty's mouth. Ryder had his hands in his hair, gripping the side of his head as if he would crush his own skull. Tadesse leaned all his weight on Rusty's chest and Amber watched in horror as a slick of mercury and black blood welled up and out of Rusty's mouth. Tadesse turned Rusty's head to one side and the mixture drained away onto the soil, but his eyes remained fixed and staring.

Tadesse pounded at his chest and breathed into his mouth again, once, twice, then came away spitting. Someone handed him a beaker of *tej* and Tadesse swilled it around his mouth and spat it onto the soil. Again he reached for Rusty's pulse, then he turned away and sat down, wrapping his arms around his knees.

Ryder let out a roar, a cry of such anger and pain Amber covered her ears. Everyone in the camp was awake now and the ground was washed with honey-coloured light. Murmurs and exclamations of dismay ran through the crowd. Some of the women began to cry, and seeing them, the children started to wail. Saffron came out of her hut, Leon struggling in her arms, and looking between her husband and the body, she gave a sudden sob and covered her mouth. Dan and Patch pushed their way through the workers, then stared in horror. Dan dropped to his knees and Patch punched the wall of the church with a cracking force that echoed like a rifle shot. The risen sun looked down on the crowd gathered around the corpse, making the silver of the mercury shine, the black blood a shadow on its glimmering skin.

• • •

They buried him the same day. The young priest led the way. Ryder, Patch, Dan and Rusty's two best apprentices carried the body, wrapped in white and supported on a wicker hurdle, up the hill on the far side of the valley. For some reason they felt they wanted to bury Rusty high up and opposite the Mother, where he could watch both the camp and the mine. Behind them followed half a dozen of the mineworkers with shovels over their shoulders, then everyone else. Amber and Saffron walked together in the middle of the crowd, saying nothing. The climb was steep, and halfway up Tadesse took Leon from his mother and sat him on his own shoulders. Everyone wore white, and they looked like a flock of goats moving up the hill. On a small plateau near the summit, shaded and green with the recent rains, the men dug Rusty's grave and he was lowered into it, accompanied by the prayers of the priest and the responses of the crowd. The red earth stained the cotton of the gravediggers' robes so they looked as if they were edged with dried blood. The children threw flowers over the body, deep blues and purples on the white shroud, and the earth was put tenderly back over him.

When it was done, the people turned and began to make their way back down the hillside, Amber and Saffron among them. But Ryder made no move to leave. Instead he sat down on the grass, took a cheroot from his pocket and lit it. Once he had blown the first lungful of smoke into the breeze, he said, 'OK, kid, you can come speak to me.'

Tadesse's head peered back over the sharp decline of the hill. 'I can see now why the kudu cannot hide from you, Mr Ryder.'

Ryder didn't reply, just blew out another cloud of smoke and watched it drift away.

'I wanted to speak to you alone, Mr Ryder, but not next to Mr Rusty's grave.'

Ryder leaned back on his elbows and tipped his head back so the sun hit his face. 'If you've come to talk to me about his death, I think this is as good a place as any, Tadesse.'

The slim boy took a seat by his side, cross-legged, and began to plait together the grasses in front of him.

'They say it was an accident. That he was drunk and fell in the tank and could not get out.'

'And what do you say?' Ryder asked.

The boy ran his fingers through the grasses again, releasing them. 'I helped prepare his body for burial. I looked at it. The fingers on his right hand were broken, as if . . .' He mimed a chopping motion in the air.

Ryder felt his throat tighten. 'As if they were struck with something when he tried to get out of the tank?'

'Something like a . . . crowbar,' Tadesse said.

Ryder said nothing. When he had returned to inspect the mercury reservoir, he found the tap half turned and the majority of the precious liquid metal slithering away into the ground. He and a couple of the other men had gone back and retrieved what they could when they realised Rusty was dead, and he had thought the tap knocked open when Rusty tumbled into the tank. Now he considered another, darker scenario. An act of sabotage disturbed by Rusty and then by his own arrival. He pushed his hands through his thick, dark hair.

He had made and discarded a number of plans since he carried Rusty's body into the camp, but all had foundered on one thing. Without Rusty's knowledge and experience, it would be all but impossible to make use of even the quicksilver they had left. He had lingered at the graveside because he needed to think how he would explain to his family and workers that the death of their friend would set them back months, perhaps even years.

'Mr Ryder, I think the hills do not want to give up their silver to you.'

Tadesse stood up, and whenever Ryder thought of Tigray after that day, this was the first image that came to mind: Tadesse, with his walking stick in one hand, his white shawl falling over his shoulders, looking across the impossible rising and falling peaks in the thin mountain air. A poor boy with the dignified bearing of a king.

Ryder clenched his fists. 'I will have it, Tadesse. For Rusty, for my family, for myself. I will not be threatened and bullied away from this place. It is mine and I shall master it.'

Tadesse looked back at him over his shoulder for a moment, his gaze cool and assessing, then set off back towards the village.

By the time Ryder followed him back to the river and his own home, his mind was clear. He believed the workers he had recruited for the mine were loyal, but if one had carried the superstitions regarding the working of metal into the camp and those superstitions had led to sabotage and Rusty's death, he would be discovered. He would question each of the men, and their wives, and if he had any suspicions he would dismiss the worker and his family at once. He demanded the complete loyalty of those who worked for him and would have it. He also needed to replenish their stocks of quicksilver and find a way to make use of it. Ryder knew that a man of Rusty's brilliance could not be replaced, but his friend had often spoken about the process in detail as they refined their plans. The only problem was time. He would not leave the camp until he had questioned the workers and assured himself of their loyalty, but he needed that quicksilver now.

'I'll go to Massowah,' Patch said, setting down his horn mug of *tej* on the rough wooden table in Ryder's hut when Ryder had finished telling him, Dan, Saffron and Amber his decision. 'Only problem is the lingo. And the cash.'

Amber was curled up on the earthen bench furthest from the fire. When Patch finished speaking she stood up and joined the others at the table.

'I'll go with you. I have the lingo, and the cash.'

Ryder frowned. 'I won't take money from my sister-in-law. You know I won't.'

She leaned on the table, and the firelight cast soft shadows on her face. 'It's not charity. It's an investment in the mine. You and Saffron can draw up the papers while we're gone. Don't worry, Ryder. It's only a minority stake. I won't be able to tell you how to run things here, I wouldn't try, but I believe in you and what we're doing. The gardens can cope without me for a few weeks.'

Ryder glanced at his wife. Leon was curled in her lap sleeping peacefully.

'She can do it, Ryder,' Saffron said. 'And we need you here.'

'Then that's the plan,' he replied and drained his cup.

'Dear Lord,' Evelyn Baring, the Consul-General of Egypt, said as he looked through the thick folder Sam Adams had laid on his desk. 'I thought little in the world could shock me these days, Colonel. I see I was wrong.'

He squinted at a photograph, one from a packet of several dozen contained in the folder. It showed a corpulent woman, naked apart from her extravagant, plumed hat, high-heeled shoes and stockings, being serviced by a middle-aged man. His face and figure were familiar to every subject of Queen Victoria. They were not alone in the photograph. The man was being cheered on, it seemed, by a half dozen men and women in various states of undress. One figure, dressed in a wide skirt and close-fitting blouse, also had a beard and a face familiar to all students of politics.

'No wonder the Duke of Kendal always obtained such favourable terms from the government,' Baring said, and returned the photograph to the packet.

Sam was standing, his hands behind his back, and staring fixedly at the portrait of the queen above Sir Evelyn's head.

'Yes, sir. Going through the . . . material provided, it seems the duke was the silent owner of a number of brothels in Paris, the most exclusive of their type. The camera equipment was no doubt hidden between the walls. He needed only a false mirror or two, a spyhole and he could arrange for these images to be collected whenever a choice victim decided to frequent his establishments.'

'I wonder who else they caught,' Evelyn mused. He drew another photograph from the packet and went visibly pale. 'Good God is that . . .? And is that a . . .?' He replaced it swiftly. 'And that is supposed to be pleasurable?'

'I couldn't say, sir.' The clock ticked very loudly. After an agonising pause, Sam cleared his throat. 'As to who else they caught, sir, I am told a significant amount of coded traffic emanated from the Italian, German and American consulates shortly after this was delivered to me.'

Evelyn Baring crossed his legs and stared out of the window into the blistering blue of the Cairo sky.

'And you think this is the work of Ballantyne, do you?'

'I do.'

'Why did he not simply give all of the material to us? It would have been a boon to the government, once these horrors were destroyed, of course, to have such material on our European cousins,' Sir Evelyn mused.

Sam shook his head. 'Ballantyne does not work for us. His aim was the destruction of the Duke of Kendal. I understand that proof of some of the duke's crimes – the murder and coercion of union officials and so on – has been sent to the newspapers. Penrod sends this material to us and the other consulates to demonstrate he has no interest in it or use for it.' Sam shifted uncomfortably. The old wounds in his legs seemed to hurt a great deal more whenever he thought of Penrod Ballantyne. 'He means to reassure us.'

'How very high-minded of him,' Baring said dryly. 'And what of the duke?'

'With your permission, I should like to call at his house personally and as soon as possible.'

Baring nodded, then closed the folder and pushed it across towards Sam. 'Of course. I would like you to burn those photographs first, however. Do it personally, Sam. And bury the ashes.'

• • •

Sam did as he was asked and then, taking only his adjutant, rode out to the duke's house. No guards were at the gate, and even from the roadside, Sam could see the windows were shuttered. He walked unchallenged through the gardens and up the broad steps, thinking of when he had come here with Ballantyne. The door was slightly ajar. Sam called out, but the house was silent. He could see the place had been looted, a mirror smashed on the tiles, the drawers of the heavy side tables in the hall pulled out and emptied, some items of clothing scattered down the stairs. He imagined all the duke's impressive servants grabbing whatever they could get their hands on and running.

He turned to his adjutant. 'Go back on to the street. See if you can find anyone who saw what happened here.'

The door to the duke's study was locked. Sam noticed the bloodstains on the wall outside and found the body with an arrow through its throat rolled into the drawing room. That room had been emptied of its valuables too. Sam thought of the servants stepping back and forth over the corpse.

His adjutant was quick. A water-seller had seen two of the servants of the house leading away one of the duke's chargers. The horse had been laden with hurriedly packed sacks of clothing and, indignant at being treated as a beast of burden, had broken free and galloped towards the outskirts of the city. The servants had followed, stopping to gather whatever treasures the animal managed to shake loose from its back.

'Very well,' Sam said. 'Break down the door of the study.'

He lit a cigar while the man kicked at the lock until it cracked and gave. The adjutant stumbled into the room with the momentum of his final kick. Sam heard him swear and retch. He took another puff of his cigar, then pushed the door fully open. A body was seated on one of the green leather armchairs, facing the door. It wore evening dress, and a shotgun lay on the Turkish rug beside it. The face was obliterated, a mess of tissue and bone fragments, and the wall behind the chair was splattered with a great plume of blood and brain matter.

'If you are going to vomit, Captain, do it outside,' Sam said, then approached the corpse. The hands were resting on its knees, palms up. White, delicate hands, the gold band of a signet ring on the little finger. Sam turned the left hand, feeling the stiffness of death, and saw the arms of the duke engraved on the ring. He lifted the lapel of the jacket and felt carefully in the inside pocket. A monogrammed wallet with some hundred pounds in it. Sam could find no note of any kind, only the concealed safe, concealed no more, open and empty, which was, in a way, Sam supposed, note enough. He took another long draw from his cigar and turned to his suffering adjutant.

'Inform the civil authorities and post a guard outside to prevent further looting. What was the name of the duke's secretary?'

The adjutant still looked pale but managed to reply, 'Carruthers, sir.'

'That's the one. See if you can find out where he has scuttled off to.'

The adjutant saluted, then left the room with all possible speed. Sam examined the shattered face of the corpse.

'I am glad I never made you really angry, Penrod,' he said to the lifeless room, then left to make his report to the consulate.

• • •

Amber did not realise how lonely she had been at the camp until she found herself back in Massowah. She and Patch had travelled with Ato Asfaw's son, Fassil, to guide them, and Fassil's wife, Subira, to act as Amber's maid and chaperone. Amber had insisted she needed neither, but Asfaw was firm. His sense of propriety would allow nothing less. Subira's eyes grew wide as they approached the city, glittering on the edge of the water in the heat like a mirage in the desert. They grew bigger still when they saw the Italian women, wives of the officers posted to the city, in their corsets and heeled boots, their hair piled high on their heads.

Ato Bru gave them a warm welcome, and when he heard of Rusty's death, lowered his eyes and put his hands together, offering up a silent prayer for their friend's soul. He insisted on welcoming them and their guides into his own well-appointed compound. Then rested and fed, Amber and Patch set to work. Arranging a line of credit from Amber's accounts in England was relatively straightforward, then Patch began the business of leaning on all the good will Rusty had built up in the telegraph office to find another source of mercury and arrange for its transport.

'This is going to take a month, Miss Benbrook,' he said, coming home after his first day on the wires and settling into a wicker chair on the veranda of Ato Bru's dining chamber. 'At least the men there talk English, so I don't need you translating for me.'

'I'll find us someone who understands mercury then,' Amber said cheerfully and sipped her tea. She felt Patch watching her, his mouth slightly open, and looked up again. 'What is it, Patch?'

He sniffed and scratched the pink scars that ran across the right side of his jaw. 'Only . . . I can't help wondering, Miss Amber. You made all this money from your book. Don't you want to leave this country, go live your own life? I see you love your sister, and she and Ryder are going to stick it out in Tigray, whatever gets thrown at them, but why should you stay buried out there in the wilds?'

Amber thought of the wild leap of pleasure and excitement she had felt coming into a city again, even one as small and out of the way as Massowah. Then she thought of the sights and sounds of Cairo, and the fizz of champagne on her tongue. Patch was right, she had the money to go anywhere and her book had won her admirers in every European capital. For a moment the idea glimmered with promise, then she thought of Penrod. He was out there somewhere, probably married to Lady Agatha by now. To see them together would kill her, and the dread of seeing them cast deep shadows over every fantasy of life in Cairo or London or Paris her mind could conjure up. At least in Tigray she was free of that fear.

She shook her head. 'Don't fret about me, Patch. I have work to do.'

●　●　●

It took three weeks of patient enquiry to find the man Amber needed. Stefano Di Moze was a trader who had been brought up in the silver mining town of Argentiera in Sardinia and studied chemical engineering for some years before taking up his current profession. Amber could not persuade him or his wife to come to

Tigray, but she did arrange to buy from him a number of technical works, souvenirs of his studies, which included useful entries and tables about the use of quicksilver. Amber was so delighted to have them, along with a bundle of old journals and a volume called *Metalworking Among the Ancients*, the fact they were all in Italian seemed only a minor difficulty. Stefano's wife, Valentina, insisted on giving Amber an Italian–English dictionary. The English wife of an officer made her a present of *A Grammar of the Italian Language Arranged in Twenty Lessons*, and a pair of other similar well-thumbed volumes. Valentina also thrust into her hands a copy of *The Betrothed* by Alessandro Manzoni in Italian, 'Because it is impossible,' she said, her hands sketching patterns in the air, 'you should learn my beautiful language reading only books such as *Nuovo Trattato di Chimica Industriale*.'

They were taking tea together and discussing the final arrangements for Amber's journey back to Courtney Mine when Valentina put an English newspaper into her hands.

'Amber, I hope you do not think me rude. But I read your book with much pleasure and I had friends in Cairo who told me a little of this Lady Agatha and how she was . . . tangled in your affairs. I thought perhaps you might not have heard of her sad end, and that of her papa.'

Amber didn't reply, but put down the coffee cup with a shaking hand and took the newspaper from her hostess. She had to reread it three times before the words started to make sense. Lady Agatha was dead, her father had committed suicide and his empire had collapsed in scandal. Agatha gone! She felt a strange stab of pity. Amber could not blame her beautiful rival for loving Penrod, after all.

'Are you ill, Amber? Did I do wrong to show this to you?'

Amber tore her eyes from the newsprint. Her hostess's face was crumpled with concern.

'No, no. Thank you, Valentina. I am glad you showed it to me. Only I admit it is a great shock.'

She had to read the article again before she managed to understand what the carefully constructed paragraphs were hinting at: that the Duke of Kendal's actions had led to Lady Agatha's death, and that the collapse of his business seemed to be the act of some avenging angel. Amber had no doubt as to whom that avenging angel was. This was Penrod's work. No one else could have managed it. She felt a burst of pride in her chest, then a confusion of pain as she thought how he had done this remarkable thing for Agatha. She bit her lip. Where was he now? She could not help herself. She imagined sitting on the veranda, not of this small house in cramped and waterless Massowah, but of Shepheard's Hotel, seeing Penrod walking by, the moment he would turn and look at her.

Saffron will understand, she thought to herself. And Ryder is so good at languages, he'll make sense of the books in the end. If I could just see Penrod one more time . . .

'May I keep this?' she said at last, and Valentina nodded.

For another half hour they discussed the best places in Massowah to buy seeds for Amber's garden, then shaking hands with cheerful cordiality, Amber left to thread her way back through the chatter and bustle of the marketplace to Ato Bru's compound, stopping only to book her passage on the next sailing back to Cairo.

• • •

The night before the sailing, Amber wrote a long letter to her sister and another, shorter one to Ryder, explaining the books she had bought and where the seeds she enclosed should be planted. Not that Ryder would plant them, but she was sure he'd put someone responsible in charge of her gardens – Tadesse, perhaps. Then she had a cheerful farewell supper with Patch and Ato Bru. An hour before the steamer was due to sail, she found herself seated in the first-class salon, with an iced glass of seltzer water in front of her, her travel bag safely stowed and a sense of delighted excitement fizzing through her blood. She had been watching the activity on the shoreline for a while when a liveried steward offered her a folded copy of the *Pall*

Mall Gazette. She took it from him, revelling in the crisp unread pages of print. Every newspaper that reached them in the highlands had passed through a hundred hands before they saw it, so to have a clean copy of her own felt like giddy luxury. She turned a few pages, humming softly under her breath as she did, then came to a sudden halt.

Another victim? the headline read. The report was only a few paragraphs long. A woman, Mrs Gloria Martin, and her son had been found murdered just outside the city limits of San Francisco. The house where they were found had been rented by a man who worked for the Duke of Kendal and it was reported in the neighbourhood that neither mother nor son had been seen in several months. The newspaperman speculated that they might have been held captive for some reason. A thorough search of the house had produced no clue as to the murderer's destination, only a telegram from Cairo dated on the day that Kendal had blown his brains out. It read: *Burn everything and get out.*

Amber felt sick. She remembered where she had seen the name of the victim, Gloria Martin, before – on the back of the photographic postcard that had fallen from Dan's hand just before Rusty was killed. The card with the message 'we depend on you' written in shaking handwriting on the back. Amber had a strange sensation, as if a key had just turned in her mind and a door had swung open, casting a clear, bright light over everything that had happened over the last few months. It was Dan. Dan had been blackmailed to make sure the mine failed, and they had used this woman to force him to comply. He had tried to convince them the mission was doomed, and when Rusty had succeeded in bringing them the quicksilver, which might make the mine a success, then – Amber almost gagged as the realisation hit her – he had murdered him.

The liveried steward heard a crash behind him and turned. The beautiful young woman to whom he had offered the newspaper only a few minutes ago had disappeared, knocking over her chair in her haste to be gone. He raised his eyebrows and crossed to the table to set the chair on its legs again. The ice in the seltzer glass crackled and a movement on the gangplank caught his attention. The young woman was dashing back to the shore, holding her wide straw hat on her head with one gloved hand. The crowd waiting to board parted and she disappeared from sight back into the city.

Ryder drove his people hard in the weeks following Rusty's death, but as no one worked with more dedication than he did himself, the men lowered their heads and responded to the task ahead of them with a determination that matched his own. He ordered two men, who he believed thought the mine cursed, to leave and he was certain he could trust the men who remained.

Operations below ground were suspended, and all efforts were bent towards building the processing works according to what they recalled of Rusty's instructions. First the arrastra was begun, a shallow circular pit some twelve feet in diameter where the smashed and sorted ore would be ground and quicksilver and water added. Dan went up into the hills to find the slabs of rock that would line it and the huge grinding stones that mules would drag through the ore to reduce it to a fine pulp. He came back after three days, having found a place further up the valley where they could mine blocks of quartz-porphyry, then float them down on rafts to the mine as they were needed. Ryder sent a dozen of his best men and food for a week back upstream to fetch the blocks.

While they were gone, Ryder led the construction of a flume leading down from the Lion Dam. His design included a series of gates and traps, so the water could be distributed around the processing works as it was needed. The river below them was too changeable in its flow and force to serve their needs, but the small dam they had built before the rains in a higher valley would provide a reliable resource for the workings. For a week the camp echoed to the sound of axes striking wood rather than stone, and the men came home smelling of sawdust and resin.

As the flumes were being built and tested, the arrastra lined, and the grinding stones fitted at the correct height and angle, work began on the patio where the ground ore would be mixed with salt, copper sulphate and more quicksilver. It would need to be turned and trodden by men and animals every other day for at least a month, but when those weeks were over, the waste pulp would be washed away, leaving an amalgam of silver and mercury.

Then the process would become one of fire rather than water. The amalgam would be hauled up the other side of the valley to the bank of furnaces, built where the breezes would carry off the fumes, and close to the wooded slopes where their charcoal was made. Heat would persuade the mercury to loosen its grip on the precious silver. What was left was further refined via a retort and furnace. Then, and only then, after weeks of labour and the actions of mercury, water and heat, would Courtney Mine produce its first ingot of silver bullion. If, that was, Patch and Amber returned with more quicksilver and they could work out the proportions in which it should be used with the ore they had recovered.

When he was certain he had done all he could to prepare, Ryder set the men to digging out more ore and watched the horizon for Patch, Amber and their precious cargo.

Gebre, the head metalworker at the mine who supervised the building of the furnaces, and on his own forge worked their precious supplies of iron into brackets and rivets, staples and chains, came to see Ryder in his hut that evening.

Saffron made him welcome and put a drink in his hand, then returned to playing with Leon in the far corner of the room; mother and child were passing each other pebbles and sticks with great solemnity. After a little talk of the work still to be done, Gebre handed Ryder a heavy roll of cloth.

Ryder opened it and found in its soft folds an iron stamp.

'What is this, Ato Gebre?' he asked, peering at it in the firelight.

Instead of replying, Gebre took it from him and cleared aside a few of the rushes on the earth floor at his feet, then pressed the stamp into the surface. The stamp was a simple circle around the interlocked initials 'C' and 'M'.

'For Courtney Mine,' Gebre said shyly. 'You must stamp it on the ingots as they cool. Miss Amber showed me the lettering before she left.'

'Do you like it?' Saffron said, grinning up from her play with Leon.

'I do,' Ryder said, taking the stamp from Gebre again. 'I do, very much.'

He heard a sniff at the doorway and turned. Dan was watching from the shadows, his arms folded across his chest.

'Any word from Massowah, Mr Courtney?' he asked.

'Not yet, Dan,' Ryder replied evenly. Dan had grown increasingly morose in the weeks since Rusty died and he was beginning to try Ryder's patience with his constant pessimism.

'Perhaps they'll have no luck there at all,' Dan added.

Saffron laughed. 'Don't be silly, Dan. You know Amber. She'll be back here any day with the quicksilver and a man who knows what to do with it.' She widened her eyes and leaned forward towards Leon. 'And perhaps a toy for her nephew too!'

Dan blinked. 'I suppose so. Mr Courtney, I want to show you a spot up on the Mother's east flank. Think there may be another seam there, so there'll be no shortage of ore when Miss Amber and Patch get here.'

'We can go at first light, Dan.' Ryder got to his feet and shook hands with Gebre. 'Thank you, Ato Gebre. We shall need this stamp and soon. I feel it in my bones.'

He ushered the two men out of his house and looked at his wife. She had settled Leon in his cot and now turned towards him, a familiar hungry glint in her eye.

'How shall we fill the hours till Amber gets home, Filfil?' he asked.

She sashayed across the earthen floor towards him and put her arms around his neck. 'I'm sure we'll think of something, Ryder.'

• • •

The runner arrived midway through the morning. Saffron heard her name being called and stepped out of the relative cool of the shade by the church and shielded her eyes. A young man was racing down the path on the other side of the valley, a bundle of papers in his hand. Saffron picked up her skirts and splashed across the low flowing river to meet him, recognising him as one of Ato Asfew's sons – Amber's guide to Massowah.

'My sister?' she cried out as soon as he was in calling distance.

'She comes – even now, with Mr Patch,' the young man panted, thrusting the papers into her hand. 'She told me to run ahead. To give you these papers. She says tell Mrs Saffron the woman in the article, Mrs Martin, is beloved of Mr Dan. She says: "Saffy, read fast. Tell Ryder."'

Saffron unfolded the sheets of newsprint. First she read the article about the Duke of Kendal, then the second about the murder of the woman and boy near San Francisco. Then her confusion was replaced by a terrible cold clarity singing through her blood. She did not need to ask how Amber knew about the connection between Mrs Martin and Dan. If Amber said this woman had been important to him, that was enough for her.

'Oh, Ryder!' she whispered. Then, with the newspapers clutched in her hand, she raced down to the river and towards the mine.

Tesfaye was the first man she saw, testing the harness on the mule that would drag around the grinding stones in the arrastra.

'Mrs Saffron, I hope you are well?'

'Yes, yes, where is Ryder, Tesfaye? I need him at once. And where is Mr Dan?'

Tesfaye was puzzled. They had seen tragedy at the mine and disaster, yet he had never seen Saffron look as distracted as this.

'They are together, yonder,' he said, waving towards the other side of the slope. 'Mr Dan took your man up to show him a place he thinks he has found more ore.'

Saffron lifted up her skirts and ran.

• • •

The path up the far side of the slope was rocky and lined with thorns. They tore at Saffron's hair and her clothes, but she dragged and willed her way up, then half fell, exhausted and bruised as the track dropped sharply again. She looked around her. Dan and Ryder were perhaps a dozen yards away, where the track broadened into another narrow plateau, like a giant step cut from the side of the mountain. Ryder was crouching by the rock face, examining a pile of rocks, then looking up to see the place from which it had fallen. Even from here Saffron could see that the colour of the rock was different, the blue-grey of silver-bearing ore rather than the rust-coloured sandstone that surrounded it, but it was not the stone that caught her attention and squeezed her heart. Dan was standing perhaps ten feet from Ryder's exposed back and he had already taken his revolver from his belt.

Saffron screamed and pulled herself to her feet, then ran on. Ryder spun around as soon as he heard her cry. He could see his wife struggling towards them, and then Dan, his revolver raised and cocked and pointed straight at Ryder's chest.

Dan kept the gun level and shifted around so the sheer rise of the cliff was at his back. He shouted at Saffron over his shoulder. 'Stay where you are! And look away, Mrs Courtney. You can't get to me in time. You know that. And I'd be sorry if you saw your man die. But die he must.'

Saffron ran past him and into her husband's arms.

Ryder cursed her. 'Saffy, get out of the way! Don't you dare put yourself in front of a gun for me,' he said.

'I'm not moving. If he wants to kill you, he'll have to kill me first,' she panted.

Dan still had his gun trained on them. He looked sorry, but resolute.

'I don't want to shoot you, Mrs C. But I will.'

'Dan! It's over!' Saffron screamed. 'They are dead and killing Ryder can't save them.'

Dan rocked back, as if she had struck him.

'Please, Dan, if you've ever cared for us at all, listen to me.' Saffron could hardly speak, hardly think. Her words felt like they were tearing her lungs apart. She could see nothing but that gun. She felt Ryder's hands on her shoulders. She knew he would fling her sideways as soon as he saw Dan's trigger finger tighten, that the round from the powerful handgun would slam into his chest and rip it apart unless Dan listened to her now.

'What are you saying?' Dan said, still staring over her shoulder at Ryder.

'Gloria Martin and her son James. They were found murdered in San Francisco. Who are they?'

'My sister and her child,' Dan said dully.

'Oh, Danny!' Saffron exclaimed and covered her mouth.

Dan lifted the revolver again, but his hand was shaking. 'You're lying! You're trying to trick me! They can't be dead. I was promised. They came to me in Massowah, after the steamer sank. They said they had Gloria but if I did what they said . . .' He pointed the gun straight at Saffron. 'You found out somehow, Mrs C,' he said. 'And now you are trying to trick me to save your man. It won't work.'

'Amber sent a runner ahead of her, Dan, with these newspapers. She said Mrs Martin was your beloved. I don't know how she knew, but look!' She held up the fistful of paper in front of her, as if it would stop the bullet.

'The photograph,' Dan said quietly. 'I had their photograph, one of the girls gave it back to me . . . Miss Amber must have seen it . . .' The gun shook slightly.

'What the hell is happening? Explain this to me, Saffy,' Ryder said urgently. He put his arm around her and she held on to it, feeling the thick muscles of his forearm.

'Someone took them, Ryder!' she said, still clinging to him and watching the muzzle of the wavering gun. 'I think that's why Dan did what he did to Rusty. To save them. But they're dead, Dan. It's in the newspaper. They killed them anyway.'

'Dan murdered Rusty?' Ryder hissed. 'The cracked stones, the cave-in last month – you've been sabotaging us this whole time?'

'Read it to me,' Dan said.

Saffron smoothed the paper with shaking fingers but she couldn't see it. She sniffed and brushed away the tears that were blinding her with the back of her hand and managed to stutter out the paragraph: throats cut, missing for some time, brutal slaughter, suspicion of kidnapping and blackmail. As she read, she saw Dan lean against the wall behind him and let the revolver hang by his side.

'Who took them, Dan?' Ryder said. His voice was filled with dark rage and Saffron could feel it, his pain at the betrayal, his grief and shock vibrating through his muscles.

Dan had tilted his head back, half slumped against the rock as if he no longer had the strength to hold himself upright.

'I don't know. But if I wanted Gloria and James to live, this mine could never produce silver. That was the deal.'

'Something went wrong,' Saffron said. 'They killed them to stop them going to the police.'

'When?' Dan said. The word was a whisper.

Saffron, deafened by the thumping of blood in her ears, could hardly hear him. 'What, Dan?'

Now he roared. 'Were they dead when I killed Rusty?'

Saffron groaned. 'I don't know, Dan.'

'When was that newspaper printed?' he shouted. 'Were they already dead when I killed my friend?'

Saffron tried to look at the paper. The breeze flicked it, as if trying to playfully pull it from her fingers. Her hands were still shaking so hard she could hardly read the paper. She cursed herself and pulled it tight. She focused on the date – 29 April 1888 – then checked the wording of the report.

'Yes. Yes, oh, Dan. They were murdered the day before.'

Dan seemed to collapse from within. He groaned and sank to the ground, his arms slack beside him, his head lowered.

Saffron began to shiver uncontrollably. If Ryder had not been holding her, she would have fallen in the dust. It took her a moment to realise Dan was speaking.

'I hardly knew them. My sister and her boy. But when I heard they were taken. God, what is it? That pull in your blood that means you'll do anything for your kin? They gave me a letter from her, when we were in Massowah, and a photograph of her and the boy. They even got the boy to send me a note. He said that he'd been told I was a great man and would save them. And I tried, God, I tried. Why? What good did it do to kill them? I was doing what . . . God, Rusty . . . I sold my soul to save them and it did no good.'

'The men who took them were tying up loose ends. Who brought you the letters? Who made the deal?' Ryder said.

'A man named Carruthers. He came in on the next sailing from Cairo and said he was working for some Englishman who was interested in this strike. Wanted you stopped so he could take it over himself when the time came. God, they knew everything.'

Saffron looked up at her husband. 'Ryder, it was the Duke of Kendal. It's a great scandal. He was corrupt and was exposed somehow. They say he shot himself. It's all in the newspaper.'

Ryder's grip on her was like iron.

Dan slowly lifted the loaded gun to his temple and began to wrap his finger around the trigger. Ryder released his wife and launched himself forward. He caught Dan's wrist and wrenched it back so the shot went straight up into the sky. Dan cried out and let the pistol fall. Saffron sprang forward into the dust to grab it and flicked open the chamber, the unspent bullets ringing against the rocks as they fell.

Dan twisted around to look at Ryder. 'Let me die.'

'No,' Ryder said. He raised his fist and punched Dan once in the jaw with a force that sent the man sprawling in the dust. Ryder towered over him, his fists clenched.

'Ryder, don't . . .' Saffron said.

He ignored her, staring at Dan with such intensity of loathing, Dan shrank away from him. Ryder spoke only to him.

'Not before you've explained yourself to the people here. They deserve better than a second-hand truth from me.'

Saffron handed Ryder her scarf and he used it to tie Dan's hands behind his back before making him walk in front of them to camp. Amber and Patch had arrived while they were gone and Saffron dashed into her sister's arms, while Ryder forced Dan to his knees in front of the church.

'Oh God, Amber! Thank you! I was only just in time.'

Amber felt her breath release in a shuddering sigh as she held Saffron's shaking body against her.

'I'm here, Filfil. I'm here. And we have quicksilver. It will be here in a few days.'

• • •

They held Dan's trial, if that was what it could be called, that afternoon. The priest officiated. The workers and their families were all collected on the open ground in front of the church. Dan was still bound to stop him making another attempt on his own life. He was seated beside the priest. In front of them was a heap of pebbles, some white, some black. They had been gathered from the river by the children who thought it all a great game.

Ryder did not think he'd be able to control his feelings, so gave the role of interpreter to Tadesse. Amber and Saffron sat with the women, while some of the older girls took the younger children off to play at a distance, where their questions and demands would not disturb their elders. The priest, looking a little unsure, first offered his blessing to the crowd, then asked Dan if he wished to confess to the people. He nodded. Amber listened to both Dan's own words and Tadesse's translation. The story sounded better in Amharic, somehow more simple and more tragic, like some ancient epic told by the fireside. Dan made no attempt to deny his guilt, no attempt to excuse himself, other than to say he had never intended to kill Rusty. He had only meant to delay the amalgamation of the ore by draining off the quicksilver, but when Rusty had stumbled into it, he felt he had no choice. Amber was glad he confessed, though she could hardly believe it even now. She had thought Dan was their friend. She thought he was like an uncle to her and Saffron. He had helped her with the garden and her dams and waterways. She did not understand how he could have done so with all that blood on his conscience.

The priest asked Dan about his sister and her son. He told him their letters, passed to him by the blackmailer in Massowah, were hidden under his bunk. One of Dan's work crew went to fetch them and Tadesse translated them for the crowd, while the photograph of the woman and boy was passed around. A murmur of sympathy could be heard among the women, but the men remained stony-faced. Amber was asked to relate what she had learned in Massowah about the duke and how she had realised the importance of the names of the murdered woman and child in the second article. Then Saffron told them of the scene on the high plateau. Ryder spoke only to confirm what she had said. The priest asked if anyone wished to speak for Dan. Alem and Silas, who had both been learning about tunnel propping under Dan, stood up and stated that he had been a fair boss, a good teacher and cared about the safety of his men, avoiding injuring them even as he sabotaged the workings. They did so while looking at the ground, compelled by a sense of justice, perhaps, but it was clear they took no great pleasure in defending him. The priest then asked if anyone wished to speak against him and Patch got to his feet.

'We grieve for this man's sister, and her boy,' he said in English, and Tadesse translated quietly. 'We all have family. We have all in our lives lost people we love. We know the greater evil was done by the man who took Gloria and her boy, forced Dan to do what he did and then took their lives anyway.' They were looking at him now, a quiet, serious regard. 'But

Rusty Tompkins was also my friend. He was a good man and he died with his lungs full of quicksilver, not at the hands of some agent in Massowah, but by those hands –' he pointed at Dan – 'the hands of a man he would have gone through fire for. A man he trusted and loved like a brother. Dan says he did not know what to do. I know what he should have done.' Patch turned directly to Dan. 'You should have told us, Dan. You should have told Ryder, you should have told me, you should have told Rusty. This man had power, this duke. Fine. Well, Ryder had money back then too. And between us we had a thousand friends in San Francisco. We might have been able to save them. We might have been able to come up with some lie to make this duke think you had done his bidding. We have all poured our hearts into this mine, this camp. It's made us family and we would have done anything to save you, but you were trying to destroy all our work from the start.'

Dan dropped his head and stared at the dust under his boots. 'I could not risk it, Patch. I could not risk their blood on my hands.'

Patch's face flushed red, making the scars on his skin stand out. He balled his fists.

'You could not risk their lives? You couldn't risk *their* lives so you killed Rusty? To avoid risking your sister, you murdered him and you would have murdered Ryder too. Because you did not wish to risk the deaths of two people already dead.'

He turned away from Dan and addressed the crowd. 'I will pity the woman and her son. I will not pity this man. I will not. And only one punishment is fitting for his crime. Hang him. Hang him like the Judas he is over Rusty's grave.'

He stalked back to his place in the crowd and sat down. The men nearest him squeezed his shoulder and a whispered approval passed across the crowd like a breeze. Amber shivered.

The priest looked solemn. 'What say you, Mr Ryder?'

Ryder did not stand up. 'In such matters I am only one voice among you,' he said. 'But I agree with Patch. I say he should hang.'

'We vote,' the priest said. 'He has confessed his guilt. If you vote for mercy, he will be sent away. He may take food and water – enough for one day – and a knife, but nothing more. If he is seen by any of us within a day's walk of here after sunrise on the second day, he may be killed like a wolf who strays too near the cattle. Vote against mercy and he shall be hanged at dawn tomorrow in the place we buried Mr Rusty.' He held up his hands. 'Let each working man or married woman cast their vote as their heart tells them they must. The white pebbles are for mercy, the black for death.'

The people got to their feet, made their selection from the pile and dropped them into the priest's folded shawl. The only sound was the click of the pebbles.

Once they were collected, the votes were counted in silence. Below the camp they could hear the children laughing and splashing in the river. At last Tadesse whispered to the priest. He got to his feet once more.

'Dan Matthews shall be hanged at first light.'

The whole crowd sighed at once.

'I shall lock him in the church tonight so he may be close to God and beg his forgiveness for his many and grievous sins.'

Amber stared down into the dust. The priest looked around the crowd, then spoke again.

'This is a heavy day. Let us fast tonight. Let no fires be lit. Quiet the children and keep to your own houses. Offer your hunger to God and pray for the dead.'

He lifted up his silver cross, the sign of his office, and most of the workers took a moment to kiss it and receive the priest's blessing. No one protested about the ordained fast. It seemed they were all grateful, somehow, to shoulder a little of the pain.

Dan was led into the church and the door barred behind him. The men and women began to drift to their own houses without looking at each other. Amber grabbed Saffron's arm.

'Saffy, this can't happen,' she whispered.

'What? Why not?' Saffron stared at her blankly. 'The vote was taken. He killed Rusty and he would have killed Ryder. If they want someone to tie the knot in the rope, I'll do it for them.'

'But Saffy! Is this how we want the camp to begin? With a hanging? How can we be happy here if every time we look up there we see the place we hanged Dan? I want Rusty's spirit watching over us, not Dan's ghost!'

Saffron pulled her arm away. 'This isn't a fairy tale, Amber. You don't get happy ever after.'

'Every penny this mine makes will be tainted with blood.'

Saffron didn't answer her, only turned away. Amber stood, trembling and alone, in front of the church. It was a moment before she realised that Tadesse was still waiting in the shade of the church's overhanging reed roof.

'What was the count, Tadesse?'

'It is supposed to be secret, Miss Amber.'

'Just tell me.'

'Seventy-five votes for exile and mercy. For his hanging, seventy-six,' Tadesse said. He was tracing imaginary patterns on the lime-washed wall of the church, not looking at her.

'Which way did you vote, Tadesse?'

He shrugged. 'I am not yet sixteen or married, so I have no vote.'

'But if you could have voted . . .'

'For mercy . . .' He stopped drawing, flattened his palm on the church wall and looked up towards Rusty's burial place. 'But it is not mercy, so much, Miss Amber, as faith. Dan deserves to be punished and Mr Patch was right. Mr Dan could have asked for help, and he would have received that help. But I still think Mr Dan is not evil. I have faith that if he were sent away he would grieve. He would suffer more for what he did and have to atone for it or go mad. That is a strange sort of mercy, but it is faith.'

Amber joined him and leaned her back against the church wall. Evening was thickening around them, but it was strangely quiet. No crackle of fires and chatter, no smells of spiced bean stews or the rising sour tang of *injera*. Soon the light would fade.

Amber spoke again. 'I am not married. I did not get to vote either, Tadesse. And the two of us deserve a vote.'

• • •

The church was not locked. Only one bar had been placed across the door to stop Dan escaping, and Amber was strong enough to lift it on her own. She slipped in and lit her hurricane lamp. Dan was kneeling in front of the altar, but she had disturbed his prayers opening the door and he was twisted around, shielding his eyes from the light, trying to see who had come in. She moved the light closer to her face so he could see her.

'Miss Amber?'

'Hush, Dan.'

'I thought perhaps some of the people could not wait for dawn and were here to hang me now.'

The church was small, not really big enough for the growing camp, but it was already loved. The walls and low ceiling were painted with scenes from the Bible and the traditional saints of Tigray, Madonnas and Christs with olive faces, a St George in the regalia of one of Emperor John's warriors slaying a surprised dragon with rippling emerald scales. The light from Amber's lamp made them live and move. St Christopher loomed and faded above them, the Christ child held casually on his shoulder.

'No, Dan,' Amber said. 'I have decided you should go free.'

She lifted a bundle from her shoulder and handed it to him. He sat cross-legged on the floor and she watched while he examined its contents. His boots and coat, a water bottle and knife, a package of *injera* bread wrapped in cloth and one of the Courtneys' last Maria Theresa dollars.

'I should pay for what I have done, Miss Amber.'

'Yes. You should.' She drew her knees up to her chest and settled her shawl around her shoulders. 'But it's a big debt, Dan. It'll take more than a night to pay for it.'

He began to cry, covering his eyes. They were the stifled sobs of a man not used to weeping. Amber looked up at the saints watching her from the walls and wished they might give her some inspiration. They looked only quietly curious.

'I think hanging you would kill the camp, Dan,' she said at last. 'I do. It could be a fine place, but it doesn't need blood on its foundations. I think mercy is a better sacrifice. I know you'd rather die. But you'd be cursing us. I want you to go. I don't want your blood on Ryder's hands, or on Saffron's.'

He still wouldn't look at her, but she knew he was listening.

'If you want to make some amends for what you have done to us, you'll go. That is all.' She stood again and picked up the lamp. 'And I can't see Rusty liking it. Your hanging, I mean. Ryder is a bull, a lion. He charges at whatever is in front of him and that, at the moment, is you. Rusty thought three steps ahead. Always. I think he'd agree with me. But it's your choice, Dan. Take it on your shoulders and do us a favour, or stay and be hanged and let your guilt poison this place.'

She picked up the lamp and left, leaving the door unfastened behind her, then returned to her bed and slept.

· · ·

The shouts awoke Amber in the early light. She stumbled out of the hut and into the morning. A number of men, Ryder among them, were gathered at the church door. Ryder was yelling and the priest was trying to calm him.

'What has happened?' Amber asked one of the women next to her. It was Selam, wife of one of Dan's crew.

'A miracle,' Selam said, half hiding her face under her white shawl, her voice slightly awestruck. 'Or that is what the priest says. The church was closed up this morning, just as it should be, but Mr Dan is gone.'

Amber returned to her house and dressed properly, then climbed the slope to the east to see to her garden, taking a hunk of bread for breakfast with her. She had been alone for an hour, spacing out the strongest of the nut bushes she had managed to coax into some growth, when Ryder found her.

'Amber!'

She got slowly to her feet. The earth was dusty, desperate for rain, and clung to her skirts.

'Ryder. What can I do for you?'

He seized her shoulders and pushed her up against the trunk of the juniper tree that was shading her garden.

'What have you done? How dare you? By what right?'

The speed and violence shook her and the bark of the tree pressed into her back. She lifted her head and looked at him calmly. His handsome, friendly face was distorted with fury.

'I took the chance to vote. Turned out it was the deciding one,' she told him.

He raised his fist and for a second she thought he was going to hit her and she braced herself, but Ryder just diverted the blow and punched the tree instead, then shoved her away from him.

'This was because you are angry you didn't have a vote, Amber?' He spoke more quietly now. She looked at his knuckles. They were bleeding.

'No. Not entirely. You know why I did it. This place has the chance to be something good. You don't start something good with an execution.'

He had frightened her, but she didn't want him to see it. She crouched to the soil again and continued with her work, settling the seedling in its new home. A little sun, a little shade, a little water from one of her pools and this would take root and grow this time. It just needed to be done right.

Ryder's shadow still lay over her. 'Justice must be done,' he said, his voice thick.

'This is justice, Ryder. And you know it.'

He said nothing more but began to walk away from her down the slope. She patted the soil into place.

'And I know he thinks that,' she spoke to the seedling. 'Otherwise he would have put a guard on the door of the church.'

• • •

Two days later, Ato Bru arrived with the new supply of quicksilver and Amber's bundle of books. If Ato Bru noticed the tense atmosphere in the camp he ignored it, but he stayed only one night with them before beginning the return journey.

Amber set to work translating the books she had bought with steady diligence, her grammar and dictionary by her side. She had learned some Italian as a schoolgirl. A rumour had reached her family that her father would be posted to Rome, but then the government asked him instead to take up the fatal posting in Khartoum and her education in Arabic began. After escaping the harem of Osman Atalan, she learned that Penrod spoke fluent Italian and loved that country, so she had tried to learn a little more herself during her stay in Europe. She couldn't help thinking of him as she sank into the language again now. Still the books on mining and amalgamation gave her headaches. Each afternoon she wrote out her translations and handed them to Ryder. He still was not speaking to her properly, but he managed to thank her, and one evening forgot he was angry with her long enough to say they would have wasted half of the new quicksilver without her work.

In the evenings she studied her novel and, as her Italian improved, she started reading chapters aloud to anyone who wished to listen, translating into Amharic as she went. Before long the whole camp was entranced by the adventures of the star-crossed lovers and the dastardly forces ranged against them. Amber's heart ached as she read, and a careful observer might have noticed the hero ended up looking rather more like Penrod in her translation than the Italian original, but the story united them and the children could be heard rehearsing their favourite scenes together as they watched the goats on the flanks of the hills. Amber was whispering lines to herself as she finished her planting in her high garden, enjoying the music of the words on her lips when she felt a cold, heavy drop land on her neck. She sat back and looked out across the valley. A sudden tumble of clouds were rearing up like a wave across the vast sky. The rains were coming. She prayed they would be ready.

Lucio Angelo Carlo Zola was not the first man who came to Cairo looking for Penrod Ballantyne in the months that followed the fall of the Duke of Kendal. Rumours linking the mysterious British intelligence officer and the duke had reached the courts of Europe very quickly. The European royal families had reacted with embarrassment and relief when the images were returned to them, then, when they realised they were to be blackmailed no more, they had all become curious as to who their anonymous saviour was. The name Penrod Ballantyne was soon being whispered in the corridors of power in Rome, Berlin and London, but the name was, at first, all they had. After some discreet enquiries, heads of state across Europe were presented with neat typescripts of their agents' discoveries. These covered the schooling and family of the former major, and full, occasionally florid, accounts of his selfless bravery on the battlefield of El Obeid and his heroism carrying information in and out of Khartoum during the siege of 1884. They all included a summary of known events in Cairo: the engagement with the young writer Amber Benbrook, its end, and Penrod's affair with the unfortunate Lady Agatha. But at the moment of Agatha's death, all certain knowledge ceased. One London agent discovered that Penrod Ballantyne's account at Coutts bank had been drained. The heads of the European states looked towards Cairo and wondered. The French and German governments sent their best intelligence officers to the city, but they returned bemused and empty-handed. The city of rumours had greeted them with silence.

Lucio, however, had one great advantage over his German and French counterparts. He knew Penrod Ballantyne personally. Lucio had spent some time in school in England and had shared a study with the dashing young man. They had discovered a mutual love of fencing and spent many hours practising with the short blade while their fellows went looking for women in the nearest town. When Penrod had decided against going up to Oxford, he had visited Lucio in Italy, and they had spent a summer in fierce competition hunting in the hills above Florence and sharpening their skills with the sword. Lucio had seen his friend's almost magical ability to absorb another language at first hand. Penrod had scarcely a dozen words of Italian when he arrived, but when he left four months later, he could charm secrets from a gamekeeper or a duchess in their native tongue, and could discuss horseflesh or international politics with a fluency that would make anyone believe him a native, born and bred, were it not for his blond hair and blue eyes. More than one of Lucio's female cousins lapsed into Latin after an evening in his company, repeating the words of Pope Gregory when he met the blond English slaves in the market of Rome: *non Angli, sed Angeli* – they are not English, but angels.

However, the two men had not seen or spoken to each other for at least ten years. While Penrod earned his medals, Lucio devoted himself to the needs of his own country and king. His work earned him less public renown, but was just as dangerous as Penrod's at times. He was among the first to know that the material the Duke of Kendal had held on the king's brother had been returned. He read the file of Penrod's career before it was passed to the king and stood in the Royal Chamber while the king read it himself.

'He wants nothing?'

'It would seem not, Your Highness,' Lucio replied.

'We are in his debt. I would not want him to think us ungrateful. Make the attempt.'

'Majesty,' Lucio replied and backed out of the audience chamber. He left for Cairo that evening.

Lucio spoke no Arabic, but as well as his personal connection with Penrod, he had another advantage over the other agents who came to the city looking for him. The Italians and their forebears had been in Egypt for a millennium. They were a community of merchants and artisans, and though most lived in the Venetian Quarter of the city and kept their Christian faith, many had adopted the dress and customs of the Egyptians. They knew the city as intimately as any Cairene, and understood the unspoken languages and rhythms of the street.

It still took Lucio a month to find Penrod. He learned first about Yakub, then Adnan. Then he began to watch. His superiors might have expected him, on discovering where Penrod was, to go to him at once. But he did not. Instead Lucio returned to his hotel and spent the evening in deep thought, considering how the gratitude of his king could be best expressed in the circumstances. By dawn he had decided. The arrangements took a further week.

• • •

Penrod Ballantyne never spoke again in his life about the events of the evening of 15 August 1888. He would claim later to have only the vaguest recollection of them. In truth, he remembered them only too well. Bringing down the duke had cost him his fortune. He had taken a room in his old friend Yakub's poorest boarding house and waited for the opium to kill him. He knew it might take years, but hazed and cocooned by the drug, time had very little meaning for him. The destruction of the duke had brought him satisfaction, but no peace. The distress and frustration of Yakub and Adnan did not touch him. He grew thin, thought of Amber, and waited only for his body to fail.

That evening he drifted between dreaming and waking, deep in his intoxication. Slowly he became aware of an unfamiliar presence in the room. An Egyptian dressed in Western clothes. He raised his head from the cushion on which he reclined.

'I know you,' he said. His voice cracked with lack of use.

'We met once at the Duke of Kendal's house,' the Egyptian said. 'My name is Farouk al-Rahmi and I have been sent to fetch you from hell.'

'I have grown accustomed to it. Leave me here.'

'No,' the Egyptian said simply and smiled.

The attack came from behind. A cloth was held across Penrod's face and he smelled the powerful aroma of chloroform.

'Forgive me, *effendi*,' he heard Yakub's voice say. 'But for the sake of my own soul, this must be done.'

• • •

Penrod awoke in a bare, whitewashed room. It seemed unbearably bright. He tried to cover his eyes but found that his wrists were tied. He remembered the bed on which Agatha had died and how she had been chained to it. His limbs were already twisting with cramp, the harbinger of the agony of opium withdrawal. He moved his head slightly. A young man in a dove grey suit was sitting in an armchair next to his bed. He was reading. On seeing that Penrod had opened his eyes, he closed his book and set it aside.

'Ah, my friend. You are awake.'

'Lucio? What in God's name are you doing here?'

The Italian smiled. 'I came to tell you that you have been awarded the Order of the King's Guardians of Rome. It's terribly prestigious. A small token from a grateful monarch. But then I realised perhaps we could thank you in a more . . . material way.'

'Release me at once.'

Lucio settled himself in his chair and took up his book again. 'You know I shall not. Our esteemed doctor is attending to his other patients at the moment. Would you like me to read to you as you wait? No? Well, I am going to anyway. I thought, given the day we are likely to have, Dante would be appropriate.'

'I will kill you when I am free.'

'I shall take that as a sign you are unhappy with me, rather than with my choice of reading material. Now, let us begin at the beginning.' He cleared his throat and began to read. The medieval Italian verses rolled through the air, shimmering like oil on water.

'When I had journeyed halfway through my life, I found myself in a deep forest, for I had lost my true way . . .'

A wave of nausea struck Penrod and at the same time the cramp in his limbs intensified. The pain was sudden and white-hot. He felt his body buckle and he pulled against his restraints.

Lucio carried on reading. '*It was hardly less bitter than death* . . .'

Penrod felt himself disappear under the agony and began to scream.

• • •

Penrod was not sure how long he had been unconscious. A boy was sitting on the chair where Lucio had been. As soon as Penrod opened his eyes, the child scooted off his perch and dashed away. Penrod had the fleeting impression that something was wrong with the boy's face, as if the features had melted somehow, and he moved with a strange scuttle as he fled the room. Penrod assumed he was in some sort of hospital. Perhaps the child was a burn victim. The room was cool. Penrod's limbs ached, but it was a deep soreness rather than the burning agony of the cramps he had felt before. He knew he was feverish and his perception seemed clouded. Time was folded, somehow. He remembered the Egyptian doctor arriving in his boarding house and the attack just as the same man appeared before him now, as if he had materialised out of the memory.

'Farouk al-Rahmi,' Penrod said, and the man nodded. He was not wearing Western clothes now, but a simple pale blue *galabiyya*, such as the water carriers wore.

'Well remembered, Penrod,' he said.

Penrod was so used to being addressed as *effendi*, or by the honorary titles given to him by his Arab friends, the use of his Christian name made him frown. The doctor noticed, and it seemed to amuse him. Penrod tried to move, but he found he was still restrained.

'How are you feeling? I have been treating you for your opium addiction, but I'm sure you have worked that out for yourself. I'm not giving you the drug, but we have a number of concoctions that are known to ease the pains.'

'How long have I been here?' Penrod said. His voice felt weak and cracked.

'Four days,' Farouk said. He came around to the head of the bed and sat in the chair Lucio and then the boy had occupied before him.

'I insist you let me go at once.'

'Not yet, Penrod. Lucio will be here in a little while to read to you. You may tell him you wish to leave. He will also refuse to let you go, but perhaps you will feel better when you have shouted at him some more.' The thought seemed to cheer him. 'You know, when he started reading Dante to you, I did wonder if it was a bit close to the bone, but now he is following Dante towards Paradise, I rather enjoy the symmetry.'

Penrod listened to his voice, the choice of words.

'You were educated in England.'

'Oxford. But not just there. I studied philosophy in Tehran and medicine with the local masters here in Cairo.'

'We are still in Cairo then?'

Farouk stood up and filled a glass from a jug standing on a small table next to Penrod's bed. Penrod twisted his head on his pillow to watch him. The table had a book on it, a copy of Dante's *Divina Comedia*, a bookmark carefully marking a place halfway through the poet's journey. Farouk put the glass to Penrod's lips and he drank. The liquid had a bitter, complex taste but it seemed to cool his throat as he swallowed.

'Near enough. Are you hungry?'

Farouk took the glass away and set it on the table again. Penrod guessed he was in his late thirties, a little older than Penrod himself. His high cheekbones, large eyes and long lashes gave him an almost feminine appearance.

'Yes, I am. Does that I mean I'm cured?' Penrod could not keep the sneer out of his voice.

'I must see to my other patients. No, you are not cured yet. You must spend a little more time in purgatory.' He tapped the copy of Dante. 'This moment, Penrod – it is like the moment when a drowning man breaks through the surface of the water for a moment, tastes air and light. Then he sinks again. But we will pull you from the depths at last. You will suffer more pain, however, before we can drag you ashore.'

'I am not afraid,' Penrod said bitterly. It was difficult to form the words. They came out slightly slurred. He found he could not focus on the doctor's face.

'You should be,' Farouk said sadly, and the world disappeared.

• • •

Days and nights became confused and fragmented. At times Penrod was conscious of a soul-shattering agony, as if he were caught on some devilish rack. Sometimes he was aware of Lucio sitting by him and could hear the fourteenth-century poetry of Dante speaking of angels and devils. At other times semi-human figures bent over him, their hands melted by hellfire. Cups of strange-smelling liquid were forced between his lips. Sometimes he accepted them, sometimes he spat them out at the demons. Farouk appeared and disappeared. Then, slowly, time seemed to repair itself and night followed day in the proper fashion. He could hear and understand what Lucio was saying for longer periods of time. The demons that tended to him, washing his flesh, manipulating his body, began to look more human.

One afternoon, as Lucio read, Penrod licked his lips and tried his voice.

'This is a leper colony.'

Lucio closed the book at once and set it aside. 'Yes, it is. Once they are cured, few of Farouk's patients dare to go back to their villages; the stigma is too great, so many stay on here. We have a farm, you know. A mill. It's terribly well organised. High walls all around, but I'm not sure if that is to keep the lepers in or keep them safe.'

'Ask Farouk.'

'I don't think he knows either. And he's a Sufi, rather a well-regarded one, so he'd probably just tell me some enigmatic story about a donkey, which suggests it's all the same thing.'

Lucio waited, but Penrod was silent for such a long time he picked up his book again and cleared his throat.

'By whose authority am I held here, Lucio?'

Lucio looked up towards the ceiling and considered. 'Mine. The King of Italy's. Somewhere in between the two. Penrod, I know why you destroyed the Duke of Kendal, and it was a very dashing gesture to release half of the royal families of Europe from his grip and ask for nothing in return. I even have a pretty good idea of how you managed it. But why, when you had accomplished such a thing, did you not dress in your best attire and go and break open a bottle of champagne at the Gheziera Club? You could probably have won back your fortune at the card table on the same evening, then taken up your commission again the next day. Why did you instead – and I mean no offence to our dear friend, Yakub – lock yourself in a hovel and try to smoke yourself to death?' He leaned forward with his hands on his knees, his head turned to one side, and blinked at Penrod with an owlish curiosity.

'I don't know,' Penrod said and turned away.

Lucio sat back in his chair and crossed his legs. 'Very strange behaviour, my friend. That is all.'

'I can do as I please.'

'That is true. And so may I. And I was pleased to have you chained up here. Perhaps Farouk has another story about a donkey to explain you, too. You have had half of Europe in a puzzle.' He held up his hands. 'Of course, you will never admit what you did to the duke, I understand, but you will be rewarded, whether you want to be or not.'

'And being chained up among the lepers is a reward, is it?' Penrod yanked at his restraints. His muscles were aching and he felt weak as a child. The frustration made his eyes and skin prickle.

Lucio scratched the back of his head. 'They are very nice lepers, Penrod. And very gentle with you, I have noticed. You know as well as I do the disease is not as contagious as was once believed, and only those who are cured wait on you.' He sniffed. 'And considering under what circumstances I found you, do not try and convince me you are concerned about your health.' He picked up the book again. 'Have we had enough chatter? Let us see if poetry can lift your spirits a little.' He paused. 'I got married, you know. Lovely girl. She died giving birth to my son. I was terribly angry. Shouted at the priests, cursed my own child as a murderer. It was reading Dante that returned me to sanity. Now my boy is growing, living with his doting grandparents and learning to hunt and ride on the same estates where we spent that summer together.'

'So your plan is to read me into sanity?'

'It's worth a try, I think.'

'You will have to release me sometime. What is to stop me returning to my hovel and my pipe then?'

Lucio wrinkled his fine Roman nose. 'You'll be too weak to walk for a while. Hopefully you'll have changed your mind before you get your strength back. Now, where were we?'

Penrod sighed. The room was cool and clean, and in spite of his weakness and the ache in his bones and head, his thoughts were clearer than they had been for many weeks.

'How did you find Farouk?'

Lucio snorted. 'My ancestors have been in Egypt for a long time, Penrod. Cleopatra brought the whole country to Rome as dowry while you English were still painting yourselves blue and sacrificing each other to oak trees. We remember our way around. Now, yes, here we are . . .'

Roughly a week later Lucio announced he was leaving Cairo. Penrod was surprised to find that the idea disturbed him. He had cursed Lucio every time he had visited and sworn as soon as he could escape that he would return to his old ways in the city, but when Lucio told him that this visit would be his last, Penrod felt as if the rope that was towing him to safe shore had been cut. He did not think he gave any sign, but Lucio must have noticed something in his expression.

'We have finished reading *Paradiso*, after all, Penrod. And I must return to Italy. Pleasant as this has been, my masters in Rome would like me to return and I have duties I would not shirk.'

'You are leaving me here then, tied to a bed.'

Lucio reached out and put his hand on Penrod's shoulder. It was the first time he had touched him.

'No. Farouk has told me you are fit to be untied. The drug has left your body, Penrod. You must feel it. Now it is your soul that must be repaired and I leave that in Farouk's care.'

'My soul?'

'Your soul,' Lucio said with great seriousness. 'But first I am to have *my* reward.'

He got to his feet and without further ceremony unlocked and unbuckled the padded leather cuffs around Penrod's wrists and ankles.

'Now, if I help you, can you sit up?'

He did not wait for an answer but put his arm under Penrod's shoulder and lifted him. Penrod's vision swam and a terrible nausea made him clutch at the mattress. He had never in his life felt so utterly helpless. He shivered.

'Very good,' Lucio said quietly. He sat next to him on the bed, supporting his thin frame against his shoulder. 'Now, Penrod Charles Augustus Ballantyne, I bestow upon you the grateful thanks of my king. In recognition of your valour, your honour and good character . . .' Penrod almost laughed, but Lucio carried on with careful emphasis, 'your great, good character, I name you knight in His Majesty's Order of the Guardians of Rome and bestow on you all the privileges and honours sacred to that order. So it is spoken. You may lie down again, my dear.'

He helped Penrod fall back onto the bed and arranged the sheet over him like a careful nursemaid. Penrod felt as if he had battled giants, such was the pain in his head and the exhaustion in his limbs. Dear God, he thought, will I ever be well again?

Lucio picked up his book, then set it down again. 'I shall leave this for you – a memento of our time together. I hope you read it again as you recover. This poetry has lasted longer than empires for a reason.'

'Lucio . . .' Penrod wanted to thank him, but his pride seemed to fill his mouth with rocks. After all, he could not yet tell if he was glad or sorry that Lucio had saved his life.

'Yes, Penrod?'

'Are there any plums among those rights and privileges?'

Lucio put his head back and laughed. 'Ah, my friend Penrod is in there somewhere! I knew it and I am glad of it. Let me think. Oh yes, I am almost certain you have the right to sell goat's milk cheese on the forum on the first Saturday of every month.'

'Cheese?'

'Yes, only goat's milk, though. Goodbye, Penrod. I hope we meet again.' He touched his fingers to his forehead in salute, then left the room.

· · ·

Penrod began to recover. Every morning when he woke he forced himself to sit and then to stand. His attendants only knew about this regimen when they noticed bruises blooming on his arms and thighs from his frequent falls. They said nothing, but the food he was given became more substantial and before a week was out he had managed to walk the length of his room and return to bed without his legs collapsing under him. He reminded himself of when he had been in Osman Atalan's hands. He had been starved and beaten almost to death then too, but he had recovered. He would do so now. He still had no idea what his life might be outside these walls, but he concentrated only on his muscles. Beyond that, he would wait and see.

One morning when Farouk entered, he asked directly how far Penrod could now walk.

'Ten times across the room,' Penrod said, his voice neutral and even.

Farouk looked mildly impressed. 'I have brought you a present, Penrod.' He lifted his hand and Penrod noticed he was carrying a pair of cheap camel-hide sandals. 'Sit up, please.'

Penrod did so and Farouk dropped into a crouch and slipped the sandals over Penrod's feet, then helped him to stand. Penrod was wearing his usual white shift. Farouk handed him a blue *galabiyya* like his own and helped him put it on.

'Let me show you the colony,' Farouk said and offered Penrod his arm.

Penrod put his hand to his face and felt the thick growth of his beard. 'I must look like John the Baptist,' he said and Farouk laughed.

'Yes, you do! We have not told anyone here who you are. Perhaps I shall introduce you as John.'

Farouk led Penrod out of the room that had been his world for so many weeks. It opened on to a wide corridor, white-washed, with several open doors leading off it. Penrod glanced through them as they walked slowly towards the open door at the far end. He saw that most were the same size as his own, but each had at least a dozen beds in them. In some, patients lay unmoving on their beds, but in others, patients were chatting and laughing with each other, collected in small groups. Penrod heard the rattle of a dice box, the shouts of pleasure or distress as the dice landed. Farouk saw him making his observations.

'Your friend Lucio arranged some privacy for you and we were more than happy to oblige. His generosity has allowed us to make various improvements to the colony. From today you shall have a smaller room, but it shall be yours alone, and you will take your exercise outside. Now, shield your eyes. It will take a moment for you to become accustomed to full daylight.'

As he spoke they stepped through the door at the end of the corridor and out onto a gravel path. Penrod was blinded at first, and Farouk waited patiently while his sight adjusted and he began to make out what was in front of him. Some hundred yards away, down a gravel path lined with young palm trees, he could see what must be the gates to the colony. They were high and made from great timbers. Hanging on the inside was a small bell, and a hatch had been cut into the wood. A neat gatehouse stood just inside them. On either side extended a stone wall, some twelve feet high, again whitewashed. As Penrod watched, the small bell jangled, and an old man emerged from the gatehouse and slid back the communication hatch. They were too far away to hear what was said. But once the hatch was closed, the old man unlocked a panel set into the wall and slid out a large drawer. He took a sack from it, which he handed to one of several lurking children, who ran off with it down another pathway.

'Offerings,' Farouk said. 'The prejudice against lepers in my country runs deep and strong, but many local people pay us a sort of tithe. Much of our food arrives in this way. Shall we walk on a little?'

Penrod allowed himself to be led on and Farouk told him about the colony with a quiet pride. The walled compound extended over five acres and contained the hospital building where Penrod had been staying, a mixture of barracks and smaller houses for lepers who had recovered but did not wish to leave the safety of the place, and a small stone-built office for Farouk and his most trusted lieutenants. Farouk also pointed out the colony's coffee house and mill, the little storefront where members of the colony could buy supplies and necessities, and the large communal dining hall where most of the residents took their meals.

'My practice in Cairo helps fund the establishment here. I have aided many of the Europeans who come here in the hopes the climate will cure their illness, and I am glad to say no more generous patrons exist than a man or a woman who feels they have had a miraculous recovery.'

'I have no money of my own any more. So your lepers will have to manage without my help,' Penrod said.

He was beginning to tire and Farouk's pride irritated him. Still, the lepers obviously loved him. Everyone who saw them offered blessings, and some of the children came running up to him with garbled greetings or news of some disputes among their fellows. Some of the children appeared healthy. Others were missing noses, ears or fingers. Among the population moving from place to place, some had similar deformities, others had wrists, hands or feet bandaged. Penrod felt a visceral dislike of the place, an animal, instinctive disgust for the disease and its sufferers.

'I have already told you we have been well rewarded for your care,' Farouk said. 'Still, now you are well enough, it is time for you to take your turn working here.'

'I have no wish to become a resident. As soon as my strength has returned, I shall leave you.'

Farouk did not seem angry or disappointed. He said calmly, 'And you may do so. But at the moment you would not be able to reach the gate unaided, let alone walk the ten miles back to Cairo, and I assure you the locals here are very resistant to picking up anyone they see coming from the direction of the colony. Let me show you your new room. From tomorrow you will work in the infirmary and if you wish to eat, you will do so in the dining hall, Penrod.'

Penrod stiffened. 'And this will heal my soul, will it?'

'Perhaps.'

Farouk said nothing more until he led Penrod into a small, cell-like chamber in one of the barracks. It held a bed, a chair and a small desk, and light poured in from a good-sized window high up on one wall. Someone had already put Lucio's copy of Dante on the desk. Next to it was another book that Penrod did not recognise. Farouk noticed him looking.

'A gift from me. Have you read the works of Rumi?'

'I have not.'

'Ah, well, it is very beautiful. Better in Persian, of course, but the Arabic translation I have left you is a fair attempt. I think you have achieved great things, Penrod, but your anger has almost killed you. This is a book about compassion.'

This was the furthest Penrod had walked since he had broken into the Duke of Kendal's house. He felt weak and was shivering, but he removed his arm from Farouk's and did not reply. Farouk waited for a moment, then left without further comment. As soon as the door closed, Penrod sat down heavily on the bed.

Very well. He would serve until he was strong enough to walk back to Cairo. The lepers seemed well fed, and with proper food and exercise he should be healthy enough to leave in a week or so. His soul might be tattered and dark, but it was his own, and he did not want any man meddling with it.

• • •

One of the young men who had tended Penrod during his illness came to fetch him at first light the next day. He was a bizarre-looking creature, the disease having taken his nose and three of the fingers from his right hand, but he made no attempt to hide his deformities. He chattered away in the Arabic of a street urchin, cheerfully describing his duties and the personalities of the other workers in the infirmary. Penrod learned a woman called Cleopatra ruled it, with a rod of iron, it seemed. This young man, Hamon, and two others worked under her, taking care of the regular rebandaging and cleaning of the sores and infected injuries of their fellow inmates. Penrod ignored most of what he heard, but after washing in the warm water Hamon brought, he shuffled over to the infirmary behind him. A neat queue of the sick and maimed was already waiting outside the doors.

They went inside. The infirmary itself consisted of two rooms: one where women were treated and the other for the men. Cleopatra was a sour, fleshy woman with heavy features, small eyes, a false foot of wood and leather, and no small talk. She sat in a large wicker armchair, which gave her a view into both rooms and the waiting area. From this position she sent the patients to one nursing station or another. Hamon showed Penrod his place, which consisted of a pair of stools and a cabinet containing a dozen pots of an astringent-smelling ointment. A bucket and bowl stood by for the washing of wounds, and a pile of bandages sat on top of the cabinet. The bandages were obviously used, but they had been boiled and pressed. Hamon explained that he was to sit with Penrod today and supervise his work. From tomorrow he would be on his own.

The doors were opened and Cleopatra greeted each arrival by name, asked about their health and then named the person who would dress their wounds. The first man who was sent to Penrod looked shocked when he saw a European waiting to tend to him and had a fierce whispered exchange with Cleopatra. The outcome was hardly in doubt. The man approached Penrod nervously and took a seat. Hamon managed to keep up a stream of conversation with the patient, while also instructing Penrod how to unwrap the ulceration on his shin and wash the flesh. The smell was not as bad as Penrod had anticipated, but it still turned his stomach. He washed, anointed and rebandaged his patient, and as soon as he had shuffled to the stone sink in the back of the room to empty his basin, another patient was sent to him. Hamon proved to be an able instructor and the morning passed quickly enough. In the afternoon, something one of the patients said reminded Penrod of a story he had heard on the back streets of Cairo and he shared it. The patient, an elderly man who had been a silk merchant before he began to show signs of the disease, was at first shocked into silence at hearing the foreigner speak

Arabic with such easy fluency, but eventually he dared to ask Penrod some questions about where he had been in Egypt. Penrod told him a few of the places and this led to a fierce discussion about which were the best coffee shops in Alexandria, and where a traveller might expect to find a decent chess player. The discussion lasted longer than the bandaging. The merchant was driven off by Cleopatra when she noticed, and another patient was soon occupying the stool.

That evening Penrod ate in the dining hall. Hamon showed him where to fetch his food and where he might sit, then, thinking his duty done, Hamon went to sit with some other men of his own age. Penrod did not mind; he had no wish for company. Just as he finished his meal, however, the silk merchant appeared at his side, a board under his arm and a box of chess pieces in his healthy hand.

'Let us play,' he said simply, and set up the game. They were evenly matched, but Penrod was exhausted, and at the fatal moment he missed the silk merchant's trap and it was sprung.

'You must sleep, John,' the merchant said in Arabic. 'But I am glad to find such an opponent here. I play with Teacher Farouk, but he is often engaged.'

Penrod helped put the pieces back into their case. They were beautifully carved, the castles covered in vines, the queen represented by a rose in full bloom. 'Teacher Farouk? Yes, I was told he is a Sufi master.'

The silk merchant sighed. 'A man of many talents. I would give what this disease took from me again to only possess half of them. But I thank Allah for his many blessings. I was angry when I discovered my illness. It cost me my business, my family. But now I thank Allah for guiding me, in his mercy, to Farouk. I am a better man, better able to love the world now, even though it rejects me. I learned I must give up everything I had, willingly, to allow true grace to enter me. Now I am far richer than ever I was.'

Penrod laughed. 'Well, I have nothing. Does that make me blessed?'

'You are proud, John. Suppose you were told that Farouk suggested I play with you. That I try and offer you a little healing. Does your pride hiss like a cat? I think it does. I think you expected Farouk himself to try and help you. You meant to reject that help, of course, but you expected it to be offered by Farouk. You are an important Englishman, after all.'

Penrod realised the silk merchant was right. Even sick and destitute as he was, he had expected to be treated with certain deference. The knowledge surprised and puzzled him. He was not a man used to introspection, but he knew he had always accepted the best of everything as nothing less than his due. He felt an uncomfortable itch in his heart, asking himself why he had regarded Amber as his right. He had never asked himself if he deserved her. When she had levelled that gun at him and told him he did not, he had been angry. That anger had sent him to Agatha, then it had turned into bitterness and guilt and opium. It had made him ruin himself, gladly ruin himself, to destroy the Duke of Kendal.

He cleared his throat. 'So Farouk wishes to break my pride, does he?'

'Oh, my friend, you are not a horse! No, John. We wish to give you a great gift to temper your pride: compassion.' Penrod snorted and the merchant smiled. 'It will make you stronger, not weaker, and you will learn how to control your pride and your anger in the future. These are the tools we shall put into your hands. How you use them will be your choice.'

As he spoke, it seemed he had torn a small hole in the dark veil that covered Penrod's soul. He did not see the blinding light of holy revelation behind it, however, only confusion, and somewhere in that confusion the faintest breath of hope.

Penrod stood up from the table and looked around him at the men and women of the colony.

'Shall we play again tomorrow?'

The silk merchant lifted his hand. '*Inshallah.*'

The rains in the highlands of Ethiopia had been mercurial and ill-tempered that year. Sudden raging downpours that threatened to overwhelm Courtney Camp and Mine were followed by days of suffocating heat, so that when it rained again, the soil was washed away rather than refreshed. Amber spent her time repairing the dams around her gardens – urgent, back-breaking work that left her half crazed with exhaustion. She had chosen the wife of one of Patch's best foundry men to help her, but even with Belito at her side it was a desperate struggle. Seedlings were washed away and replanted as lightning crackled over the sky. The river was sluggish one moment and a torrent the next. Very few travellers passed through the valley and their supplies of pepper and salt dwindled alarmingly.

Twice the mine was flooded, the second time filling so quickly one man was drowned before he could reach the surface. It was a painful loss. Ryder learned quickly, reading and rereading the pages Amber had prepared for him, but the process of salting the ore was delicate. Sometimes the reactions on the patio went too fast and hot, at others the pulp was so diluted with rain they stopped entirely. In late September they lost half of their remaining quicksilver when the torrents of water coming off the mountainside washed away the foundations of the store.

Then the rains stopped and the earth began to bloom. Patch went to Massowah again and, on Saffron's instructions, bought more quicksilver with the last funds from her London bank. He asked Amber if she wanted to come with him again, but she refused. Her work in the garden had tied her to the soil and those few minutes sitting on the Cairo steamer seemed like a dream now. She needed to see the fruits of her labour before she left Tigray.

Patch returned more quickly than they expected. An uneasy truce was holding between the Ethiopian Emperor John and the Italians on the coast, which made acquiring the mercury simpler, and now Patch knew his way around the city and its people too.

At the feast of St John the rains stopped, and by Christmas the camp's storage bins were filling slowly with grains, nuts and peas. The children enjoyed first precious fruits from Amber's trees.

Amber worked in the gardens or the kitchen huts with the other women and became involved in their lives and hopes. Patch had long been eyeing the eldest daughter of one of his senior foremen with shy admiration. The girl, Marta, knew it and was flattered. She liked Patch. She was afraid, however, of throwing herself away on a man with a ruined face and no cattle. Amber became confidante to them both. She taught Marta English as they worked together grinding grain, and Patch made an effort to learn more Amharic than the words of command and praise he found necessary at the mine. Then Amber found him teaching Marta and her brother to play poker before the evening meal one night, and realised that she had nothing more to do in that matter.

• • •

They were making slow progress with the recovery of the silver from the ore, and then, just after the New Year, they had their first success.

The day the first ingot of silver was cast, the whole camp went to see it emerge from the furnace and be poured. Tesfaye and Alem struck it out of the mould and it hit the red dust of the ground outside the furnace house with a hard thump. The crowd sighed. It looked dirty and black, a lump of charcoal. But Ryder picked it up the moment it was cool enough to handle and, in spite of Saffron's little mew of distress, started to polish it with one corner of his last good shirt. The crowd watched, then laughed when he held it up. Below the covering of ash the glint of pure silver was clear to all.

The bar was passed through the crowd, each man and woman rubbing it a little, some because they wanted to see more of that rich lustre, others because they thought it lucky. By the time it had gone through the hands of every man, woman and child in the camp, it glowed. Amber was one of the last to hold it. Its weight astonished her. She rubbed it with the corner of her skirt, then handed it back to her brother-in-law.

'Congratulations, Ryder,' she said.

He managed to nod at her.

She wondered if he had heard the same rumours she had, of a white man turned monk living in one of the high monasteries. She hoped the rumours were true, that it was Dan, and that he remembered them in his prayers.

• • •

The short rains came and went. One ingot became two, and then five. Ryder calculated what each one had cost him and shuddered. They must find a way to improve the yield without using so much quicksilver.

Patch married Marta and the celebrations were lavish, though Saffron worried her husband's cheer was forced. The children put on a performance of *The Betrothed*, and this time the hero wore an eyepatch.

A week after the wedding, Amber was working at her sister's side, helping to make *injera*, closely supervised by the elder women of the camp, Selma and Tena. As they spread the batter over the skillet and watched it bubble, Saffron suddenly hissed with a sharp discomfort and stood up. Amber flicked and folded the bread into the basket waiting for it, then got up too. Selma sniffed at Amber's work and took her place by the fire.

'Saffy? What is it, darling?' Amber looked hard into her twin's face. The curls of her hair seemed different, and something about the curve of her cheek had changed. 'You're pregnant.'

Saffron wrinkled her nose. 'Yes, I rather think I am.'

Amber laughed with pleasure, and Selma and Tena turned to see what was happening.

'Mr Ryder has mined for treasures and brought riches among us,' Amber said in Amharic, with a sly glance at Saffron's belly.

The women caught both meanings at once and showered congratulations on them: for Saffron's child and for Amber's quick and clever tongue.

• • •

Amber's verse travelled around the camp with the news that Ryder was going to be a father again. Within a quarter of an hour Ryder came charging into the camp and swept his wife off her feet, spinning her around to the applause of the women. When he set her down, he beckoned Amber towards him and grinned.

'Mined for treasures, is it, Amber? You have become a witty witch since I first met you.'

She made an elaborate curtsy to him and, as she stood again, he grabbed her around the wrist, pulled her towards him, then kissed the top of her head.

'I suppose I'll have to stop being angry with you now, al-Zahra.'

She looked up and felt a burst of affection for him, a sudden blossoming after long-awaited rain. Then she saw something over his shoulder and frowned. Ryder caught the change in her expression and followed her gaze. High on the plateau above them they could see the silhouette of a man. He held the long spear of a warrior upright in his right hand, and the outline of the traditional round shield on his left arm was clear. Then, as they watched, the man crumpled to the ground.

'Ryder?' Saffron said.

'Tadesse, come with me. Saffy, get Geriel and Maki. Tell them to prepare a stretcher and follow.'

Before he had even finished giving his orders, Ryder was racing up the track that led upwards to the place where the warrior had fallen.

Ryder recognised the young man when they were within five yards. Tadesse, scrabbling up the path like a goat behind him, recognised him too.

'It is Iyasu! Son of Asfaw.'

Ryder did not speak but kneeled on the dry ground and supported the fallen warrior's head, then tried to give him water from the leather bottle he always carried at his waist. The man's eyes fluttered open for a moment, then closed again. It was a miracle he had been able to stand at all. His robes were ragged and hard with blood; a great slash across his muscled chest looked to Ryder like the wound of a dervish blade. Someone had bandaged it roughly, but the binding had come loose. Another deep wound was visible on the outside of Iyasu's thigh. Ryder moved the man's leather shield aside and hissed. Iyasu's left hand had been severed. The stump was crudely wrapped and stank of rotting flesh. The bandages were black and stiff with dried pus.

Tadesse had made his own inventory of the man's injuries. He sucked air between his teeth.

'I can do nothing here. We should be able to carry him to camp without the wounds breaking open again. Then we can clean and treat him in camp. Why has he come alone? What has happened, that a warrior wanders by himself so far?'

Iyasu groaned and stirred. Ryder could hear the sound of Geriel and Maki approaching up the steep path. He tried to remember how old this boy was – twenty, perhaps? He was an athlete and the pride of his village, gone to win glory in the army of the emperor.

'Iyasu, you are at Courtney Camp. We shall look after you and send for your father. You have my word. What happened?' Ryder asked.

His eyes opened again, huge and dark. Ryder knew that look: these were the eyes of a man replaying horrors in his own mind rather than seeing what was in front of him.

'Mr Ryder, he is dead. Emperor John, the King of Kings, is dead.'

They carried Iyasu carefully into the village, into Ryder's own hut, and laid him on a wooden pallet by the open fire. As soon as Ryder had sent the fastest runner in the village to take the news of Iyasu's return to his father, he joined Tadesse at the injured man's side.

The darkness had fallen swiftly. Ryder held a hurricane lamp above Iyasu as Tadesse worked, examining the wounds and carefully suturing those on the warrior's chest and thigh. Iyasu had not regained consciousness.

'How long do you believe it will take Ato Asfaw to reach us?' Tadesse asked.

Ryder calculated quickly. Asfaw's village was three miles away – not far for an old warrior like himself – but it was rough ground. If he were at home. He had many duties as headman of his parish that took him often to outlying hamlets and markets.

'Some hours yet, Tadesse.'

The boy sat back on his heels. 'You must make a choice. The wrist is infected, Mr Ryder. If I do nothing but try and ease his pain, he will live till dawn. If we do the other thing – cut off the arm high up where the infection has not yet reached – we must do it now, at once. The shock of it might kill him, but if he survives it he might live yet to be an old man.'

Ryder looked down at Iyasu, so strong and so near death.

'What are his chances?' he asked.

'What is that thing I have seen you do?' Tadesse said, squinting up at him. 'Throw a coin in the air. It is like that.'

Ryder tried to imagine his own infant son grown into a man, a man injured and suffering like this. What would Ryder want done if strangers were standing around his son's bed? For a moment, like a dream, he saw Leon as a man, as a soldier of Iyasu's age, lying on an earth floor and in the care of others. The answer was clear.

'He must have the chance to live.'

Tadesse nodded. 'It will be here. The infection has taken the rest.' He pointed at a place just above the elbow on Iyasu's left arm. 'Mr Ryder, I have not the strength. If you can do it in one blow, it may save him.'

'Make the arrangements, Tadesse. I shall do it.'

Tadesse got to his feet, but Ryder stopped him.

'Mrs Saffy is with child. If we need more help, ask Miss Amber.'

Tadesse considered for a moment. 'We shall need more help. I will tell her.'

• • •

Tadesse consulted with the men of the village and they brought their weapons from their homes, curved *shotels* were examined for sharpness and weight, while one man, Hadash, scarred from battle, brought an axe he had used to fashion the timber supports of the mine. They agreed this would be the best instrument. The blade had to cut through bone without shattering it – only an edge with the weight of this axe could be trusted. Hadash asked for half an hour to grind the edge to an ultimate sharpness. Tadesse hesitated, then told them to do it, but take no longer.

Amber watched as the men worked the circular grindstone, sweeping the blade across it in a delicate arc. It did not spark, the metal only seemed to sigh as it found its edge. Amber joined Ryder in his hut.

Iyasu was still unconscious and his skin had taken on a yellow hue in the lamplight. Amber carried strips of leather over one shoulder, linen over the other and fresh water in a bowl in her hands. Ryder saw her pause in the doorway, knocked back by the smell of rotting flesh, but without making a sound she came in and set out what she had brought.

'They are nearly ready. Are you?' she said.

'Yes. Where is Saffy?'

'By the church with Leon. The priest is leading prayers.'

'I am glad you came with us, al-Zahra,' Ryder said.

She turned to look at him and he felt as if he were seeing her for the first time. He remembered her as a little girl under her father's protection in Khartoum, begging him for treats and showing off her party dresses. His words had made her happy, and he realised he had not seen her look so since the day before she broke her engagement with Penrod. She blushed and took one of the leather strips from her shoulder and tied it tightly around the highest point of Iyasu's arm.

Iyasu moaned and, as if in reply, they heard a warning shout from outside. Tadesse came in first and behind him, Hadash. Hadash handed the axe to Ryder, then went at once to the head of the bed so he could hold Iyasu's shoulders. Tadesse took hold of Iyasu's diseased arm and drew it out at a right angle from his body. Amber leaned in and placed a thick bundle of cured hides under the arm where the blow had to fall, then took hold of Iyasu's legs. The warrior began to fight and scream. Ryder felt the weight of the axe, then swung it above his head. Its glittering edge burned a pattern into the gloom as he shifted forward, then brought the axe down with every ounce of his weight and strength behind it. The blade sliced through flesh and bone and buried itself in the hides. Iyasu's eyes opened and he let out one terrible moan before his eyes rolled back into his head and his jaw went slack.

Tadesse pinched the oozing arteries of the wound together and sewed them closed, then began packing the wound with linen. Ryder stepped back.

Amber was assisting Tadesse, watching carefully and handing him what he required. Ryder moved further away from them and sat with his back to the wall of his home, the muscles in his shoulders stinging, and watched them as they tended to the wound. As long as they were working he knew Iyasu was not yet dead.

• • •

Ryder must have slept. He felt someone shaking his shoulder and he woke up with a start. It was Amber. She was offering him a cup, and he smelled the welcome aroma of strong coffee. The lamp had been extinguished and the hut was filled with the light of a new day. He looked about him while Amber settled herself on the floor beside him. The severed arm was gone, as was the axe. Tadesse was crouching by Iyasu, blocking Ryder's view.

'He is still alive,' Amber said, answering his thoughts.

'Thank you for the coffee.'

She pushed the hair back from her face and Ryder noticed she looked pale with fatigue.

'Saffron is waiting for you outside with Leon. Please do not tell her I woke you.'

He laughed. 'I shall not. But you should rest yourself.'

She drank deeply from her own cup. 'Not yet. I want Tadesse to sleep for a while. When he has rested I will sleep, not before.'

Ryder stood and patted her on the shoulder then went outside, his coffee cup still in his hands, warming them in the morning chill. His wife sprang up like a cat from her place by the path to the water, carrying Leon on her hip, and flung herself against his chest. He caught her and lifted her face, kissing her hard. Leon struggled between them. Saffron set him down and he toddled off bravely in pursuit of a chicken.

'Ryder, we've had news from Ato Asfaw's people. He has gone to buy cattle at the market in Adrigat. They sent word and sent us three sheep and a great cask of honey. That is his son Fassil's doing, I think.'

'A generous gift.'

'A proper gift,' Saffron said, releasing herself and smoothing down her skirts. 'You have saved Iyasu's life.'

He finished his coffee and she took the mug from him. 'Saffy, we don't know if he will live yet, and if anyone saved him it was Tadesse.'

'Pah!' she said. Saffron would never believe her husband was anything less than the hero and saviour of any situation in which he found himself.

'Well, you saved Tadesse, so it's the same thing anyway. The men didn't know what to do with the arm so they put it in a box and gave it to the priest. He prayed over it, which everyone felt was the right thing, and then took it off somewhere.'

They sat together on the log benches in front of the church. Ryder wanted to go to the mine and see what progress they were making. He needed to talk to Patch and the senior workers about timber, and discuss what repairs were needed on the flumes, which led their precious water through the works. He also wanted to be sure he was in the village when Ato Asfaw arrived.

'Ryder, did Iyasu really say that Emperor John is dead?' Saffron whispered.

'He did.'

'Then who will rule? His only son is already dead! Was Emperor John killed fighting the Italians? It will be much more difficult to get things from Massowah if war has broken out.'

Ryder looked out across the flowing valley, up the hillside to the plateau where they had first noticed Iyasu yesterday, and beyond the purple peaks marching towards Adrigat and Axum. He could feel success, just beyond his reach, like an itch in his blood. If they could only improve the process of extracting the silver from the ore, the painful trickle of treasure would become a steady stream. He just needed more time, another mining engineer to replace Dan. He wondered if Iyasu was the harbinger of some greater danger approaching, something that would sweep them and all their workings away.

Saffron tapped his shoulder and pointed across the river. 'Look, Ato Asfaw is coming.'

• • •

For two days they watched and waited to see if Iyasu would live or die, then on the third morning he opened his eyes and recognised his father. Tadesse ordered the women to make a teff porridge with his own mix of herbs and flowers added to it, and fed this to Iyasu with a horn spoon, like a mother bird feeds her first chicks.

When the workers had returned from the mine and the families ate their evening meal, Ryder was invited to Iyasu's bedside to hear his story.

Iyasu was supported on a pile of straw-stuffed pillows. His skin was dusty and grey, but he recognised Ryder and smiled at him. Ato Asfaw got to his feet as Ryder came in and embraced him.

'A stool for Mr Ryder, Tadesse, my boy. Here, just next to mine.' Asfaw's eyes widened and he covered his mouth with his hand. 'Father, forgive me! I am inviting you to sit in your own house!'

Ryder laughed. 'While Iyasu is here, my friend, it is your house.'

Tadesse brought the stool and the two men sat, while Tadesse crouched on the other side of Iyasu's bed, watching like a hawk.

'Good evening, Mr Ryder,' Iyasu said. 'Are you well?'

'Thanks be to God, I am well. And you?'

'Thanks be to God, I am well.' Iyasu sighed and moved slightly, then winced as his stump brushed against the pillows on which he lay. Tadesse jumped up with a scowl and moved the pillows and coverings to make him more comfortable.

'It is too soon to talk,' Tadesse said sullenly. 'You should open your mouth for food and water, and that only.'

Ryder thought Tadesse might be right, but he was desperate for news.

'Peace, little brother,' Iyasu said weakly. 'You know this must be told.'

Tadesse gave a quick nod, then dropped again into his watchful crouch. Iyasu shifted his gaze back to his father and Ryder.

'I have been with Emperor John for two years,' he said, 'under the flag of Ras Alula of Tigray. Last year he led us close to the Italians, but John and Alula are wise men. They saw the Italians were dug in firmly in their places in Saahati and we had not men nor guns to push them back into the sea. John heard rumours that Menelik of Shoa was offering to make war on our flank.' He paused and Ryder watched while Tadesse poured *tej* from an earthenware jug into a cup and lifted it to Iyasu's lips. While he drank, Asfaw spoke.

'You know of King Menelik, Mr Ryder?'

Ryder nodded. 'He has made his kingdom within Ethiopia into a great power, but he seems like a careful man.'

Iyasu closed his eyes for a moment and began speaking again.

'Emperor John was very unhappy. He has been less than himself since his eldest son died. We heard he had talked of giving up the throne itself, but his advisors, Ras Alula among them, told him he could not abandon his sacred duty. He seemed to grow strong again, and walked among us with his head held high. He stood above us and proclaimed a war against the dervishes. "Their attacks against the northern border can no longer be endured," he said. "They must be beaten out of our territory like the dogs they are."' Iyasu smiled. 'His words warmed our hearts and lifted us. We marched to Metemma and we attacked in great fury. Ras Alula led us on the flank and though we had warned them of our coming, they could not withstand us.'

'They are brave fighters,' Ryder said. 'I have seen the dervishes attack and it is like a flood or a firestorm. Few can withstand them.'

Iyasu's eyes sparkled. 'They are best at a charge; they do not like to defend a position. And you have not seen the Ethiopians fight, Mr Ryder. With our princes and our emperor among us, we can make the dervishes squeal and cry like children.'

Ryder imagined the battle, the tearing of flesh, the spears of the Abyssinians and arrows of the dervishes, the rifles each had won from European armies by trade or plunder, an ancient and a modern war unfolding in one place and between two armies who had no fear of death, devoted to their leaders. It must have been a terrible slaughter.

'We had them. We cut them down like straw. Then . . . Then it was as if a terrible curse fell on us. From the middle of the battle came a dervish in a green turban mounted on a black charger, an animal that must have been sired by the devil himself. He galloped through us and not one of our shots or spears could touch him. In his right hand he held a blade, bloodied from tip to hilt, and in the other, held high so we could all see it, he held the head of Emperor John.'

Ryder thought he knew who that particular dervish was. Osman Atalan. The warlord who had held Amber and Penrod captive, who still held his own sister-in-law, Rebecca Benbrook, as his concubine.

Tadesse spooned more of the *tej* between Iyasu's lips.

'Enough.' Iyasu pushed him gently away and turned his head back towards Asfaw and Ryder. 'It broke our spirit. To see that devil holding the good emperor's head by his hair. Our warriors collapsed. The dervishes were inflamed and in that moment the battle turned and we were scattered.' He touched the binding on his chest. 'I took this wound in the moments after I saw it, and this –' he touched his thigh – 'within a minute more. Where a moment before I had been fighting with my brothers, now I was floundering among their corpses. One man rushed at me and I managed to raise my shield against his blow, then another came from my left and sliced through my wrist. I thought they were my last moments on earth. But then I thought of my home and my father, and I wrapped my wound with the cloth of one of my fellows. I tried to reach Ras Alula, but night came. I fell to the ground, and when I woke, my only company was the dead. The army had fled.'

The fire behind them crackled.

'How came you here?' Ryder asked at last.

'I walked one day, then another. I did not know where the army had gone and I thought only of my home. I met a shepherd who washed my wounds and would have had me stay with him, but after one day of rest, I felt stronger and walked on. Then the pain began to grow in my wrist, and I knew the wound was going bad. But I thought I could still outpace the hurt of it.'

'Does Ras Alula still live?' Ryder asked. 'Who now is emperor?'

Iyasu's eyes fluttered closed again. 'I do not know,' he whispered.

'Enough,' Tadesse said. 'He must sleep, Mr Ryder.'

Ryder placed his hand on the boy's chest. 'Rest now, Iyasu. And thank you for your news and the pain you took to tell it. Ato Asfaw, will you speak of these things with me? I think I must see Ras Alula in Axum. If he lives, he will be there.'

The older man stood up. 'I am glad you go, and yes, let us speak. I know Tadesse will care for my son while we talk.'

They went out into the gathering night.

Ryder reached Axum three days later and news of his coming had obviously travelled ahead of him. As he reached the final crest and looked down on to the plain where the town nestled on the golden, crop-covered plateau between the astonishing sugarloaf mountains of red and purple, a party of warriors was already on its way to meet him. They were high-caste, Ryder could tell that even at this distance by the glimmer of silver decorating their hide shields, and the skins – leopard and lion – they wore across their shoulders. Some, Ryder noticed, carried rifles and wore cartridge belts. Others still held the tall, flat-bladed spears that had been the weapon of the Abyssinian warrior since the time of the Queen of Sheba.

Ryder called a halt. He travelled with only two pack mules, and for their protection against bandits, he brought Geriel and Maki. Ryder did not want to make any grand display, and every move he made, including waiting here, high above the town, was designed to convey only respect and friendship. They had brought the first dozen silver ingots from the mine with them in offering, and four fat sheep ambled alongside their little caravan. Ryder had calculated the gift carefully. To bring too little would be insulting – Alula was governor of the entire region and his authority should be recognised – but too much would look like arrogance. Ryder also brought Tadesse, who had volunteered his services to the wounded among Ras Alula's followers. Saffron had wanted to come, of course, but the new pregnancy was making her sick and in the end even she agreed that the trip to Axum would be too much.

The warriors reached them in the heat of the early afternoon and Ryder exchanged formal greetings with them, asked for news of Alula and offered his gifts. The warriors gave them no news, of course, but accepted the gifts with dignified approval and told them that a compound in Axum belonging to the Ras himself was being prepared for them. The prince asked them to visit him during the evening.

Ryder had visited Axum many times as a trader, but it never failed to astonish him. The houses were the usual thatched round huts of wood or stone, arranged in compounds, and a wide, open area in the middle of the town served as a marketplace most mornings, shaded by fig and acacia trees. But Axum was more than a provincial city. This had been the capital of one of the greatest African empires, and the Axumite rulers who had held sway here for five hundred years had left their monuments behind them. Huge carved granite columns marked their tombs, rearing up to a height of eighty feet, like the great obelisks of ancient Egypt. To the west of the town stood the ruins of a great palace, bleached and worn, where the local people said the Queen of Sheba herself had once lived.

Ryder counted dozens of wounded men watching from doorways or lying insensible in the shade before they reached the compound Alula had selected for them. He saw the tight, worried expression on Tadesse's face and put a hand on the boy's shoulder.

'You must do what you can, Tadesse, but do not try and save them all. Begin with those that can be saved, not the ones who are most sick. Do you understand me? We shall say Geriel and Maki are your brothers. They will go with you and make sure that your decisions are respected.'

'Thank you,' the boy said quietly. 'But it is not necessary, I have friends here.'

He had slipped away before Ryder had time to argue, so Geriel and Maki led the animals to the compound set aside for them.

• • •

The night was drawing in and cooking fires had been lit outside several of the doorways. The atmosphere was dark: an uneasy mix of confusion and defeat as Ryder made his way to meet Ras Alula. The audience chamber itself was in a large, stone-built hall, and when Ryder entered he saw a group of men, the senior advisors of Ras Alula, gathered at the far end. They were men of mature years, and though they were dressed in the same simple white robes, kaftans and trousers all the men of the region wore, the small details of their clothing, ornaments on their shoulders and silver fittings at their hips marked them as an elite group. As Ryder entered they fell silent and parted to reveal Ras Alula seated on a raised platform against the far wall. He was a man in his late fifties, short and stocky, with a long straight nose and his skin a deep bronze. His beard was more white than black and his face deeply lined, but no one could mistake the sense of physical power he exuded. He was wearing an embroidered kaftan of purple and green, chased around the throat and wrists with gold thread. The stool on which he sat was upholstered in purple and decorated with silver trimmings, including a cascade of silver bells. His shield, also decorated with silver, was propped up against this throne on his left and his rifle leaned within reach of his right hand.

As soon as he saw Ryder he stood up, then stepped down from his platform and walked towards him with his arms held wide. As he reached Ryder he placed his hands on his shoulders, and both bowed until their foreheads touched.

'I thank you for the pretty bars of silver, my friend.'

'I am glad they please you,' Ryder replied.

And he was speaking the truth. The good opinion of Alula was not only useful but important to him. Alula was perhaps the only military man for whom Ryder held genuine admiration. He has been poor in his youth and the elite of Tigray resented his position as right-hand man to Emperor John and governor of the region. He had won his position through loyalty and bravery. He had held on to it by using his wits as well as his muscles, and he knew and loved every inch of his land.

Now he put his arm around Ryder's shoulder and led him towards one of the long mud benches at the end of the hall, dismissing his advisors with a wave. They drifted away and within a few moments Ryder found himself sitting alone with Alula in the quiet of the empty chamber.

'Our grief at the death of Emperor John is profound,' Ryder said at last. 'And all the greater because we know the loss you have suffered.'

Alula leaned forward, his elbows on his knees. 'I know it, and I thank you. How did you come to hear of our troubles so quickly?'

Ryder described the arrival of Iyasu in the village and his account of the death of Emperor John.

'The King of Kings had a premonition the night before the battle,' Alula said when Ryder had finished. 'He sent for his council and told us if he were killed that his natural son by his brother's wife was to become emperor.'

'Ras Mengesha?' Ryder said, frowning. 'He is young.'

Alula stiffened slightly but ignored Ryder's remark.

'We swore allegiance to him, of course, for who would refuse the King of Kings? But we never believed the dervish could defeat us. Emperor John sent me a message when our victory seemed complete, telling me I was right to put no faith in his dream, that the battle was won. The messenger was still speaking those words when that devil of hell rode through our men with the emperor's severed head held high.' He drew his shawl across his shoulders. 'Our men were distraught, the dervishes regained the momentum of battle and we were scattered. You see how few returned with us. Others have, we hope, returned to their homes. Many more feed the carrion eaters at Metemma.'

Ryder said nothing, but the news disturbed him profoundly. Ras Mengesha was a boy, and as far as Ryder could recall, not a particularly impressive one. He was spoiled and unformed, hardly a man to lead when Ethiopia was challenged by the Italians on one side and by the dervishes on the other.

'Menelik, King of Shoa, has declared himself King of Kings,' Alula continued. 'He is in Wuchale even now, negotiating a treaty with the Italians.'

The news was darker then than Ryder had thought. Contesting claims had been made to the throne. Ryder knew Menelik was a powerful leader who had opened up trade routes in the south, even while he challenged Emperor John. Ryder had heard rumours the Italians had sold him a great number of rifles, hoping to win his support and his approval of the expanding Italian presence around Massowah. Ryder felt his heart growing heavy with dread. His camp in the valley, his pregnant wife and their son, the workers who trusted him, they were so close to these competing kings and the Italian army. And all this when it seemed they were close to wringing from the earth some recompense for their work and sacrifice.

Alula seemed to read his thoughts. 'You should have bought cattle, not dug in the earth,' he said gruffly. 'When a man puts his money in cattle and the wind changes, he may sell his beasts or drive them to another place. You are tied to your mine.'

'And you?'

'I also am tied to my land and to my prince.'

'You will not submit to Menelik, then?' Ryder asked.

It was a dangerous question. Alula sat up straight and smoothed the embroidered sleeves of his kaftan. He looked severe. Ryder examined his profile in the flickering torchlight. He looked like the portraits on the Axumite coins found scattered around the ancient monuments of the city.

He replied in a low growl. 'I told you. Menelik negotiates with the Italians even now. The same Italians who have sent troops into my lands once more. They have dug in at Asmara while I fought the dervish alongside my emperor.'

Ryder absorbed the news in silence. Alula did not have the necessary weaponry to dislodge a modern European army from a well-fortified position, no matter the bravery of his warriors. If Menelik was willing to let the Italians keep that territory in exchange for their support of his claim to be overall ruler of Ethiopia, it would leave Alula weak. Ryder realised that Alula was watching him shrewdly.

'The Italians are my enemies, Ryder. They were the enemies of Emperor John. They are the enemies of John's son and heir, my lord Ras Mengesha, so no, I will not submit to Menelik.' Alula spat out the words, his low, powerful voice seeming to fill the empty chamber. 'Your mine is failing, Ryder. You think I do not know what those ingots have cost you? You think I am a blind old man? Even with dervish blood warm on my blade I have followed your every struggle. The men who will not work for you, your murderous engineer, the loss and waste of your quicksilver.'

Ryder narrowed his eyes. He knew the traders who passed through the valley would carry news to Ras Alula, but how could he know so much from them? Ras Alula was watching him and laughed, his chuckle rasping and low, then clapped his hands. One of his warriors came into the tent, pushing Tadesse in front of him.

'Tadesse?' Ryder hissed. 'You have been a spy in my home?'

The boy only stared at the ground in front of him.

'What?' Alula's face twisted. 'You thought I would let you take the land and do what you would without having my eyes on you, Ryder? I ordered Ato Bru to send a servant with you, and he chose Tadesse after he saw the boy already had your trust. We are not fools. So yes, I know all your troubles. Go home, Ryder. Go back to Cairo. Stop grubbing in the soil. Your presence is a complication I do not like.'

'This is my home!' Ryder raised his voice. 'You call yourself a loyal servant of Emperor John – he granted me the land and the right to work it, and in his name I demand you honour that agreement.'

'Your agreement!' Alula said sharply. 'What do such words mean in the mouth of a white man?' He lifted his finger and his face grew dark. 'You know the British promised Massowah to Emperor John in return for his help saving your soldiers from the dervish? They promised. Then when their soldiers are all safe, they say, "Oh, sorry, we gave it to Italy instead." Why? Did the Italians simply ask more politely, do you think?'

The grief, anger and passion that must have been building up in Alula since the death of John was now bursting forth in a torrent.

'Then the Italians say, "No, we just want to stay here by the sea, we will be no trouble." Next I find them sending their soldiers up into the highlands and they say, "No, no, do not be concerned, we are only protecting our caravans from your nasty savage bandits. Your *shifta*." All lies!'

Ryder waited and did not try to interrupt the old man as yet. He had to let this quick fire burn out, not add fuel to it.

'And they will trick Menelik too!' Alula gripped the edge of his seat till his knuckles paled. 'He thinks he can deal with them. But no! You are all *liars*.'

'My lord,' Ryder said firmly.

The warrior who had brought in Tadesse bristled to attention, and the old man met Ryder's eye unflinchingly. Then he looked away and lifted his hand. The warrior relaxed his stance.

'Great Prince . . .' Tadesse said softly. 'May I speak?'

Ras Alula's raised hand became a gesture of permission.

'Mr Ryder cannot stop by his own will, my lord. He will always carry on unless he is beaten senseless and carried away. He will fight for his silver until he and his wife and Miss Amber are ruined, or until his heart stops, and even then it will probably take a little time for him to notice. The lion cannot decide to stop hunting; the rain cannot decide to stop falling. He cannot *decide* to abandon this mine.'

The prince nodded. 'Go on, boy.'

'Mr Ryder treats his workers well and deals honourably with them. Though I believe work of this kind with metal is . . . tainted, if any man could use it to bring wealth to our nation, he will do it. His love of our country is not pretended. His respect for our ways is sincere.'

Ras Alula looked at Ryder again and raised his eyebrow. 'Is that so, Ryder?'

'I have fought at your side, my lord. You know it is true.'

Now the passion had left him, Ras Alula looked weary. 'Very well, Ryder. I shall not hinder your work. I have only one condition. You must take this boy back with you and know then I have my eye on you.' Tadesse gasped. 'Treat him well. For the rest, you are our guest this evening.'

He stood up and clapped his hands twice. At once the heavy doors to the hall opened and his guests and servants began to stream in. The women in bright skirts and richly coloured shawls carried great platters of food. Alula kept his hand on Ryder's shoulder.

'Tonight we shall eat like the friends and neighbours we are. Tomorrow I shall take you part of your way home, then God protect us both, my friend.'

When Ryder woke in the morning and began to prepare the mules with Geriel and Maki, he noticed that Tadesse's face was ashen with fatigue. The boy tried to speak to him, but Ryder turned his back on him, telling him curtly to go and sit by the fire.

As they breakfasted, two of Alula's advisors arrived with gifts from their host and his good wishes. He sent brightly woven cloth for Saffron and Amber, and local brandy for Ryder. They were thoughtful presents and Ryder was grateful to him.

Once breakfast was over, Alula himself arrived with half a dozen of his men. On seeing that Ryder had no horse, he sent his own back to be stabled. Alula would never ride while his guest walked, and so they left Axum side by side, past the monuments of other ages, and the ancient wild fig tree next to the cathedral where, so tradition said, the Ark of the Covenant itself lay hidden from human eyes and protected by the priests of Axum.

Ryder and Alula avoided any further talk of politics, and instead swapped stories of the hunt on the first steep ascent and descent of the track.

Both men were strong and even at this altitude and climbing such paths, they did not need to pause in the flow of their talk. As they reached the bottom of a narrow gorge, however, they let the pack mules drink in the icy stream and enjoyed the cool shade offered by a stand of sweet-smelling juniper trees growing beside the water for an hour before setting off again.

The track would take them south along the shady gorge for some two or three miles, then would climb again steeply to take them further east. Ryder glanced over his shoulder and noticed Maki, who led one of the pack mules, stiffen and frown up into the heights ahead. Even as he caught Maki's look of surprise, he saw something on the eastern wall of the gorge behind them. A puff of dust, and a small trickle of loose pebbles from a high ledge he never would have noticed had he not been looking directly at the spot. He felt an animal twitch of disquiet in his gut. Calmly he gave a word of excuse to Alula and slowed his pace. The rest of the party began to overtake him and soon he was walking by Maki's side.

'What did you see?' he asked him.

'I'm not sure, Mr Ryder. It was there and gone again almost immediately, merely a faint movement in the thorn bushes. Fifty yards ahead, three quarters of the way up the slope.' He spoke quietly and did not point at the place.

Ryder looked casually up and down the twisting valley. The precipitous sides of the gorge were covered in patches of low scrub that had found a hold on the narrow sandstone ledges. The path alongside the stream was wide enough for two men to walk abreast, and the river itself was some twenty feet wide and shallow. During the rains it would be a dangerous and fast-flowing torrent, but at this time of year it merely provided refreshment for the travellers who chose this route. Only a minute before, the gorge had seemed a calm and restful place; now Ryder saw it with new eyes. It was the perfect location for an ambush. A small attacking force taking up positions north and south of them could fire down into their party, trapping them at the base of the steep slopes and cutting off any possible escape. Ryder hesitated. Perhaps they had only spotted the movements of animals on the gorge walls – the wild mountain goats could graze on a cliff face, and the fact they happened to be in places ideal for bandits planning an attack could be simply coincidence. But Ryder's instinct told him differently. They needed cover and they had to get to it before the men stalking them along the valley walls realised they had been spotted and opened fire.

Three hundred feet in front of them the river and track turned sharply west. The attack must come before they reached that point. Ryder thought quickly. About twenty yards in front of the head of their column was a recent rockfall. At its base grew a pair of young fig trees, and around them a low bank of poinciana. The poinciana was dense with bright green, feathered foliage, and sprinkled with crimson flowers. It would have to do.

'You see the rockfall?' Ryder said quietly to Maki, and the young man nodded. 'Five yards short of it, cut the rope on the mule's load. Then shout about it. Complain. Tell me it is my fault for letting the animals drink and unbalance their load. Do not touch your rifle until we are fired on.'

'How many, Mr Ryder?' Maki's eyes widened, but he kept his voice steady. 'I think I see another in front.'

'I do not know. Now laugh as if I've just made an excellent joke.'

Maki did. Ryder grinned and slapped him on the shoulder, then lengthened his stride slightly until he was beside Alula again.

'My lord, I think we are about to be ambushed,' Ryder said, his voice tense and urgent. 'Maki has seen two in front of us; I've seen two behind. We must take cover at once. If they take us in the open they will kill us all.'

Alula looked at him as if he were insane. 'No one would dare attack me or those who travel with me so close to my home, my friend. Your eyes are playing tricks on you.'

Before Ryder could open his mouth to answer him, they heard a crash behind them and Maki began to curse the mule and its master. It was a poor ruse, perhaps, but Maki was an impressive actor. He shouted for Ryder to come see the disaster for himself, throwing the packs from the mule towards the edge of the gully. Alula and Ryder turned back towards the rear of the column.

'Come,' Alula said to his own men. Three followed quickly enough, the others, probably thinking that dealing with the pack animals was beneath their dignity, were slower. Ryder jogged back along the track and, as soon as he was close enough, sharply ordered Geriel and Tadesse to take cover between the rockfall and the fig trees. Tadesse looked bemused, but Geriel recognised the tone of Ryder's voice and moved fast, grabbing the boy and the fallen pack from the animal, and pulling them both into the bank of poinciana as the first shot rang out. The sound snapped and echoed around the valley walls as one of Alula's men went down. The bullet tore into his back, sending him sprawling in the path, coughing up gouts of blood. The rest of the party dived for shelter between the rocks and the fig trees. Alula's remaining men scrambled to load their rifles under the thin cover of the shivering poinciana leaves and the thick packs from the mule. Ryder flattened himself against the valley wall. At first the shots seemed to come from every direction at once, the rounds thudding into the soil and kicking up small sprays of earth as the riflemen on the valley walls judged their range and picked out their targets. Ryder concentrated on locating their positions. There were two in front, on the east and west walls of the gorge, and two behind – again one each side.

Ryder heard another bullet thud into the trunk of the fig behind him. The tree shuddered. Alula's man downed on the path was struggling to breathe, slowly suffocating in his own blood. His hands scrabbled in the dust as he twisted and retched, his eyes wide with fear. They could do nothing for him; any attempt to reach him would be suicide. Instead they had to watch him die as the bullets ripped through the air, and listen to the wet rattle of his final breaths.

Another of Alula's men was trying to crawl closer to the rock-fall when a round from one of the attackers at their rear hit him in the back of his head. A splatter of his blood rained down on the bright green poinciana leaves and he stopped moving.

Ryder had his rifle upright in front of him, but he had no room to aim and fire.

The two mules brayed and bucked, frightened by the noise and the smell of blood, but the riflemen on the slopes did not target them. They were too valuable. It was the men they wanted dead. Ryder felt a surge of anger running through his body. He concentrated on the forward positions, twisting his head so that his face pressed against the red sandstone to try to pick out exactly the location on the east side of the valley where the bandit was concealed. Then abruptly he had it. A contrary movement of the branch of a nut bush on the ledge cut out of the valley flank. Gently he lowered his rifle until the peep sight covered the target. He waited for the next enemy movement. He saw the muzzle of a rifle barrel prod cautiously around the base of the nut bush. He adjusted his aim slightly and squeezed off the shot. The nut bush erupted in violent movement and a human form rolled into full view and began to slide down the hillside. Almost immediately he jammed in another low bush and struggled there, trying to free himself. However, both his hands were clamped to his face and blood spurted between his fingers. Ryder cycled another round into the chamber of his rifle and fired again. The wounded man jerked and then lay deathly still.

Ryder turned his face towards Alula, who was lying close against the low tumble of rocks and staring up the valley.

'They planned to ambush us there.' Ryder pointed up the path. 'Where the track is bare to the walls. That is where their main force will be waiting.'

'The perfidious swine,' Alula said quietly. 'May they rot eternally.' He spat on the ground. 'Cowards.'

Another bullet hit the rocks inches above Alula's head and kicked up a spray of fragments, which fell over his white shawl. He brushed them away.

'Silas, Amlak, take up position at the rear. You will kill the two men behind us. Silas, take the one on the east, Amlak the one on the west. Tamrat, when they are ready, offer the snipers another target.'

No man questioned his orders. Silas and Amlak slid silently into the green cover on their stomachs, pulling themselves forward on their elbows. A minute of quiet followed, then each man clicked his tongue softly against the roof of his mouth. Another bullet slammed into the tree trunk, and Ryder felt the force of it through the wood. If both the rear enemy snipers fired on Tamrat, Alula's men would be able to spot their positions and return fire. Ryder hoped Amlak and Silas were exceptional marksmen. They had to be if any of the party on the valley floor were to survive.

Tamrat lifted himself into a half crouch at the rear edge of the cover. Two shots echoed from close behind them. Tamrat dropped at once and then the answering shots came from Amlak's and Silas's guns. On the rear west slope a body tumbled off one of the scrub-matted ledges and thumped sickeningly onto the path behind them. Amlak had found his mark. Silas had not. Ryder heard the click and scrape of the reload and the brassy ring of a discharged cartridge hitting stone. Then Silas fired again and they heard a scream behind them from the east. The body did not fall but was caught on the thorns and they could see him now, half visible, hanging in the ash-coloured branches, still.

Ryder reached for Tamrat, but he had already crawled into cover again, clutching his rifle to his chest and apparently unharmed. He must have the luck of the devil.

Even with the rear riflemen dead, they could not retreat north along the gorge. The two snipers in front of them would have them in range for long enough to shoot them all in the back before they found more cover.

Ryder touched Alula's shoulder and pointed up the gully, where the rockfall had cut a narrow wedge into the steep wall.

'Keep their attention,' he said.

Alula nodded and started hissing orders. The men changed their positions. The two forward snipers were increasing their rate of fire, nervous now that their companions had been killed. The shots were not as accurate, but so packed were they in the patch of cover, the riflemen only needed a little luck now.

Ryder had to move fast. He needed to climb up the side of the canyon and take out the snipers to the fore and east. The attacker to the west would see him, and Ryder's broad back would be an excellent target unless the fire coming from the men on the valley floor could distract him.

Ryder leaped up the slope like a leopard. The earth was loose and dry, and slid away treacherously under his boots. He dug his hands into the rock, pulling himself up by his fingertips. His muscles began to burn and he felt his skin beginning to bead with sweat. He forced his boot into a crevice and felt the sharp pull of gravity as he released his handhold, then reached up, his chest flat against the sheer rock, and hauled himself higher.

Three quarters of the way up the slope where the shallow cover of the gully ended, he went sideways, grabbing on to a low thorn bush and praying the roots had dug their way in deep enough to hold his weight. He felt the skin on his palms tear on the thorns, and brought up his right leg and looked ahead, the sun and sweat almost blinding him. The rifles of Alula's men cracked again in the ravine below, but he could see the sniper now, three yards in front of him, and the angle of the slope here meant he could take those three yards at a run. He yanked himself into a crouch just as a round buried itself into the soil next to him. The sniper on the opposite flank had spotted him, but too late. He plunged towards the sniper's nest, his knife already in his hand.

The enemy rifleman heard Ryder coming at the last moment, turned and took aim. Ryder was moving too quickly. He crashed into the man's chest with his shoulder. The rifle flew out of the man's grip and dropped onto a lower ledge. Ryder felt his blade slide between the man's ribs. He was lying across him, the hilt bruising his own shoulder. He felt the man's blood jetting out over both of them. Their faces were an inch apart. Ryder saw the surprise and shock in his opponent's eyes, and then the life faded out of them.

The force of his fall had thrown them both out of cover. Another bullet kicked dust close to Ryder's head. He rolled over so the body of the man he had just killed was on top of him. He felt another bullet hit the corpse and a sudden burn in his side. Then he thrust the body from him, pushing the dead man off his knife, and scrambled back to the narrow protection of his nest. He was breathing hard.

Geriel had taken his chance: while the sniper on the west bank was firing at Ryder, he sprinted across the shallow river and scrambled up the almost vertical incline, hauling himself up ledge by ledge, the muscles on his shoulders bulging.

Ryder took his rifle from his shoulder and reloaded it, his movements swift and practised from years of hunting. He did not wait to aim precisely. He had to keep the sniper opposite him from seeing the danger of Geriel's approach. He shot by instinct and heard an answering bullet strike the rocks to his left. Ryder watched Geriel spring upwards, as if he had wings, pulling his knife from his belt. Even as Ryder heard the bandit's scream, he twisted around and looked up the valley. He could see much further from this new vantage point. Men were waiting around the curve of the river. Ryder counted fifteen of them, waiting to pounce on anyone who survived the sniper's alley of the gorge. He turned back towards his own party and signalled the number, punching upwards with his clenched fist three times.

How long was it since Maki had cut the mule's rope? Five minutes, perhaps. Ryder couldn't understand why these men hadn't attacked already. They looked as if they were arguing. Ryder reloaded, picked a target in the middle of the group, breathed out very steadily and smoothly squeezed the trigger. His man fell like a puppet with his strings cut. One of his fellows bent over him as if he could not understand what was happening. Ryder reloaded and shot again. It was a clean shot. The second man dropped on top of the corpse of his friend.

One of the others aimed what looked like a musket in Ryder's direction and fired. The gun had no more effect than a child's catapult at this range. Ryder realised the bandits on the valley floor had no modern rifles. Those must have gone to the men on the hillside.

He took aim again. The remaining bandits began running along the valley floor in a final effort to swamp Alula and his men. They threw themselves forward with desperate war cries, but as they came around the curve of the river they were exposed to Geriel's rifle and those of Alula's men from behind the rockfall. The rifles opened fire and the ambush became a slaughterhouse. Ryder bowled over another man before they closed on Alula's position. It seemed as if Geriel took another two, judging by the angle. Alula's men had time to shoot, reload and shoot again before the men could reach them and they made each shot count. One after another of the enemy fell as they sprinted forward, caught by the well-aimed fire from Alula's men. Three of them made it through the hail of bullets. Maki took the one on the right with his knife, then Ryder watched as Ras Alula rose like a ghost and in the same movement brought his curved sword up hard into another man's guts. His blood spattered the old man's robes and his viscera poured from his belly as if from a butcher's slop bucket. Alula turned and, with the grace of a dancer, sliced the same blade right and high through the throat of the last surviving attacker. The body collapsed sideways onto the rocky slope.

Silence fell across the valley. Ryder could hear only the gurgle of the river. He reached down for the rifle of the sniper he had killed and shouldered it, wiped his knife and returned it to its sheath, then kicked the body so it tumbled and bounced down the steep incline in front of him. He began to clamber down after it. On the other side of the gorge, Geriel did the same.

When Ryder reached the path, Alula bowed to him as if they were greeting each other for the first time that day.

'Are you hurt, my friend?'

Only then did Ryder remember the burn of the shot when he was using his enemy's corpse as a shield. He noticed a patch of wetness across the bottom of his shirt and across his hip. He smelled alcohol and cursed as he lifted his shirt. The bullet had struck his hip flask. Ryder took it from its loop on his belt and shook it. The bullet rattled inside and some of the men laughed.

'Don't mock me, gentlemen,' he said. 'That was damned fine whisky. Are my people well?'

Alula stepped back so Ryder could see Tadesse tending to a thin, clean wound on Maki's shoulder, the graze of one of the snipers' bullets.

'It is nothing,' Maki said. 'My little son has given me worse injuries.'

Alula was looking with distaste at the blood that had spattered his white robe. 'We shall bury these men here, and my men with them,' he said. 'I will not have the paths through my lands befouled with their corpses.'

'We shall help you,' Ryder replied, but Alula shook his head.

'No, do not delay, if you are to arrive home before the end of tomorrow you should go. Besides, I am out of humour now. That these *shifta* bastards should attack so close to Axum – I am vexed. Leave an old man in his bad mood and take my greetings to Mrs Saffron home with you.'

Geriel was already reloading the pack mule.

'If that is your wish.' Ryder was looking at the bodies of the slain men. They looked thin. He wondered why they had been chosen for ambush. Most *shifta* waited until some lightly guarded caravan crossed their path. Why would they attack such a well-armed group as theirs? Even with their superior numbers and the element of surprise, it had been a dangerous gambit. It smelled of desperation.

Alula followed his gaze. 'They were weak and they knew it. They were badly led.'

'Is that why they dared to make the attack, my lord?' Ryder asked.

Alula shrugged. For all his calm and self-possession during the attack, the fact of the ambush had obviously ruffled him.

'So it would seem. Now go. You must return to your wife. I hear she is with child?'

'The quality of your information is always impressive, my lord,' Ryder replied, casting a bitter glance at Tadesse.

Alula closed his eyes and tilted his head upwards, as if offering some prayer, then he looked at Ryder again. His shoulders relaxed and some of the anger left his large dark eyes, to be replaced by a weary hopelessness.

'Do not forget the boy spoke for you, Ryder,' he said. 'Come, embrace me!'

Alula opened his arms and Ryder bent forward so the old warrior could encircle his shoulders, but he wondered for a brief moment if he was going to feel Alula's knife between his ribs. Alula put his hand around the back of Ryder's neck. It was an affectionate gesture, fatherly and resigned.

'No, Ryder. You have fought beside me. You brought me silver from your mine, when you might have kept it. You have been honest with me and a courteous guest in our lands.'

He clasped his hands around Ryder's face, then brushed his blood-dampened fingers through Ryder's thick black hair. Ryder remained still. The gesture felt like the blessing an old man gives to his child when they know their ways are parting.

'Go now, my friend, and go in peace,' Alula said, releasing him. 'But guard your people well. This is the start of our troubles, not their end. May we always fight side by side when the battles begin.'

'I hope we shall, my lord.' Ryder swung the rifle he had taken from the bandit and offered it to Alula with a low bow.

The old warrior took it and examined it carefully. 'Italian-made, I think, like your own, Ryder. Now farewell.'

With that he turned and walked away. Tadesse, Geriel and Maki were ready, the mules loaded. Ryder led them across the battlefield in silence and towards home.

• • •

Amber was trying to keep a watch on her sister without Saffron noticing. Saffron's pregnancy with Leon had been straightforward, but she had been frightened when the birth pangs arrived, and Amber had never seen her sister scared before that day. The birth had been quick and Saffron was dismissive of the pain she had endured as soon as it was over. But that had been in Cairo. If anything had gone wrong in the city, Ryder and Amber could have ordered in an army of specialists, European or Egyptian, to help her. In Tigray they had only the help of the other women in the camp and half of them liked to entertain Saffron with stories of dying mothers and stillborn monsters. Amber told them not to frighten her sister, but they looked at her as if she were an idiot and told her Saffron should be prepared. Tadesse had told them, firmly, that childbirth was not his business, though Amber believed he would not abandon her sister if anything went wrong.

'Not that anything will go wrong,' she said aloud. She was grinding pepper for the evening meal and wondering which of the chickens she should pick for the pot. It was an extravagance to kill another bird, but Amber had an Englishwoman's faith in chicken as a sort of universal cure. It must, therefore, be effective against morning sickness. She would kill and cook it while Saffron was resting. Her sister would hardly refuse to eat it if it were dead already.

They had at last begun to produce silver, but the process was painfully slow and Ryder had taken what they had produced to Ras Alula. Even the little they had made since was worth no more than the stones in the river bed until they could be transported and sold, and given what they had heard from Iyasu, Amber had no idea when that would happen.

She tipped the ground pepper carefully into the saucepot, then left the hut in search of an unlucky hen. The chickens wandered the camp in perfect freedom. They were the responsibility of the children – those too old to spend their time constantly with their mothers but too young to act as shepherds or help in the fields. They guarded the grain bins and searched for eggs where the hens liked to lay. Amber consulted with one of the little girls about which birds were the best producers, so should be saved, and together they solemnly marked for death a fat but bad-tempered bird who had provided nothing for her keep for a week.

Amber was fond of the animals, but not sentimental about their deaths. The bird was caught and killed with the minimum of fuss. She set her little co-conspirator to plucking and preparing it, then looked about her, considering the next of her domestic tasks to be tackled. Her gaze was caught by a movement on the ridge above the camp and she looked up, shielding her eyes. She saw the silhouette of a man and her heart quickened. They were not expecting Ryder home until tomorrow at the earliest, but perhaps he had come ahead of time. Another figure appeared on the ridge next to the first, then another. It was not Ryder, nor was it Maki or Geriel or Tadesse.

'Saffy!' she called sharply. Then she grabbed one of the young boys of the camp. 'Go get Patch. And the others.'

The little boy dashed off and Saffron emerged from her hut. She wore a skirt and blouse in the English fashion, but both women now went barefoot in the camp and wore the thin gauzy *netela* veil over their hair. She joined Amber and squinted upwards. Perhaps twenty men were now lining the ridge. Amber could make out the shapes of their shields and rifles, either held at their sides or worn slung across their backs. She felt Saffron slip a hand into her own. Soon the ridge was completely lined with warriors, silent and watchful. Then those in the centre moved away to the flanks and a new shadow appeared on the horizon. It was a man on horseback.

'Saffy, what shall we do?' Amber hissed.

Instead of answering her sister, Saffron lifted her head, cupped her hands around her mouth and called out in Amharic. She used the high-pitched, carrying singsong voice that the highland shepherds and travellers used to swap news and messages over miles. It had a sort of chanting rhythm to it, which was both beautiful and slightly unearthly. Her veil slipped back from her hair.

'Great lord,' she called, 'come down and be our guest, honour us with your presence. Let us offer you our home and the best of our meat and drink.' She lowered her hands and waited.

In the camp and on the ridge no one moved or spoke. Even the animals seemed to feel the heavy tension of the moment and became still. The man on horseback leaned forward in his saddle. The man whom he spoke to then stepped forward to the edge of the escarpment and cupped his hands to his mouth.

'He comes. Menelik of Shoa, King of Kings, Emperor of Ethiopia approaches,' he called, then, as the horseman dismounted, the spokesman lifted up his arms and let out a cry. It reminded Amber of the ululation of the women during the religious ceremonies. This, too, was devout, but warlike and powerful. The other men along the ridge lifted their arms and took up the shout, then drummed their fists on their shields. The sound echoed like thunder up and down the gorge. Already a group was separating from the rest, starting down the steep trail towards them.

Saffron licked her lips. 'Amber, you might need another chicken,' she said.

R yder approached the camp the following day in the late morning. They had made good progress since parting from Ras Alula. Ryder always moved quickly when he was thinking and he hardly saw or felt the miles of trails, the steep climbs and trackless descents, the views of the impossible mountains, the golden craters of the high plains, the groups of shepherds and farmers moving through the landscape.

He felt his heart lift as he reached the familiar landscape within ten miles of his home and began to watch for signs of game, the spoor of the mountain ibex and nyala, the pad prints of the leopard, marking them in his mind for the next time he came out with his rifle to provide something extra for the feasts. Perhaps the political problems of Ethiopia would pass them by after all.

Then, where the trail towards his home crossed the path that led from Mekelle in the south to Adrigat in the north, he stopped dead and called for Maki to join him.

Maki whistled between his teeth, examining the scuffed sandy soil. 'Many men, Mr Ryder, and turning towards our camp.'

He pointed at one mark with his walking stick and the wood glimmered in the sunlight. Ryder looked at the place he was pointing. A hoof print, walked over by many barefooted men, but it was certainly a hoof print and that of a horse rather than a mule or donkey. Very few men could afford to ride horses in the highlands. Mules and asses were far more sure-footed on the leaping and plunging trails. Only princes and kings rode horses. Ryder felt his skin prickle and his mouth grew dry.

'Not bandits. A big man. A very big man,' Maki said, his voice low and serious.

'How long ago?' Ryder asked.

'A day, and they only go towards the camp. None coming back. Whoever they might be, they are still there.' Maki turned towards him again, and his words came quick and urgent. He had a wife and children at the camp too.

'Let me run on, Mr Ryder. I swear by Mary and St George, I will only look and then return. No matter what I see.'

Ryder did not reply, only began walking more quickly up the trail to the escarpment. Maki decided silence meant consent. He tossed his walking stick to Geriel, who caught it out of the air, and ran off ahead of them with the graceful, fluid lope of a born runner. He was soon out of sight.

Ryder and the others followed in silence. They saw the fires as they reached the summit of the next long gradual climb. When Ryder noticed the smoke, his imagination filled with horrors: Saffron dead, the camp destroyed. He had an image of little Leon face down in the river, of Amber eviscerated like the bandit in the gorge. He was about to break into a run himself, then they heard someone approaching. It was Maki. He ran up the hillside towards them and, as he came closer, Ryder tried to read his expression. He clenched his teeth to stop himself calling out for news at once.

Maki reached them, panting from his climb, bending over and breathing deeply. He reached out and put his hand on Ryder's shoulder.

'It's all right, Mr Ryder. All is well! They are cooking fires. But it is Menelik himself who has come, the new emperor. He has fifty warriors camped on the escarpment, more servants with them. He himself is in the village with his guard. But why has he come?'

Ryder breathed out slowly, as if he too had been running over the narrow, rocky trails, and remembered the moment he had sat in the steamer wondering what the penalties of success in the mine could be.

'I think he has heard about our silver.'

• • •

Ryder changed his clothes before going any further. Not that any of his clothes were particularly clean, but he thought it wise not to appear in camp with blood still staining his shirt.

Tadesse, Maki and Geriel also washed themselves in a small, clear stream that trickled towards the valley. As Ryder washed the blood from his arms, pinking the shallow water, he tried to remember everything he had heard about Menelik. He had ruled Shoa for many years and opened up his territory to traders before any other of the regional rulers of Abyssinia. The Italians at Massowah had spoken of him as a politician, but done so in that light, smiling way a parent might speak of a precocious child. He had come to some accommodation with the French at Djibouti, and a number of Russians had travelled from the heart of their own vast empire to offer their respects.

Ryder let the sun dry his skin and stared out into the pale turquoise sky. If the people of Ethiopia had a choice between Emperor John's young, untried son Ras Mengesha and this older man, a proven ruler, they would naturally choose Menelik, no matter what Ras Alula said. Ryder might even agree with them.

Tadesse brought him a shirt from his pack. It was a little threadbare from much washing, but it was not bloodstained.

So that's all that I know about Menelik, Ryder thought. But what does Menelik know about me? Alula had said he was negotiating with the Italians at Wuchale. Had the Italians told him about Courtney Mine? Perhaps he came only out of curiosity, but it was a long way to come on an idle whim, and Ryder did not think Menelik was the sort of man to do anything idly.

• • •

They were soon spotted by the men camped on the ridge and Ryder found himself exchanging greetings with one of Menelik's lieutenants. The lieutenant had brought an Arab man with him as he walked towards Ryder on the trail, but as soon as he realised no need for a translator existed, he dismissed the man with a wave of his hand. Both Ryder and the lieutenant addressed each other with careful formality.

Ryder noticed that Menelik's men carried themselves with great dignity, and each wore decorations – armbands of leather and silver, fur collars and short woollen cloaks – to demonstrate their status, but saw no sign of unnecessary show about them. They had a sort of quiet confidence that Ryder recognised and respected.

Once the initial exchanges were over, with a slight bow the lieutenant offered to accompany Ryder into camp. The offer was made with courtesy, but it was obvious it was not an offer to be refused, so Ryder found himself being led, as if he were a guest, into his own home.

Ryder took in the scene as he followed the track towards the valley floor. In the middle of the central square of the camp, in between the church and the fire pit, a chair and canopy had been set up. On the chair – the traditional wooden stool of any headman, but larger and more ornately carved – sat a man in a traditional kaftan and loose white trousers, but over his shoulders he wore a long purple cloak. He also wore a white turban – the mark of priests and aristocrats. Ryder knew then that it was Menelik himself. The canopy above his chair was of green and gold cloth, and fringed with long, silver tassels. Around him stood two or three older men, all dressed in similar fashion, though without turbans, and forming a semicircle around them were half a dozen warriors with decorated shields and modern rifles on their backs. In front of the throne, and to Menelik's right, the log benches had been rearranged. Saffron, Amber and Patch sat along one like schoolchildren. Along the other sat the senior men of the mine. Ryder realised he could hear no signs of working coming from the valley. The lack of the usual rumble of rock being pounded and shifted gave the whole scene an unfamiliar air. Ryder could see the rest of the men and women of the camp gathered by their own huts. The women were still working at their usual tasks. The men simply sat in the shade and watched. He glanced upwards. The children had been allowed to take the livestock out to graze, he noticed.

As he reached the base of the valley and followed his guides across the causeway, then up the track to the camp, he saw something else. There was a series of neat stacks of rifles piled outside the church. Ryder was quite certain they were the rifles that were normally carried by his men. He hoped that Menelik had not asked Amber to add her father's revolver to the pile.

As Ryder walked into the camp, Menelik rose to his feet. Ryder realised the King of Shoa was much taller than he had thought, looking at him from afar. The broad set of his shoulders made him look stocky when he was seated, but as he stood up and opened out his arms, Ryder realised that Menelik had a build very much like his own: broad-shouldered and muscular, but still standing at over six feet. His skin was darker than that of the inhabitants of Tigray, but he had the narrow nose and lips of the highlanders.

Ryder could feel his wife's gaze, but he did not dare look at her yet.

Menelik smiled. 'Mr Ryder, of Courtney Mine and Camp. In the name of our Lord, of Mary the Mother of Christ, and of Saint George, I greet you.'

Ryder stopped on the patch of bare earth between Menelik and the fire pit and bowed.

'I greet you, my lord,' he replied.

'I was told your Amharic is good. You do not need a translator to understand me?'

'I do not.'

Menelik waited for a while before he spoke again. 'This is uncomfortable, is it not, Mr Ryder? I greet you as if you are my guest, but the entire valley is yours, as you see it. To invite me, a king, to be seated would be a gross insult. If I tell you to sit, and you do, then I am usurping your authority and you are submitting. A puzzle indeed.' He looked amused, and cupped his chin in his hand. Then his expression changed. He became more serious, and his voice became lower.

'You have a claim on this place. That I do not deny, Mr Ryder. But I am the King of Kings. Your authority flows through me, or you have none.'

Ryder swung his rifle from his shoulder. Menelik did not flinch; from his guards came a sudden ripple of movement, a series of clicks and snaps as they loaded their own weapons, and lifted them to their shoulders and levelled the barrels at Ryder. Ryder heard Saffron squeak, but she managed to stop herself making any other noise. Ryder could imagine her biting the inside of her lip until it bled. He could almost taste her blood, metallic and warm in his own mouth.

He extended his arms away from his body, holding his rifle loosely in his right hand. Then, without speaking, he carried the rifle over to the pile of weaponry in front of the church. Menelik's guards followed his movements with the muzzles of their guns. Still with both arms extending from his body, Ryder carefully placed his rifle on top of the rest. He heard Menelik give a word of command, and his men lowered their rifles.

Ryder nodded to Maki and Geriel. They followed his example and Ryder noticed Tadesse slip into an empty place next to Amber. She put her arm around his thin shoulders. Then Ryder returned to his place in front of Menelik. The King of Shoa was watching him, his head on one side and a smile twitching the corner of his mouth.

'I hope, my lord, you have enjoyed the hospitality of my family?'

Menelik stepped out from under the canopy and offered Ryder his hand. Ryder took it. The palm was warm and dry, and the grip strong.

'I have, Mr Ryder.' He pointed towards Amber. 'Miss Amber makes a chicken stew almost as good as an Abyssinian woman. And Mr Patch has been showing me around the mine.'

'I am surprised, my lord, that the men are not working today,' Ryder said.

Menelik shrugged. 'They are ashamed. Men should work in the fields or take up arms and serve their lord in battle. They will not do this labour while their emperor is in their midst. You found Ras Alula well?'

Ryder was careful not to show any sign of surprise. 'He is well. He grieves for Emperor John.'

Menelik still had hold of Ryder's hand. 'He has nothing to grieve for. Emperor John died in battle defending his country. It is the best death a man might wish for.'

Ryder did not reply. Menelik studied his face for a moment more, then let his hand go.

'You wish to greet your family. Do so. We will talk more this evening. You shall sit by my side as we eat. For now, I have other duties. Word of my visit has spread, and you see, many of my people wish to have sight of me.'

Ryder turned around. One of the men from the escarpment was bringing a procession of men and women down the track – peasant farmers from the look of them. They must have come from miles around. Each carried a basket on their back or head. Offerings for their new lord. These neighbours had never visited the camp before, convinced that the mineworkers would be, like other metalworkers, infected with the evil eye. Perhaps they thought Menelik's presence made them immune.

Ryder realised that the king was still watching him. 'I look forward to our conversation, my lord,' he said, then walked swiftly towards the hut he shared with Saffron. He heard his family and friends stand and follow him. He did not look back, but as soon as they had reached the relative privacy of the interior, he spun around and caught up Saffron in his arms.

'Ryder, I thought they would shoot you!'

He buried his face in her neck, drinking in the scent of her, the softness of her skin, the warmth where her hands clasped his shoulders.

'Where is Leon?' he asked.

'One of Menelik's servants is playing with him and the other little ones. He has so many servants! It's all done very politely, but he frightens me. It was the same with the rifles. He made it all sound very sensible and reasonable, but it was terrifying. He just arrived and we didn't know what to do. I offered him our house, but he has a huge tent on the escarpment. Sometimes he seems very kind, and then a moment later he has this look in his eye and I'm afraid he'll cut my throat. I just can't tell. Oh, I've been so frightened and I'm so glad you are home!'

All this was said in a muffled, whispered rush. He stroked the hair from her face, rocking her gently as if comforting a child. He put out his hand to Amber, who clasped it briefly, her blue eyes looking old with worry, then he held it out to Patch, who shook it firmly.

'He's a clever man, Ryder,' Patch said. 'No mistaking that. He wanted to know everything about the mine, and he had a fellow with him the whole time making notes.'

'Where is Tadesse?' Ryder asked.

'I sent him to our hut, Ryder,' Amber answered. 'What happened?'

Ryder released his wife and sat down heavily on one of the benches in the middle of the room.

'What did Ras Alula say?' Amber asked. 'How can he resist Menelik?' She pointed towards the door. 'You see how he is. Mengesha and Alula can't challenge *him*, and the people like the look of him.' She crossed her arms around her chest. 'He certainly acts like the King of Kings, Ryder.'

'Alula knows that,' Ryder replied. 'He would not admit it, though. He's promised to leave us in peace. So now everything depends on Menelik. If he tries to take the mine from me, I swear he'll have to kill me first.' He looked around the faces of his friends. 'And another thing: Tadesse has been acting as Ras Alula's eyes and ears here since we arrived.'

Saffron gasped and Amber bit her lip and turned away as Ryder told them what had happened in Axum, and Alula's insistence that Tadesse remain with them. As he finished he saw the boy himself in the doorway. He held a small canvas-wrapped package in his hands. Ryder would not look at him. Tadesse glanced around him, seeing the disappointed looks of the two women and Patch's hunched shoulders.

'Mr Ryder?' he said softly, holding out the package. Ryder did not take it or speak to him. 'When Mr Rusty was killed, and I prepared his body for the grave, I saw his notebook was gone.'

'I asked Dan about it after the trial,' Patch said, confused. 'He said he'd destroyed it.'

Tadesse shook his head. 'He tried. He hid it under rocks in one of the water channels. I found it before the channel filled.'

Ryder's eyes widened and he snatched the package from Tadesse's hands. He removed the canvas wrapping and flicked through the pages of the thick notebook. It was filled with sketches and careful notes, all Rusty's missing genius neatly caught on the page. Ryder felt a surge of hope. This might be it. The missing piece that would turn the trickle of silver he had managed to extract from the mountain into a steady stream. Deciphering the notes might take weeks, but it would be worth it. He looked up at the faces surrounding him, then back at Tadesse.

'You kept this from me?'

Tadesse shrunk away from him. 'I believed the mine would kill you all, Mr Ryder. I thought you had to leave to save your family. I believed the work cursed.'

Ryder could barely contain his rage, but Saffron put her hand on his thigh and leaned forward.

'You don't believe that any longer, Tadesse?'

The boy shook his head.

'Why not?'

He began to weep. Ryder had never seen the boy give any sign of deep emotion before and he felt his rage retreat, at least enough to allow him to listen to his words.

'In Axum, I tried to save a man who was beyond saving. When he breathed his last, his family cursed me as a witch. I told Geriel and Maki and they said to me: "Do not mind them, little brother. They are ignorant people." And I thought: they are good men, though they work in your mine. Ato Gebre, who made the stamp for your ingots, is kind, though he has worked metal all his life. I thought perhaps I have been an ignorant person. I will not betray you again, Mr Ryder.'

Saffron glanced between the boy and her husband.

'Tadesse, go now,' she said. 'Such things are not forgotten in a moment, but I hear you, and I do not forget the good you have done here.'

The boy nodded and slipped away. When he was gone, Patch put out his hand and Ryder handed him the notebook. He thumbed through the pages and whistled.

'This could change everything. If Menelik gives us the chance to make use of it.'

Ryder felt a touch on his shoulder. Saffron was offering him a horn beaker of *tulla*. He drank it down and she took her place next to him.

'Ryder, try and forgive Tadesse,' she said. 'For me.'

'For you, Saffy, I will try.'

Amber and Patch had taken their places now around the central fire pit. Ryder felt the *tulla* warming his blood and Saffron's slim arm snake over his shoulder, the touch of her fingers on his neck. He closed his eyes for a moment to enjoy the promise of her comfort. Patch was frowning and scratching the scarring on his face. Ryder knew by now it was a sign he wanted to ask something, but didn't think he was going to like the answer.

'What is it, Patch?' he asked.

'Just how much silver is Menelik going to want? We've just handed everything we have to Ras Alula,' Patch answered.

Ryder always forgot that most Europeans had no idea how business was conducted in Africa. They expected to pay official taxes, buy permits and permissions. They never realised that in a land of kings and princes, a world of warriors and vast distances, it was a matter of friendships and patronage, an infinitely complex system of influence and favours. Ryder had always known that some of his silver would be spent buying those favours and earning that status. But it was a fragile system. The rivalries of princes and kings in danger of breaking out into new violence could tear the whole web apart and leave them with nothing.

'And we have earned Alula's friendship with them,' Ryder said. 'But if we are going to survive here now Emperor John is dead, we're going to need to come to some sort of arrangement with Menelik too.'

Patch seemed to struggle for a moment, then gave a short nod and lapsed into silence. Perhaps he was learning something of this world from his new Abyssinian wife after all.

Seeing that Patch was done, Amber spoke. 'Ryder, I don't think getting workers for the mine is going to be a problem any more. I think we are going to have plenty of new recruits in the coming months,' she said.

Ryder frowned. 'Why? I think we'll always need good men, especially ones who are willing and smart enough to do the work in the processing sheds, but you know as well as I do how hard it is to tempt an Abyssinian from his land and his cattle.'

He noticed Amber looking at his wife, and saw out of the corner of his eye Saffron give a microscopic nod.

'I went with Ato Asfaw back to his village to see Iyasu home. He's recovering well, and telling everyone how you and Tadesse saved his life,' Amber said. 'Ryder, disease has broken out among the cattle. Rinderpest. Even if this year's rains are good, I'm not sure half the farmers will have oxen left to plough their ground properly. They could starve, and some people are going to come to us. Perhaps a lot.'

Ryder thought of the thin frames of the bandits who had attacked them, the flicker in Ato Asfaw's eyes when Ryder had asked in the usual way about his cattle and fields. He straightened his back.

'Very well. Amber, work out how we'll cope if we end up with refugees arriving at the camp. Chances are they won't come until after the rains, but we should get ready. But first see if you can get any more news from Menelik's people. I want to know what he's agreed with the Italians before I start negotiating with him, not wait weeks until the official proclamations. Patch, start work on Rusty's notebook.' He felt Saffron's fingers under the collar of his shirt, touching the warm skin around his collar-bone. 'See Menelik and his men have everything they want.'

Patch and Amber nodded, and left the hut without saying anything more.

• • •

An hour later, Ryder sat up from the bed and reached for his shirt. Saffron laid her hand on his thigh.

'I missed you,' she said softly, and curled around so she could kiss the bruise at the top of his hip.

'I am going to see if Patch has made any progress with Rusty's notebook. I want to have some idea of what it means before I talk to Menelik.'

'Must you?'

He made the mistake of looking down at her, her sensual smile, her honey-coloured hair falling over her naked shoulders. She met his gaze, looking up at him through her dark lashes, and licked her lower lip. He groaned and pushed her back onto the bed, lying against her, feeling himself harden. She arched her back, lifting her breasts towards him. They were fuller already. He cupped one, weighing it in his hand, and she moaned very softly, then as he lowered his mouth to kiss it, he let his other hand run up her inner thigh till he met the softness of her mound. She gasped and he lifted his mouth from her nipple. Perhaps Rusty might profit from a little more time alone with the notebook.

'Quietly, my darling. We don't wish to disturb the emperor.'

She giggled and twisted her head to one side so she could smother the sound of her arousal by biting on the flesh of her arm. He brought her near to the peak of her excitement before shifting on top of her. She clasped her hands on his shoulders and bit her lip as he slid into her.

Amber went in search of one of Menelik's servants, who had been pointed out to her as a scribe. If anyone was likely to know and tell her about the details of the treaty with the Italians, it would be him. She decided she would ask him how he made his ink. She was running low on her own supply, and her attempts to make a substitute had been unsatisfactory. It stained everything but paper.

The man was welcoming and respectful, and happily shared the secrets of his trade. He was obviously pleased to discuss his work with such a beautiful young woman and one who could speak such excellent Amharic. He pressed her to accept a quantity of his own ink, and Amber asked if she might see some of his work. The treaty, perhaps? He hesitated, but Amber smiled and reminded him that in a few days the treaty would be read to both the parliament of Italy and to the princes loyal to Menelik in Addis. He looked reassured and carefully unrolled the treaty Menelik had just signed with the Italians in Wuchale.

Amber traced the lettering with her fingers. The script of Amharic was very beautiful to her, a series of strange shapes that looked like monuments, crosses and squares arranged in neat lines across the vellum, like a map of some ancient land strewn with fantastic ruins. The scribe blushed and shrugged at her praise, then fetched from his strong box the Italian version of the same treaty. He knew no Italian, but the cursive script, so different from his own, fascinated him. They bent their heads over Amber's notebook and she showed him how to write his own name in Latin letters, and they compared, laughing, his attempts with the copperplate flow of Italian penmanship. As they worked, Amber took careful note of the lands granted to the Italians as part of their colony of Eritrea. Courtney Mine remained firmly in the territory controlled by Menelik.

Then Amber frowned. She blinked, then asked, trying to keep her voice light, to see again the matching clause in the Amharic version. She read them both several times, committing the phrases to memory in both languages, then before the scribe noticed anything wrong, started to talk once more about pens, papers and ink. When she left she gave her second best fountain pen to the scribe, a gift that made tears start in his eyes, and left in a sombre mood to look for Ryder.

• • •

The guards were surprised to see Ryder and Amber appear on the escarpment late in the afternoon, but they were civil, and it was not long before they were ushered into the huge tent in the centre of the camp and the king's presence. Menelik was reclining on a heap of cushions in the middle of the room like an Arab. He invited them to sit with him. One of his servants was roasting coffee on a small brazier among the rich carpets and wall hangings, perfuming the enclosed space with those dark and astringent aromas. They talked politely about the roads and the weather until they were served their coffee, black and thick in small china cups, then Menelik dismissed the servant.

'You may speak freely now, my friends,' he said, sipping his coffee. 'I thought we had agreed to negotiate this evening, Mr Ryder. I hope you will persuade me it is in my interest to allow your works to continue.'

'I look forward to our discussion, sire. I come because my wife's sister wishes to bring something to your attention,' Ryder said, and Menelik turned his thoughtful gaze on Amber.

Amber had met and spoken to many important men while she was in Europe, but she felt nervous and afraid before Menelik. She had spent the last hour thinking through the implications of what she had learned and they terrified her. She thought of her parents and of her sisters, and told herself to be brave.

'I was speaking with your scribe this afternoon, sire,' she said in her low, clear voice. 'He did me the great honour of showing me some of his work – the treaty you have just signed with the Italian government.'

Menelik took another sip of his coffee and continued to watch her.

'I know something of the Italian language, and I noticed something that troubled me.' Her mouth went dry.

'Continue,' Menelik said. His voice was gentle, but no one could mistake the tone of command with which he spoke.

Amber shifted her gaze to the richly woven carpet at her feet. Red and bright yellow, patterns that might be abstract but that resolved somehow into birds of paradise, mountains and pastures.

'My lord,' she said, not daring to look up, 'clause seventeen of the treaty in Amharic says that you, King of Kings, may, *if you wish*, make use of the Italian government and their diplomats to communicate with the other great powers of the world in Europe and beyond.'

Menelik studied the remaining coffee in his cup, tipping it back and forth, but not letting any of it spill. 'Until I have men I can send out as ambassadors into the world, Miss Amber, to make use of our Italian friends in such a way is both practical and sensible. Do you not agree?'

She glanced at him quickly, then returned her attention to the carpet. 'Yes, sire, of course. But I looked at the Italian version too. In that it says you *must* make use of the Italians in that way.'

She felt her face flush red. She and Ryder had spoken in whispers about the clause in the camp. The Italian clause would be like a declaration to all of Europe and the whole world beyond that Ethiopia, all the vast territory now under Menelik's authority, was in effect the protectorate of Italy, unable to make her own sovereign arrangements with foreign powers. In the Amharic version, Abyssinia remained an independent nation.

Menelik was silent a long time. Amber had expected him to rage, for his anger to be swift and terrible, but somehow this heavy silence was more frightening than an explosion of wrath would have been.

'I do not know more than a few phrases in Italian,' he said at last. 'But I read the treaty written in my own tongue with great care. You agree, Miss Amber, that in my language it says I *may* consult.'

'Without doubt, sire.'

'But you are certain that in the Italian it says "must"?'

'It may be an oversight, a simple error of transcription, sire, but I am certain, the official version in the Italian language that bears your signature and seal says "must".'

Amber could swear she smelled lightning. Her hands had formed into tight fists at her side and she dared not look up. She felt Ryder's strong fingers close over her own and squeeze them briefly. She felt such a profound gratitude for his comfort in that moment, she swore she would never tease or annoy him again.

Menelik stood, and Amber and Ryder did the same.

'A mistake in the transcription,' he said quietly. 'That is almost certainly the case. To think my Italian friends were attempting something . . . underhand would distress me.'

'Yes, sire,' Amber said, staring at the carpet again.

'I thank you for bringing this matter to my attention, as you put it.' He turned to Ryder. 'Mr Ryder, I am very glad I decided to visit you here. It seems to me you and your people are excellent diplomats.'

Ryder thanked him, his voice even and calm.

'I can assume, I think, that this mistake will not be spoken of outside your family?'

Ryder nodded.

'Good,' Menelik continued. 'Now, Mr Ryder, my Italian friends would very much like me to drive Ras Alula from power in this region, and snuff out the claims of Ras Mengesha to my throne at once. I find, however, that I have been away from my capital and my queen for too long already. When I have enjoyed one more night at Courtney Camp, and we have concluded our negotiations, I will take my men south.'

Ryder was listening very carefully, both to the words and to the layers of meaning under them. He did not wish to miss the gold under the wax. Menelik turned away from them both for a moment, choosing his words and their weight with the same care as the Ethiopian poets and minstrels.

'I have the greatest respect for Ras Alula,' Menelik said, facing them again. 'He wishes to serve the emperor, who is dead. It is a mistake, but a mistake made for honourable reasons. Now I have given the Italians the right to protect themselves in the area surrounding Massowah, to that he must submit. But you may, Mr Ryder, tell Alula and Mengesha they still have my love, for I love them just as a father must love even his most wayward children. And you may tell him that, for the moment at least, I shall make no move against him. If he provokes my Italian allies, the consequences must fall upon his head. But if he does not move against me, he need not fear an attack from the warriors of Shoa.'

'I understand, my lord,' Ryder said.

Menelik clapped his hands together sharply. Three of his servants entered the tent, and Amber caught a glimpse of dusk behind them.

'We will join you in the camp in a little while,' Menelik said. Then he addressed his servants, pointing down at the carpet under his feet. 'This is to be taken down into Courtney Camp. A present from myself to Miss Amber.'

Amber gasped. 'Thank you, sire. It is beautiful.'

Menelik smiled, and everything felt cool and welcoming again. He put a hand on her shoulder. 'Little sister, you seemed to find the carpet so fascinating while we spoke. It must be yours.'

• • •

The feast that night was a triumph. Freshly woven straw mats were laid across the central square and torches and oil lamps were lit around the church and along the fences that held back the livestock, as if fuel were as plentiful as sand. The smell of roasting meat filled the camp and Menelik summoned his musicians from the escarpment to entertain the camp. The women dressed in their best, braided and oiled their hair, and draped gauzy shawls of turquoise and gold over their shoulders. The young girls brought out the wicker *massob* baskets on which the spongy sour pancakes of *injera* sat, and in the centre of each were piled hotly spiced chicken and lamb stews and fragrant pepper and bean sauces. The older children wove between the guests, carrying heavy gourds of *tulla*, filling the beakers.

Menelik sent his canopy and stool back up the hill and sat next to Ryder on one of the tree trunk benches. Ryder offered him the basket and Menelik tore off a piece of *injera* and used it to scoop up some of the stew from the central mound, put it into his mouth and chewed with his eyes slightly closed, then grinned and clapped his hands together as he swallowed.

'Excellent, excellent!' he said, and nodded towards Saffron. It was the signal for everyone else to begin, and soon everyone was ripping strips of *injera* off the shared platters, eating or handing morsels back to the waiting children. Conversation became general and loud, and the musicians started a fresh tune with a jangling, bouncing rhythm that made the flames of the bonfire dance. The tension of the afternoon seemed to have melted away in the firelight and as Ryder looked around the faces in the crowd, he saw only laughter and pride.

Menelik took another bite and leaned slightly towards Ryder. 'How many ingots have you now?'

'Very few, my lord,' Ryder replied evenly, and Menelik grunted. 'Our small stock of refined silver I took to Ras Alula in tribute.'

'Perhaps I should take this land from you and put it in more skilful hands,' Menelik said. 'Many foreigners come to my court now, engineers and miners among them.'

Ryder breathed slowly. 'I have sunk my fortune into this land, and I know it better than my own face. At last, I see the path ahead of me clearly, and the wealth the land promises is within reach. I may go about in rags today, but give me time, my lord, and I shall fill your treasury with silver.'

'And your own pockets.'

Ryder nodded. 'Yes. But *I* shall deal with you and your people honestly.'

It was dangerous to refer to the differences in the Italian treaty in this way, and Ryder knew it, but Menelik had to give him time. He watched the firelight play across the face of the King of Kings. Ryder thought he looked angry, but Ryder could not tell if that anger was directed towards him or the Italians.

'How much time?' Menelik asked.

Ryder calculated swiftly in his head. 'To reach full production? Five years.'

Menelik snorted and waved his hand. 'Five years? Mrs Saffron's art and Mrs Amber's book have made them rich. Go home, and let your wife buy silk shirts for your whole family.'

Ryder was surprised, and it must have shown in his face. Menelik glanced at him, his eyes glinting with satisfaction.

'We receive visitors from France, Russia and even Britain, Mr Ryder,' Menelik continued. 'I did not come here without knowing something of your family and your history. I intend to buy a printing press and set it up in Entoto. I shall have Mrs Amber's book translated.'

Ryder controlled his temper. He was not going to pour his blood and treasure into the ground and have nothing to show for it but a copy of his sister-in-law's book in Amharic.

'Great King, I cannot be reduced to the slave of my young wife. You cannot ask it of me, sire. You say you know me; then you must know I mean what I say. I will wrest the silver from these hills, and I will make proper tribute. Yes, five years seems long, but what is five years in the history of kings and empires?'

Menelik lifted his beaker to his mouth and took a deep draught, looking up into the star-scattered sky.

'So now I am your great king? Good. Very well. You may continue to work for now. My coronation will be held after the rains. Attend me then, and bring me one hundred ingots of silver. Do that, four times a year for five years, and I shall confirm your right to this land and its wealth for ever.'

Ryder felt his heart freeze. To produce a dozen ingots had taken months. Even if Rusty's notebook allowed them to increase production fivefold it would be almost impossible. Then to have to hand over every shining bar to Menelik for five years?

His head filled with images of loss and sacrifice, the steamer, Rusty. He thought of the days and weeks spent struggling against the rock and ore alongside his men, and his hands clenched. If Menelik stood by this insane demand, Ryder would dynamite the workings himself, then take up his rifle and go and fight along Ras Alula until the bandits or Menelik's troops gutted him.

Menelik tore off more of the *injera* and used it to spoon up the stew.

'Bring it to me, Mr Ryder, and I shall sell it through Djbouti on your behalf. Twenty out of every hundred ingots I shall keep for myself. Perhaps I will sell them, perhaps I shall just build a silver throne out of them for my coronation.'

Menelik was pleased with the trick he had played and he watched the emotions chasing each other across Ryder's face with glee.

'It is a test, Mr Ryder. Prove to me you can wrest wealth from these hills and we shall work together. From this point forward I will guarantee the safe transit of your silver, and you shall pay no other tithe to any other ruler or official in my empire. In return you shall promise to sell your silver only through me. This is not a raid, my friend; it is the beginning, I hope, of a partnership. Now, do you agree?'

Ryder made a series of swift calculations in his head. It was a steep tax, and made no allowances for what he had lost in the enterprise so far, but he had known that whatever route he chose to market with his silver would involve bribes, fines and a mounting range of taxes in every province he passed through. The route to Massowah meant passing between the people of Ras Alula and the Italians; to go via Entoto was a longer route, but with Menelik's protection it would be a safer one. If he could produce the quantity Menelik required: four hundred ingots a year for five years. It was impossible, but it must be done.

'I will be at your coronation, sire. With one hundred ingots.'

Menelik looked satisfied, but Ryder saw the flickering threat in his eyes.

'See that you are, Mr Ryder. Or I will give this land to men who can deliver what they say they will.'

• • •

Menelik's caravan left late the next morning. The great tents were collapsed and piled onto innumerable light wagons.

Ryder stood on the escarpment, holding Saffron's hand on one side, and a curious Leon's on the other. Patch, his wife Marta and Amber were standing with them, and together they watched the royal caravan begin its stately progress south towards Menelik's capital. Saffron put her free hand over the early swell of her belly.

'What will happen? Can we trust him, Ryder?' she asked.

Ryder watched the dust kicked up by the horses and mules, the carts, the warriors and servants of Menelik's retinue.

'I hope so, Saffy,' he said at last, then turned away and led them back towards their camp.

As soon as she was back in her own house, Amber bent over her notebook, considering the question of the refugees who might arrive in the camp after the rains, and writing a collection of neat lists. Tadesse would help her, and the priest. She used the fresh ink she had got from Menelik's scribe to sketch a plan for another orchard and fruit garden in the adjoining valley. If they were planted in the next few weeks and they managed to control the flow of some of the springs of that flank, it could provide a bountiful harvest. From time to time memories of the starving masses in Khartoum filled her mind. Men and women driven mad with hunger and fear. She had witnessed Ryder's compound being overrun by a mob driven wild by the notion that he was storing food and seen the slaughter that followed in spite of all Ryder's attempts to prevent it.

The night drew in. She lit her lamp and continued her work.

• • •

Ryder and Patch spent the next three days bent over Rusty's notebook, with the sheaf of papers Amber had translated scattered over the rough tabletop in the hut they called their office by the new works. The process, the measurements, a thousand technical details were worked out and recorded in Rusty's neat, heavy handwriting. It was as if he had climbed out of his grave and spoken to them.

Ryder thumbed through the pages. It was mostly dry, technical stuff, but occasionally in the margins Rusty had written something more personal. A few words of Amharic and their translations, a tiny sketch of Ryder himself battering away at the side of the mountain. Ryder felt a fresh burst of grief for his friend, and saw him again lying on the earth with the mercury sliding from his nostrils. He closed the book.

Patch was sitting opposite him and reworking his calculations on the back of Amber's pages according to what they had deciphered so far. He glanced up.

'Sort of hurts harder, don't it?' he said. 'Having his voice in our hands again.'

Ryder said nothing and Patch worked on a while before clearing his throat and trying again. 'Three days, and then we can make the changes to the arrastra and build the new amalgamation pit. What else?'

'Have you seen his design for a reverberatory furnace?' Ryder asked.

Patch shook his head. Ryder found the page and spun it around to face his friend. Patch frowned as he read the notes under the diagram, then whistled.

'If he's right, this could be the making of us. We'll save on quicksilver and fuel. Think it will work with charcoal?'

Ryder felt a warmth in his blood. 'Rusty believed it would, and I trust him. Let's get Ato Gebre in here. I want these built and tested before the month is out.'

Patch picked up the book and kissed it with a resounding smack, and for the first time in weeks, Ryder laughed.

I t was impossible to tell, looking back, the moment Penrod began to recover. He became aware slowly, over many weeks, that he had, from time to time, forgotten to be angry. He moved through the days mechanically, tending to the sick, eating the plain food in the dining hall and discussing Sufism with the silk merchant as an intellectual diversion, just as he moved through innumerable chess games, testing his mental powers.

Then one day he came away from the infirmary and found himself laughing at something one of his patients had said. On another he discovered the pleasures of gently teasing the formidable Cleopatra. Then came a moment, as he was cleaning the ulcerated wound of a child, that he forgot himself. Caring for the frightened little boy, he was no longer Penrod Ballantyne, VC, the hero who had brought down a corrupt monster and saved the royal houses of Europe from deep and damaging scandal, he was simply a means to help this one child. A sensation flashed through him, but he could not identify it at first. It was like a sudden light of startling intensity but without heat or pain. Crouched among the bandages, murmuring soothing nonsense to the child as he worked, it struck him with such force he felt as if his heart had exploded in his chest.

A little shaken, he finished the work at hand and went to empty out the dirty water and fetch fresh, his head lowered. Cleopatra sent him his next patient and he greeted him, an ancient beggar with a reputation for foul if colourful language. As Penrod kneeled and began to unwrap the old, discoloured bandages, he put a name to the feeling he had just experienced: peace – but a peace more profound than anything he had ever felt before. It puzzled him.

He tried to explain it to the silk merchant that evening as they played a game of chess. The merchant took his knight's pawn.

'Freedom from your raging heart, Penrod. That is what you have discovered. We shall make a Sufi of you yet.'

Penrod took his rook. 'I am not sure I believe in God.'

The silk merchant raised his eyebrows. 'That is a little churlish, my friend, given it seems you have just met Him.' He studied the board. 'Now here is a pretty problem you have set me. Let me concentrate.'

As the weeks unfolded, Penrod began to discover a lightness he had not known before. He experienced no more blinding flashes, but that peace began to enfold him. He thought of nothing other than the work at hand. When he had leisure, he read the volume of Rumi that Farouk had left him and watched his fellows go about the colony. He was sitting with the volume on his lap one afternoon when Farouk found him. Seeing who it was, Penrod made to stand, but Farouk waved him back and sat next to him on the sandy soil. They were shaded by a young palm tree, and the occasional breezes were heavy with the scent of jasmine. It was the first time Farouk had sought his company since the day Penrod had emerged from the hospital building.

For a few minutes they sat in silence. Some of the children were playing cricket, as far as their disabilities would allow. Once or twice they appealed to Penrod for advice or a decision. He gave both lightly and they thanked him, called him 'uncle', and returned to their game. Farouk noticed his reading and for a while they discussed some of the teachings in the book, then Farouk shrugged and looked back at the boys playing their games.

'Not all wisdom is contained in them, however, Penrod.' He spoke in English and Penrod replied in the same language. The words felt strange on his tongue; it had been so long since he had spoken anything but Arabic.

'What do you mean?'

'You know the parable of the talents, I think. You are still a young man. Might the time come when you should leave this place and make use of your skills in the wider world again?'

The idea seemed odd to Penrod. 'It might, but I have no wish to leave.'

Farouk patted his knee comfortingly. 'You are welcome to stay with us until you die of old age, my friend, but I think you should consider that parable.'

'Perhaps my talents are best left buried,' Penrod said. 'My skills seem to be for death.'

Farouk seemed to consider. 'I think there is more to you than that, Penrod. You are a leader of men, and a man of great intelligence. The kings and prime ministers who control the fates of people such as myself, people such as these children, need men like you to guide and advise them, and yes, at times fight for them. I am a man of peace, but that does not mean I despise men ready to fight for their people. But enough of that, I have a great favour to ask you. I have been treating an American lady in Cairo. She is now quite recovered and has made a generous contribution to the colony. I think we may build two or three more family homes and a barracks for some of the children who arrive here alone. I would like you to supervise the building. Will you do that for me?'

'I will do whatever you ask, Farouk.'

'Very good,' Farouk said and got to his feet again. 'Come and see me in my office in the morning and we shall discuss it.'

He put his hands in his pockets and sauntered back to the office building, leaving Penrod to stare at the pages in front of him, seeing nothing.

• • •

The construction work took a month. Every day Penrod instructed the crew and, stripped to his waist, worked alongside them mixing lime cement, shifting the great stone blocks of the barracks into place and supervising the workers. He felt himself growing stronger from the physical labour, and found, as Farouk had suggested, that his ability to lead men was undiminished.

As they were finishing the tiling work on the roof of the barracks, the fierce sun beating down on their backs, absorbed with the repetitive nature of the work, Penrod wiped the sweat from the corner of his eye and felt again that shock of lightness, a joy deeper than pleasure. It lasted longer this time. He felt it fill him, warming his limbs. He closed his eyes for a moment and realised he was offering up a prayer of thanks, and though he did not know to whom he was praying, he felt his words were heard.

The construction was not without its challenges. They had hired workmen from the city, and though most were willing and knew their trades, Penrod was suspicious of one and kept a close watch on him.

When the buildings were complete they held a celebration at the colony. Fires were lit, songs were sung and the children put on a play teasing the older members of the colony. A little girl dressed as Cleopatra scolded the others about bandages and ointments, one boy whitened his face with flour and leaped about the stage carrying empty cartons that represented stone blocks with debonair ease, while his friends dragged theirs about very slowly and groaned. Penrod laughed and applauded with the rest, and it was late when he left the company and began to make his way across the yard to his cell.

He heard something. A shout cut off. It came from the back of the offices. He jogged around the corner and one of the children from the play barrelled into him. Penrod caught hold of him.

'What is it, son?'

'Men – they are trying to break into Papa Farouk's office.'

A cloud shifted away from the moon and Penrod caught a glimpse of the boy's face, wide-eyed and tearful.

'Go, get the others,' Penrod said, and the boy dashed towards the dining hall.

Penrod moved quietly to the edge of the building. An old crutch was leaning up against the corner, a single rod with a padded crosspiece, but strong enough to bear the weight of a man. He picked it up, tore off the padded crosspiece and tossed it aside, and, weighing the shaft in his hands, turned the corner.

Three men, and he could tell from the shape and bulk of him that one was the worker he had distrusted. So they had taken the opportunity provided by the party to break in and try to rifle through the cash box. They were already clambering out of the office window again. Penrod glanced towards the wall of the compound. It was only twenty feet behind them and a rope hung over it. No doubt some conspirator was waiting on the road beyond. Penrod thought of what Farouk had said, how at times a man with talents such as his own was necessary in the world.

He had no time to wait for help from the others. Penrod put his lips together and began to whistle – it was a tune from his youth, something about lochs and fair maidens. He strolled out into the middle of the space between the office and the wall, where the moonlight would catch him.

• • •

Three minutes later, when Farouk, the silk merchant and a great number of other members of the colony rushed out to his aid, Penrod was still whistling the same old tune. At his feet lay three men. One was unconscious. A second one with a knife still clutched in his hand was dead. The third one was lying on his back, groaning at the unsympathetic sky.

Part III
November 1889

The rains ended just as the last of the first one hundred ingots was stamped at Courtney Mine. Ryder, Saffron and Amber left for Addis at once, and on the morning they arrived in the capital, Ryder presented his treasure to the emperor's steward. He felt a bone-deep thrill of satisfaction as the ingots were counted and recounted before being placed into teak chests, ribbed with metal bands. The emperor's seal was set in wax over their locks.

Menelik's steward presented Ryder with a small chest of Maria Theresa dollars, and explained his master had instructed him that if Courtney could produce the silver as agreed, he should be paid the market price at once, minus the tax they had negotiated. The steward also provided him with a sheaf of papers, heavy with seals, guaranteeing him safe transit for his silver for the next five years.

Saffron and Amber were waiting for him when he rejoined them in the compound they had been assigned, but he showed them the papers and the dollars with a frown.

'Aren't you pleased, Ryder?' Saffron had said, arranging the folds of the dress she had made for the coronation ceremony around her. She had refused to stay at the mine in spite of the advanced stage of her pregnancy, and looking at her now, aglow with pride and excitement, Ryder was glad she had come.

'Yes. But we must get that second seam opened and working if we are to continue.'

Without Rusty's notebook, the sudden leap in production would not have been possible and it would need to leap upwards again if they were to reach the goals Menelik had set. Opening up the new seam Dan had discovered would be key, but to do that they needed more men, and a mining engineer to lead them.

Saffron threaded her arm through her sister's. 'But today we can enjoy the coronation, can't we, darling? It is not every day one sees an emperor crowned, is it?'

Ryder bowed to the two sisters with a flourish, which made them both giggle.

'Yes, Saffy. Today we celebrate.'

•   •   •

Menelik's coronation was a spectacular pageant, a demonstration of power and authority unprecedented in Africa, and Amber recorded every detail in her notebook. The waiting congregation in the new cathedral shone in silks and gold. The women wore their hair high and woven with silver braid. The Ethiopian noblemen wore short purple capes fastened with elaborate silver clasps, and collars and headdresses fashioned from the manes of lions.

A scattering of other Europeans was visible in the crowd, some in the uniforms of the Italian or Russian diplomatic service; others, like Ryder, wore civilian dress. Amber stole a glance at her brother-in-law. Considering he spent most of his life in rough working clothes, he looked remarkably at ease in a frock coat. Saffron had arranged the tailoring, of course, so it fitted perfectly across his broad shoulders.

Outside the walls of the cathedral, a huge mass of men, women and children watched the invited guests arrive as they waited for Menelik and his Empress Taitu. Verses of praise for Menelik were picked up and repeated across the crowd, calls and responses that made them burst into fits of laughter or applause, which echoed against the cathedral walls and flowed down the slopes of Mount Entoto in a joyful chorus.

The emperor's procession began with a dozen priests dressed in pure white, calling down blessings on the new King of Kings. Behind them came a menagerie of camels, horses and elephants, chained lions and leopards, bears, muzzled and walking upright alongside their keepers, then a dozen horsemen, princes of the territories of Ethiopia in all their pomp and splendour.

Menelik wore robes of dazzling white and was carried through his people on an open litter lined with silk. His empress followed on her own litter borne by the women of her household. Bringing up the rear were the massed ranks of Menelik's personal bodyguard, the most elite warriors of the nation. Each man carried a richly decorated shield, chased with complex repeating designs in silver and brass, and the sunlight blazed from the leaf-shaped points of their spears and the decorated hilts of the curved *shotels* hanging at their hips. Every one of them had a shining new Italian rifle hanging on his shoulder.

The voices of the priests reached those inside the cathedral and the archbishop of the Ethiopian Church stood at the door to receive the coronation party. Servants ran forward to take the heads of the horses while the princes dismounted and then the animals were led away. The songs of the people outside reached new ecstatic crescendos as the congregation came to its feet to welcome Menelik and his wife.

Amber drank it all in, overwhelmed by the splendour of it all. As he passed, she could have sworn Menelik caught her eye and winked.

●　●　●

After the ceremony, the new city of Addis Ababa erupted in one gigantic party. Menelik ordered a dozen oxen roasted whole and great vats of *tulla* were offered to the people. The bread that had been brought to him as a traditional offering was given back to the crowds and, as the sky darkened, bonfires were lit and the music grew louder. Everything smelled of roasting meat, woodsmoke and gunpowder as guns and rifles were fired, volley after volley, in honour of the new rulers. The people danced and feasted, and the children ran wild, looking for treats from their laughing elders.

Amber wandered through it all, happy to find herself in such a crowd again. The last few months had been hard. Each day had been full of back-breaking work as she expanded her gardens and fought the rains when they threatened to overwhelm her careful system of dams and channels. She had argued constantly with Ryder and Patch, spending her days fighting for the wood and labour to set up a large kitchen and a dozen shelters while they were still struggling to build the new furnaces and produce the necessary hundred ingots of silver for Menelik. Saffron had found this pregnancy harder than the last, so was in no mood to play peacemaker. Amber had managed in the end, cajoling, bribing and occasionally stamping her foot until she got what she needed. She had even built a second storey on the hut she shared with Tadesse, reached by an outside staircase, and its floor was covered with the magnificent carpet Menelik had given her. It was a sanctuary for her, but was damp and smoky. When she tried to write she could not help thinking of Penrod, how his help and encouragement had made her work on *Slaves of the Mahdi* a delight, and how she ached for him still.

As she continued to wander around, Amber hoped her brother-in-law had managed to forget his worries about the mine for a little while during the ceremony. Now it occurred to her suddenly that she had not seen Saffron or Ryder for a while. She walked between the fires, the singers and laughing crowds, searching through the faces in the light of the flames. At last she saw Ryder, but Saffron was not with him. Apparently ignoring the dancing and songs around him, Ryder was deep in conversation with a European man. Amber walked up to them and put a hand on Ryder's arm.

'Where is Saffron?'

'I thought she was with you,' Ryder said, his brow furrowing with concern.

Amber gave him a swift, tight smile. 'Don't worry. She wouldn't want to disturb you. I'll find her.'

The man Ryder was talking to put out his hand and Amber shook it, already looking over his shoulder to see if she could spot her sister in the throng.

'Amber, this is Bill Peters. He's a mining engineer.'

Amber looked at him properly and smiled. 'Oh, how wonderful!' she breathed.

He was rather older than Ryder – indeed, the thick hair of his head and beard were almost white, but he had only the faintest lines around his eyes. His grip was firm and cool, though perhaps he held on to her hand a moment too long.

'So glad to meet you,' she added, then plunged back into the crowd.

• • •

Amber hated it when people said twins had a particular bond, but suddenly she was heading directly back to their little stone house as if she knew what she would find. Everything was dark. She lit the lamp by the door and held it up.

'Saffron?'

She heard a groan. Saffron was lying in the middle of the floor, still wearing her beautiful dress from the coronation, and great lengths of green and blue material swirled around her on the sandy floor like the waters of an oasis.

'Saffy? Saffy, speak to me!'

'I called,' Saffron whispered, struggling to her feet, 'but the singing – no one could hear me. The baby is coming, Amber.'

Amber did not waste time with words. She ran back to the edge of the crowd and grabbed the shoulder of a young boy watching the festivities from a safe distance. At first the child was too shocked to hear a white woman speaking Amharic to understand what she was saying, but as soon as he had grasped her meaning, he ran off into the darkness in search of Ryder.

Amber returned to her sister. She was leaning with her hands flat on the rough table in the middle of the room and panting hard.

'It's coming quickly, Amber.'

'We must cut you out of the dress.'

'No, don't do that!' Saffron's head jerked up. 'You'll ruin . . .' Then she bent forward suddenly and let herself fall to her knees on the earth floor, her forehead resting on the wood.

'Fine, cut it off, cut it off!'

Amber moved quickly, grabbing her knife from her travel bag, then crouching behind her sister and using it to slit through the ribbon lacing, the dress easing open with a sigh.

'Hurry, I can hardly breathe,' Saffy said in a gasp. 'Where is Ryder?'

'He's coming, darling,' Amber said firmly, then pulled Saffron's arms free from the tight sleeves of the dress as if she were a doll, and half lifted her out of it, kicking it aside before allowing Saffron to drop to her knees again, still in her long, white shift. Amber took the shawl from her own shoulders and wrapped it around Saffron's.

She groaned again. 'Amber, it doesn't feel right.'

Amber put her arms around her sister's shoulders. 'Do you need to stand up?'

'Yes.' She leaned against Amber as she tried to lift her, then cried out again. 'No, no . . . let me down. Amber, something is wrong!'

Her face was drawn and her hair was damp with sweat. A wave of brutal pain made her cry out and Amber suppressed a squeal as she felt her sister's fingers crush the bones of her wrist together. For another five agonising minutes she could do nothing but murmur soothing words. Saffron was horribly pale and breathing hard.

'Hang on, darling! Ryder is coming . . . Then I shall fetch a doctor.'

As soon as she said it she realised she had no idea where she might find one. Would the empress help her, perhaps? They had met very briefly only the day before, and she was rather cold towards them. Someone at the court would know whom to fetch. How long would it take her to find someone?

Saffron cried out again, just as Ryder arrived at a run. As soon as he had taken Saffron in his arms, Amber sprang to her feet.

'I must find a doctor!'

Ryder only nodded as he cradled Saffron against him. In the doorway she almost ran into Bill Peters, the engineer Ryder had been talking to earlier.

'Excuse me, I have to find—'

'A doctor?' Bill said. 'When I heard what the matter was, I took the liberty . . .'

He stepped aside and Amber saw for the first time that he was not alone. A small white man in eyeglasses and a European suit was standing beside him, holding a large medical bag.

'This is Doctor Yuri Alexandrovich Mishkin. He is here as part of the Russian mission.'

'Oh, thank you!' Amber exclaimed. 'This way, doctor.' She pulled him into the hut, where Saffron and Ryder were huddled together by the table. 'Ryder, Saffy, this is Doctor Yuri Alexandrovich Mishkin.'

Ryder only nodded. Saffron looked up and Amber felt her heart freeze as she saw the fear in her sister's eyes. The doctor must have seen it too.

'Mrs Courtney,' Mishkin said, smiling broadly as he set down his bag and took off his jacket, 'I have delivered a hundred healthy babies in peasant shacks, and half of those in snowstorms. This place is a palace in comparison. You are safe with me. Now first we need to make you comfortable.'

He gave his orders with precision and assurance. Amber dashed to and fro, fetching clean linen and hot water, while Ryder remained with his wife, holding her hand in his great paw as she rode the agony of her contractions.

Once the linen and water were fetched, Amber knelt at her sister's side, echoing the doctor's gentle words of encouragement. She had almost convinced herself that her feeling of dread was just foolish imagination when Saffron gasped, squealed and shifted her hips sideways. Amber turned to look at Yuri Alexandrovich Mishkin and heard him mutter something short and sharp in Russian under his breath.

'Doctor?'

'One moment, I must check the baby's position. Forgive me, my dear.' His tone was firm and clear. He bent over Saffron. She screamed and writhed away from him.

'For God's sake, what's happening?' Ryder said.

'The baby's shoulder is stuck behind the pelvic bone,' the doctor said. 'The child is not getting the air it needs. Keep Mrs Courtney calm. She must not push.'

Saffy's eyes were wild and dancing. 'I must, I must, Amber!'

Amber took hold of her sister's face and turned it towards her, staring into her eyes, seeing the light of the bonfires outside reflected in them.

'Saffy! Saffy, look at me! Do you remember when I was sick in Khartoum?'

Some sense returned to her sister's glazed expression. 'Cholera, you were dying.'

'I was, but I had you, and Ryder saved me, because I did what I was told.'

'But, Amber—'

'Saffron Benbrook! No excuses! Do *not* push!'

Saffron pulled her head away and screamed, the muscles and veins in her neck standing out as she fought the urge.

'Not much longer, Saffy, I swear it,' Ryder said. 'Doctor?'

Mishkin's face was pink and his eyes looked huge and swimming behind his glasses. 'One moment, just one moment. I nearly have it.'

Saffron groaned and Amber looked up and saw Ryder's face. The agony of tension in Saffron's face was reflected in his.

'Saffy! Think of Ryder, think of Leon!' Amber said.

She felt Saffron's fingers squeeze her own again. The doctor twisted sideways and Saffron screamed again.

'Now!' Mishkin shouted. As he slid his glasses back up his nose, his fingers left a bloody smear across his cheek. 'Push now, Mrs Courtney!'

Saffron lifted her hips and back off the rough blankets and arched her spine with effort as she pushed. The shriek she gave ended with a groan and she collapsed sideways onto Ryder's chest.

'Yes, Mrs Courtney!' Mishkin called out. 'Once more.'

Saffron's cry was animal, torn from her through gritted teeth. Ryder gripped her shoulders as if she would slip away from him into hell.

'Good! Excellent,' Mishkin breathed.

Amber could smell blood and heard the slippery rush of flesh and fluid. She twisted around and saw the doctor was cradling something in his arms, bloody and still. Saffron sighed and her head fell back against Ryder again.

'Come on, my little one,' Mishkin whispered into the sudden, terrible stillness, broken only by Saffron's ragged breaths. He was wiping roughly at the baby's face with his handkerchief. 'Come join us in the world, my treasure.'

A cough and then a thin wail. Amber saw the baby raise its fist, stretching out into the air for the first time. Mishkin took hold of the tiny hand, testing the baby's limbs, then nodded to himself. '*Ochen horosho.* Very good!'

'Is everything all right, doctor?' Amber asked, a tremble creeping into her voice.

He smiled at her warmly. 'Mr and Mrs Courtney,' Mishkin said gently, as Saffron's eyes opened. 'You have a healthy daughter.'

He passed the baby to her mother, then cut the cord, and Amber let out a long sigh. Ryder did not try to speak, but stared down at the tiny infant nestling against his wife's chest. Amber lifted the lamp so they could see her face. Her eyelids fluttered open as the light fell across them and she gave a breathy hiccup.

Ryder felt a sudden shift as his world broke apart, reformed around his love for the little girl.

Mishkin adjusted Saffron's shift and laid a blanket over her, then stood, leaning heavily on the rickety table.

'What shall we call her, Saffy?' Ryder asked.

Saffron could not speak above a whisper. 'Doctor, what was your mother's name?' she asked.

Amber held a beaker of brandy and water to her sister's mouth, and Saffy took a sip as she waited for him to reply.

Mishkin was already washing and packing his instruments. 'My mother was an Englishwoman, madam. A painter who came to the Russian court and met my father during her stay. Her name was Penelope.'

Saffron looked at her husband and he nodded.

'Penelope Courtney, then. You have all our thanks, doctor.'

'*Neechevo*, which in Russian means: "don't mention it". It was a pleasure to bring such a pretty child into the world.'

Amber showed him out, but did not go back into the house at once. Ryder and Saffron would want to be alone with Penelope for a little while.

Something moved in the shadows and Amber jumped.

'I'm so sorry, I did not wish to startle you.' It was Bill Peters. 'I hope all is well.'

Amber put out both her hands to him. 'Yes, indeed it is, and all our thanks to you. Where did you find that wonderful man?'

He laughed. 'I came over here with the Russian delegation. So when I heard Mrs Courtney was in labour, I thought of Yuri.'

Amber wrinkled her nose in surprise. 'But I thought you were English by your accent?'

'So I am. Born in England, then began to travel as soon as my apprenticeship was over. Silver mines in Bohemia, then I began working in the Urals, but the climate is unforgiving in that region. When I heard some men from St Petersburg were coming to see Menelik, I signed up to join them and try my luck here.'

He smiled at her and Amber felt some strange sliver of fear in her belly, but could not for the life of her think why. Perhaps it was because the smile did not seem to reach Bill's eyes, which remained oddly cold and blank. The bonfire nearest to them suddenly crackled and flared, sending up a great fountain of sparks. The crowd gathered around it shouted and laughed, then the music started up again – bouncing, joyful melodies, a chorus of delight and new beginnings.

Bill offered Amber his arm with a slight bow. 'Perhaps I can bore you with my whole life story while we have a walk through the crowds, Miss Benbrook?'

She was being ridiculous. It had been just some trick of the night, the smoke and excitements of the day.

She put her hand lightly on his arm. 'Call me Amber. That would be delightful, Bill.'

The following morning, when Ryder told them he had asked Bill to join them at Courtney Mine and Camp, Amber was determined to be pleased. They were desperate for an engineer at the mine and now one had fallen into their laps like a gift from heaven. She had managed to ignore her strange reaction to Bill's smile and remember the debt they all owed him for finding the wonderful Doctor Yuri. His company had been very pleasant. Bill had told her all about his travels and asked sensible questions about Khartoum and Amber's rescue from the harem. She nevertheless felt an itch at the back of her mind that she could not quite name. Perhaps it was the easy fluency with which Bill told her about his life. She was a storyteller herself and she heard a note in his account that seemed not quite right, like when a string of an instrument is out of tune, and that false tone keeps creeping in, no matter the skill of the player. She told herself she was being fanciful, and set about cooking Saffron something to eat.

Empress Taitu was gracious enough to act as godmother to Penelope, and Ryder spent far too much of the money he received from Menelik's steward entertaining every man, woman and child who came to offer their congratulations. Menelik sent presents for the whole family, including oil paints and canvas for a delighted Saffron and a typewriter for Amber. The sisters pounced on these treasures with shrieks of delight and Saffron at once sent a note to the empress asking permission to paint her portrait as soon as she had recovered from the birth. Permission was graciously granted and by the time the portrait was complete, both Saffron and Amber had come to love the fierce little empress, and she in her turn let it be known the sisters were under her particular protection.

Of Menelik they saw very little, and they heard no discussion about the treaty while they were in Addis. The Italian envoy seemed very at home in the court. Amber asked Ryder one evening what he thought as they all sat together in front of their temporary home. Among the emperor's presents had been a set of very comfortable camp chairs, shipped, apparently, direct from Harrods.

'Does Menelik not care? Or do you think he means to accept that Ethiopia is a protectorate of Italy?'

Ryder undid the top button on his collar and stretched out his legs. Saffron handed him his glass of whisky and settled Penelope on her shoulder, patting her tiny back.

'He cares. And he'll never accept Italy's "protection",' Ryder said. 'He is playing a long game. And the Italians are so keen to keep him from complaining about the treaty and their new colony, Eritrea, they are selling him every rifle he wants to buy.'

'The empress told us he is spending his share of your silver on guns,' Amber said and sipped her tea. She did not like whisky and in any case, Saffron would never allow anyone other than Ryder to help themselves to the spirit.

'From what I've seen of Menelik,' Ryder said, 'when he has enough of those guns, he'll use them to deal with anyone who challenges his authority in Ethiopia. Including the Italians.'

Ryder stopped speaking and his face broke into a broad smile. A heavily veiled woman was approaching them through the crowd, and by her side was a white man, respectably dressed but looking uncomfortable in his smart clothes. His grey hair stuck up at all sorts of strange angles from his head, making him look like an alarmed sheepdog. Amber recognised him at once. He had once worked for Ryder as engineer of his steam ship, the *Sacred Ibis*, and had suffered the horrors of Khartoum at their side.

'Why, Jock!' she shouted, and bounced up to him, catching him by the shoulders and kissing him firmly on his pink scrubbed face.

He blushed furiously. 'Is that little Miss Amber? Why, what a treat you've grown up into. We are just coming to visit your sister. We heard she'd had a baby and wish to offer our congratulations.'

Saffron gave a cry of delight. 'Oh, how wonderful!'

She passed the baby to Amber and stood up a little awkwardly so she could take her turn at embarrassing Jock with a kiss.

Ryder clapped him on the shoulder and shook his hand hard. 'Jock, it's good to see you! How is the *Sacred Ibis*? How are you?'

Jock looked both pleased and embarrassed by the warmth of his reception, and answered in a broad Scottish accent, untempered by years of adventure in Africa. 'Oh, I'm right enough. And the *Sacred Ibis* is still the best little steamer on the Blue Nile, though she is called *Durkhan Sama* now, you know. Madam pays a good wage.'

Ryder turned to the veiled lady, who was watching these reunions with a friendly eye and bowed very low.

'Bakhita, I heard rumours of your illness, and I am glad to see you well again,' he said.

She inclined her head. 'Thanks to Allah, the most merciful, I have been blessed. The illness took all my beauty and my vanity with it.'

Amber blinked rapidly. So this was the famous Bakhita, trader of antiquities and a woman who had managed to amass great fortune and influence in a world of violent, dangerous men. She had once been Penrod's lover, and had helped rescue them both from Osman Atalan. Part of Amber was grateful to her and sorry for her to have lost so much, but part of her was glad that Bakhita was not beautiful any more, because she had known what it was to be with Penrod, to run her hands over his body, to pull him into her. The very idea of it made Amber's eyes fill with hot, jealous tears.

She managed to curtsy and said, in a rather choked voice, 'I am so glad to meet you. You helped save me. Thank you.'

Bakhita took her hand and Amber lifted her gaze to look into her wide, dark eyes. Whatever the smallpox had done to her famously lovely face, those eyes were still beautiful.

'And I am glad to meet you, al-Zahra. You were well named, and I would do anything to serve a friend of Penrod Ballantyne.'

'Do you . . .' Amber spoke very quietly. 'Do you have any news of him?'

. . .

Bill Peters appeared in the Courtneys' yard an hour or so later looking for Ryder. He found Saffron seated outside with the baby in her arms. She was chatting quietly with some of the ladies of Bakhita's entourage, delighted to be speaking Arabic again and swapping stories of babies and their care. They also had some excellent ideas about how to recover from a difficult birth.

Bill waited at a distance until she noticed him and looked up with a welcoming smile.

'I've come in search of your husband, Mrs Courtney. I'm sorry, I did not mean to disturb you.'

'Oh, not at all,' Saffron replied with great cheerfulness. Penelope sneezed in her arms, then sighed happily and shut her eyes again. 'Ryder's met an old friend and they have gone off to tell each other stories. We shall not see him again today. And our friend Bakhita is telling Amber tales of Penrod Ballantyne, which is making them both cry, so they are doing that inside while we have a comfortable evening out here.'

Bill frowned. 'Ballantyne. I know that name.'

Saffron lifted the baby on her shoulder and patted her back. 'Yes, he was a war hero and all sorts of things. He and Amber were engaged for a little while before we came to the mine.'

'I thought he meant to marry the daughter of some aristocrat?' Bill said lightly.

'What, Lady Agatha? No, he never loved her. Penrod was fond of Bakhita too, but Amber is the only woman he ever loved, I think.'

The baby began to fuss and Saffron turned her attention to her child, marvelling at her small perfection, her thick eyelashes and the soft down of her hair. When she looked up again, Bill was gone.

Bakhita emerged a little while later and took her entourage with her. Saffron was surprised when Amber did not come out to see her off, so went in search of her. She found her sister curled against the wall of the hut, trying to stifle her sobs in her scarf.

'Amber! What is it? Are you ill?'

Amber gulped and looked up at her sister with swollen eyes. 'Oh, Saffy! Bakhita says Penrod is dead!'

Saffron felt the strength leave her legs and she sat heavily on the ground next to her sister, holding Penelope's fragile weight to her with one hand while she felt for her sister's fingers with the other.

'After he ruined the duke, he disappeared in Cairo, and Bakhita was told by people she trusts that he died in one of the opium dens!' Amber cried. 'If I had only gone back when I had the chance . . . I could have saved him.'

'Gone back?' Saffron said wonderingly. 'What do you mean?'

She pieced the story together from Amber's tear-soaked account: how she had bought a ticket and boarded the ship, but fled again when she had worked out Dan was a traitor.

'I thought as soon as the mine was safe, I'd go back. But now it's too late!'

'Oh, Amber. I'm so sorry,' Saffron said, and let her tears fall with her sister's onto the beaten earth of the floor. 'But you saved us – me and Ryder and the mine. I'm so sorry you couldn't save Penrod too.'

Amber swallowed hard. 'I just keep thinking of that line from that Italian novel, *The Betrothed*: *Questo matrimonio non s'ha da fare, né domani, né mai*. It's haunting me.'

'What does it mean?' Saffron asked, leaning closer so their foreheads touched.

'This marriage will not be performed, not tomorrow, not ever.' Amber pulled away and covered her face with her hands.

'Oh, Saffy, it was not much, but I had just a little hope and now it is gone.'

• • •

They spent several weeks in Addis while Saffron recovered from the birth, painted the portrait of the empress and spent a few of their precious dollars. The city was filling up with all sorts of interesting items being shipped in by enterprising traders, and while Amber kept quietly to their compound, Saffron hunted through their stocks for cheap cooking pots and hurricane lamps and a case of reasonably priced whisky. The rest of their money would be spent on quicksilver.

Saffron steadily regained her strength, but Amber looked sick and pale, and Saffron caught her several times weeping when she thought no one was looking. Saffron told Ryder and Bill that Penrod was dead, and asked that they return to the mine at a gentle pace. Amber needed time to recover from the news and she hoped that the peace of the journey and the sight of the flowering rain-recovered lands would give her some comfort. Bill offered to go on ahead at once to start work and Ryder sent him with his thanks.

A day's ride from the mine, they heard the shepherd boys calling to each other in the high singing voice they used to communicate over long distances. They were spreading news of their arrival and word that Mrs Saffron had a baby girl.

Patch came to meet them. He fussed over the baby and seemed to delight in Saffron's account of the coronation, but Ryder's first thought was for the mine. Patch was able to report that Bill was already settled in and proving to be worth his weight in pure silver. The second seam had been opened and was producing ore of excellent quality. When Ryder told him they had the money for more quicksilver, Patch clapped his hands.

'We might manage it yet, Mr Courtney! I can set out for Massowah tomorrow,' he exclaimed. 'Three days out of every five here I think we've been mad to try, but I think you might be proved right at last.' He hesitated. 'We certainly have men enough willing to wield a pick now, when they have the strength for it.'

'What do you mean, Patch?' Ryder asked.

'I've been wondering how to tell you, Mr Courtney,' he said, and scratched his chin, 'but you'll see for yourself in a minute. The cattle plague has spread from Asmara to Adowa, and the harvest has been poor. Not enough beasts were left to plough the land properly. People are starving.'

Amber put her hand on Patch's arm. 'Have any of them come to us?'

If he noticed this was the first thing she'd said since they met, or the shadows under her eyes, Patch didn't remark on it.

'See for yourself, Miss Amber.'

As he spoke they climbed the rise that would lead them to the great plateau above the mine and camp.

'Oh, Lord,' Amber said.

Before them, around the kitchen building and shelters Amber had built through the rainy season, and across the wide back of the hill, were small groups of men, women and children among the waving grasses. They looked up as Amber and the others appeared on the horizon. All of them appeared dazed, gaunt and exhausted. Some of the children had swollen bellies. Others lay without moving, as if they had no strength left to even lift their heads. She guessed they numbered at least a hundred.

Amber heard Saffron gasp, and her own eyes stung with hot tears. She thought of the luxuries of Addis, those roasting oxen, the profusion of the marketplace, and she felt a hot rush of anger and shame. Tigray was suffering and starving even as the flowers bloomed around them in such beauty; it seemed terribly cruel.

Amber recognised Patch's wife, Marta, and other women of the camp moving among them, offering handfuls of bread from their baskets and filling beakers of water from the skins they carried over their shoulders.

'They began arriving a week ago, Miss Amber, from all over Tigray, and it's the same story every time: bandits or soldiers taking what food they have, and the cattle dying in their droves,' Patch said, scratching at the stubble under his chin. 'Young Tadesse and my missus have been organising the help until you returned. And I tell you now, I'm sorry for every cross word I gave you while you were stealing my prop wood for those shelters, and being so strict with your supplies. The women have been baking bread all night in shifts and the priest prays here with them every day. It seems to give them some comfort.'

Amber did not answer him, but walked across the low grass to join Marta. No help would come from Addis while Menelik and Ras Alula were at odds. It was up to them.

Saffron watched her sister go. She did not think for a moment caring for these people would stop her sister grieving for Penrod, but at least it would keep her working and stop her disappearing into that grief entirely. For a moment she was grateful for the plague, then she caught herself and shook her head. The baby gurgled.

'Sometimes, Penelope, your mother is not a good person at all,' she whispered to the child. Then, with Ryder and Patch, followed Amber towards the camp.

Penrod left the colony, quietly, the day after he defeated the three men trying to rob them. He said goodbye only to Farouk, who told him to keep the translation of the Rumi, and to the silk merchant, who gave him the ivory queen from his chess set. The men spoke few words of farewell, but they did with warmth on both sides.

Penrod walked the ten miles into Cairo thinking about the violence of the previous day. His skills as a fighter did not seem to have suffered from lack of use, and his mind felt clearer, his senses sharper than they ever had before. He had felt no anger during the fight and had killed the man who threatened his own life with neither pleasure nor guilt. He had acted as he had to defend the people he cared for, and that made him stronger. The simmering rage, which had for so long been his companion, had left him, his pride was tempered by compassion and he saw the world around him with a new clarity. When he reached the city, however, and heard the babble of voices around him, the assault on his senses of noise and colour, he felt again that joy he had experienced in the infirmary and on the rooftop in the sun. It made him smile. He hitched his bundle over his shoulder and went to find Yakub.

Penrod embraced him and was surprised to see his old friend burst into tears. Adnan appeared, wondering what the noise was, and Penrod was shocked to see the boy he had chased across the rooftops was now a youth, tall and slim with his jet-black hair cut rather long.

Once they were sure he was not a ghost, they set about making Penrod look like a European again. Yakub had kept a trunk of his old possessions waiting for him, including a number of items of value. Gold tiepins and cufflinks, and the 18-carat half-hunter pocket watch that Amber had given him. Penrod kept the watch. The rest he asked Adnan to sell. Then he used the money to buy cricket equipment and a pretty tin of rosewater sweetmeats for Cleopatra, and had it all sent to the colony so his friends would know he was still thinking of them.

Yakub insisted on doing Penrod's barbering himself and when he presented Penrod with a mahogany hand mirror, Penrod looked at himself in surprise. He was looking at a familiar stranger.

Yakub brushed the stray hairs from his collar. 'So, *effendi*, where next?'

• • •

Colonel Sam Adams was at the club as usual that evening. He had spent the day buried deep in telegrams and briefings from London, trying to work out which way the political winds were blowing in Europe, and now was keen to put such concerns behind him. Yet they still flickered through his mind as he drank his first cocktail at the bar. One of his junior officers was trying to impress him with his own thoughts on the current climate in Africa, the latest conferences in Berlin, the ambitions of the French and the current situation in Sudan. Sam tried to keep up a pretence of polite grunts while ignoring the man, when he sensed a presence at his side. It was another junior officer, fresh off the boat, but looking strangely nervous. Sam sensed the boy's disquiet was due to more than finding himself in such a crowd of senior officers. Sam held up his hand to stop the flow of the other fellow.

'What is it, Patterson?'

'Sir, a man is waiting to see you. He would not come in. He says he is no longer a member.' Patterson ran a shaking hand through his hair and his voice dropped to a whisper. 'Sir, he says his name is *Penrod Ballantyne*.'

Sam put his glass down on the marble bar and immediately followed Patterson through the hall, past the fountains and ferns, the women draped in jewels and the men in their uniforms or evening dress, through the popping of champagne corks and hubbub of self-satisfied conversation, into the cool lobby and out onto the driveway.

A man was standing in the shadows on the far side of the drive. Sam hurried towards him, at first sceptical, then as he saw again that familiar face and figure he almost broke into a run. He came to a halt a yard away from the man. It was him, though Sam thought he could see something different in his bearing. He looked older and was lean, but his hair and moustache were neatly trimmed and his dress, a well-cut but unassuming suit in the European style, was pristine.

'Penrod!' Sam said. 'I thought you were dead!'

Penrod laughed. 'I came close, Sam.' He put out his hand and his eyes grew serious. 'I have come to ask your forgiveness, Sam. You tried to help me, and I treated you very badly.'

He said no more, and offered no self-justification. He had no arrogant sneer in his voice to render an apology meaningless, just that sincere tone and open hand.

Sam took it and pulled Penrod into a rough embrace, then held him by his shoulders at arm's length. He was surprised to feel his throat tighten and his own voice cracked a little as he replied.

'I am glad you are alive, Penrod.'

'That is much better than I deserve, my friend. Now, I find myself at something of a loose end. Can you or Her Majesty make use of me, do you think?'

The torches that lined the driveway flickered in the light evening breezes, chasing shadows across their faces. Sam thought of the piles of paper on his desk, the strange currents chasing each other across Europe and Africa, and the reports he had been reading about the relationship between the government in Rome and the new Emperor of Ethiopia, an interesting warrior king named Menelik.

'So you are back?' Sam said. 'And you wish to put on a uniform again? Serve as my intelligence officer?'

'I am, and I do, if you'll have me.'

He thumped Penrod on the shoulder. 'I'll have you, dear chap. Of course I'll have you.'

* * *

Colonel Sam Adams first broached the subject of the fall of the Duke of Kendal with Penrod a few days after their reunion. Penrod refused to confirm that he had been in any way involved. Sam goaded him, tempted him with wild rumours, flattered him and ordered the best champagne up from the cellars, but still Penrod remained impassive. Eventually Sam conceded defeat and threw up his hands.

'Keep your secrets, then! Good Lord, you could teach an oyster to be close-mouthed.'

They were seated in a quiet corner of the veranda at Shepheard's Hotel, a bottle of perfectly chilled Krug, swaddled like a baby in crisp linen, in the silver ice bucket between them. Outside, beyond the wicker armchairs and linen tablecloths, the usual dramas of Cairo rolled past them in explosions of colour and a babel of competing tongues.

'Surely discretion is not a bad characteristic in an intelligence officer,' Penrod said mildly.

'True enough,' Sam grunted, 'but I suppose, even though you have no personal connection with the case, you might be interested in an eyewitness account of the finding of the duke's body?'

'I suppose I would,' Penrod replied, lifting his glass to examine the bursting of the bubbles with an expert eye. Rumi called over-richness a subtle disease, but then the poet also recommended living life with enthusiasm, and the 1881 vintage was superb.

Sam told him all he had seen: the destruction of the house, the locked office, the empty safe and the horribly disfigured corpse. Penrod's face maintained an expression of polite interest throughout.

'And did you find the secretary, Carruthers?'

'Not a trace of him,' Sam said, stretching out his legs and crossing his ankles. 'We looked, and we weren't the only ones. He had no family living, and though we kept an eye on some of his known haunts and associates in Paris and London, he never turned up.'

'Strange,' Penrod said quietly. 'And the safe was completely empty, you say?'

'It was. Why do you ask?'

Penrod drank his champagne, savouring the complex flavours of flint and fruit with proper attention.

'Idle curiosity, Sam. That is all.'

• • •

After a month in Cairo, Penrod travelled to England to see his brother, the baronet, and his sister-in-law, Jane. They were overwhelmed with happiness to see him alive and forgave his disappearance with an alacrity that humbled him. For some weeks Penrod was kept in London in talks with the War Office about the situation in the Sudan, and dining with senior officers and politicians. At last they managed to escape to the Scottish estates for some shooting and Jane took the opportunity to ask about Amber.

'I grew very fond of Miss Benbrook,' she said as he raised his gun. 'Do you have any news of her?'

'I have not,' he said and fired. It was the only shot he missed all day and Jane did not try to press him further.

On his return to Cairo some months later he was summoned to the offices of the commander-in-chief, General Kitchener. He found Sam Adams in the sirdar's office as he arrived and delivered to them both his report on the current condition of the camel cavalry corps, along with his suggestions for further training. Kitchener approved his suggestions without comment.

'Very good. At ease, Major.'

Penrod clasped his hands behind his back.

'Major Ballantyne, you have done a good job with these men, but your behaviour has not always been what I would expect from a man of your rank and experience. Colonel Adams tells me that I may trust you and I have a task for which you are uniquely suited. It requires a man on whom I can rely to act independently, but not like a damned renegade. Are you that man?'

'I am, sir.'

He felt the general's penetrating gaze on him. Kitchener was a bold, decisive commander in the field and a superb leader. He was demanding, but he was also loyal and he trusted his instincts. Penrod knew that the decision this muscular gladiator of a man made now would be the deciding factor in his future military career. He found, to his surprise, he did want to take his place in the centre of events again. Farouk had been right.

'Very well,' Kitchener said at last. 'I need you in Massowah. I want to know what the Italians are doing in Eritrea and what they're planning. I need an assessment of the Mahdist strength and leadership in south Sudan and I want to know if our friends in Aden and Somaliland need to concern themselves with this new Emperor Menelik. I want regular reports, and I expect you to get the best possible information from the senior Italian officers. Do you understand?'

'Yes, sir.'

'You'll be on your own. Our agreement with our Italian friends is that you are to advise them on their battles with the dervish and exchange information about the recruiting and training of native troops. They are damned proud of their *askari*. See if we can learn anything of use to our own forces. And get me that information too.'

'Sir.'

'I understand you have friends in royal circles. The Italians wouldn't be so welcoming to any other officer,' Kitchener added. He glanced at a briefing paper on the polished desk in front of him, covered with Sam Adams' neat, heavy writing. 'What on earth is the Order of the Guardians of Rome?'

'I understand I may sell goat's cheese in the forum, sir,' Penrod said. 'But only on certain Saturdays.'

Kitchener's mouth twitched in a rare smile. 'Excellent. You will leave for Massowah on Friday.'

• • •

Penrod made arrangements for his departure. Yakub and Adnan lavished great attention on his kit, and his lodgings echoed with their orders and curses when they found any item of clothing less than perfect.

Penrod's new role was to be something between an intelligence officer and a diplomat. He was to observe and advise the Italians, but more than that, he needed to give Kitchener his own opinions about the shifting currents in Eritrea. His fluent Arabic as well as his fluent Italian would give him the opportunity to study the land and the people, and he felt sure the clarity and thoughtfulness he had discovered in the colony would prove equally advantageous.

And he would be closer to Amber. She was never far from his thoughts and his old arrogant assumption that she was his by right still pained him. He would never love another woman as he had loved her, and he hoped if their paths ever crossed again she would see he had changed. In the meantime he wished sincerely for her happiness and prepared for his mission with quiet diligence.

The number of refugees that arrived at Courtney Camp in the following months, desperate for help, waxed and waned. As soon as people had recovered their strength, most either tried to return to their farmlands or headed south towards areas still untroubled by rinderpest or drought. Some stayed. The men asked for work at the mine and their families built more permanent homes near the church. The population of Courtney Camp swelled, but such was the richness of the second seam, work was available for any who wanted it.

Not every family reached them in time. More than once a mother, emaciated and exhausted, put her child into Amber's arms, sat down on the ground and never got up again. The little graveyard grew full.

The refugees were fed on bread, goat's milk, nuts and fruits. It was a meagre enough diet, but it gave them some respite and a chance to recover their strength. But Ryder made it clear that the workers must be fed first. Hunger led to carelessness, and in the punishing world of the mine, that led to accident and death. They still had to strain every sinew to meet Menelik's targets. The workers' families must remain well fed too. If a man's children were hungry, he would share his ration with them, so it was vital they were all kept well supplied no matter the want of the refugees. Nevertheless, Ryder noticed some of his workers seemed to be losing weight, and discovered to his rage that the women were still taking rations to the refugees. It was then he decided to issue each man and boy with rifle and ammunition from the camp armoury. When they were not working in the mine, they were sent hunting. The small deer and game birds they shot were taken to the refugee kitchen to be made into nourishing broths and soups. Morale improved dramatically, and the men began to boast of their prowess with a rifle.

The months became a year, then two. Travellers and traders stopped from time to time at the camp and brought them news of the outside world. Menelik issued an official protest to the

Italian King Umberto about the disputed clause in the treaty, while Ras Alula and Mengesha had made an uneasy peace with Italy. Once they received a letter from Bakhita. She told them she had seen their sister Rebecca, that she was the favourite wife of Osman Atalan and had now two children: a son and a daughter as brave and beautiful as she had once been. Bakhita's own health, however, was fading and they should not expect to hear from her again.

Amber went hunting too in the gorges and valleys near the camp. The responsibilities she had assumed weighed on her, but she found she could forget them for a while as she followed the trails deep into the mountains. Tadesse was the companion she normally took with her. He never tried to distract her with chatter and had no interest in shooting. He came in search of plants and herbs he could use to heal. He still kept clear of Ryder and worked mostly with Amber among the refugees.

One afternoon, towards the end of the dry season, they had gone further from the camp than usual, travelling in a wide arc into a section of the mountains they did not know. As they crested a ridge, Amber noticed an isolated *tukul* half a mile away on the next rise. She pointed it out to Tadesse.

'No smoke, no people, Miss Amber. We should stay away. I can smell death on it from here.'

Amber hesitated, then shook her head. 'Come or not as you wish, but I shall go. Perhaps someone is still alive inside, too weak to leave.'

Tadesse rolled his eyes. 'No animals, and the field is unploughed. They are dead and have been for some time. I do not wish to see it. Enough death walks into camp every day.'

Amber's temper flared. 'Stay here then,' she said. I shall not be able to rest without going to see.'

Tadesse sat down, and Amber stamped off without looking back at him. Her irritation carried her into the sandy gully and up the rise to the narrow plateau where the round, thatched hut stood. As soon as she reached the level ground, her heart sank. Tadesse had been right. She could feel the suffering in the air.

The thorn hedges built to protect the livestock were tumbled and broken. A few animal bones, tossed about by predators and scavengers, lay in the dust. And the silence – it had a depth to it, a quality that Amber knew meant she was in the presence of death. She looked over her shoulder. Tadesse was sitting on the ground with his knees pulled up to his chest, plucking at the pale, dry grasses at his feet. Amber felt a flash of anger, but not with Tadesse. This was a terrible place to set up a homestead. The earth was thin and the vegetation sparse. How they had expected to survive the dry season even in a good year amazed her. She wove her way through the thorn barricade and called out a greeting. No answer came. Even the natural sounds of wind and bird song seemed to have dropped away to nothing. She paused in the doorway of the hut as a wave of a sweet, dusty smell hit her and she covered her mouth with her scarf. Three bodies lay in the middle of the earth floor, semi-mummified in the dry air. Judging by what remained of their clothing, it was a family – a man, woman and child. They lay close together, the mother cradling the child and the man with his arm around them both, drawing them to him with his last strength. Amber wondered if they had already been dead when he took his place next to them.

The animals that had feasted on the bodies of the livestock had left them undisturbed. Amber spoke a few words of the funeral ceremony of the Coptic Church – Lord knows she had heard it often enough since the refugees had started arriving – then she slipped out of the door and pushed the thorn bushes back across. They were probably young, too young to afford decent farming land, but they had married anyway. She imagined them coming here, full of hope with one or two oxen, how that hope must have turned to desperation when the animals suddenly sickened and died.

She began to walk back down the trail again, lost in her imaginings of the dead family, and it was not until she was halfway down the slope that she looked up and saw Tadesse gesticulating at her. She wondered why he didn't call out to her. Perhaps a dik-dik or a wild goat was hidden in the cover at the bottom of the gully. She stood still, took her rifle from her shoulder and loaded it, then looked at Tadesse again, waiting for him to point out where her prey might be. She wondered how he would mime to her what was hidden in the undergrowth. Perhaps he'd flap his arms for a mountain partridge, or give himself horns with his hands for a kudu, though it was unlikely one of those creatures would have allowed her to get so close. Tadesse spread out his fingers and mimed great swiping claws.

Amber froze. Tadesse was pointing down and to her right. At once she heard a low snarling growl and turned. It was a lioness, less than ten feet away, her ears back, her lips pulled back from her three-inch fangs, head down and shoulders raised, ready to spring forward. Time stopped as the great beast made her leap, a blur of movement, tawny hide, muscle and light, and the flash of those terrible yellow eyes. Amber shot from her hip, the bullet tore through the lioness's fore-shoulder, but she was carried through the air by the momentum of her jump. Amber stepped backwards, just out of reach of the swiping claws, and the lioness fell sprawled in front of her. Her huge paws scrabbled in the dust as she struggled to stand again. Amber reloaded and fired a second time, carefully aiming between the lioness's glaring yellow eyes. The creature bucked backwards and collapsed on its side.

Amber felt her legs turn weak, and she found she was sitting on the track, a sudden shivering running over her as if she had been doused in cold water. Tadesse ran down the slope towards her, but when he arrived she could do no more than gape at him.

'What . . .?' Tadesse gasped.

He put a hand on her shoulder while she continued to shake. 'Miss Amber?'

'*Dehina nenyi* – I'm fine, Tadesse,' she said and reached for her canteen of water, but her fingers were trembling too violently to undo the screw of the lid. He took it from her, opened it and handed it to her, then turned his back until she could recover her composure.

She drank deeply and the edge of the canteen rattled against her teeth.

Tadesse had bent down and was stroking the warm flank of the lion with great reverence. Amber got to her feet. To kill a lion was a badge of great honour in Tigray. The lions had learned as much and kept a decent distance from humans, unless they were sick or hungry, and even then they would only take straying animals from the edge of villages. Amber could not understand why the creature had attacked. She had a sudden vision of teeth and claws again and, shuddering, picked up her rifle.

'Shh . . .' Tadesse hissed, and pointed towards the wavering scrub. Amber struggled to reload, but her fingers were clumsy now and she could hardly see. The world became a confusion of light and her eyes misted. Then she saw Tadesse relax, and she blinked hard to clear her vision. A cub, no more than a few weeks old, appeared at the edge of the cover and examined them, its head on one side, flicking its black ears. They did not move, and so it padded forward and pushed its muzzle into its dead mother's flanks. It gasped and mewled, then sat down rather awkwardly and sneezed.

'Kill it, Miss Amber,' Tadesse said. 'It is kinder to waste a bullet than to let it starve here.'

Amber looked at the cub. It had got back on to its four feet, its black-tipped tail sticking out straight behind it. Again it grunted and keened as it shoved its nose into its mother's side and received no response from the cooling corpse. Amber ran her hand through her own golden hair, watching it, a little beast alone in the wilderness.

'No. It is mine, I'm taking her home.'

Tadesse looked up at her sideways. 'Mr Ryder will not be pleased. It will kill the chickens and frighten the women.'

Amber lifted her chin. 'I shall call her Hagos and I shall take her up above the orchard. I will teach her to hunt. Mr Ryder is not my husband – he cannot tell me what to do.'

'Hagos – you name the lion "happiness"? You are crazy, Miss Amber,' Tadesse said.

'I need some joy, Tadesse, and perhaps I am crazy, but now I am a crazy lady with a lion.'

• • •

Amber moved her things up to the ground above the orchard that afternoon, pitched a tent and made herself comfortable with her little lioness. Hagos cried the first night, little mewling gasps that broke Amber's heart, and she refused to eat, but shortly before dawn she found her way to Amber's camp bed and agreed to take goat's milk in the morning.

It was two days before Amber dared go back into camp and face the music. She found Saffron with her children on the pebbled riverbank. Leon had been inclined to be jealous of the baby when they came back from Addis. He thought Penelope was a gift, like Saffron's paints and Amber's typewriter, and kept telling them to give her back. Over the last few months, however, he had grown rather protective of the little girl and was almost as pleased as her parents when she took her first steps.

Penelope obviously thought her brother was some sort of god, and cried when he ran off with his friends faster than she could toddle after him. Now she had him to herself as he showed her the secrets of the riverbank, while Saffron watched from a careful distance. Amber came and sat down next to her sister.

'Is Ryder very cross with me, Saffy?' she said after a moment.

Saffron didn't turn around, but Amber saw her smile.

'Yes, he is rather. He calls it another of your stunts. Don't worry, they are trying out a new method to save more of the quicksilver on the arrastra tomorrow, and he won't be able to think about anything other than that for a week or two. Just make sure you keep Hagos out of his way.'

Amber twisted the trailing edge of her thin headscarf between her fingers. 'I'm sorry.'

Saffron shrugged. 'I don't mind. But you do keep fighting with him, Amber. And fighting with Ryder is *my* job.'

She shifted her seat so she could look at her sister. Amber lifted her shoulder a bit, trying to hide from that rather searching look.

'You don't want to marry Bill, do you? Then you could fight with him.'

Amber shook her head, but Saffron persisted.

'Are you sure? He is a bit old, but he knows about books and you need someone who can talk to you about things like that. And he likes you. I've seen him staring; we all have.'

Amber reached down and picked up one of the grey, smooth river pebbles and turned it over and over in her palm.

'No. I don't like the way he stares, Saffy. Something is not quite right about him. Don't you think? He says all the right things, and behaves in the right way, but it's as if he's made of paper. I feel like I could poke a finger straight through him. Does Ryder like him?'

Saffron fidgeted. 'Not really. He said almost the same thing, though not in such a writerly way.'

They were silent for a while. Leon handed Penelope a stone and she stared at it, transfixed with gratitude, while he wandered a little further away. Amber let the stone she was holding fall back on the shore.

'I can't help it, Saffy. Unless I meet another man like Penrod, I think you are stuck with me. And I don't think I'd make a very good Ethiopian wife.'

Saffy gave a little gurgling laugh. 'No, you'd be hammering away at your typewriter while the stew burned, and spend so long staring at the stars you'd never get up early enough to make breakfast.' She put her hand over her sister's. 'You think of Penrod all the time, don't you?'

Amber stared into the water. 'Yes.'

'But you know, even if you had gone back to Cairo, you couldn't have saved him from the opium, don't you?'

'I know, Saffy. It hurts me, but I know Penrod was the sort of man who needed to make his own path. I suppose, though, I always hoped it would lead back to me. Part of me will never accept he's gone.' Saffy squeezed her fingers and Amber straightened her back. 'Hagos and I will stay up above the orchard. I'll still take care of the gardens and the refugees, and I've started writing again, Saffy. Really writing.'

Saffron sighed lustily. 'That's good, I suppose. You won't get lonely, will you?'

Amber laughed. 'I shall see you every day, my darling. So no, I will not get lonely.'

When Penrod arrived in Massowah, he found the port of the new colony of Eritrea bustling and confident. Italian settlers had begun cultivating the land around Asmara. The port itself was full of new buildings and the streets were thronged with Italian uniforms. He went first to the governor's residence to present his credentials and letters of introduction. One of the latter came from Lucio, and if ever Penrod needed a demonstration of his schoolfriend's power and influence, he found it in the reaction to his signature and seal. Penrod was shown into the presence of General Baratieri, military and civilian governor of the new colony.

The formalities over and his accommodation arranged, Penrod strolled through the streets, watching the people and tasting the mood of the city like a connoisseur tastes wine. The sun cast a silvery brilliance over the whole scene. Arabs bargained noisily with ebony-skinned traders from the interior. Women with tightly braided hair, their wrists and ankles tinkling with delicate silver bangles and bracelets, teased the stallholders and called greetings back and forth in Arabic, Amharic and Italian. White officers walked through the market, their arms threaded through those of local women, and each woman who had an officer on her arm also had a servant running behind her with a brightly coloured fringed parasol. One particular beauty saw him looking at her and raised her delicate eyebrows in inquiry. He gave a microscopic, regretful shake of the head and she returned an equally small shrug with a lazy smile. It was an entire flirtation in the space of ten yards. So the inhabitants, he felt, were ready to take advantage of the new arrivals, and live in a peaceable manner with them, here at least.

Penrod heard his name called, and saw a group of Italian officers sitting under the awning of a nearby café. He joined them and found that one of them, a Captain Toselli, was sharing his digs. As he sat down, the waiter heard him being hailed as an Englishman, and the ragtag orchestra in the interior of the café launched into a brave attempt at the British national anthem.

The officers laughed and with good humour toasted Penrod's queen and country, before explaining that the band performed this courtesy for all new arrivals, though the Italian national anthem was now their speciality.

'So you have met Baratieri?' Toselli asked. He was slightly below medium height and with such thick, black hair and long eyelashes that he looked almost feminine, but he had an energy to him like that of a gun dog.

'I have met him,' Penrod replied. 'Although we exchanged little more than pleasantries.'

Toselli nodded rapidly. 'He is a man of vision. This country has such potential. It will make Italy rich!'

The other men around the table groaned, but Toselli dismissed them with a wave of his hand and only spoke more loudly.

'It has! These fellows are idiots. Ignore them. I tell you, the land here is excellent.' He kissed his fingertips, as if praising a fine dinner. 'The soil of Italy is exhausted, we have farmed it for five thousand years, but here is a place our peasants can come and grow such food, such vines! The wines of Eritrea will be the envy of the world. The French will go and drown themselves in the English Channel in despair!'

That, at least, got a cheer from his fellow officers.

'And the goods that come from the interior! Civet, musk, the best coffee in creation, and it all arrives here so bountiful and cheap. For the price of a cup in Rome, you may buy enough green beans to load a camel.'

Penrod was given a glass and he took it with a nod of thanks and drank. The wine was cheap and rough, but had a sort of earthy honesty to it.

'Toselli,' he said, 'are you by any chance Pietro Toselli? The author of *Pro Africa Italia*?'

The officers cheered and Pietro swept his arms widely, as if to gather in the applause.

'You have read it?'

'I have. My friend Lucio gave it to me. You are a passionate advocate.'

'I am,' Pietro said with great pride. 'And do you have any questions, Major, having read my humble offering?'

'Only one,' Penrod said. 'What do the natives think of your plans?'

Pietro beamed. 'They are delighted we are here! They have grown tired of all their little kings and warlords fighting over their farms. We bring stability, civilisation.'

An older officer, the same rank as Toselli, but twice his age, grunted. Penrod looked sideways at him, wondering if it was incompetence or lack of connections that had stopped him advancing in the military. He was unshaven and his skin and eyes had the unhealthy tinge of the disappointed drunkard.

'You are a fool, Toselli. You only meet recruits who want your one and a half lira a day, market traders, or women who want to pick your pocket,' he said.

'I speak to many, many people, Marco,' Toselli replied with comic indignation, then added over his shoulder to Penrod, 'this is Marco Nazzari, our resident naysayer.'

The older man shook his large head and laid his meaty hands flat on the table. 'I was with Baldesseri when he blundered into Tigray. I tell you, you could feel it. You know when you take a seat on some unbroken horse, some great, beautiful beast, and even if it's standing quiet for you, you can feel it, feel it in your bones that it hates you, that it's only waiting for its chance to throw you to the ground and dash your brains out, if it can? That's what it felt like every day we were on the far side of the Mareb River. Your *askari* are good fellows, but they're from here, near the coast, where traders have been coming and going for a thousand years. Half of them are Muslim and half of them speak Arabic. However, up in the highlands,' he nodded towards the interior, 'they don't want anything we're selling, apart from rifles, and they've bought plenty of those already.'

Penrod decided it was probably Nazzari's tendency to speak his own mind that had slowed his progression through the ranks. But that meant he would likely be an excellent source of information. Penrod made a mental note of his name.

Pietro shrugged elaborately. 'All we have to trouble us in Tigray is Alula, the old bandit, and we've forced a peace with him. I'd say we have to worry about the dervish too, but now we have Major Ballantyne with us, and he can tell us how to defeat them.' He turned away from the older man and stared wide-eyed at Penrod. 'You were at the battle of Abu Klea, were you not? Will you not describe the action?'

Penrod was happy to oblige. The tabletop became a plan of the wadi, and the carafes and glasses became the Desert Column forming a square under sniper fire from dervish salt cellars, until the square was ambushed by a massive force of Mahdist forks.

Penrod described the action well, rattling off quick replies to the questions that came in a flood from the men around the table. By the time he reached his account of the final attack, where the dervish broke into the square before being driven out by the troops in the rear, most of the patrons of the café were listening intently and craning over the shoulders of the men in uniform to watch the final stages of the battle.

Penrod provided a dramatic finish, sweeping the dervish off the table, and the officers and observers cheered and the scratch orchestra broke into an encore of 'God Save the Queen'.

• • •

The following morning, after a very dull dinner at Baratieri's residence, where a woman, wife of a General Albertone, dripping in pearls and ignorance, lectured him extensively about the beautiful simplicity of the African soul, Penrod was awake early and had already breakfasted when Marco Nazzari called on him.

'I am seeing new recruits today,' Nazzari told him. 'I thought it might be interesting for you to see how we manage them. I'd be very grateful for your thoughts.'

Penrod was glad he had stood Nazzari a few drinks the previous evening.

They rode together to a dusty training ground on the edge of Massowah. Perhaps a hundred men and boys, barefoot and dressed in the loose tunics and trousers of the region, were standing in the sun, applying to join one of the native battalions. Penrod was surprised to see so many and said so.

'Oh, we have suffered bad rains in the last year or two, and a cattle plague,' Nazzari said. 'Many of the farmers have lost everything and hope to regain the fortunes of their families by serving us. We let them live with their families and the pay is enough that if they are sober and careful after a year or two with us, they can then afford some land and animals.'

Nazzari strode along the lines of recruits, his back straight and his expression stern, stopping whenever a recruit seemed too young or too old, or too wasted with disease or hunger to be worth the trouble. The men he dismissed did not show their disappointment or attempt to argue, only turned and walked away into their uncertain futures.

Once Nazzari had thinned the field to about half the original number, he nodded to his *askari* sergeant, a bright-eyed man of about Penrod's age wearing the battalion sash over his white tunic and trousers.

The sergeant saluted, spoke a few swift, sharp sentences to the remaining men, then set off out of the camp at a steady jog. The men followed him.

'Where is he taking them?' Penrod asked.

'Sergeant Ariam will lead them up the slopes to the north, then in a wide zigzag back here. He will go as far as he needs to until only some twenty remain. Those will be our recruits for today,' Marco said. He spoke with satisfaction. He might be sceptical about Pietro Toselli's ambitions for the colony, but he was obviously proud of the native soldiers.

'And how far is that?'

'Twenty miles, perhaps, depending on the heat of the day.'

Penrod watched the body of men moving swiftly away along a narrow path into the misted highlands. He felt a twinge of envy. When he had been a captive of Osman Atalan, he had been forced to run alongside his tormentor's horse. What had begun as torture had become a pleasure.

'I almost envy them,' he said.

Nazzari looked at him with a frown, but said nothing.

They discussed questions of training and discipline until Sergeant Ariam led the remaining men back into the parade ground three hours later. Nazzari officially recruited them into the Italian army and sent them to the quartermaster for their uniforms.

Penrod spent the rest of the day making some judicious friendships in the marketplace. The Arab speakers were delighted to hear their language spoken so fluently by a white man and Penrod was sure one or two of them might prove useful as sources of information.

It wasn't until much later that Penrod found his remark about envying the *askari* recruits had spread like wildfire through the whites of the colony. General Albertone's wife had publicly declared she would give her famous pearls to the Englishman if he could keep up with the recruits and repeated her declaration so often, the general was forced to seek out Penrod in the Greek café. The officers leaped to attention. Albertone waved them back into their seats and bowed to Penrod.

'I apologise for my wife's challenge, Major Ballantyne. I'm sure your comment was only an idle one. I shall happily explain to her that the remark was made in jest. We Italians love to boast too.'

The table had grown very quiet. Penrod studied the man with careful interest. He already knew that Albertone was not popular with his officers, and thought that Baratieri did not much appreciate his patrician attitudes either. To cut the general down to size a little, under the guise of a friendly sporting wager, might win Penrod some new friends and encourage others to share their opinions with him more openly. He was sure many of the senior Italian officers would be delighted to see that self-satisfied smile removed from the general's face.

'Not at all. I am delighted to accept the wager,' Penrod said. 'Shall we say tomorrow morning?'

The general stopped smiling, but agreed and left to ironic cheers. Penrod stayed late in the café and spent freely.

The whole of the white population of the town was in attendance when Penrod arrived at the parade ground the next morning, and a large proportion of the natives and traders had come to see the fun also. Penrod was amused to overhear the odds being laid against him in Arabic as he passed through the crowd. Pietro had nominated himself as Penrod's second and strode in front of him, ostentatiously clearing the way for the 'crazy Englishman who wants to die running with the *askari*', as he put it. No wonder the odds being given were not in Penrod's favour. He spotted the owner of the Greek café in the crowd and beckoned him over.

'Friend, place a wager for me.' He pulled out the gold half-hunter Amber had given him and put it in the man's hand. 'Use that as my stake, but take great care of it.'

'You wish me to wager you will live?' the man said, then whistled as he saw the quality of the watch.

'That I will finish among the recruits,' Penrod replied abruptly. 'And remember, not a scratch on it when I return.'

The café owner looked dubious but agreed, and Penrod thanked him before retiring into the barracks to change from his uniform into borrowed knee breeches, a short-sleeved vest and tennis shoes donated by the officers who shared his digs.

He was out on the ground again in time to see Nazzari doing the first winnowing of that day's recruits. He watched for a minute, then frowned and approached.

'Nazzari, what are you doing?'

Nazarri drew his heavy brows together and puffed out his cheeks. 'My duty, Major Ballantyne.'

'No, you are not,' Penrod said simply. 'That last man you sent away is in the prime of life and this fellow –' he nodded to one of the recruits Nazzari had selected for the run – 'must be at least sixty. Captain Nazzari, this is no act of friendship. I insist you select the men who are to run exactly as you would on any other day.'

'Oh, very well,' Nazzari said with a scowl. 'But you will be dead or humiliated by the end of the day if I do.'

Penrod looked behind him at General Albertone and his wife. They looked sleek and confident in the morning light and were standing with Baratieri, who appeared more troubled. No doubt he was worrying about Penrod's fate and what Lucio might have to say about it. He cast occasional irritated looks at Albertone, and Penrod was confident his assessment of the relationship between the two men had been correct.

'Trust me, Nazzari,' he said.

• • •

The runners set out to loud, if rather ironic, cheers, the recruits and Sergeant Ariam going barefoot as usual. Most of the potential new recruits seemed more amused by Penrod's company than anything else; white men, in their experience, did not run. One young man with thickly muscled legs, who ran with an angry hunch, tried to barge him as the path narrowed on the first gradual climb. Penrod sidestepped him, then half a mile later caught the man on a corner, shouldering him into an awkward stumble. He dropped out soon afterwards and the other recruits paid Penrod no further attention, concentrating on their own endurance.

For the first three miles, climbing steadily from the dry plain around the port and into the hills, Penrod's muscles began to ache. It did not concern him overmuch. He was used to pain and trusted that it would soon fade as his body began to understand what he needed from it. He was right. After another twenty minutes the cramps and soreness passed and he began to enjoy himself. He lifted his head and drew the air steadily into his lungs, letting his chest expand. Two or three more of the potential recruits had already given up, but the rest seemed to be quite comfortable. Sergeant Ariam looked behind him and obviously came to the same conclusion, for he increased his pace. Penrod remembered what it was to run like this and he relaxed even as he picked up speed. The breathing of the man next to him became ragged and gasping. As the path turned, Penrod glanced back towards the parade ground. They had perhaps gone six miles now, curving higher in slow arcs. The port lay far below them, a scattering of stone next to the jewel brightness of the Red Sea. The sergeant took a narrow path heading north, and for a while Penrod had to watch the ground in front of him to avoid missing his footing.

'*Effendi, effendi* . . .' One of the other runners was calling to him. 'You speak the language of the Prophet, peace be upon him, is that so?'

'I do,' Penrod said.

'What do they call you in our language?'

'He who never turns back.'

The man laughed richly and translated the name into Amharic for the other runners nearby. The pack had thinned. Some hundred yards behind them a group of stragglers were slowing to a despairing walk. It was an excellent way to discover which of the men were suited to long marches, Penrod thought, looking to his right and left. The men running with him now possessed the endurance and steady fortitude that were the attributes of an ideal soldier. He wondered how his desert warriors would take to the idea of running in this way. Not well, he thought. They were horsemen, riders. To run like this would be a humiliation. Penrod felt a sudden rush of pleasure. They were wrong. He felt a purity and purpose in the exercise and he revelled in it.

• • •

At twelve miles the route took them on a slow curve back towards the port. The sergeant had kept up a punishing pace, but Penrod's breathing was still deep and regular. He shook out his arms and stretched out his shoulders. By now only a few more than thirty runners remained, and several of them were struggling. Penrod felt a dream-like calm. He thought of Agatha and Amber, of Farouk and his books of Rumi's and Dante's poetry. He let favourite verses drift through his head and his body found the rhythm of the lines.

The sergeant glanced over his shoulder and nodded to himself. Penrod came out of his daze and saw he had already won his bet for only twenty recruits were left. Now the sergeant had done his duty and whittled down the pack to the proper number, he had no need to push these men to exhaustion. He slowed a little and Penrod felt a stab of disappointment. The parade ground was in sight. The man who had spoken to him in Arabic was still beside him. He was looking a little grey, but was facing this last mile or two with dogged determination.

'Translate for me,' Penrod said. 'I want to speak to the sergeant, but I do not speak Tigre.' He was pleased to know he had breath enough for the words.

'I can speak Arabic also, sir,' Sergeant Ariam replied, dropping back a little to run at Penrod's side. Penrod's friend looked glad he could keep his own breath for his running.

'These men have all succeeded, yes?' Penrod said, snatching his words as he exhaled. 'Whatever happens, you will take them into the native battalion?'

'We shall.'

'Then can I make all of you men an offer? I want a race. I'll pay ten lire to anyone who gives me one, and a hundred lire to anyone who beats me. If the sergeant agrees.'

The sergeant's eyes glittered. 'Agreed!'

He translated into Tigre for the rest of the squad and they gave a ragged cheer. They had about a mile to go. Immediately they surged forward, each man finding unsuspected reserves of energy in his limbs.

Penrod lifted his head and kicked out his legs, making his strides longer and faster. After a hundred yards he, the sergeant and one other had separated from the rest. Penrod swung his arms. The path between here and the parade ground was flat and wide; their feet kicked up explosions of dust from the earth.

Penrod felt his lungs beginning to ache. A suspicion flitted across his mind.

'Ariam, anything less than your best . . .' he sucked in a lungful of hot, salted air, 'and I'll beat you bloody with my own hands.'

The sergeant put his head down and began to drive, hard.

Penrod could hear the cheers of the crowd now, cries of amazement and whistles. He lifted his head high, so his lungs could suck all the air they were able to, and his heart drummed an impossible rhythm in his chest. The pain shot through his entire body with renewed force. He knew his feet were bleeding, and his body was starved of oxygen. Every fibre of his being screamed at him for cessation, but he took a contrary pleasure in overruling his heart and lungs. It was just the sergeant and him now. He would breathe later.

Ahead of him he saw Marco Nazzari and Pietro Toselli. Once they had seen what was happening, they had found a length of ribbon from somewhere and stretched it out across the entrance to the parade ground. The crowd was on its feet, yelling out in a dozen languages. The sergeant started to pull slightly ahead, but Penrod had a crucial advantage. Forced to run over the desert sands, lashed to the halter of Osman Atalan's stallion with his wrists bound and bloody, he knew exactly what his body could endure and survive. He threw himself on, ignoring his shrieking muscles and his bursting heart, and thrust his chest forward, reaching the ribbon a fraction of a second before the sergeant. He slowed to a jog and took long, even breaths.

The crowd poured forward to congratulate him. He felt Pietro thumping him between his shoulder blades and his right hand being pumped by innumerable strangers. He wiped the sweat out of his eyes and offered his hand to the sergeant, before they were separated by the throng of his admirers. Penrod allowed himself to be lifted onto the shoulders of some of the officers and carried to the centre of the parade ground, where Signora Albertone was waiting with her husband and General Baratieri. She held a velvet case under her arm and looked miserable. Baratieri was grinning from ear to ear.

Once the officers had deposited Penrod in front of them, Baratieri held up his hands to quieten the crowd.

'The contest has been completed, and as Governor of Eritrea, it gives me great pleasure to announce that our English guest, Major Ballantyne, has won, and won convincingly! As a mark of his singular success, I am pleased to award him the rank of Honorary Major in our Native Eighth Battalion!'

The parade ground rang with laughter and applause, and Penrod made a low bow to the company.

'But,' Baratieri said loudly, raising his finger for silence again, 'although the contest has been completed, the wager has not! Signora Albertone, you made a wager, the wager was witnessed and the wager was lost.'

The signora looked sick, and Penrod felt a flicker of compassion. She opened the case and Penrod and the crowd stared at the thick rope of pearls. It was worth a thousand pounds at the very least.

General Albertone looked almost as ill as his wife. The signora put the case in Penrod's hands and he took it with a quiet thank you, then turned around slowly, holding it above his head to whoops and cheers, making his decision as he did. He could gain another advantage here. He turned back to General Albertone and his wife, then returned the case to her.

'I have no wish to take so fine an ornament from so fair a daughter of Italy,' he said loudly and clearly.

For a moment she did not understand him and looked in confusion at her husband. Then, with eyes cast down, she took back the case. The cheers became ecstatic.

'I am in your debt,' General Albertone said quietly.

'You are,' Penrod replied as quietly, 'and I always collect my debts in the end, General.'

Penrod was lifted onto the shoulders of the other officers again and carried with much song and laughter all the way to the Greek café. In vain, he protested he wanted a bath. It was not allowed. They were determined to toast his victory first.

'God Save the Queen' was sung with enthusiasm and variable accuracy at twice the usual volume, and Penrod found that the owner's store of champagne had been raided and dispensed in his honour. It was not Krug, but it was certainly refreshing after his run. When the first flush of celebration was done, the owner approached and handed Penrod his watch, along with a thick leather pouch.

Penrod opened it and raised his eyebrows. 'This is a great deal more than I expected.'

The Greek tapped the side of his nose. 'Ahh, when I saw you in that last half mile, I could not help myself: I bet double or quits you would win.'

When Penrod had staked his watch on his success, he had been perfectly confident – he knew that he would be able to keep up with the recruits – but the idea he might have lost it in that final race made his blood freeze momentarily in his veins. It did not matter how long it had been since he had laid eyes on Amber Benbrook; as long as he held the watch he felt as if some tie still existed that bound them together, a bond that neither time nor distance could destroy. The watch was somehow a witness to him becoming a better man. The idea he could have lost it thanks to the good-natured bravado of the café owner made the world spin sickly for a second. No sign of this appeared on Penrod's face. He looked into the beaming visage of the Greek, then lifted his champagne glass and toasted him heartily.

Amber developed a routine. Early each morning she would visit the refugee camp, and soon the inmates grew accustomed to the sight of Amber and Hagos walking down the slope towards them just as the fires were being lit for the morning meal. Amber had stolen some of the canvas they had bought in Addis to make a halter for Hagos – a careful construction with adjustable straps to allow for her rapid growth. The lioness hated it, but she hated letting Amber out of her sight even more and so she submitted. Some hundred yards from the edge of the camp, Hagos would allow the halter to be fitted over her muscular shoulders, affecting a weary disdain for the process, and permit herself to be tethered to a nearby tree trunk. She managed to convey the impression she had been planning to stop here anyway.

Amber then joined Marta and Tadesse, and spent an hour or two talking to the refugees about their homes, their recovery and their plans for the future. She checked supplies, made notes and gave instructions, then returned to Hagos and took the lioness hunting with her, north and west of the camp where she knew she had a good chance of finding game, but with no risk of stumbling on people. Not that Hagos would have hurt them; she was used to human company and did not see them as food. Occasionally a new arrival at the refugee camp would panic and protest at the sight of a grown lioness taking her ease so nearby, but one of the older residents would explain and point out both the halter and the fact that the eccentric *ferengi* who kept the animal as a pet was the one who was busy saving their lives and the lives of their children.

Stories of Amber spread across Tigray as refugees found the strength to move on. She was fast becoming the new and exotic patron saint of the hungry and dispossessed. They called her the lion lady. She built Hagos a playground of ropes and log swings in the clearing by the cabin and watched her for hours, instinctively stalking the swinging shadows, pouncing on them with a shake of her hindquarters and sharpening her claws on the bark of the trees. Amber paid for local farmers to bring her goats to feed the growing lioness, but made sure they were slaughtered and prepared in the camp, so Hagos never learned to associate the penned and bleating animals with the excellent meat provided for her dinner. Amber wanted to be sure Hagos never thought of goats and cattle as prey. The lioness needed to accept animals came in two sorts: the humans and beasts of the camp among whom she lived peaceably, and then the game she and Amber brought down on their hunts. Eventually Amber changed her strategy: if Hagos failed to stalk and kill an animal on the hunt, she got no food in the evening, and Amber, careful not to provoke her with cooking smells, did not eat either. When her hunt was successful, they dined together. It took some time, and some hungry days when Amber kept well away from the camp, but in the end, it worked.

· · ·

Late one morning, when Hagos was almost full-grown, Amber and the lioness were relaxing in their own fashions after a successful hunt. Hagos buried her face into the torn belly of the antelope and began to eat with a satisfied purr.

'You have horrible table manners,' Amber said as she watched the lioness rip into her kill, her muzzle already red with blood. Hagos ignored her.

Amber drank from her canteen, then stretched out her legs and leaned on her elbows to enjoy the sun. Something caught her eye. A flash of reflected light to the west. She wondered if it was Bill again, searching for more exotic birds, and felt a familiar shiver of dislike. She suspected he was following her on her hunting trips with Hagos, but when she had mentioned seeing him, Saffron had told her he shared a passion for the local flora and fauna with Ryder, and now that work on the second seam was proceeding smoothly, he had begun to wander further afield in search of new animals and plants. Yes, there he was in a patch of withered thorn bushes, pale skeletons of themselves among the knee-high grass. She wondered again if he had come out looking for her, and hoped he had missed seeing Hagos and the kill. Perhaps he would move on before she had to acknowledge his presence.

She slid back further on her elbows so the tall pale grass would shield her, still looking in his direction and willing him to leave. Then she realised he was talking to someone. A man was with him in the copse of thorns, an Abyssinian, but not a man Amber recognised. She squinted, trying to see more clearly as a breeze stirred the stalks around her. The Abyssinian wore a rather dirty *shamma* edged with green and carried a rifle over his shoulders. After a few minutes of conversation, he bowed and moved away. Bill remained where he was for a while, then left also, walking in the other direction with easy, confident strides.

• • •

When Amber and Hagos returned to her camp at the top of the cliff later that afternoon, they found Tadesse waiting for them. He was sitting cross-legged in the shade, but as he heard them approach he stood up and stepped into the sunlight.

He visited Amber several times a week to discuss the arrangements for the refugees and offer her his tally of deaths and survivals, arrivals and departures. Hagos padded across to the tent, took up her usual position outside it by Amber's chair and began to groom herself with her long, curling tongue. Amber and Tadesse exchanged greetings and Amber invited the young man to take a seat beside her. He did so cautiously, keeping an eye on Hagos. The lioness paused to watch him sit, then blinked her yellow eyes and returned to her grooming.

Three orphans were currently in the camp: two girls and a boy for whom they needed to find foster parents. Some family or another nearby always wanted an extra boy to work in the fields and tend the animals, but girls were more difficult. It was a case of finding a family that would be glad to have an extra pair of hands in the home, but would not treat the child as a slave. One of the girls provided a particularly difficult problem. She had a squint, and had said nothing since she arrived in the camp. Amber was inclined to think that she was still too stunned with the horrors of her journey to talk, but she was gaining the reputation of an idiot.

'Someone will help her. I'm sure with kindness she will recover.'

'Perhaps, Miss Amber.' He rested his head in his hands and sighed. 'For now, no one is taking care of her. I am afraid she will be taken by bandits if we do not find her a place of safety soon.'

'Bandits?' Amber said. The tone of her voice disturbed Hagos, who lifted her head and made a low warning sound in her throat. Tadesse said nothing, until Amber had leaned down and stroked the lioness's head with her knuckles and scratched her muzzle. Hagos huffed approvingly.

'I have heard stories in the camp,' Tadesse said. '*Shifta* between here and Axum taking children from the parties coming here for help. They will make the boys fight, I suppose, and the girls will be their slaves.'

'Why have I not heard of this?' Amber said, but she spoke calmly, not wanting Hagos to grow agitated again.

'The people are afraid. They do not want to be blamed for not defending the children,' he replied with a sad smile.

'I would not blame them. They hardly have the strength to reach us. How could they fight off bandits? But do you think they are in danger even in the camp?'

'They are coming closer, and the camp is getting larger. I think we should move the supplies down the escarpment. No bandit would dare attack Courtney Camp itself, and we might move the families with children into the centre of the rest.' He clicked his tongue against the roof of his mouth. 'But I fear they will not all move. They want their privacy, even here.'

'Do what you can, Tadesse,' Amber said.

. . .

The following morning Amber arrived at the camp at her usual time, slipped Hagos's halter on and went down to join the others. She had meant to talk to Tadesse about the orphan girl with the squint, but soon got caught up in the latest tragedies and victories of the refugees. A new family had arrived just after dawn. The two elder children looked strong, but the mother and her youngest were both struggling to breathe. Amber arranged for someone to help the older children and left the father keeping vigil over his wife and the baby. He watched with such intensity, refusing all attempts to make him rest. He fed his wife by hand and – it seemed to Amber – was spending every last ounce of his remaining strength in willing them to live.

The sight made her feel rather hollow and alone, and it wasn't until she had rejoined Hagos and walked half a mile from the camp that she remembered the orphan.

'Damn,' she said aloud and stopped. Hagos turned her beautiful head towards her mistress and twitched the black tuft of her tail as Amber turned around to retrace her steps.

'Please, Hagos?' she said. The lioness shook her head and sneezed, then followed. When Amber re-tethered her, she crouched down in the dust and Hagos, in a forgiving mood, put her great paws on Amber's shoulders and pushed her head into Amber's chest. Amber lost her balance and fell back under the lioness's weight. She laughed, scratching the lion's neck and pulling at her muzzle. Knowing that she had been forgiven for delaying the hunt, she scrambled upright and was just about to head off in search of Tadesse when she noticed they were not alone. The orphan girl herself was standing a little way off, biting the side of her thumb and swinging from side to side as she watched Amber and Hagos at play.

'Do not touch the lion,' Amber said to her.

The girl looked at her as if she thought she was quite mad, which, Amber had to admit, was probably fair. She was wondering if she should say more when she heard the crack of a rifle shot below her. She looked down into the camp. Some sort of confrontation was going on at the edge of the flat ground at the bottom of the slope nearest to her. Three men, all strangers and all armed. Two were holding refugee children by their wrists and pulling them away. The third was still holding his rifle, and Amber could see a man sprawled out on the grass. One of the children was reaching for him and shouting, 'Papa, Papa!'

'Stay here!' Amber shouted to the little girl, and ran down the slope.

Some of the refugees were taking flight, gathering up their children and fleeing the armed men, but others were rushing over from the kitchen tent to help.

The men had not expected an attack from this direction.

Amber grabbed on to one of the children, a little girl, and wrenched her from the grip of the bandit holding her, her outrage and his surprise giving her a sudden, brief advantage.

'How dare you!' she screamed.

The rifleman shifted his grip and swung upwards with the butt of his gun, catching Amber on the jaw and sending her flying backwards. She landed heavily next to the boy's murdered father. She saw his eyes, empty and lifeless, staring into hers and seeing nothing. The other man tried to grab the girl again, but she was too quick for him, racing full pelt towards her weeping mother.

The rifleman was reloading. Amber tried to get up but the blow had stunned her and she was too slow. She saw his face as he raised his gun; she saw the green border on his *shamma*.

'No!' It was Bill's voice.

The bandit hesitated, then his eyes hardened and Amber saw his finger squeezing the trigger. She tried to scramble backwards, but her hands slipped in the blood of the murdered man. All she could hear was the sound of weeping, Tadesse shouting and the hysterical shouts of the little boy still held captive.

Then she saw Hagos. The lioness was bounding towards them in great fluid leaps. The bandit with the boy shouted out a warning and the gunman turned. Hagos leaped into the air as he fired, but his shot went wide. Hagos twisted her head mid-air and went straight for his throat, her huge white teeth clamping into his neck. He screamed and tried to reach for her eyes as she snarled and shook him. When she released him, a fountain of blood erupted from the wound in his neck. Then she reared back, growling deep in her throat, and with a swipe of her paw sliced open his belly.

His two followers turned and ran, leaving the boy to fall weeping at his father's side. His mother swooped down and picked him up. He kicked and shouted, but she would not let him go again, carrying him with grim determination away from the blood and the lion.

Hagos's victim was still screaming, a gurgling, choking cry. Hagos grunted, then bent her great head and tore out his throat. The body went limp and Hagos dragged it a short distance away.

Tadesse and Bill had reached Amber now, but when they put out their hands for her, Hagos looked up from the corpse and roared. Tadesse took Bill by the arm and pulled him away.

'Don't touch me,' he said, shaking him off, but he did not try to approach again.

Hagos paced around the corpse, her tail thrashing and her ears back, uttering a constant low growl that seemed to make the ground shiver.

Amber began talking to her, softly and soothingly. The refugees, Bill and the rest were still watching her from a careful distance.

'Don't stare at her,' Amber said, loudly enough for them to hear, but still in a light singsong voice. 'Please move away, but don't turn your backs.'

The growls grew softer and Hagos's tail stopped whipping so fast, although it kept up a regular twitch.

Amber glanced to her right. The orphan girl was still standing high on the slope, not far from where Amber had left her, still biting the side of her thumb, but in her other hand she was holding Hagos's tether loosely at her side. Amber realised that she had freed the lioness to allow her to attack the bandit and save them from his clutches.

The lioness stopped pacing and padded across to Amber. She had to steel herself to reach out her hand. It was as if the earth and sky were holding their breath.

'Hello, my darling,' Amber said. 'Hello, you beautiful beast.'

The great cat huffed and pushed her bloodstained jaws against Amber's hand, then sat down heavily beside her and rested her chin on Amber's lap.

'Tadesse,' Amber said. 'I think you can come and get the bodies now.'

• • •

They buried the bandit and the man he had killed that afternoon, and the orphan girl was adopted by the widowed mother. Amber was concerned at first – it seemed foolish for the woman to take on another mouth to feed when she had lost her husband – but she insisted. The little girl had proven she was clever and brave, the widow said; she had saved her son and avenged her murdered husband while his blood was still warm. Reluctantly Amber acquiesced.

As the priest read the prayer for the dead, Amber remained at the back of the crowd. Hagos was safely tethered at a distance, but the lioness was still unsettled, and Amber wanted to make sure they did not lose sight of each other.

Bill found his way to Amber's side. She ignored him at first, but when he had bent forward to whisper his delight that she was safe, she moved away from him.

'You knew the bandit,' she said.

He blinked and shook his head slowly.

'I saw you,' she insisted, 'talking to him only yesterday while I was out hunting with Hagos.'

Ryder must have caught sight of them for he was suddenly at her shoulder. Bill leaned away from them both slightly on his heels and Amber felt immediately safer.

'What's this?' Ryder said.

Amber shifted a little closer to him. 'Bill was talking to the bandit yesterday,' she said simply. 'I saw him.'

'Well?' Ryder said to Bill.

Bill made a little humming noise and studied the sky above Ryder's head.

'I did meet a young man yesterday while I was out walking. He said he was on a pilgrimage, searching for one of the mountain churches south of here. I told him the way to the road. Was that the same man who attacked the camp? How terrible! I'm afraid I can't tell them apart yet.'

'Why would a pilgrim have a rifle?' Ryder asked sharply.

'To shoot game, perhaps?' Bill replied, blinking. 'I am sorry. Of course I shall mention it if anything similar occurs.'

Amber glanced at Ryder. He looked faintly disgusted, but not suspicious.

'I'm surprised you could manage to give him directions, your Amharic is so bad. Geriel needs you on the second seam. You can recognise him, can't you?' Ryder said.

Bill gave another blank smile and left. Ryder put his hand on Amber's shoulder and she sighed. They waited until the priest had finished his prayers, then Ryder walked with her back to Hagos. The lioness sat up on her haunches as they approached and gave a wide yawn. Ryder reached down and scratched her muzzle. Hagos lifted a heavy paw and placed it on his wrist while she pushed her muzzle into his palm. Ryder was the only other person in the camp that Hagos would allow to touch her and he had, reluctantly, grown fond of her.

'Flirt,' Amber said and the lioness sneezed. Then she untied the tether and the three of them walked slowly back to Amber's camp. After they had walked in silence a little way, Amber spoke quietly. 'She did not eat him, Ryder.'

He laughed. 'Did you think I was going to say we should kill her? No, she was defending you – we all know that. I was going to tell you that I've asked Ato Gebre to cast a bell. It will serve as an alarm if anyone makes another attempt against the refugees and I will set half a dozen men to guard the camp, night and day.'

'Thank you,' she answered softly.

'Though I don't think the bandits will attack again when this story about Hagos becomes common knowledge,' he added.

When they reached Amber's tent, she and Ryder sat together, while Hagos dropped at their feet and huffed contentedly. Ryder noticed Amber's typewriter on the camp table and the thick pile of typewritten pages next to it, held down with a rock to save it from the mischievous breezes of the highlands.

'How is her training going?' Ryder asked.

'Very well,' Amber said, with a sudden, dazzling smile. 'She has stopped chasing game as if it is nothing but play, and is learning to wait until the game comes to her. It is fascinating to watch. I was just writing about it this morning, before—'

'The time is coming when you must release her, Amber.'

She touched her stack of typewritten pages and her shoulders slumped a little.

'I realise that. But I shall not release her, Ryder,' she said. Then she caught his look of disapproval. 'No, I don't mean to keep her either. I think she will choose when to leave. I suspect it will not be long before she decides it is time for her to find a mate. I will simply wake up one morning and she will be gone.'

'And when that time comes, will you return to camp?'

'Yes, of course.'

She spoke briskly, but Ryder knew it would not be easy for her. She had grown independent up here; to be folded back into the domestic life below would be a challenge.

'I have come to ask you if you would like me to dismiss Bill before you return. I know his attentions make you uncomfortable. And do you honestly suspect him of having something to do with the attack this morning?'

'That is kind,' she said slowly. She thought about the way he had said 'no' to the gunman, as if it were an order. 'But what would he get from working with *shifta*? It's much more likely the man was scouting the area and pretended to be a pilgrim when he met Bill, just as he said.' She threw back her head, letting the last of the day's sun fall over her like a blessing. 'I don't know what to say, Ryder. I don't trust Bill and I hate the way he stares at me sometimes . . . But he is useful to you, isn't he?'

'Yes,' Ryder said simply. 'I would never have been able to keep up with Menelik's conditions this long without him, but I do not like him much either, so would be happy to give him his marching orders if that would please you, al-Zahra.'

Amber folded her arms. 'It is strange. You and Patch, you give your orders, but you are never above doing the work yourselves. I've seen you both swinging pickaxes a thousand times. But Bill never does that.'

'He certainly has soft hands for an engineer,' Ryder agreed. 'He knows his work, though, and the orders he gives are good ones.'

'Thank you, Ryder, for the offer, but when Hagos leaves I shall return to camp, and Bill may stare all he likes. I have you to protect me. You will not lose the mine because of me.'

The corner of his mouth twitched in a smile. 'We would never have kept it this long without you.'

'Thank you, Ryder.'

'Very well,' he said, clearing his throat. 'And another thing: can you manage without Tadesse for a week or two? I want to send him to Addis with this quarter's load of silver.'

'I can. Have you forgiven him for acting as Ras Alula's spy, Ryder?'

He stretched out his legs and sighed. 'I have accepted it. And every time we make use of Rusty's notebook, I remember it is only because of Tadesse's quick thinking that it was not destroyed, even if he did keep it from us for a while.' He rubbed his chin. Since Tadesse had been exposed as Ras Alula's man, the flow of information had at least run in two directions. 'He tells me Ras Alula has decided to submit to Menelik. I have no doubt he will be welcomed as a prodigal in Addis. Forgiveness, though, is a difficult thing. Have you heard a certain holy man has taken up residence in the hills between here and Adowa?'

Amber blushed. 'Ah, yes. That is Dan. Will you ever forgive me for releasing him, Ryder?'

'Him I will never forgive. You, al-Zahra, were forgiven long ago. I thank you for not ordering me to run Bill Peters out of the camp.'

He raised his hand in farewell and left her smiling. The idea of anyone ordering Ryder to do anything was ridiculous. She reached out and scratched the lioness's ear, eliciting a growling purr.

Hagos left her three months later. For a week she had absented herself for longer and longer periods during the day, returning to walk in circles around Amber's camp in the evening, as if she could not make up her mind what to do. Then one morning Hagos was gone when Amber woke and she knew it was for good. She moved back into the camp with Saffron and Ryder that afternoon.

Word that Ras Mengesha and Ras Alula had gone to pay homage to Menelik in Addis reached Penrod and the Italian colonial officers in November 1894. General Arimondi, Commander of the Second Operational Corps, rolled his eyes at the news, saying it was impossible to keep up with the shifting alliances of the Ethiopian princes, and predicted Mengesha would be back and asking for favours before the end of the year. Penrod's network of informers among the traders and his friends among the *askari* saw things differently. Mengesha and Alula had carried heavy stones on their shoulders as they approached the emperor. It was a formal, sacred act of submission not to be confused with more informal alliances of the past.

Penrod sent a report to Cairo detailing what he had learned and travelled to Asmara the following day to take stock of the situation. He spent some time with Captain Nazzari, observing the native battalion drills and suggesting some improvements to their bayonet training, which Nazzari approved.

'The more of that sort of work we do the better,' he said gruffly. 'The brass want all of Tigray to add to their colony. Too greedy. We don't have the men to hold it.'

Penrod was returning from the training ground when he found himself summoned to Major Toselli's office. Pietro was holding a telegram.

'From Baratieri,' he said, waving it in the air with an elegant flourish. 'The telegraph lines to Saganeiti have failed and the old man is nervous. You've managed to convince him rebellion is imminent.'

'It's a possibility,' Penrod said. 'Though I did not think Batha Agos would be the one to cause trouble.'

Batha Agos was the Abyssinian ruler of the area around Saganeiti, very much a client of the Italians, and no friend of Alula or Mengesha. Penrod examined the map of Eritrea and Tigray pinned to the wall of Toselli's office. It was spotted with pins showing the positions of Italian troops and allies, forts and defensible towns. It was impossible not to notice the vast distances between them.

'No hint of trouble from your man in the town?' Penrod asked.

'None.' Pietro shrugged expansively. 'I think he was planning to invite Batha to dinner this week. Still, we shall go and see for ourselves, but under cover of a route march. How quickly do you think we can manage it? It is some fifty miles, perhaps.'

'I shall get ready,' Penrod said.

• • •

They were within twelve miles of the town when word reached them that Batha Agos had taken the Italian resident, a Lieutenant Sanguineti, as a hostage. Pietro at once began to negotiate for the man's release while planning a dawn attack.

'Let me go down and take a look,' Penrod said as they stood together on high ground just outside the town, scanning the haphazard sprawl of low buildings. Toselli looked at him as if he were mad, but when Penrod presented himself in the guise of an Arab trader an hour later, he gave his consent.

Penrod walked into town alone late in the evening, his revolver hidden in the folds of his *galabiyya* and a rough pack of borrowed trade goods on his back. The town was very quiet. Occasional lights of cooking fires could be made out inside some of the houses, but he saw no groups of armed men. Penrod became convinced that Batha had already fled. He had not the skill or cunning to conceal a fighting force so effectively. When Penrod found the house of the Italian lieutenant, the only stone building off the deserted marketplace, he found it unguarded and simply walked in. He expected to find Sanguineti dead, but the young man was in his empty dining chamber, gagged and tied to a chair.

Penrod released him and put an end to his spluttered gratitude with a swift order to be quiet. Then he guided him back through the dark and silent streets, arriving at the Italian camp just as dawn was breaking and Pietro was giving his junior officers their orders.

Pietro stared, then burst into fits of laughter. 'Who needs fifteen hundred men when you have Penrod Ballantyne?' he said to the room at large.

The officers around the camp table joined in the laughter, then quietened as Pietro put one polished boot on his camp stool and quietly asked for the lieutenant's report. Penrod listened too, leaning against one of the tent poles with his arms crossed.

'I asked Batha why he had turned against us, for Italy is a great power,' the man stuttered. 'He said Ethiopia is greater, and though one may recover from the bite of the black snake, the bite of the white snake is always fatal.'

'A child's riddle!' one of the Italian officers, fresh off the boat from Naples, said loudly.

Pietro looked at Penrod. 'What do you think, Ballantyne?'

'Batha goes where the wind blows. And he seems to think it is blowing in Menelik's direction. Where might he strike? Where could he attempt to win some easy victory against Italian forces?'

Pietro's face darkened. 'But we have complete control of the region.' Nevertheless he stared hard at the maps laid out across the table in front of him. 'Halai. It is a small fort to the north with only one company under Captain Castellazzi. It is vulnerable.'

'Surely Batha will just run away into the hills?' said a junior officer rather plaintively.

'I shall not risk another slaughter there,' Pietro said. 'We march for Halai in an hour.'

• • •

When Penrod wrote his next report from Adrigat, the officers were dizzy with twin successes against Batha's men at Halai in December and Mengesha's forces at Coatit the following month, ignoring the fact both leaders had managed to escape the Italians with most of their forces intact.

Baratieri acted as if Tigray had already been added to the colony of Eritrea and sent a rather pompous document to the government in Rome demanding the funds and personnel necessary to occupy and settle the land. Lucio wrote discreetly to Penrod asking his opinion and Penrod replied that the campaign had resembled a man striking his sword through the water and declaring himself king of the sea. Baratieri was summoned to Italy to consult in person, and, according to the few newspapers that reached Adrigat, was treated as a conquering hero. Penrod received glowing praise for his reports from London and Cairo, and was told to advise or assist the Italians as he saw fit. Penrod was glad to be keeping his own government informed while being of use to his Italian friends, though he felt their successes in the field were tempting them to act with a dangerous lack of caution. The forward movement of the Italian troops was also drawing him nearer to Courtney Mine. He could feel the proximity of Amber Benbrook like an electric charge in the air.

'It is no good, my friend. You must either go, or go mad. And if you go mad, then your friend Lucio will blame me. And you know how important he is these days, always standing close to the king, we are told. So go.'

Pietro and Penrod were playing cards together at company headquarters, confined by the thundering afternoon rains. Penrod gathered the cards and began to shuffle them, enjoying the ripple of colours as he turned, split and reformed the pack.

'I have no idea what you mean.'

Pietro leaned back and crossed his legs, watching how Penrod handled the cards with pleasure.

'You do. You are my friend, but you are also the officer of a foreign power. Did you really think I would not take steps to find out a little about you before we got so friendly? You know as well as I do that your former fiancée, the acclaimed Miss Amber Benbrook, is living somewhere in the hills to the west of here. I see you looking in that direction as if she might appear at any moment. I see how you look through the crowds at the market in case she has come into town for supplies. You probably also know that she killed a lioness and brought up its cub, before releasing it back into the wild, and that she is regarded as something of a saint for the help she has given to the starving of the region during the poor harvests of recent years. Also that her brother-in-law is now on the verge of becoming as rich as a king from his silver mine, but still lives in a wooden hut.'

Penrod spoke very quietly. 'My relationship with Miss Benbrook is ancient history.'

He began to deal quickly, spinning the cards across the table with a sharp flick.

Pietro raised his eyebrows. 'Yet you still carry the watch she gave you.'

Penrod paused with his deal and looked up.

'I looked at the engraving one day while you were training with the company,' Pietro admitted. 'Perhaps I should be an intelligence officer.'

Penrod said nothing. Pietro had the good sense not to pursue the subject further, and soon found it required all his concentration not to lose his entire pay to his English friend.

• • •

Penrod woke the next morning with a sudden craving for the pipe. It came with such force it seemed to drive the air from his body. Pietro was right. He needed to see Amber. He wanted to know if she still hated him, or if time had worn down her rage. If she was still beautiful. He asked himself if he would fall on his knees in front of her and beg her forgiveness. No. Forgiveness had to be earned and freely given, not wrung out of someone with tears. He would willingly acknowledge the wrong he had done, seducing her sister and concealing the fact, then he would walk away. He dressed with particular care and then, leaving a message for Nazzari that he had gone hunting and might spend the night camping in the hills, set out with a servant towards Courtney Camp.

The rains had turned the highlands into a series of pleasant pastures littered with purple and white flowers, and the thin air was gently perfumed with their scent. Penrod's Amharic was enough to greet the farmers passing along the tracks, and they gave him directions for Courtney Camp that set him along the right path.

When he thought himself within a reasonable striking distance, he left his horse and told his servant to make camp for the night, then he walked the final mile or two along steadily rising ground until he found himself looking down into a wide valley. The distant sounds of the mine drifted up towards him, but from where he stood he could see only the family houses grouped around a church. He saw gardens and orchards thick with blossom, and on the hills above were ploughed fields already pushing forth new growth.

He lifted his field glasses and swept them around in a slow arc, spotting another camp to the south, though it seemed sparsely occupied. No doubt that was where Amber had been caring for those driven from their land by hunger and disease.

A flash of gold caught his eye and he looked down into the camp. It was her. He knew it without needing to lift the glasses to his eyes. He watched her slim figure as she crossed the open square in front of the church and joined a woman, a native woman, who was grinding grain outside one of the huts. They were talking, laughing, it seemed. Amber turned and looked towards the river and Penrod lifted the glasses. Her face was in front of him again. He had seen it every day since they had parted, but in that image she had never aged, she had remained a child of sixteen. He had wondered how she would look now, but he had never expected this. She was more beautiful than he could have imagined. A young woman, confident and graceful, laughing easily with a friend. A man was coming towards her, a white man in a wide-brimmed slouch hat, but it was certainly not Ryder. Penrod would know his bull-like frame from any distance. This was a man more of his own build. She smiled at the stranger and Penrod felt his heart tighten like a fist. A sudden glimmer of light raced across the earth towards her. A child, a girl with Amber's thick blonde hair. She bent down and swept the infant up in her arms, spinning her around, and even from this distance Penrod thought he could hear the girl's delighted laughter.

Penrod lowered the glasses and walked back down the slope into the shade of a low sycamore. She had a child. Of course she had married and he was glad that she had done so. She deserved to be happy and he would not disturb her happiness with his presence. He had no claim on her and would never make one. He wished her only well. He examined his feelings and made his decision. If he ever saw another man touch her, he would kill him stone dead. Nothing he had gone through in the years since they had last met could change that, not even his wish that she be happy. So he must stay away.

He heard a metallic click and froze, listening.

'Hold, and state your business.'

He recognised the voice. He lifted his hands to shoulder level, then turned around.

'Courtney. A pleasure, as always.'

Ryder emerged from the high grass, pausing to gaze at Penrod for a long moment, then slinging his rifle over his shoulder as he approached. He hadn't changed a great deal, Penrod noticed. His muscle had not run to fat; if anything he seemed stronger than he had in Cairo. His skin was burned to a permanent bronze and his thick, unruly hair was still black as pitch.

'Ballantyne. We were told you were dead.'

'You were misinformed.'

Ryder was only a yard away from him now, and Penrod felt himself being closely observed. Let Courtney look. Penrod had a few more lines about his eyes, but other than that he was content he would pass muster. His blond hair and thick moustache showed no signs of grey. His riding boots were polished to a fine gloss, and in spite of the ride, the dust and the heat, his uniform was smart as always. The last time the two men had seen each other was in the lobby of the Shepheard's Hotel, bloody and hot with rage, panting among the shards of the shattered chandelier.

Ryder put out his hand and Penrod shook it.

'We were also told you brought down the Duke of Kendal, before your supposed death. That man caused us a great deal of hurt, so I thank you for that. Unless we were misinformed about that too?'

'I am just rejoining my servant. Would you have a cup of coffee with me and a cigar?'

'Like that, is it?' Ryder said. 'Well, I can respect a man keeping such business to himself. I'll take the coffee and the cigar.'

They walked across the plateau and into the next gully where Penrod's servant had made camp. Seeing another white man approach with his master, he set up another camp stool for him and before long Penrod and Courtney were drinking their coffee and drawing on a pair of very fine cigars as the air cooled.

'What brings you here, Ballantyne?' Ryder said, looking about him. 'I'd say your kit and your servant come out of Massowah. Are you working with the Italians?'

Penrod crossed his legs and blew out a cloud of smoke and explained, briefly, his diplomatic mission in Eritrea.

'I have news of Rebecca,' Ryder said when he had finished. 'Would you like to hear it?'

'Yes.'

'First wife of Osman Atalan and mother to two children. Treated with respect by his people.'

'I have heard the same,' Penrod said. 'I hope she has found some peace, but the British will retake Sudan eventually and when they do I shall find her husband and kill him.'

'I understand,' Ryder replied.

They both studied the landscape in front of them in silence.

'So tell me what you think, Courtney,' Penrod said at last. 'The Italians are convinced that it will be a simple business to take over Tigray and force Menelik to accept a protectorate over Ethiopia.'

Ryder grunted. 'The only people who can think that are the ones who have never met him.'

Penrod raised an eyebrow. 'You think they are wrong? The victory at Coatit was straightforward. The Ethiopian fighters are many, I admit that, but they could not withstand the discipline of European troops, or the *askari* troops the Italians have trained.'

Ryder examined the glowing end of his cigar. 'You and I have had our disagreements in the past, Penrod. But I know you're not a fool. The battle at Coatit was a skirmish with a local ruler. If the Italians force a claim on any more territory, they will be dealing with the emperor himself. The *askari* are good, but you haven't enough of them. The emperor's troops are just as fast, just as disciplined, just as well armed. And he has a lot more of them.'

Penrod looked sceptical. 'As well armed? Half of Mengesha's men at Coatit had only spears and swords.'

'Menelik wasn't going to provide his rival with the best of his weaponry. Not yet. Last time I was in Addis I saw crates of new rifles in the storehouses they hadn't even bothered opening yet. The French and the Russians are happy to supply Menelik when the Italians decide they do not wish to do so. Italian aggression will unite the country. Then Menelik will share his stockpile with Mengesha and Alula.'

'The Italian informants are telling them that Menelik cannot raise more than thirty thousand men.'

Ryder laughed. 'The Italians should believe nothing they do not see with their own eyes. Intrigue is a national sport here, and they are masters at it.' Then he grew more serious. 'And one thing every Ethiopian agrees on is that you can never trust a white man. They chant a song. "From the sting of the black snake, one can recover, but the bite of the white snake is deadly." They will not only betray the Italians because of the power and prestige of Menelik, they will do it joyfully as a patriotic duty.'

'I have heard that rhyme before.'

'It is fast becoming a national proverb. My people are left alone here because we are under Menelik's protection. No other white man will be safe in Tigray soon.'

'How many men do you think Menelik could muster?' Penrod asked.

'Against the Italians?' Ryder scratched his chin. 'A hundred thousand at least.'

Penrod whistled. 'That seems unlikely.'

Ryder felt a burst of irritation, but sipped his coffee. 'You may believe me or not as you see fit. The Italians will find out sooner or later, then they must make peace and get out of Tigray.'

Penrod blew out an even stream of smoke. 'No. They would lose too much face in Europe and at home. It is a question of national pride.'

'Then a lot of brave men will die,' Ryder answered, his dislike of military posturing overwhelming him. 'Italy has done what even Menelik could not. She has united Ethiopia against her. Will you stay and fight alongside the Italians?'

'I shall,' Penrod replied and made no further comment.

Neither of them spoke for a while. In the past Penrod would have deliberately goaded him, but he resisted the temptation. Ryder had a good sense of this country after his years of residence and Penrod had taken careful note of his opinion.

'I saw Amber, and the child,' he said.

Ryder understood at once. Penrod had seen Amber with Penelope, and had assumed the girl was hers. He considered. He could tell Penrod the truth, and bring him to the camp. Word would quickly reach Ras Alula and Menelik that Ryder had received him, and they might well conclude Ryder was trying to make some underhand deal with the Italians. Amber had grieved deeply when she thought Penrod was dead; what good would it do her to let her know he was alive now just as he was about to ride against Menelik with his Italian friends? Let Penrod think Penelope was Amber's if that sent him back to the Italians and left her in peace.

He kept his voice even. 'Amber is well. You saw the camp on the opposite escarpment, and the orchards?'

'I did.'

'All her work. She has saved a great many lives in these past years.'

Penrod did not speak, and Ryder tipped the ash off his cigar.

'Penrod, you and I will never be friends, but Amber was fond of you at one time, so for her sake, I'll give you this advice: go back to Massowah; go back to Cairo. To fight with the Italians in this country is suicide.'

Ryder glanced sideways at the rigid line of Penrod's jaw. He didn't expect he'd persuade the man to leave the Italians to their fate, but for his sister-in-law's sake, he made one last attempt.

'Amber found a lion cub when it was weak and young,' he continued. 'She fed it, cared for it, taught it to hunt. But she is not a fool. She has released it, not tried to keep it on a silver chain. She recognises its strength.'

'I think you have picked up this nation's love of riddles,' Penrod said with a drawl. 'You draw some parallel, I suspect. Are you saying that the Italians thought they could treat Menelik as a pet?'

Ryder let the smoke of the cigar trickle deliciously between his lips. 'So it seems to me. Look at this country, Penrod.' He swept his arm out over the horizon. 'It is vast, proud. The idea that Italy can claim control over it with a few thousand men is nonsense. It is as if Menelik sent a dozen Ethiopians into St James's Park and claimed to be governor of England. It is ridiculous, and insulting.'

Penrod said nothing, even though he had given the same opinion to Rome and London on various occasions.

'If you had your way, Courtney, no army would ever leave its own shores.'

'That is true. Are you married yet, Penrod?'

'I am not.' He cleared his throat. 'You have built something remarkable here, Courtney.'

Ryder drained his coffee cup and stood up. 'Almost, Penrod. I have almost built something remarkable. And now every evening I pray to God the greed of your Italian friends will not destroy it just when it is beginning to work. Goodbye.'

'Goodbye, Courtney. And good luck,' Penrod replied, and turned his attention back to the horizon.

The day after Ryder met Penrod in the uplands, he was lying with Saffron in the sleepy haze that followed the heat of their lovemaking, when she lifted herself up on her elbow and looked at him with her most stern expression.

'Ryder, what are you thinking? I know something is bothering you, and I think it is time you told me, don't you?'

He lay back on the blankets and stared up into the thick thatch of the roof while Saffron sat up properly, pulling her shift over her shoulders and tying up her hair, then he sat up and reached for his shirt.

'I met an old acquaintance of ours while I was hunting yesterday,' he eventually said.

She was tying her skirt at her waist, gradually changing again from his lover to his wife, the mother of his children.

'Someone from Ato Asfaw's village?'

'No. Penrod Ballantyne.'

She spun around towards him, her hand over her mouth. 'Oh, my Lord! Penrod is alive? Why did you not bring him to camp? Have you told Amber? I must find her at once.'

He took hold of her wrists and pulled her down to sit on the bed beside him and told her exactly what Penrod had said, watching the play of emotions across her face. She seemed thoughtful and quiet, but as soon as he released his grip, her hand flew up and she struck him, quick as a snake with the flat of her hand.

'You let him believe she was married!'

She raised her hand again, but this time he caught her and pulled her to him.

'Saffron! Listen to me! I could not have Penrod, who is attached to the Italian general staff, in this camp,' he hissed. 'Not just at the moment we are about to achieve the levels of production we swore to Menelik we'd reach and gain our security here!' She frowned and tried to pull away, but he held on to her. 'How can we go to Addis and expect Menelik to take our word if we've been entertaining an ally of the Italians in our camp? For God's sake, Saffy, Penrod Ballantyne has caused your sister nothing but pain, and if he stays with the Italians he's as good as dead anyway. I did what was best.'

'You did what was best for you, Ryder! You know Amber has not forgotten him. You cannot sacrifice her chance of happiness for the sake of this place!'

Ryder stared into her flashing eyes. 'What about our sacrifice? What about Rusty's sacrifice? What about Amber's? Would you have me risk everything for the sake of a sentimental reunion? He thinks she is married; she thinks he is dead. Let it be!'

Her breathing began to slow and she lowered her head for a moment. 'You are right. We have all sacrificed a great deal.' Saffron was shaking. 'Have we saved the mine, Ryder?'

He released her hands, trying to judge the deep emphasis in her voice. 'If . . . If we can take the final shipment of ingots to Addis the moment the rains ease, and defend the camp until Ethiopia is at peace again, then yes, we will have saved the mine.'

She stared at him, her eyes shining in the shadows. 'Then that is what we shall do. And then we will leave.'

'Leave?' Ryder said in a dangerous bark, moving away from her.

She followed him and put her hands on his shoulders. He could still feel the tremble of nerves in her fingertips.

'I know you, Ryder Courtney. The moment our capital and the mine is secure, you will need another challenge. Why wait? And I want to take Amber back to Cairo. If Penrod survives, and has become worthy of her, then we will give them our blessing. If he does not live, the best chance Amber has to be happy again is still there, not here. We owe it to her. You know we do.'

Ryder watched her for a long moment before he spoke. 'I will fight till my last breath to save this place, Saffron. But if we manage that miracle, I will put Patch in charge and take you and Amber back to Cairo.'

'Thank you,' she said as he pulled her into his arms.

· · ·

Saffron told Amber an hour later that Penrod was alive, and that Ryder had seen him. The news seemed to strike her like a physical blow and for a full minute she could not utter a word. Saffron stroked her shoulder.

'I was so angry with Ryder, Amber. But he didn't want a known friend of the Italians coming into camp, and Penrod thought you were married, so—'

'Saffy, stop! Just explain it all to me again.'

She did, whispering every detail she could remember to her sister and holding her close, wishing she could take some of the pain and confusion from her.

'I wonder if he has changed, Saffy?' Amber said at last.

'Why do you say that, my sweet?'

'He came all that way, then left so he might not disturb me when he thought I was married. But when we were in Cairo last time, he flaunted his affair with Lady Agatha all over town.'

'I suppose that is possible,' Saffron said softly. 'Do you still love him that much, Amber?'

Amber wiped her eyes. 'I think I do, Saffy. Even after all these years. I've tried very hard not to.'

Amber knew with an absolute certainty the moment Penrod had been watching her. She had been outside the church talking to Marta, and little Penelope, who, despite her parents' darker colouring, had inherited the Benbrook blond mane, had run over to her. Bill had been in the square too and they had spoken briefly as she was holding Penelope in her arms. As she held her little niece she had felt a sensation of light and warmth, then suddenly darkness. She turned instinctively up to look at the escarpment above the camp, but it was already empty. The feeling of loss had followed her like a ghost all evening. She struggled to understand her own feelings. She was angry with Ryder, angry with Penrod for not simply walking down to the camp and speaking to her, but at the same time she felt something else. Hope.

She pushed herself away from the wall. 'I'm going to think for a while, Saffy.'

'You go, I'll see to dinner,' Saffron said and watched her go. 'Penrod Ballantyne,' she said between gritted teeth. 'If you get yourself killed now, I will never forgive you.'

'Did you say Ballantyne?'

Saffron jumped. Bill Peters had appeared out of nowhere, an annoying habit of his.

'Yes, an old acquaintance of ours. Penrod Ballantyne.'

Bill blinked rapidly. 'I thought he was dead.'

'Yes, we all thought that. But no, he's on some diplomatic liaison exchange with the Italians.' Saffron suddenly felt tired. She didn't want to be near Bill with his soft hands and strange blank stare. She strode away without saying goodbye.

• • •

The last ingot was ready just as the rains began to ease. With luck they would reach Addis just in time to meet the agreement with Menelik and secure the right to the land in perpetuity. They would also receive the money due to them for the silver sent to the capital over the last eighteen months and be able to restock the mine. Hostilities between Menelik and the Italians would throttle the usual trade routes and there was no telling when they would open again.

Bill asked to make the journey with them, and Saffron wanted Amber to come too so she could help with the decisions about what they would need if they found themselves under a virtual siege. They left at the first possible moment, a grim determination to get to Addis as quickly as possible spurring them on. Their usual route lay on lower ground alongside the range of heights that divided the bulk of Ethiopia from the coast and the Red Sea, but Ryder decided that they would use the tracks which wound their way between the hills. The route was more difficult and longer, but the Italian army had now occupied several strategic points between Adrigat and Mekelle, and Ryder felt it would be safer to avoid entanglement with the military whenever possible.

They led half a dozen mules loaded with silver ingots, as well as several more laden with camping equipment. Penelope and Leon walked with them, or rode when they were tired, chattering to the guards or their family depending on who was willing to pay them attention at that time.

Ryder kept up a punishing pace. Until the silver was in Menelik's treasury he was vulnerable, and he knew that they were still in danger from late rains, but he could not delay any longer. They made excellent progress on the first three days, but late on the afternoon of the fourth day Geriel tapped Ryder on the shoulder and pointed west. The sky had grown purple and bruised with rain clouds. Ryder swore under his breath as he looked at them. Their route had taken them into a steep-sided ravine with a broad, flat base to it. Ryder gave his orders and Geriel set off ahead of the convoy at a steady run.

'What is happening, Ryder?' Amber asked.

When he replied, he spoke loudly enough for the whole party to hear him. 'A heavy rainstorm is coming in from the west, and it could flash flood the valley. We need to get up to higher ground and set camp, and we need to do it quickly. Geriel's gone on ahead to see if he can find a place where we can get off the valley floor before the main track turns off.'

None of them wasted time with questions or exclamations. Ryder took Leon on his shoulders, Bill carried Penelope and they set off along the track. The air still felt cool and dry, but they had all seen the clouds behind them.

Half a mile further along the track they heard Geriel calling them. He had found a path that led from an S-bend in the river's course to a broadening plateau about halfway up the valley walls. The ground was sloping and uneven, but it was large enough to put up the tents and tether the animals. Ryder nodded, and they began the climb, driving and leading the patient mules with them. Even those loaded with the silver ingots managed the incline with the remarkable stoicism of their kind.

Amber scrambled up beside one of the animals loaded with camping equipment. The air was becoming quickly colder and the breeze began to pull at her clothing. The animal baulked, then sprang up the rocky ladder of the path. She dragged herself after it. They were lucky. With the rain coming from the west, the twist in the course of the river meant the ravine walls would provide some cover. As soon as they reached level ground, she began to help unloading and setting up the tents, while Ryder drove stakes into the ground to tether the animals.

The heavy canvas began to whip in the air, and already Amber had to shout to make herself heard above the rush of the wind. A crackle of light was followed by a low rumble of thunder that broke over the valley behind them. Amber glanced down at the shallow river below. It was already deepening and spreading over the path they had been walking on such a short time before.

She pulled the guy ropes taut and tried to hammer in the tent pegs. The ground was dry and crumbling, unable to offer a hold.

'The trees!' Ryder shouted and she understood. The acacia and juniper scattered over the plateau had been working their roots into the rocks for years. She led the guy ropes to them, tying them off as quickly as she could. Maki came to help her and they felt the first fat drops of rain beginning to fall.

Saffron hurried the children into the tent, while Amber fetched the sack of what she thought of as her emergency rations from one of the nervous beasts – thick breads baked before they left camp and dried fruit. It was not much, but it would be something. They could not light cooking fires now. A sudden gust of wind tore at her skirts – a force so abrupt and violent it almost knocked her off her feet.

Geriel was working with Ryder to unload the ingots from the other mules.

'Get under cover, al-Zahra,' Ryder called to her.

Before she had time to obey, another flash of light brightened the sky, and at the same moment Amber was deafened by a clap of thunder. The rain began to fall in a sudden torrent, sending plumes of dust up from the soil. Ryder and Geriel were soaked at once, but continued to work as if the ripping wind and lash of the rain were nothing to them.

'Now!' Ryder called again, and Amber scuttled inside to join Saffron and the children.

Leon and Penelope were curled up on a pile of blankets, wrapped around each other. As Amber came in and pushed her wet hair off her face, she smiled bravely at Leon.

'I'm not scared,' he said loudly. 'Only Penelope does not like the thunder.'

'She is lucky she has you to look after her then,' Amber said.

The sides of the tent quivered and shook, but the ropes held. Amber unpacked half of her rations, then prepared to dash out again to take the rest to the tent where the men slept, but Saffron called her back.

'Amber! Take these – spare blankets for the men.'

Amber gathered them in her arms, then ran the few feet to the other tent. Already the ground was slippery. The low trees whistled and shook. She ducked in and handed the blankets and food to Maki, who took them with thanks. Ryder, Geriel and Bill followed her in.

'How are the children?' Ryder asked.

'Leon is being brave for his sister,' she answered and Ryder nodded, proud, but not wishing to show it.

'Go back to them, and thank you for the food.'

'The mules?'

'Not happy,' Bill said. 'But secure and in the lee of the slope, so they have some shelter.'

Bill had taken off his soaking shirt and was drying himself off with one of the blankets. Amber had never noticed before how well defined the muscles of his chest and arms were. He noticed her looking at him and smiled. It was a look that made her shiver, and she was glad of the storm and the rain to wash it from her again before she rejoined Saffron and her niece and nephew.

• • •

The violence of the storm seemed only to grow and thicken. The flashes of lightning came so quickly they seemed to form a constant flickering illumination and the thunder broke in one deafening clap after another. The tent sagged under the weight of the rain, pressing in on the two sisters, Leon and little Penelope. Again and again they thought the worst must be over, only to hear the cannonade of thunder start once more, closer and more fierce.

Amber dozed fitfully and the whole night took on the feeling of a dream. She thought she saw dervish warriors in the flashes of light, and that the starving hordes of Khartoum were breaking into the tent. She was staring into Penrod's angry eyes the moment she broke their engagement. She was on the lifeboat, watching flaming bodies fall from the side of the steamship, Saffron's blood sticky on her fingers. Rusty's body was in the tent with them, bleeding quicksilver.

Suddenly she was awake. Bill was shaking her shoulder and hissing at her.

'Amber, the animals are loose. Help me.'

If she had been properly awake or at least not fogged with the ghosts of her past, she would have been suspicious, woken Saffron, asked some questions, but she only responded with a dazed understanding and stumbled out of the tent. The rain was still coming down hard. Bill had a lantern that fought against the thick, wet darkness, but it cast only a murky light around him. The lightning flickered.

Where is Ryder? Amber thought. Where are Maki and Geriel?

Bill was already striding away towards the patch of cover where they had tethered the animals. She followed him, her mind still groggy. Another flash of lightning and the wind began to pick up, throwing the rain against her face with such force it felt as if she was being pelted with gravel. The mules were all where they should be – miserable and huddled together, but tethered. Two, though, she saw had been loaded with some of the small boxes that contained the silver ingots from the mine.

'What is happening, Bill?' she yelled above the thunder of rain, the wind whipping the words away from her. 'The animals are not loose.'

'Not yet,' he shouted over his shoulder and she watched, horrified, as he began to untie the ropes that tethered and hobbled the unloaded animals.

She ran towards him, trying to catch the ropes. He dealt her a single backhanded blow that sent her sprawling in the rust-coloured mud.

'It's time for me to go, Amber,' he said, 'and I'm taking you with me. Come along now.'

'Go where? I'm not going anywhere with you! Are you insane?'

The mules were confused by their sudden freedom, but they showed no sign of wishing to escape, staying in their huddle.

'Ryder!' Amber screamed. 'Ryder!'

Bill looked at her with a sort of pitying contempt and slapped one of the mules hard. It shrank from him, but did not run.

Amber struggled to her feet and screamed for Ryder again, hoping by some miracle that the others might hear her over the rage of the storm.

'Stupid animals,' Bill said, almost to himself. He took his revolver from his waistband and fired a shot just above the mules' heads. It was enough. They brayed and bucked and ran in a haphazard panic towards the camp or further up the slope as their instincts led them. Amber had to leap backwards to avoid their frantic escape. She felt Bill grip her upper arm in a vicious hold and he dragged her towards the two animals that were still tied and laden with silver. He unhitched them without letting go of her, moving with an easy confidence as if the rain and wind did not exist for him.

Amber started to fight and scream, but the strength of his hold was like iron. And then she felt the cold pressure of the muzzle of his gun in the small of her back.

'Keep moving,' he said.

S affron started out of her uneasy sleep into a world of sudden chaos. She could hear animals braying and Ryder shouting.

Leon was awake and staring at her with wide, frightened eyes. Amber was gone.

'Leon, will you be a brave lad for me?'

The little boy nodded.

'Good. I need you to stay here and keep Penelope with you. Just bundle up together and don't move. It's very important.'

'I want to help you and Daddy.'

He was such a strong little boy; she felt a sudden pride and reached out to touch his smooth cheek.

'This is helping me and Daddy. This is helping us a lot. Look after your sister.'

He seemed convinced. 'I shall, Mummy.'

'Thank you,' she said. Then she leaned forward and kissed them both, firmly and quickly on the tops of their heads, before diving out into the rain.

The lightning flashed and Saffron saw Ryder, his shirt soaked and clinging to the broad muscles of his chest and shoulders. He already had a grip on two of the mules and was shouting out orders to Geriel and Maki.

Geriel was climbing up towards a narrow ledge where one of the panicked creatures had stranded itself. Ryder made a grab for its trailing tether, but the animal kicked out with both its back legs and caught Geriel on his right shoulder, throwing him backwards. He fell and slithered to the edge of the narrow plateau. Ryder sprang forward, then threw himself full length on the mud, reaching out for Geriel as he did. Geriel saw him and made a lunge for Ryder's outstretched hand, scrabbling for some purchase in the mud. Saffron screamed. Geriel was going to go over the edge; it was impossible he could be stopped, he was moving so quickly. Then Ryder caught Geriel's wrist. It slowed and twisted his fall. He scrambled up into a crouch as Ryder released him, panting and holding his shoulder. Ryder did not even pause. At once he was on his feet, gathering the tethers of the mules and leading them back towards their cover. Maki went to Geriel, but Geriel shook his head, got to his feet and went after the mule on the ledge again.

Saffron could feel her clothes beginning to stick to her skin and struggled to marshal her thoughts. Lanterns. That's what they needed. She went first into the men's tent, only to find their hurricane lantern had been overturned and smashed. She ducked back into her own tent. Leon stared up at her. Penelope was curled tightly against his chest.

'Darling boy,' Saffron said as calmly as she could, 'I need the lamp to help Daddy.'

He understood at once. 'We don't mind the dark, Mummy,' he said.

She took it and staggered through the rain towards the tethering spot. Ryder took the lantern from her without a word.

'Where is Bill? And where's Amber?' Saffron said.

Ryder looked around him. 'Amber is not with the children?'

'Leon is looking after his sister, they are perfectly all right,' she said with more confidence than she felt.

Before Ryder could answer, Geriel loomed out of the darkness. He had cuts and grazes on the side of his face and he was panting hard.

'Mr Ryder, two mules still missing and I think . . . I think some of the silver has gone.'

'Bill?' Saffron said in wonder. 'Ryder, it can't be.'

'Did you see another path down from here, Geriel?' Ryder demanded. 'One that does not lead through the camp?'

'A goat track, that way.' He pointed past the tethering point.

'Secure the other animals; I'll fetch my gun,' Ryder said.

Even as he turned, Saffron was plunging past him.

'Saffron!'

'He has Amber,' she screamed over the fresh howls of the wind. 'Hurry!'

• • •

The path was steep and slick with the rain. In the flashes of lightning that still came in regular bursts, turning the sky purple and grey, Amber could see how it led towards the valley floor. A new sound struck her: the rush of water. The placid stream they had walked by earlier in the day had already become a river, deep brown and speckled with foam.

'You've worked with us for years, and now you have turned thief?' Amber shouted. 'Why?'

'I was always only waiting to take what I wanted, my dear,' he said.

Amber went as slowly as she could. She was surefooted after years in the highlands, but now she moved as cautiously as an old woman.

'So take the silver and let me go.'

The narrow mouth of the revolver jabbed her in the back. 'Oh no, Amber. I couldn't leave without you. I have the most wonderful plans for us once we join my friends.'

'Who are your friends?'

He chuckled. 'I think you know. Once your lion left, it got a lot easier to meet them from time to time. Offer a little friendly advice.'

'The bandits! You *were* talking to them.'

'Obviously.'

She turned around and stared at him. The rain had soaked them both to the skin; it beaded across his high cheekbones, and his eyes seemed darker and fiercer than they had been. No longer dead and blank, but suffused with a grey light. She felt a deep and instinctive revulsion – and fear. He came closer to her, so she could feel his heat against her body. The hard, cold gun was still pressed tight against her belly.

'You do not love me,' she said. 'Why would you run this risk to take me?'

'You shall see. Fate put you in my hands, my dear. How could I refuse such a perfect gift?' He jammed the gun harder into her belly. 'Now stop playing for time, Miss Benbrook, or I shall get angry.'

She turned away from him and took another step down the track. He was a good shot. She wondered how far she would have to get away from him to have a chance of him missing her. She looked right and left, searching for cover in the darkness.

'Amber!'

It was Saffron's voice, faint above the sound of the wind and lashing rain. He did not even look around but pushed her forward. Out of the corner of her eye she saw him wrap the tether ropes of the mules more firmly around his lower arm.

'Amber!'

The shout was louder, closer. She heard something else, a deeper note in the roar of the water pounding along the river bed, but she had no time to wonder what it might be. If Saffron was coming after her, so was Ryder, and they were both marksmen of the first order. She dared a glance over her shoulder and longed for a flash of lightning.

Bill threw his lamp away in a wide arc. A shot cracked behind them and it shattered in mid-air. The roaring noise further up the valley had increased in volume and the temperature of the air suddenly seemed to drop. Sheet lightning flickered over the other side of the gorge and in its brief illumination Amber saw and understood. The torrent of the river was being pushed higher. Forced forward, she blinked into the darkness and saw a wall of dark, churning water racing towards them. Bill saw it too.

'Up! Move!' he yelled.

Amber stumbled on to her knees and began to clamber hand over hand up the mud-slicked stone. The mules brayed and pulled backwards on their tethers. Amber desperately dragged herself higher up the slope as the roar of the water approached. Another flicker of light and she saw Ryder above her on the main path, his rifle raised. She was between him and Bill. He moved the rifle very slightly and fired.

Amber spun around in time to see as his shot felled one of the two loaded mules. The animal went down and Bill was jerked sharply backwards by the sudden weight on the tether. The other animal tried to scramble past them. Bill roared and launched himself forward. Amber felt his fingers fasten around her ankle.

The first wave of the flash flood caught her, dragging her away from the side of the path. She grabbed on to the woody root of a thorn bush just above her head and felt it begin to give at once. Bill's grip on her ankle did not weaken, but as he was caught by the force of the flood, Amber felt his weight pull on her ferociously. It felt as if her joints were being ripped apart. She cried out and her mouth filled with mud and water, debris from the river struck her in the side, and everything was agony and confusion.

'Amber!' Saffron's voice was strong and close.

Amber tried to move, then felt her sister's slim, strong arms grabbing her around the chest, trying to pull her free of the surging waters. Amber lifted her head above water, screamed and kicked out hard, slamming the heel of her free foot against Bill's hold. Once, twice, then suddenly she was released and Saffron dragged her free of the waters.

For a minute the two sisters lay together on the edge of the torrent, panting, then Saffron pulled herself up into a sitting position and gathered Amber to her with a groan.

'Saffy?'

'Ryder! We're here. Both of us.'

He was beside them a second later. The sudden flood was already abating and the waters were scouring the lower slope of the gorge. The rain had stopped and the sudden African dawn was almost with them. The storm was passing, rolling south and west until its rage faded into the wide sky. Of Bill and the two mules, they could see no sign.

'Is he dead? Why did he try and take you?' Saffron asked.

'That was a brilliant shot, Ryder,' Amber said as he put his arms around them both and held them in the softening rain. 'I don't know, Saffy. He said he had plans for me.' She shuddered. 'And he said he's been talking to the bandits. But I don't understand.'

Saffron suddenly put out her hand and took her husband's. 'Ryder! We don't have the full load of silver any more! Will Menelik still grant us the land?'

'He must,' Ryder said. 'He must.'

Menelik had heard news of their coming and sent men to meet them. A certain excitement pervaded the atmosphere that Ryder did not recognise. As they made their way into the city and towards the house Menelik had assigned for them, Ryder noticed representatives of every people of Ethiopia among the crowd. He made some comment about what he had seen to his escort, but he only smiled and said he thought the rains were better this year than they had been for some time, and that he hoped the worst of the cattle plague was over.

Ryder left Amber, Saffron and the children at the house, then went on to the new palace to see his silver counted into Menelik's treasury. When the count came up short, he calmly asked for an audience with the King of Kings. It was granted, and Ryder took Geriel and Maki with him. They were shown not into the main audience hall, but a small side chamber, and found Menelik alone, seated on a velvet-covered stool, the table at his side covered in papers. Geriel and Maki dropped to one knee and Ryder made a low bow.

'So in the end you could not manage the count, Mr Ryder,' Menelik said. 'Your land is forfeit.'

'My lord,' Ryder said firmly, 'I ask you to hear the testimony of these two men.'

Menelik nodded, and after exchanging nervous glances, Geriel and Maki told the King of Kings about the treachery of Bill Peters and swore to the number of ingots they'd carried when they left Courtney Mine.

Menelik listened carefully, then dismissed them, asking Ryder to remain and inviting him to sit opposite him.

'You do well to offer me my own people as witnesses, Ryder,' Menelik said when they were alone. 'I hope Miss Amber is not hurt.'

'Thanks be to God, she is well. My lord, I have a request. If the loan of my share of this last load of silver might be of any use to you, I beg you to accept it. I naturally would ask no interest in this time of trouble. I wish also to inform you that once the grant in perpetuity is given, and the nation is at peace, I mean to return to Cairo with my family and put the management of the mine under Tom Western, who we know as Patch.'

Menelik studied him carefully. 'You are a clever man. A tactful man. If I thought the life of a courtier held any interest for you, I would keep you in Addis. Yes, the loan of your silver would be useful. Though I insist you keep for yourself in ready money whatever is needful for the coming months.'

Menelik paused and Ryder examined his face. The emperor looked grave.

'But I cannot grant you the land,' he continued. 'I am watched from all sides for weakness and I can show none. Today is not the day I can renegotiate to my disadvantage with a white man.'

'You cannot take the mine from me,' Ryder said fiercely, getting to his feet.

Menelik stood and threw out his hand, a grand, sweeping gesture that seemed to tear the air. 'Do not say "cannot" to an emperor, Mr Ryder!' he roared. 'I will not be commanded by you.'

Ryder rocked backwards on his heels, but stood his ground. 'Is this justice?' he spat out.

Menelik took two long strides until their faces were inches apart. Ryder could feel his breath hot on his face as they stared into each other's eyes.

'If *I* speak it,' Menelik said, slowly and distinctly, 'it is justice, law and truth.' Then he turned away and lifted his hands.

Ryder felt the audience coming to an end. He had to find the right words now, before Menelik could clap his palms together and summon his servants, or he would lose everything.

'Time then,' Ryder said, and Menelik paused, waiting. 'You mean to call my men to fight at your side, as is your right and their duty. When they return after your victory to their home at the mine, give me a month to make up the shortfall.'

Menelik let his hands fall and did not reply at once. Instead he took his seat on the raised stool again. The silver bells that edged its velvet cover rang with their soft tongues.

'If I lose this war, Mr Ryder,' he said more gently, 'whoever is put in my place will not give you another month. They will take your mine and all the silver that sits unsold in my treasury.'

'But you will *not* lose, my lord,' Ryder replied.

Menelik looked up at him. 'You are betting everything on my success? You are not tempted to run to the Italians and try to shelter under their wing?'

Ryder shook his head. 'Emperor John awarded me the Star of Solomon and Judea, and I have carried it with pride every day since. I will not betray it, his memory, or you. Grant me a month after your victory, sire.'

Menelik leaned his elbow on the table. 'You have fed many people at your camp during the cattle plague, have you not?'

Ryder hesitated. 'That was Miss Amber's doing, my lord.'

Menelik smiled. 'Honest Ryder, even at this moment! I know it was her doing, but you did not drive the refugees away. You let her do what was right, even when it cost you labour and timber and time. So I return you that time.'

Ryder felt his breath steady.

'You will have your month, but no more. I will have to remain firm in victory, if God grants me victory, but I shall give you that month.'

· · ·

Amber, Saffron and Ryder were with the children in the marketplace when the war drums began to beat. Saffron took Penelope on her hip and Ryder walked with Leon on his shoulders, and together they joined the excited crowd moving towards the centre of the square.

The head of the emperor's bodyguard waited for the masses to approach. He was mounted on a chestnut stallion and wearing his full regalia: a lion-skin headdress and cape with a decorated leather panel that covered his chest. Under his cape he wore a tunic of rippling green silk and trousers of pure white. His shield was decorated with bronze, and as well as his sword he had a M1870 Vetterli rifle over his shoulder.

On either side of him a man beat a *negarit*, the huge war drum, whose deep, echoing boom summoned the people from their businesses, their homes, their fields. Once the crowd had gathered, the horseman gave a word of command and the drummers ceased. The sudden silence was almost shocking.

Ryder lifted Leon down from his shoulders, but kept hold of his small hand as the horseman began to speak.

'I am the mouth of your Emperor Menelik, King of Kings, Lion of Judah. Hear me!'

The crowd's attention was so complete it seemed they had even stopped breathing to listen.

'An enemy is come across the sea. He has broken through our frontiers in order to destroy our fatherland and our faith. I allowed him to seize my possessions and I entered upon lengthy negotiations with him in the hopes of obtaining justice without bloodshed. But the enemy refuses to listen. He continues to advance. Enough! With the help of God I will defend the inheritance of my forefathers and drive back the invader by force of arms. Let every man who has sufficient strength accompany me! And if he has not, let him pray for us!'

As soon as Menelik's herald had finished speaking, he touched the reins of his horse and, with the drummers following, forced a way back through the crowd towards the palace. The crowd dispersed quickly. Runners and riders would already be on their way to regional capitals and market towns with copies of the proclamation and details as to where and when to muster.

'So it has come to this at last,' Amber said.

'It was inevitable from the moment you told Menelik about the treaty,' Ryder said.

Before Amber could protest that it was hardly fair to blame her for an entire war, they heard someone calling Saffron's name. They saw a rather elderly white man approaching them across the square. It was Saffron who recognised him first.

'Yuri Alexandrovich! Penelope, my love, this is the doctor who helped Mummy the night you were born.'

Penelope had a sudden fit of shyness and hid her face in her mother's neck.

'Doctor, I am glad to see you!' Saffron said.

'As I am you. And you, little Penelope.' He reached out a finger to stroke the girl's cheek and she rewarded him with a brief dazzling smile. 'But I must speak to you all. I have heard rumours in St Petersburg that your engineer, Bill Peters, is not the man we thought he was.'

'We know,' Amber said simply. 'He tried to kidnap me and steal our silver, and died in the attempt.'

The doctor blinked in surprise. 'Bill Peters did exist,' he said, 'but he died in Bohemia some years ago, it seems.'

'Come with us, doctor,' Ryder said. 'And we shall tell each other all we can.'

* * *

Menelik's army had their first victory three months later. Major Pietro Toselli and his men were caught thirty miles ahead of the rest of the Italian troops at Amba Alagi by Menelik's advance guard and were slaughtered. Penrod blamed General Arimondi for his vague orders, and he blamed the Italian telegraph officers for mangling them still further. He blamed Pietro for holding his position with a thousand men when he realised the advance guard of Menelik's army consisted of at least twenty times that number. But Toselli had been expecting reinforcements and believed his orders were to hold his position. The march of Arimondi and his men, advancing towards Amba Alagi, and then leading a fighting retreat back to Mekelle with the traumatised remnants of Toselli's forces, was a remarkable act of military skill and bravery.

Penrod would have blown up the fort at Mekelle and continued the retreat until Arimondi could join up with Baratieri's forces, but the general would not do so. Mekelle was full of valuable supplies, and he believed the fort would be a perfect base for future offensive actions against the natives.

He left a garrison of twelve hundred men under Captain Galliano.

'We will be back in a few days,' he said and left.

Within a week Menelik's vast army had surrounded them.

B ack at Courtney Mine, Christmas came and went. It was strangely quiet in the camp as most of the men had gone to fight with Menelik. Ryder trained the men too young or too old to join their emperor to use their rifles, and sent regular patrols in sweeping arcs around his land. They heard that thousands of reinforcements were arriving from Italy every day, and in early February an elder from a hamlet three miles to the west visited them with the news the fort of Mekelle had been taken.

'The Italians fought like lions,' he told them, drawing a plan of the fort on the dirt in front of the church, 'so Menelik said they should be allowed to march out with full military honours. Now why did he do that, do you think?'

The little boys and girls of the camp who had clustered around him, Leon and Penelope among them, shook their heads.

'I shall tell you! Our emperor is a wily one. Now look! The Italian dogs are here.' He drew a line – the English road that led through Tigray all the way to Addis Ababa – and stabbed it where the Italians held a strong position at Adagamus. 'Now Menelik does not want to fight them between those hills! He wants to give battle to the west –' he swung his stick towards Adowa – 'where he has room to move about. But he does not want to show them his soft belly as he passes by. They might shoot him.' The stick became a rifle. 'Bang, bang!'

The children shrieked and giggled.

'So what has he done, Grandfather?' Leon piped up.

'Well, my little cub, he has made all those brave Italians from Mekelle walk alongside him, so now, as he turns towards Adowa, where he wants to be . . .'

'The Italians cannot shoot him!' Leon shouted. 'They might hit their own soldiers!'

'Just so, my boy,' the old man answered.

Ryder and Saffron were watching from a few paces away. Saffron looked up at her husband.

'This cannot go on much longer, can it, Ryder? Menelik's men must run out of forage soon.'

He held her slim body close to him but did not answer her. He had not forgotten what Menelik had said. If the King of Kings lost this war, they would lose the mine.

• • •

The alarm woke Saffron in the thick of the night: the sound of a bell being struck on the escarpment; a rapid jangling suddenly cut off. Before she had opened her eyes, Ryder was out of bed and pulling on his breeches. He grabbed his rifle from the rack by the door and went out. Saffron did the same, but before she put her hand on the latch she heard a patter of steps behind her. Leon had woken.

'Mummy, where are you going? Why do you have your gun?'

'Stay here and keep your sister safe, Leon,' she said quickly.

'But I always have to look after her!'

Saffron crouched down so she could look in to his eyes. 'Leon, someday it will be your job to run out of the house when the alarm rings, I know it shall, but for now your job is to look after Penelope for Daddy and me. And that is a very important job. Do you understand?'

'I think so.'

'Thank you, Leon.'

He drew back a step and Saffron left.

The women and children of the camp, woken by the bell, had stumbled out in to the chill dawn. Ryder could see nothing through the mist lifting from the river. He ordered Patch and the older boys to take rifles and ammunition and find cover behind the heavy wooden log benches. Most of the good rifles had gone into battle with the men. The women carried knives. He ordered them into the church with the children.

Bandits. The bastards had seen their chance, but Ryder still had a dozen men, skilled workers too old to join the army and endure the rigours of the march but bred with the martial pride of their people.

Once the bandits realised he had some armed men in camp, they would retreat in search of easier prey. Ryder was irritated, but neither surprised nor afraid. Every Ethiopian warrior worth his salt was with Menelik or harassing the Italian supply routes. Whoever was waiting in the mist could pose no real threat to him or his people.

'You'll find no easy meat here, you jackals!' he shouted into the darkness.

Ryder gave the order and the camp's defenders fired a single warning volley into the air.

'Now run like the cowards you are, or the next shots will hit home!'

Ryder expected to hear the sounds of retreat immediately, but none came. Instead, out of the mist, a volley was returned. It was disciplined and focused. The dirt in front of the church sprang up in dozens of neat fountains.

He heard a click beside him. It was his wife, still tousled with sleep, calmly loading her revolver.

'What on earth? Ryder, that must be twenty guns.'

A voice spoke out of the mist, in English. 'Good morning, Courtney,' it said.

'Bill Peters! I so hoped he was dead!' Saffron exclaimed. She stepped forward and fired into the mist. They heard the bullet strike stone.

'And Mrs Saffron is here!' Bill laughed.

Saffron looked up indignantly at her husband. 'How did he know it was me?'

'No one else here would fire without word from me, and I wouldn't shoot straight into the mist like an idiot,' Ryder said.

Saffron pouted. 'He sounds different, doesn't he?'

Bill's fine drawl echoed across the square. 'Still, lovely as it is to chat, one of my men has a message for the members of your camp.'

A loud voice began to speak in Amharic.

Patch dashed across to their position in a low crouch. 'What's he saying? I can't make it out.'

Ryder translated, his gut growing cold. 'He's saying that they do not want to kill their countrymen and women. If our people turn over the whites to them, they will not be hurt. If they resist then they will kill us all.'

'God damn him. What are our chances?'

'I trust our people,' Ryder said, his eyes dark with anger.

It was easy to say, but they had a dozen rifles to protect fifty women and almost as many children. If Bill had twenty rifles under his command, this could turn into a slaughter.

A movement caught Ryder's eye. Women were slipping out of the church, scrambling up into the shadows.

'What is your answer, men of Tigray?' the voice in the mist asked.

It was Tadesse who answered from the other side of the square. 'One minute, we are deciding!'

'I'll kill him!' Saffron hissed.

'Bring them out to the front,' the voice answered.

Tadesse crept up to them in the shadows, Amber with him.

'Mr Ryder, Balito, Agnes and Marta have gone up the far path with their eldest boys. Old John and Simon are crossing the river by the mine. Can you keep Bill talking a while?'

'I shall. Send Kassa and Adera north.'

'Yes, Mr Ryder.'

The voice came from the mist again. 'Now, grandfathers and children of Tigray!'

'We will come!' Ryder shouted. 'I do not want the blood of the women and children on our hands. But who are you, Peters? Who are you really? We know the real Peters died a year before we met.'

The voice answered, lazy and clear. 'He worked for me, for a while, then I realised I wanted his papers more than his labours.'

'Tell me your name!' Ryder roared into the damp morning air. 'How did you deceive us for so long?'

Ryder could almost see him, a shape of shadow and mist.

'Go,' Peters said in bad Amharic. 'Take their weapons and tie their hands.'

Above them they heard a sudden scream and the ululation of the women. They had surprised one of the gunmen on the high path with their knives.

They heard Bill shout, 'Miss Amber is not to be harmed! Kill the rest!'

Amber flung herself forward onto the ground as the first shots peppered the earth at their feet. Patch was struck in the shoulder and went down with a gasp. Two of the women of the camp ran to him, seizing him and dragging him back under cover. Ryder and Saffron went right, ducking behind the log benches. More shots, more screams. Rifles cracked up and downstream.

The mist was finally lifting, replaced by shifting clouds of smoke. Saffron shot at the place she had seen an old-fashioned musket flash and a figure fell forward into the water.

Ryder raised his rifle and fired. Another of the bandits on the far bank fell, tumbling down the incline into the river.

'Oh God,' Saffron said.

Ryder stared at where she was pointing. A campfire had just been lit by Rusty's burial ground. Standing next to it was an archer. As they watched he held one of his arrows into the flames, and they saw it flare. Ryder had seen fire arrows before: tows just behind the head were soaked in oil and set aflame right before the archer fired. The flaming arrows could not be fired as accurately or as far, but the archer was not aiming for Ryder or his people, but for their homes. The first arrow hit the ground a few feet from Ryder's hut. Ryder turned his aim on the man, breathing steadily and quietly. The archer lit another arrow and drew his bow again. The arrow wavered in the air and fell just short. One of the children squealed and threw sand over it.

'Ryder, hurry!' Saffron whispered.

Ryder squeezed the trigger and the archer crumpled to his knees, but his third arrow was already in the air. It flew with an almost lazy grace, and buried itself in the thatch of their roof.

'The children!' Saffron turned to dash across the square, but a sputter of shots drove her back.

Ryder could see Bolta, one of Patch's protégées, crouched on the other side of the square.

'Bolta!' He pointed. 'Cover Mrs Saffron!'

They both aimed their fire at the north bank and Saffron ran to the hut, crying out for Leon. The thatch was tinder-dry. Ryder could feel the heat at his back already. He kept his fire up. A terrible groaning noise came from behind him: part of the roof was collapsing. He spun around and, as he turned, saw Amber. She was standing quite still in the centre of the smoke and confusion. For a moment he was amazed, then he saw a glint at her throat. Bill was behind her, his knife at her neck, dragging her backwards across the river.

'Ryder!' he heard his wife scream.

Amber saw him. He thought he saw her lips move, but what was spoken, he could not say. He turned and ran towards his flaming home. Saffron was in the doorway, choking; in the centre of the room he saw his son and daughter holding hands. Penelope was crying and Leon's face was white. Between them and the door was a heap of flaming thatch.

'Leon! Pick up your sister and run to me!'

'But, Daddy!' The little boy was frozen.

Ryder leaped forward, feeling his hair singe, and swept up both children in his arms. There was another crash and wave of heat behind him. He could not avoid the fire. He launched himself forward and out into the square. He felt hands all around him. Someone took the children from him, someone else threw a blanket over him to smother the flames, then he heard Tadesse shouting, and he was tumbled forward and down the slope into the river. The cold sent a deep shock across his arms and back, and then began to soothe them.

The firing had stopped. The inhabitants of the camp were returning to the square. Some of the women were wailing; it meant someone had been killed. His arms and back were starting to ache, but he could see Saffron with the children and heard them cry, both of them. Marta was giving Patch water. Tadesse was beside him in the river.

'Miss Amber?' Ryder asked. 'Where is Miss Amber?'

Tadesse's voice when he replied shook with rage. 'He took her.'

• • •

As Tadesse smoothed a mixture of oil and herbs over Ryder's forearms and shoulders where the fire had blistered his skin, they formed a plan. Ryder would track Peters as best he could, while Tadesse and Saffron would ride to Menelik's camp near Adowa and beg for help. Patch and Marta would look after the children and the injured.

Ryder flinched as Tadesse's fingers probed the burns, and as he looked up he caught Patch scratching the scarring on his jaw. 'What is it, Patch?'

'I went looking for Marta's cousin, Ryder. He was on patrol last night. We reckoned it might have been him who raised the alarm.'

Ryder felt a fresh chill in his blood. 'Did you find him?'

Patch hunched his shoulders. 'Hoped he might have got scared and run away, but no, we found him. They cut his throat while he was ringing the bell up by the furnaces.'

'I'm sorry, Patch.'

'I know it. Thing is, Mr Ryder, I was wondering: why'd they come in that way? So I went to look and . . . There ain't no end to that Bill Peters' spite. They pulled down the Lion Dam and flooded the charcoal store before they even came to us.'

Ryder stared at the earth at his feet. So that was that. Even if Menelik beat back the Italians and his workers all returned, there was no way they'd make up the shortfall in the silver now. The mine was lost. So be it. He'd made and lost fortunes in Africa before, but he was damned if he was losing Amber too. He stood up and took the shirt Saffron handed to him, shrugging it on.

'Look after our people, Patch,' he said.

They assembled their travelling kit quickly and set out on their different paths three hours after the last rifle shot had been fired.

For the first hour the track the bandits had left was clear. Ryder made good progress, then he realised he had been following a false lead. He doubled back and rediscovered the right path, but lost it again five miles from camp. These bandits were clever. He forced himself to rest and think. They must have a base. He only had to find it. He drew himself a map in the dust and marked on it every raid he had heard of. They would want somewhere near the good, fast trails, but not too near their favourite hunting grounds. He drew a circle in the dust. Somewhere near Suria. It had to be.

He got to his feet and shouldered his pack.

The Italian army, swollen with new recruits, had been camped at Suria for two weeks now. Penrod could easily spot the new arrivals, pale and wide-eyed among the sunburned men who had been in Tigray for months, as he walked in long strides towards General Baratieri's tent. When Penrod took his seat in the circle among the generals in command of the Italian forces, next to Baratieri, but with his chair pulled slightly back, Albertone regarded him with open hostility.

'Why is the Englishman here? Major Ballantyne is a good soldier, but this is our business. By what right does he sit among us?'

Penrod said nothing, but met Albertone's gaze calmly.

Baratieri spoke quickly. 'He is here at my invitation and request. Ballantyne's advice on how to repel the renewed dervish attacks on the Sudanese border has been invaluable. He has consistently offered us better information than our most trusted scouts and has ridden over the area repeatedly since we made camp here. We would have suffered far greater losses in these continual skirmishes without him.'

Albertone snorted. 'What good is that? I can give you his report myself. Dust, hills and bad roads. We've all been here long enough to see that. Our prime minister is right: these skirmishes have been nothing but military wastage rather than a campaign. It is time to act.'

Penrod showed no reaction, but he was angry. He could not resent Albertone for disliking his presence at the council, but to show contempt for Baratieri, his commanding officer, in front of the other brigade generals was disgraceful. What was worse, Baratieri pretended to ignore the insubordination. He was looking ill. Penrod thought he had the air of a man about to crumble from within. The slaughter at Amba Alagi had aged him twenty years, and the way Menelik outwitted him by using the prisoners from the fort at Mekelle to move westwards, exposing the flank of his vast army in perfect safety, had shaken and confused him. Then came that last bitter telegram from Prime Minister Crispi, which Albertone now quoted with such relish. Penrod believed Baratieri's strategy had been perfectly sound. If anyone was to blame for the current situation it was Arimondi for his handling of the situation at Mekelle, and he took his place at the table as sleek and self-satisfied as a cat.

Baratieri cleared his throat and tapped his papers together. 'The choice is simple, gentlemen. We must advance, or face the prospect of retreating from Tigray and back to Eritrea without giving battle. I believe we should retreat.'

General Vittorio Dabormida actually made a sound of disgust under his breath. Arimondi went pale and clamped his jaw. Albertone rolled his eyes.

'My reasons are as follows. Our supply lines are overextended, and since the defection of Ras Sebath and Agos Tafari to join Menelik, attacks on our caravans have increased dramatically. We have only food enough to feed our men for four days at most, even if we cut the rations still further. My second reason is that the army Menelik has assembled is collapsing under its own weight. He has stripped the countryside and our scouts tell us more and more of his men are deserting and returning home. He will not be able to pursue us if we make an orderly retreat. We will return to the borders of Eritrea with our army intact. Now, I shall hear your thoughts.'

It was Arimondi, the most senior of the generals, who replied first. He waved away Baratieri with an elegant flick of his wrist.

'We have not come so far merely to go back. The very reasons you give for retreat are those I give to attack. We have to strike a decisive blow against these savages while our men are still fed. Let us sweep Menelik's army away and with that we will revenge ourselves for the slaughter of Major Toselli and his men at Amba Alagi, and this campaign will finally deliver us a triumph worthy of our great nation.'

The other generals nodded solemnly. Outside the tent Penrod could hear the sounds of the camp: occasional laughter and calls between the men, the creak of carts and the stamp of boots as parties moved to and fro, digging defensive ditches around the camp, which had no part in either of the options that Baratieri had put forward.

Albertone spoke next in his superior drawl. 'Attack, sir. Attack. They will scatter like rats when we fire on them.'

All eyes turned to Dabormida. 'I have come here to fight. Not march around the country for no reason.'

Finally General Ellena looked around the set faces of his colleagues. 'I and my men came to fight also, and I give weight to what my comrades have said. But I would be interested in hearing what Major Ballantyne thinks.'

Baratieri glanced up at Penrod and nodded. Penrod leaned forward a little, looking at each general in turn while he spoke.

'General Albertone, Menelik's army will not melt away as the followers of Ras Mengesha did. They are better armed, better led, and they too have come a long way from their homes to seek battle with you. However, they do not wish to fight you in entrenched positions. They are waiting to draw you out into the open. Attack and you are playing into their hands.'

Albertone wrinkled his upper lip. 'I would bet on my men against Menelik's even if they had twenty times our numbers. His men are peasants.'

'The Ethiopians are farmers, but they practise the arts of war from an early age,' Penrod said urgently. 'Do not think they are as raw and untrained as a volunteer army in Europe would be. They are strong and fast, and do not fear death.'

Ellena rubbed his long nose. 'I bow to the experience of Generals Albertone and Arimondi. Menelik's men are only peasants after all.'

Baratieri made no attempt to defend his own opinion. 'Very well,' he said. 'We shall advance towards Adowa and occupy the high ground. Menelik will be forced to attack or retreat. If he attacks, his men will have to meet us where the ground will funnel his numbers towards us. If he retreats he will be, in effect, admitting the expansion of the colony of Eritrea into

Tigray. I will give you your final orders tomorrow. Then we will march at nightfall. The first Menelik will know of it is when dawn breaks and he finds our men looking down on him from the heights.'

It signalled the end of the meeting. Baratieri remained where he was, bent over his papers. Penrod did not try to speak to him, but followed the generals outside. They moved away in a group, in animated discussion. Albertone looked almost gleeful. Penrod watched him from a distance, frowning. Baratieri's plan was to force Menelik to retreat, not to launch in to a battle, but Penrod saw in Albertone's face the expression of a man who expected to fight.

He made his way back through the camp and found Nazzari at work on his diary and letters. He greeted Penrod with a quick smile, but continued writing. Penrod lay on his camp bed with his hands behind his head and stared up at the canvas ceiling.

Amber had let Bill lead her away from the camp without resisting. She'd thought only of Saffron and the children and her friends in the camp. The most important thing was to get these men away from her family; then, and only then, she would think about herself and her escape.

Bill regrouped his men half a mile away from the escarpment. He had not spoken to her as yet, only pushed her to walk quickly along the path as it climbed then fell again on a more gradual incline. After some half an hour of walking, Amber spotted the pack animals of the raiding party and their guards. She had been left untied, and as the men exchanged news of casualties and their own bravery in battle, she had to fight the impulse to flee at once. They were still too near the camp to risk it. She kept her eyes down. One of the bandits led out a riding mule for her. She mounted without comment or assistance, and made a quick count of the number of men and their weapons. A dozen of them had survived the raid uninjured and all had modern breech-loading rifles. They walked with the swagger of young men used to instilling fear by force and threat of violence.

She would wait until dark and hope the men would get drunk and sleepy with feeding. Two women were travelling with them. Possibly wives of the fighters, but more likely slaves. She guessed by the position of the rising sun that they were heading west, but not along trails she had ever used.

Bill rode at the head of the column and never looked back at her. The bandits walked alongside them and wasted few words on conversation. The dry heat began to affect her. All around the ground was parched, waiting for the rains with a desperate quiet. She felt her lips begin to stiffen and she swayed slightly in the saddle. Bill said something to one of the bandits jogging at his side. The man dropped back and offered her a canteen. She wanted nothing more than to knock it out of his hand, but if she was going to maintain her strength, she had to drink.

They did not rest at midday, but kept up the same steady pace across the rising and falling terrain. Amber lost all sense of where she was. Her back and legs were growing stiff and sore, and her belly ached with hunger. The men beside her showed no sign of fatigue, and in her confused and wandering mind they looked at times like devils, dark spirits leading her to hell. As they climbed onto another rise, she shook off her imaginings and looked about her. At first she thought she must be dreaming. Off to the north, where she should have seen fields and the occasional compound or church, she saw what looked at first like an inland sea. A great mass of shifting activity. The glitter of metal in the late afternoon sun, white canvas tents and hordes of men. Then she realised: the Italian army. A vast camp of cooking tents, stores, animals, soldiers and camp followers. A city suddenly fallen in the vast expanse of the highlands of Tigray to confront the army of Menelik.

The path curved away and the image disappeared, but it gave her hope. If she could get away from her captors, help was closer than she had hoped. The Italian or Ethiopian army – it did not matter, either one would offer her refuge.

At last Bill called a halt. One of the servants invited her to dismount and led her into a patch of shade. A bandit stood guard beside her, but still Bill did not look at her or approach. So be it. If he chose to ignore her, for the moment at least that served her purpose. She had been given water during the ride and in all likelihood she would be fed too. Then darkness would fall and bring with it the chance of escape.

• • •

The guard was changed and Amber was brought bread and fresh stew. She ate hungrily then told the servant she needed to relieve herself. The servant consulted with Bill, then returned with a rope. It was tied around her waist, but was long enough to give her some privacy in the undergrowth fifty yards from the camp. She squatted in the darkness. The scrub gave way to trees and thorn bushes in front of her in the pale moonlight. She let the servant lead her back, knowing now where she'd find cover that might conceal her as she fled.

Her chance came only a few hours later. It was a still night and the moon was heavy and clear in the star-spattered sky. She had curled up on the ground with a woollen rug over her, and made her breathing soft and regular. Slowly all noise of activity in the camp ceased. A hurricane lamp had been lit and set close by her. She half opened her eyes. Her guard was still standing by her, but he was leaning against his spear as if it was a crutch and his face was angled away from her. She was almost sure he was sleeping where he stood.

She had considered trying to shift out of the light cautiously, quietly, but once they had set the lamp next to her she had decided the only chance would be to move quickly, and try and lose herself in the darkness before her captors had a chance to react. Her heart began to thud in her chest.

Do it now, she urged herself silently. Images of rifles and spear points, ropes and blood flashed across her mind's eye, but she tightened her muscles and refused to think of them. She thought of her father, her sisters, Ryder and Penrod. She asked them to help her be brave, then she sprang to her feet and threw herself into the darkness.

'She runs!' The shout went up the moment she moved, even as she dashed headlong into the stand of acacia and blue gum trees where she'd been roped and led a few hours before. She realised that the warning cry had contained no note of surprise or alarm. A lamp appeared almost directly in front of her, dazzling her. She darted to her left and heard laughter. Another light. Her stomach twisted and she felt a sick and bitter fear run through her, which seemed to thicken her blood and slow her limbs. This was a game. They were playing with her.

'Not this way, little one!' a voice said, and she realised she had almost stumbled into one of the bandits. He bent at the waist until he could stare directly into her eyes. 'Run away!'

She felt a sob in her throat and though she already knew her chance of escape had been an illusion all along, she dashed into the tearing thorns. So many voices, calling from her right and left. She was being driven through the cover like a game bird.

She stumbled and fell out of the copse and onto the path she had hoped would lead her to safety and lifted her head. Another pair of hurricane lamps suddenly cast their yellow sickly light over her. Shaded lanterns. They had been waiting for her, laughing at her. Perhaps she was just meant to be a plaything for the whole murderous, robbing band. A beautiful little blonde gift for them all. Rage at the trick they had played replaced her fear. Bill was waiting for her with his gunmen on either side of him. Amber sprang at him. The chance of escape was gone, but she would claw his eyes out if she could. They were ready for that too. Bill didn't even flinch. Strong arms caught her wrists and held them, while another man held her around the waist. She managed to kick a third in the jaw as he bent to grab her legs, but another man took his place and she was lifted off the ground. Her frantic struggles gained her nothing.

'I knew you would run, my dear Amber,' Bill said. 'I would have been rather disappointed if you hadn't tried. But you must learn this sort of wilfulness brings punishment.'

'Why, Bill?' she shouted at him, straining against her captors. 'Why have you taken me?'

'All in good time, Amber. I promise you won't die without understanding.'

Bill took a lamp from one of his companions and moved forward. As she struggled she saw his face, smooth-shaven, his hair neatly brushed back from his forehead, looking at her with a gentle pity.

'It's no use, dear child. Submit. Ease your suffering.' Then he stepped back. 'Tie her, gag her and bring her back to the camp.'

• • •

She was left to sleep on the chill ground with her hands tied behind her back, wrenching her shoulders, while her ankles were bound with a thin rope that cut into her flesh. The gag left her mouth dry and each breath she took was an effort. She thought she might suffocate. Her heart raced and shocks of pain burned through her arms and chest. She struggled to control her breathing, yet instead of fighting the pain, she let it wash over her. She lost consciousness, but the agony in her shoulders woke her almost at once. Time inched by and she wondered if she'd be mad before dawn.

She was given water at first light, and they did not replace her gag – a miracle that made her almost tearful with gratitude. The camp was packed up and she was thrown across the back of the mule she had ridden the day before like a sack of seed. The blood rushed to her head. Waves of sickness and agony shivered across her body. Amber hoped she would go mad – anything to escape the pain even for a moment. Then all at once she remembered seeing Penrod tied to the *shebba* in the court of Osman Atalan. The thought that he too had suffered like this brought her a sudden flash of courage. She pushed away the pain, squeezing it into a tight, fiery ball in her heart so she might think, just for a minute. Submit, Bill had said. He expected her to give up, stop fighting. Perhaps if she did, just a little, next time he would not be so ready for her escape. Bill expected to break her. She would let him think he was winning for a while.

Amber began to cry, and this time she meant them to see it.

Time passed. The mule took an uneven step and a fireball of pain exploded in her back. It became all of her consciousness. She was Amber no longer, just a being in agony. Thought was impossible; she fainted, crying out when she woke. The rope around her wrists was untied, then her hands were in front of her. As the blood flowed through her arms and into her hands, it felt as if her fingers had been plunged into lava. A bolt of white-hot pain flashed across her back, then a dreaming release.

The relief was overpowering. Her guts spasmed and she vomited before slipping into a half dream again.

The path was beginning to climb. Someone gave her water and wiped her mouth. Amber started to shiver in the thinning, cooling air. A moment later a woollen blanket was thrown over her.

Perhaps I will die before they even reach wherever we're going, she thought, and the idea gave her a certain sort of peace. Her only regret was that she had never slept in Penrod's arms.

A voice broke its way into her mind. An exchange of words between her guards. She twisted her head and thought she saw someone standing above them, some hundred yards away. A white man.

Has Penrod come to take me to heaven? she wondered, lifting her head a little more. The blanket slipped sideways.

'Miss Amber?' She heard an American voice. Her whole consciousness came flooding back to her in a single moment.

'Dan?' she said, then she screamed it. 'Dan! Help me!'

She squirmed against the ropes. Dan was running towards her. She called out again. 'Dan, oh Dan!'

One of the bandits threw his spear. Amber watched its deadly arc. It struck Dan in his side and he fell backwards. Two of the bandits ran towards him. Amber fought the agony, trying to lift herself up to see if Dan was still alive, but her view was blocked by Bill. He grabbed a handful of her hair, dragging her face up towards him. His face was white with rage and his spittle splashed on her cheeks and lips. She cried out.

'I told you, Miss Benbrook: submit or be punished.'

His eyes were sparkling, feverish.

Oh God, she thought. He is completely mad.

She saw him ball his fist and draw his arm back, still holding her by her thick, tangled hair. She tried to turn from the blow but she could not pull free. He was too quick. Too powerful. She felt a flash of pain and then the world went dark.

Saffron and Tadesse bought horses in Adrigat for a price that would have purchased five acres of good growing land, and then rode as fast as they dared, stopping only when necessary to save the horses from exhaustion. They circled to the south, reaching the outskirts of Menelik's camp thirty-six hours later.

They drew curious and hostile stares as they moved through the mass of people. Warriors, servants, women and children flowed around them. The army camp was bigger than any city in the country, but it was arranged along logical lines. The emperor's red velvet tent was at the centre of everything and the camp of Ras Alula would be close by it.

They abandoned their horses and walked swiftly and with purpose. Saffron kept close to Tadesse and wrapped her hair and face in her shawl. As they approached the centre of the camp she looked around her, desperate to see a familiar face in the crowd. Most of the mineworkers had joined Alula's men, but that was only forty men out of his force of ten thousand. Perhaps they could reach the emperor's tent. One of his retinue or that of the empress would know her.

Saffron could see the wall of cloth that surrounded Menelik's compound ahead of her. Hope lifted her heart, then she felt a hand on her arm.

'Where are you going, *ferengi*?' The warrior who had grabbed her wore the mark of Alula.

Saffron stood very straight. 'My name is Mrs Saffron Courtney. I need to see the emperor. He is a very great friend of mine.'

The warrior laughed in her face.

'This is a very important lady, from the Courtney Camp and Mine!' Tadesse said.

'I have never heard of such a place, little brother,' the man said.

Tadesse tried again. 'She is sister to the lady of the lion!'

Now the warrior hesitated and looked at Saffron with slightly more respect.

'Bandits have taken her,' Saffron said. 'I have come to beg the emperor for his help.'

The warrior took a step back and bowed. 'Come, madam, little brother. I shall take you.'

• • •

They got as far as the audience chamber and were ordered to wait. At the far end of the vast tent, Saffron could see Menelik and his generals in heated discussion, though she could not hear what was said. At last the meeting seemed to end and the warrior who had brought them in approached Alula, the emperor and the empress and spoke to them.

They glanced towards them and exchanged a few words. Menelik and Alula left the chamber and, seeing them go, Saffron gave a small moan. The empress, however, came towards them.

'Mrs Saffron, are you well?'

Saffron was trembling but she dropped into a low curtsy. 'Thanks be to God, I am well. And are you well?'

'Thanks be to God I am well. I am grieved to hear of your sister, but we cannot help you.' She turned away at once and Saffron cried out.

'But madam, my sister!'

Taitu faced her again, her expression ferocious. 'My *country*, Mrs Saffron!' She passed a hand across her face and spoke again more quietly. 'We need every man, my daughter, every man. The future of the empire is about to be decided. You know we cannot help you now.'

Saffron tried to blink back her tears. 'What is happening, madam?'

'Our army is having to search ever further for supplies. If the Italians do not come out into open ground, we are lost. The princes want my husband to launch an attack at once, but our men would be destroyed in the passes between here and Suria. He will not sacrifice his men.' She balled her hands into fists.

'We shall hold here until the last possible moment. We have two days at the most and then we must retreat west of Axum or the army will starve.'

Saffron had started to cry; she could not help herself. 'What can I do? I shall go mad waiting and doing nothing for Amber!'

Taitu leaned towards her. 'Do as I do. Pray the Italians attack. And when they do I shall take you in my retinue. You will carry water and food to our warriors with the other women, and when the invaders are crushed, Ras Alula will give you men to search for your sister. That is all I can do. That is all that can be done.'

Saffron lowered her head in submission.

'Who are you, little brother?' the empress said, turning to Tadesse.

He dropped to his knees. 'My name is Tadesse, madam.'

'The healer at Courtney Camp? Ras Alula's eyes and ears? He has spoken of you. Stay here. I will find work for you. Now, Mrs Saffron, I am going to church. I suggest you come with me.'

• • •

The Italians received their orders at eight-thirty on the evening after the generals met, and by nine o'clock the columns were on the move. A force was left at Suria to guard the supplies, but the bulk of the Italian forces moved out in four columns. The maps provided were rough, but Baratieri's intentions were clear. They would move forward in silence and under cover of darkness to occupy the heights of Rebbi Arienni, some eight miles short of Adowa. Menelik and the princes who fought alongside him would wake to find the Italian army entrenched in strong positions directly in front of him. He would be forced either to attack at just such a point in the landscape where his superior forces would do him least good, or he would have to withdraw and cede the field to the Italians, and with it Tigray.

The moon was high and bright, and as the Italian troops made their way along the paths behind their native guides, they could look up into the star-studded sky, broken by the shadows of the fantastical outlines of the high peaks. The army marched in silence. The only sound was the occasional scrape of European boots on the sand and gravel of the steep tracks. The *askari* went barefoot and made no sound at all.

Penrod remained with Baratieri and his staff during the march. The general seemed calmer now than he had been the previous evening. From time to time messengers would approach, jogging along the tracks past the regular troops to deliver news to the various columns, either written or verbally.

Albertone had taken the wrong path, and Arimondi had been forced to halt his own column for more than an hour while they passed. It was an annoyance, but such mistakes were perhaps inevitable on the confused narrow tracks and in darkness. Baratieri saw Arimondi start his deployment on the eastern slope of Rebbi Arienni, and then began to climb, rather laboriously, the slope of Mount Belah, which he had chosen to give the best viewpoint of the field.

As they gained height, Penrod began to see the campfires of the Ethiopian army at the other end of the large bowl-shaped valley. They were scattered over a vast area.

'A sight to warm the blood, no?'

Penrod turned. One of the new captains had joined him.

'I hope they attack.'

Penrod did not reply.

'I have a message for you,' the officer continued. 'Word has come up the line from camp that a man has been taken. They say he is Menelik's spy, even though he is white. He has said you can vouch for him. His name is Ryder Courtney.'

'What in hell's name is Courtney doing here?'

'You do know him then?'

'A trader, mining now in the hills above Adrigat. If he's come looking for news he's picked a hell of a time for it. But yes, I vouch for him.'

The captain looked apologetic. 'No use vouching for him to me, Major. It's some of Albertone's men guarding his kit at Suria. They won't release this Courtney without a word from the general. They say his eyes are crazy.'

'Who took him?'

'Some of the new Napoli boys.'

If any of the native brigades had picked up Ryder, he'd have been able to explain to them in any one of four languages what his business was and be done with it. Penrod doubted that Ryder had ever needed to speak much Italian.

'Sorry, my friend, but you'll have to go and get Albertone's say-so to release him.'

Penrod cursed fluently and in a number of languages, and then began to make his way back through the snaking column to the point where he could join the path towards Albertone's position. Halfway down the steep zigzagging track, he stepped off it to allow a mule loaded with parts of one of the field guns to pass him. One of the junior Italian officers he had spoken to in camp once or twice slipped out of the column and joined him. He was scarcely twenty and his uniform was loose on his skinny frame. He was bravely attempting to grow a moustache, but Penrod had seen more impressive specimens on the wives of retired generals.

'Major, may I ask something? Some of the lads are saying if these blackies catch you, they, you know . . .' He pointed unhappily to his groin and then made a chopping movement with his right hand.

'It's part of the culture here, I understand,' Penrod said, and the boy went white. 'Best not to let them catch you, young fella.'

The lad nodded sadly and returned to his company. Penrod watched him trudge off into the darkness, wondering if he had ever been that young, then continued down the track and took the path to the point where he expected to find Albertone deploying across Kidane Meret.

He found no signs of deployment, however, only the rear of the column bringing up supplies that were intended for the column's breakfast. He grabbed an officer from the catering corps.

'Where is Albertone?'

The man looked at him as if he were mad and gestured forward. 'That way. An hour ahead of us at least.'

Penrod felt a thin sickness in his stomach. An hour's march along this track could put Albertone miles out of position and in a perfect place to be engulfed by Menelik's troops.

'I need a horse. Now.'

The officer shrugged. 'That is impossible.'

Penrod grabbed him by the collar, lifting him off his feet. 'Horse. Now.'

The officer called over his shoulder and a sniggering *askari* brought up a good animal. Penrod flicked open his watch, taking careful note of the time, then mounted the horse and spurred it into a gallop, his head down.

• • •

Saffron thought she might have prayed herself into a daze. The priests chanted in slow, rising cadences. Some time after midnight she realised that the sacred *tabot* over which the priests were praying was not a replica of the Ark of the Covenant, one of which was kept in every church in Ethiopia. It was the actual Ark. The legend, accepted as fact by every son or daughter of Ethiopia, was that it had been carried to Axum from Jerusalem many centuries ago by the son of King Solomon and the Queen of Sheba. Now the priests of the ancient capital had brought it to guide and protect the imperial family. Saffron was not sure if it was her exhaustion, or her fear and frustration, but she could have sworn that the Ark seemed to glow.

She heard a shout at the back of the church.

'They are coming! To arms! The Italians are coming!'

The emperor stood and helped his wife up from her knees. He bowed deeply to the priests and the Ark. Everything was still. Then he turned and swept out towards the battlefield.

Saffron shook herself awake and followed the empress.

• • •

The further he galloped through the predawn dark, the more intense the pain in the pit of Penrod's stomach grew. One mile, two, three along the straighter, wider track of the Mai Agam valley and the path became clogged with the rear of Albertone's column. Penrod swung off his sweating horse and went at a run towards the group of dark uniforms, bright sashes and white faces that showed Albertone's position on the heights in front of him.

The officers turned to watch him approach with expressions of amusement and mild disdain. Penrod went straight to the general.

'You are miles out of position. You must retreat back to Kidane at once.'

Albertone put his arm through Penrod's and led him away from the rest of the staff with a light laugh. As soon as they were out of earshot, Albertone's face became an angry mask.

'You presume to give me orders, Englishman?'

'Sir, I am only stating a fact. You are at least three miles forward of where you should be. You are practically in Menelik's camp! You must return to the line – the position you were ordered to – before the enemy discovers you and attacks. You will be encircled here.'

Albertone showed no surprise or concern. If anything, Penrod thought he looked rather satisfied, like a child whose little intrigue against his elders has succeeded.

'I doubt that, Major Ballantyne. I have chosen my position. The enemy cannot take the heights to my left or right, but will be forced forward into the fire of the guns. A few rounds and they will fly away like crows in a cornfield when the farmer comes out with his shotgun.'

'You will not retreat and take up the position you were ordered to defend?'

'I disagree with your interpretation of my orders. It was my understanding that I was instructed to occupy this point and I have done so.'

'I tell you, the other columns are three miles in the rear.'

Albertone had begun to look bored. 'I'm sure they will join us quickly enough. They will not wish to miss the fun.'

Penrod was tempted to pull his revolver and shoot the man dead on the spot. Only the knowledge that doing so would mean his immediate execution, and not result in the forces deploying their proper position, prevented him. The night was pulling away from him.

They heard scattered rifle fire coming from a point some half a mile in front of their position. Albertone handed his coffee cup to one of the servants.

'Good, Turitto has woken them up.'

He gave his orders. The mountain batteries had not yet reached the high ground, but Albertone ordered the Sixth Native Battalion to the left to hold the southern flank of his position, while the Seventh, under Major Rudolfo, was sent to the right. The Eighth would hold the centre.

Penrod watched as the artillerymen unloaded the 75mm guns from the backs of mules and began to assemble them, while others of the company drove the animals away and up the slope.

The light came quickly. Penrod was soon able to see a mass of Ethiopian forces making their way across the valley towards them. A sea of men, the early sun struck sparks from the decorations on their shields. They were not charging, but moving forward in good order directly towards their position. Penrod made a quick calculation. Ten thousand men were already in the field and their numbers continued to grow. The Ethiopians broke into an easy jog and the ground between them and Albertone's position seemed to melt away. The sound of rifle fire located the advance guard, or what might remain of it. Their position had already been overwhelmed.

Penrod gritted his teeth as Captain Henry's battery began loading. The Ethiopians were ignoring the flanks and pushing forward against the centre. Henry gave the order and the guns belched smoke and flame with a ripple of cracks that echoed up and down the valley. They were firing shrapnel rounds directly into the middle of the approaching warriors. The gunners hardly had to aim. The numbers coming against them were already so vast they came in a single wave rather than in groups. Bodies disappeared in a mist of blood and torn-up dust, and the wave drew back for the briefest of moments, then reformed and came on again.

Moments later, the remains of Turitto's advance guard struggled up the slope under cover of the guns. Two of the *askari* were dragging a wounded white officer between them. Penrod went to the man's assistance. A captain, he was pulling at the blue sash over his right shoulder. His right arm hung limp and bloody, the forearm smashed by a rifle bullet. Penrod called for a stretcher party as the wounded captain shivered and mumbled to himself.

'We walked into them,' the captain kept repeating. 'We walked into them. We had no time to take a position. They have sharpshooters. I thought they did not know how to handle guns, but they took out all our officers first. All the officers.'

A pair of stretcher-bearers carried him away at a jog. Penrod tried to calculate how long it would take them to get back to the main force of the army and the field hospital beyond at the main camp. The man didn't stand a chance. He would be dead long before he reached the hospital.

All four mountain batteries were at work now. The valley below them had become an image of hell, of flesh and dust and the screams of the injured. Each wave of attack was coming closer. Penrod lifted his field glasses. The Ethiopians had sent squads of riflemen to the right and left, working their way into cover and taking out the officers and artillerymen. The forward riflemen of the Sixth and Seventh Battalions were doing a good job of holding them off, but they were still inching forward.

Albertone was watching the action from a knot of his senior staff, issuing orders to reinforce positions on the flanks, a model of calm authority. He noticed Penrod watching him and beckoned him over. Penrod walked towards him across the plateau, his face impassive.

'You have a horse, I think, Major Ballantyne?'

'I did, General. I'm sure I can find him again.'

'Perhaps you might take this to Baratieri, then,' Albertone said, writing a short note on his field notebook, then folding it and handing it to him.

'Certainly, General,' Penrod replied. The guns boomed heavy and slow. They seemed to have plenty of ammunition, but no matter the havoc they wreaked on the Ethiopian lines, the enemy showed no signs of breaking off the attack. The outcome was inevitable. For the sake of his conscience, Penrod made one last attempt.

'General, a fighting retreat even at this stage could save the majority of your men and enable you to fight on.'

Albertone shook his head like a teacher with a particularly dense student. 'Major, these savages will wear themselves out shortly. We are the rock on which this army will break. I will not deny my men the honour of subduing them.'

Penrod did not salute. Only then did he remember the reason he had joined Albertone in the first place.

'General, an acquaintance of mine has blundered into some men under your command at Suria and they require your note to release him. They think him a spy for Menelik.'

'And is he a spy?'

'No, he is a trader and a miner. Ryder Courtney.'

Albertone still looked as if he were scanning a parade ground rather than a field of slaughter. 'I have not time to deal with it now.'

'Sir!' He waited until Albertone turned back to him. 'You owe me a debt.'

'So that race and my wife's foolish wager have come back to haunt me at last, have they?' He lowered his field glasses, and wrote another quick note. 'I've released him on your parole, Major.'

'Thank you, sir.'

• • •

Penrod found his horse among the mules that had brought up the mountain guns. The beast looked rather indignant to be left among such low company and received Penrod with a toss of her head.

He swung himself up into the saddle, and as soon as they were clear of the beasts of burden, he encouraged her into a canter. Behind him he could still hear the regular crack and echo of the guns.

Penrod left his horse where the path became a mountain track and made the rest of the ascent on foot, negotiating it with the ease of a native. The spur where Baratieri had established his command post had a good view of the ground directly in front of him, but the curves of the valley floor put Albertone's position out of view.

Penrod found Baratieri still observing the deployment of Arimondi's brigade on the western flank of Belah. He was seated at a field desk under a short stretch of tarpaulin that gave him a certain amount of shade. He looked up as Penrod approached.

'Major Ballantyne, what are those guns?'

Penrod handed him the folded sheet from Albertone and stood with his hands clasped behind his back, focusing on some point in the middle distance of the morning haze.

'Advance guard hotly engaged and reinforcements would be welcome?' Baratieri read. 'I would welcome a cold bath and a chicken dinner, but that does not mean I need them. Your report, Major.'

Penrod continued to stare directly ahead as he spoke. 'General Albertone is deployed some three miles in advance of this position, sir. The Sixth, Seventh and Eighth Native Battalions are all engaged against vast numbers of infantry. I would estimate they face twenty thousand Ethiopian warriors in the field and the enemy are moving their field guns into position. At present Albertone is holding off successive waves of frontal attack with his mountain batteries and rifles.'

Baratieri clenched his jaw. He pushed aside the papers he had been writing on so that the map of the ground between Suria and Adowa was visible.

'Show me.'

Penrod leaned forward. 'The mountain guns are here and here, on rising land.'

'And these heights?'

'General Albertone is sure that they are too steep for the Ethiopians to reach them.'

'They made it up Amba Alagi. They are as quick as mountain goats,' Baratieri said under his breath.

Penrod had not taken the time to consider what effect the news might have on the Italian commander. He was in a vulnerable position and vastly outnumbered, and now his entire plan had been wilfully destroyed by the actions of one of his most senior officers. He might have called down curses on Albertone, but he did not. He summoned his messengers and began to give his orders.

'Make all haste to Arimondi. He is ordered forward and east to protect Albertone's right flank and give him cover to retreat.' The officer he instructed saluted and scurried away. 'Albertone is to retreat back to his position with Arimondi's support. Go at once.' Off went the next messenger.

Only then did Baratieri's calm fail for a moment. He covered his eyes with a shaking hand, then removed his pince-nez and polished them vigorously on his handkerchief. A fresh burst of gunfire boomed to the south-west. A new note, distinct from the mountain guns of Albertone's brigade. They both knew what it meant. The Ethiopian artillery was in position and had commenced firing.

Baratieri looked up at Penrod and spoke quietly. 'Major Ballantyne, I understand you have some business back at Suria.'

It was a dismissal, as firm as it was tactful. Penrod understood. He would not want a foreign witness in such a situation either. He put out his hand.

'May I wish you and your men the best of luck, General?'
Baratieri shook his hand firmly. 'And to you, Major.'

• • •

Penrod reclaimed his horse once more and made his way along
the empty paths the army had covered during their silent march
the night before. His impulse was to pick up a rifle and fight
where he could, but the Italians did not want him. And now he
had to go and rescue Ryder.

It did not take Penrod long to find him. He could hear Ryder
bellowing in frustration a hundred yards from the tent.

Penrod lit a cheroot on the threshold. It seemed Ryder had
persuaded one of the native guards he was no spy. The man
was trying to talk to his white comrades in broken Italian, but
the two youths who were guarding Ryder looked stubborn and
defensive.

'Penrod, thank God!' Ryder exploded. 'Tell these idiots to
release me at once, or I swear I will release myself and kill them
both with my own hands.'

Even if his guards did not understand his words, they understood something of his intentions and flinched as Ryder glow-
ered at them.

Penrod raised his eyebrows. Ryder was in shirtsleeves, seated
on a camp stool, with his hands tied behind his back. His guards
had used a great deal of rope to secure him.

'I always knew your complete inability to look like a gentleman
would be your downfall in the end,' he said. 'The Italians think
you are some wildman of the hills – they have heard rumours of
such a creature – and that you are also a spy for Menelik. I can't
say I blame them.'

Ryder pulled at his bindings and the ropes creaked ominously.
One of the guards started fumbling for his rifle and almost
dropped it. Penrod laughed.

'We have no time for this!' Ryder shouted.

His tone stilled the laughter in Penrod's throat. He gave Albertone's note freeing Ryder into his custody to the guards and ordered them to fetch Ryder's things with a few short phrases, then, his cheroot clamped between his teeth, he went to untie the ropes himself. Ryder's struggles had fused and tightened the knot into a dense mass. Penrod took out his knife and sawed at it. Ryder's wrists were bruised a deep purple, and his forearms showed signs of recent burns.

'What's happened?'

'Amber has been taken.'

Penrod's heart stopped in his chest for a moment. He bent over the ropes again, sawing at the last fibres. 'By whom?'

Ryder burst free of the last shreds. 'Thank you.' Then he grabbed his coat and gun belt from the cowed guards.

'Can you get me food, water and more rifle ammunition?'

'Yes. Who has taken Amber?' Penrod's voice remained level.

Ryder looked at Penrod directly for the first time. 'I hired an engineer. Bill Peters. Never liked him much but he knew his work. Then he tried to kidnap Amber on our last trip to Addis during a flash flood, but he was lost in the waters. I hoped he was dead but he's been leading a group of bandits in the hills and he attacked the camp to take Amber. I've no idea who he really is, but I know he's mad and obsessed with her.'

Penrod sprang forward, driving Ryder up against the pole in the centre of the tent. Everything shook and the guy ropes creaked. The guards began to protest in fluent, high-pitched Italian, but Penrod and Ryder ignored them.

'You let him take her?'

Ryder stared back at him, but did not attempt to break his hold. '*She* let him take her, to save Saffron and the children. Penrod, listen to me!'

Penrod breathed hard, controlling his rage, trying to hear Ryder's words through the thundering of his blood.

'I'm sure his camp is nearby,' Ryder continued, 'and I came here looking for information, but the Ethiopians think I'm a spy for the Italians, and, as you see, vice versa. But I don't care if I have to search every cave and hilltop for a hundred miles. I am going to find Amber. Are you going to help?'

Penrod released him. 'Yes. Talk to that man. He's one of the scouts, though I think he's been working for Menelik too.' He turned to the sputtering guards and spoke in Italian. 'Water rations and ammunition. At once.'

They scurried out of the tent and Ryder spoke to the native scout, then he too left them.

'Well?' Penrod said.

'He does work for Menelik, and luckily he works for Ras Alula too, and we have friends in common. He's told me what he knows and is going to talk to his fellows and see if he can find out more.'

The Italians came back into the tent and dumped their spoils in front of the two men. While they both selected what they wanted from the pile of canteens and ammunition, Penrod told them in a few short sentences what had happened and where he was going. One offered his own rations from his pack. Penrod thanked him, but refused. They backed out of the tent, mumbling apologies.

'We have another problem,' Ryder said, filling his pockets with ammunition.

'What?'

'The people are rising up against the Italians and they aren't going to stop and let us explain that we are subjects of Her Majesty Queen Victoria. Any local we see will try to kill us. It's their duty.'

'Couldn't your friend Alula give us safe passage?'

'He has other business today. I won't waste time dragging you around the battlefield to his camp. Even if we survived, it will be hours before he can lend us any men.'

Penrod changed into civilian clothes. The scout slipped back into the tent and had another, shorter, conversation in Amharic with Ryder, then he shook hands with him and disappeared.

'So do you know where he has taken her?'

'He's heard rumours of a white bandit near the Three Sisters. That must be him. It's more than I had, anyway, and he will tell Alula where we are going so he can send men after us when this business with the Italians is done. Are you ready?'

'I am,' Penrod said, then stiffened. 'Listen.' He had heard the distant crackle of rifle fire.

Penrod left the tent and looked up the valley towards the passes that flanked Baratieri's command post and Arimondi's deployment, cursing. Groups of *askari* choked the paths. The wounded were being carried back to the camp in good order, but two hundred yards behind them was a mass of bodies, men pursued and pursuing and hopelessly tangled. The two Italian guards had disappeared.

Penrod lifted his field glasses. His gaze was caught by a small tableau up on the slope above the path: a white officer and a group of *askari* attempting to offer covering fire to the retreat. It was Nazzari and some of his men from the Eighth Battalion. As Penrod watched, the squad kept up an astonishing rate of fire, giving some of the *askari* enough cover to tumble by and below them towards the camp. Ethiopian riflemen took up positions on the opposite side of the gorge and began to concentrate their fire on them. Nazzari still held his ground.

'You've done enough, Nazzari, fall back,' Penrod said, his jaw clenched.

Three of Nazzari's men had been hit. One was obviously dead and one of the others continued to fire as best as he could as he lay slumped on the slope.

More Ethiopians were approaching their position from above. Still, neither Nazzari nor his men moved. As Penrod watched, Nazzari took out three of the attackers with his revolver. He was about to be overwhelmed. Penrod took a step forward and Ryder grabbed hold of his arm.

'He's too far away. You can't help him.'

The lance of one of the Ethiopian infantrymen plunged into Nazzari's thigh. He staggered, lifted his revolver and blew out his own brains.

Penrod lowered his binoculars, then reached into the press of men beginning to swirl through the camp and grabbed an *askari* by his shoulder.

'What happened?'

The man said something Penrod could not understand. Ryder translated his frightened gabble in a monotone.

'He says Albertone's left flank was turned. Officers all dead or captured. General Dabormida went north, so no protection. Ethiopian cavalry has broken the centre.'

Penrod released him. 'These men are all going to be slaughtered unless they make a fighting retreat.'

'And we'll be killed with them unless we get out of here,' Ryder replied. 'Are you coming?'

Penrod lowered his binoculars. 'No, not yet.'

'But what about Amber?' Ryder said.

Penrod felt her name like a brand on his heart. He looked at the men surging towards them, the fleeing troops breaking around the camp. Some of the *askari* NCOs were ordering the men to form up around them, but with little success. Others were carrying their wounded and dying officers from the field. It seemed no commissioned officers had survived. Where they stood, the campfires and baggage carts of Albertone's retinue provided a bulwark against the surge of men struggling back from the battlefield and their pursuers.

Penrod checked his revolver. 'You may go ahead, or remain, but I will not walk away from this. Not yet.'

Ryder hesitated. Penrod could guess his thoughts. Ryder knew he had a much better chance of rescuing Amber with his help.

'Very well,' he said at last with a growl.

'Try not to get in the way,' Penrod said, then grabbed hold of one of the *askari* running by him. 'Do you speak Italian? Arabic?'

Neither language worked and Penrod shoved the man back into the flow of soldiers, then he heard himself hailed by name. A man was struggling towards him through the crowd and Penrod put out his hand and hauled him clear. It was Ariam, the sergeant he had raced in Massowah. He had a deep wound across his cheek and his left arm hung awkwardly. His skin was ashy with exhaustion and his white jacket was streaked with dust. Penrod could read the story of his battle in his wounds, the wide stain across his chest – the same russet as his sash – where he had carried a wounded man.

'Ariam! Captain Nazzari is dead.'

The sergeant lowered his head, grief and exhaustion weighing him down like a stone. 'I had hoped . . . *Effendi*, he was the last. All the officers are gone. We are like a snake with our head cut off.'

'What now?' Ryder asked.

'These *askari* fought at Kassala and Coatit,' Penrod said quickly. 'They need only a moment to steady themselves. Sergeant, you will gather the surviving NCOs and men of the Eighth Battalion now. Follow my orders and we may yet save some of them from this rout. Are you willing?'

Already the sergeant seemed to be regaining his strength. He listened carefully to Penrod's instructions and his breathing steadied. As soon as Penrod had finished, he saluted and began to bark out orders, calling men out of the fleeing pack by name. Some of the Ethiopian warriors were already at the edge of the camp and engaging the routed *askari*.

'Ready, Sergeant?'

'Ready, *effendi*!'

The sergeant had managed to pull perhaps fifty men from the throng. Their injuries seemed to be light and Penrod was pleased to see four or five NCOs among them. The men were split into four groups and given their orders.

The mass of the pursuing Ethiopians was almost upon them, slashing at the *askari* who choked the path in front of them like men slicing through thorn bushes. The pursuit was as disorganised and leaderless as the retreat.

'Fix bayonets!' Penrod shouted and unsheathed his cavalry sabre. The blade felt alive in his hand.

Ariam was watching him like a hawk, his wounds forgotten and his whole body taut with purpose.

'Wait for it, wait for it,' Penrod snapped. The rout was dividing around them. He could do nothing for the men fleeing along the northern edge of the camp, but if they were lucky, the *askari* fleeing down this southern path might have a chance. The mass of the Ethiopian advance guard was coming level with them.

'Charge!' Penrod shouted.

He led some forty *askari* with him against the flanks of a force at least three times that number, but the Ethiopians were too focused on their prey to be aware of the threat. They were blocked by the baggage wagons and steep southern slopes that turned the path into a killing ground. Penrod picked an officer by his lion's mane headdress and attacked with a sweeping cut that severed the man's carotid artery just below his left ear. On either side of him the *askari* provided ample proof of their training, thrusting their steel into belly and chest.

The air stank of sweat and blood, and the Ethiopians, surprised by the force and ferocity of the attack, fell back. Penrod spun right. A flash of steel glimmered to his left. He rocked backwards and felt the curved blade of the *shotel* slice through the fabric of his jacket. He parried blows to his thigh and shoulder as his attacker exploited the impossible angles of attack the curved blade offered, and spun away from Penrod's sweeping counter strike. He too wore a lion's collar.

Penrod thrust forward, swinging the sabre upwards with such force the Ethiopian could not turn the blow with his shield. The glimmering steel point ripped him up from groin to rib cage. He collapsed onto the ground. Penrod changed his grip and drove the sabre through the man's heart.

As Penrod withdrew his blade, he sensed a movement to his left. An infantry swordsmen was descending on him, his blood-spattered *shamma* billowing behind him. Penrod's blade caught for a fatal second against the ribs of his dead foe. The blade that would kill him was swinging towards his neck. Then the man fell back and away onto the dust. Penrod turned in time to see Ryder Courtney lowering his rifle.

'On me!' he shouted, and the *askari* disengaged from the remains of the Ethiopian attackers. The *askari* who had not formed part of the attack opened up a steady volley with their rifles, their numbers swelled now by men who had escaped the headlong rout.

The mass of the Ethiopian troops, finding their path impeded, were swinging around to the north of the camp. But, hampered by the tents, cooking fires, animals and servants, their advance was becoming blocked. No co-ordinated attempt was made to flank Penrod's position. More men, some supporting wounded comrades, were finding their way back behind the protection of Penrod's rifles.

Ariam formed the men into two platoons and they began to retreat in good order. Penrod called the sergeant to him.

'When you are clear of any pursuit, scatter your men into small groups. Do not use the supply routes. Travel by night, post guards in the day and get to Asmara as quickly as you can.'

The sergeant saluted, then, with a slight hesitation, put out his hand, and when Penrod shook it, he said, 'Thank you, *effendi*.'

'Go with God,' Penrod answered and Ariam went to join his men.

'Done winning your latest VC yet?' Ryder asked. His pack was already on his shoulder. 'Because I think it's time we got out of here.'

'King Umberto does not give out VCs. I shall have to make do without a matching pair,' Penrod replied coolly.

A rifle round kicked up a spurt of dust between them. The Ethiopians who had overwhelmed Nazzari and his men had noticed the pocket of resistance and its source, and were finding their range.

Penrod picked up his pack. 'Now we can go.'

• • •

After two hours Ryder called a halt under a lone juniper. The shade would provide both refuge from the afternoon sun and some little concealment for them from any bands of Ethiopians searching for survivors of the battle.

'I do not need to rest,' Penrod said.

Ryder held out his canteen towards him. 'Did you have friends in the battle?'

Penrod took the canteen and allowed himself a mouthful of water. He rolled it around his mouth before he swallowed, then sat down in the dust next to Ryder.

'I knew many of the officers.'

Ryder did not offer condolences, nor did he take the chance to remind Penrod what he thought of European armies on colonial adventures. Instead he drank and carefully stoppered the canteen.

'The blonde child you saw at camp was my daughter – mine and Saffron's. Amber has not married.'

Penrod did not react at once, but when he spoke, his voice was icy. 'Do you think I am more likely to save her knowing that?'

Ryder sighed deeply. 'No. I think you would do anything to save her, married or not. But we are facing odds of at least six to one, judging by the attack on my camp. If we are going to die trying to save Amber, you should know she remained faithful to you, even when she thought you were dead.'

'Very well. What can you tell me of this man who abducted her?' Penrod asked at last.

Ryder shared what little he knew. How he had met Bill in Addis and had found him a useful and skilled addition to the camp, but never liked or trusted him. He gave a brief description of his assault on the trail to Addis before the great muster, and the revelations of the doctor.

Penrod listened intently. 'So this man who calls himself Peters, he first appeared in Bohemia?'

'According to the doctor, yes,' Ryder said, stowing the canteen in his belt pouch. 'Why?'

Penrod only shook his head and they got to their feet, but a dark and seemingly impossible suspicion had begun to bloom in his heart. 'Did you tell him I was alive and in Tigray?' he asked.

'You? No. I told Saffron you were alive and she told Amber, so I suppose he may have heard you and I met here. Why?'

Penrod only shook his head.

At the top of the next incline Penrod turned and looked back towards the plain of Adowa. At first he thought he saw a thick mist reaching up the slopes on either side of the battlefield. He lifted his field glasses and looked. It was not mist, but smoke. The Ethiopians were driving out any Italian soldiers remaining in the field by setting fire to the grass and vegetation. Penrod could imagine the scene, the wounded not allowed to die quietly among their fellows, but forced to their feet by the choking smoke, wandering through the horrid tableau of the dead into the arms of their foes.

Amber opened her eyes. Her head pounded and at first she could only make out patterns of light and shade. She was lying on some sort of bed. She tried to move. She was not tied down, and as far as she could tell her limbs were whole. She was sore and trembling and her head ached with an intensity that almost blinded her. She raised herself up and squeezed her eyes shut as a fresh wave of pain broke over her, then very carefully traced her fingers over the back of her head where the pain seemed worse. No swelling that she could feel, and no blood.

Just a bump, she told herself firmly. She carefully opened her eyes again and, moving as little as possible, looked around her.

It was a traditional round hut, though small, less than twenty feet in diameter. The final foot of the wall before it reached the thatched roof was open wickerwork that allowed the light to pour steeply into the room, casting deep shadows.

As Amber's vision adjusted, she began to make out the shapes of crates and baskets, rolls of cloth leaning against the walls, rough hessian sacks, plump with grain, small banded chests and steamer trunks. The central area had been cleared. On the rough earth floor stood a small rosewood table and a pair of elegant dining chairs. She felt the sheet of the bed on which she was sitting: soft cotton. And it was a proper bed too, with a head and foot, a mattress and a silk comforter. The door was closed. Next to the stove was a mahogany washstand, complete with a porcelain ewer and bowl decorated with small pink roses.

Amber stood up shakily and went over to the washstand. She found clean water in the jug and she poured a little over her hands and splashed her face, before glancing in the mirror and smoothing her hair from her face. Then she began to explore the chamber. It was a cave of stolen delights. At least the search took her mind off her pounding headache and her aching limbs. She dragged one of the chairs to the end of the bed and clambered shakily on top of it. Pulling herself up on to the tips of her toes, she peered out through the wicker. The air was chill and thin. She could just make out the distant mountaintops, purple against the pale sky. She lowered herself on to the flat of her feet and leaned against the walls of her prison. It had been evening when she saw Dan – evening on the second day of her capture. Had they killed him? She prayed they had not.

It was day now. Whatever Bill had planned for her, it was obviously not immediate execution. What did he want from her? Why risk the attack?

An hour or so later she heard the bar across the door being lifted. A girl of no more than fourteen slipped into the chamber. Amber caught a brief glimpse of the world outside: a dusty court-yard, the shape of other buildings, the figures of two guards, their rifles in their hands, standing by her door.

'I hope you are well,' she said to the girl.

'Thanks be to God I am well,' the child answered. 'And you?'

'Thanks be to God I am well.'

The girl was carrying a basket of bread and a beaker of some warm liquid. It steamed slightly. For a moment Amber could not place the fragrance competing with the sour yeastiness of the *injera*, then she realised with wide-eyed surprise that it was the smell of Earl Grey tea. The girl was already returning to the door.

'Sister,' Amber said, softly but urgently, 'where are we?'

The girl blinked. 'In the mountains,' she said in a husky whisper, then disappeared back into the sunlight before Amber could ask anything else.

She thought about throwing the tea to the ground, grinding the bread under her heel, but she was painfully hungry. What-ever the day held for her, she decided, it would be better for her if she faced it on a full stomach. Only when she was eating did she notice a small, polished wooden box on the table next to her. She opened it very carefully. The box held within it a beautiful, mask-like ivory carving of a man's face.

· · ·

After Amber had eaten her meal, she heard a knock at the door. Considering it was barred from the outside, this almost made her laugh, then she noticed an envelope pushed underneath. She waited for a moment, but no further sound came from outside, so she left her seat and went to pick up the envelope. It was thick, heavy paper and her name was written on it in a graceful copperplate. She returned to her chair and put the last of the *injera* in her mouth before she cracked the seal and unfolded the pages. It was a short note. Her host apologised for having to take such extreme measures to win her compliance. Amber almost choked. He went on to say in similarly formal language that he would dine with her that evening. He would be grateful if she took the opportunity to dress for dinner and said all the feminine apparel and jewellery in the room were at her disposal.

For a long time Amber stared into the gloom of her prison and considered the letter held loosely in her hand. Then she made her decision and began to open up the chests and cases surrounding her. She took her cue from the formal language of the note itself and selected a long and heavy skirt in scarlet silk, and a sky-blue bodice with loose lace-trimmed sleeves, laced at the front. As she dressed she wondered to whom these clothes had belonged. An Italian officer's wife or daughter, perhaps.

The bodice was a little tight across her chest, but the fit was close enough. The skirt hung down to the floor, and she found a pair of velvet slippers, worked with silver thread. They fitted her perfectly. She debated changing them for a little pair of boots, but those were loose on her small feet. They might seem sturdier, but in the slippers she would be able to run more quickly. Then she turned her attention to her hair, brushing and twisting it high, and fixing it in place with some little silver combs she had discovered. Looking at herself in the mirror, she felt a certain amount of pride, then laughed. She remembered going to the Gheziera Club in Cairo and feeling so uncomfortable and trapped in clothes much like these. Now she was as formally dressed as she had ever been, about to dine with her murderous kidnapper yet feeling remarkably at ease. Her years in the wilderness had somehow given her the poise and confidence of a young duchess. So be it. She began to test the stiffness in her shoulders, teaching herself to move without wincing.

Towards the middle of the afternoon the bar was lifted from the door and the servant girl came in again with another, even younger girl. Amber did not attempt to talk to them, but instead watched, fascinated, as they placed a linen cover over the table, and added candlesticks, plates, cutlery, glasses, napkins, and all the paraphernalia of fine European dining produced on an isolated hilltop in the middle of the Tigray highlands.

· · ·

Ryder halted on the edge of a garden plot, planted chest-high with fruit bushes. The back of his neck had been prickling for the last twenty minutes, a sense of being watched, but he could see no signs of anyone following them.

'Well?' Penrod asked.

Ryder pointed up to a range of narrow, fantastical, flat-topped peaks about a mile in front of them across rising ground, scattered with broadleaf trees and the skeletons of sycamores waiting for the rains.

'This is as far as the scout's directions will take us. He was told the *shifta* with the white leader have their permanent camp on top of one of those three *amba* in the middle of the range – those are the Three Sisters – but nothing he told me indicates which one.'

Penrod examined each in turn through his field glasses. 'I can't tell if any of them is inhabited. I don't see smoke either.'

Ryder shielded his eyes. 'I would wager money that you'll find a church or monastery on one or other of them. If it weren't for that damned army, we could ask any of the peasants for two miles around and they'd tell us.'

'If it weren't for the army scouts, you'd be here without any clue at all and no water,' Penrod said. 'You're a hunter. Surely we can pick up the trail? Heavily loaded pack animals, large groups of men . . .' Penrod was growing impatient, but Ryder shook his head.

'The *shifta* are hunters too. If they wish to cover their tracks, they'll use every trick in the book to do so: false trails, brushing out tracks behind them. They have fooled me already.'

'Then we climb each one in turn. We'll have to wait until dark, or we might as well announce our coming with a bugle.' Penrod examined the flat tops of the peaks again. The landscape was filled with a choice of natural fortresses. 'We'll have to go in quietly. A frontal approach would be useless,' he added.

'Agreed,' Ryder replied. 'I swear to God, though, I shall see that man die today, even if I have to give up my own life to do it.'

'We do have a secret weapon, of course.'

'What is that?' Ryder asked.

'Amber.'

• • •

Amber could sense her appearance pleased him. She felt his slow, assessing gaze, but kept her own eyes lowered.

'What a pleasure it is, my dear, to see you properly dressed,' he said.

She did not reply but only touched her neck, as if brushing away some stray strand of gold hair.

'Will you be seated and take a glass of wine? I've told the servants we shall wait upon ourselves.'

He pulled out the dining chair for her, and once she had arranged the heavy folds of her skirt, he took his own place opposite. An open crystal decanter stood on the table. He poured the wine into her goblet and the heavy fruited scent of an excellent Burgundy was released like a subtle breeze into the air. She smiled briefly and thanked him, but when he spoke again his voice had hardened a little.

'You are unusually quiet, Miss Benbrook.'

He began to put food on her plate from the serving dishes. Goat, a mash of beans, but all served as if it were côte de boeuf and gratin dauphinois.

'I was thinking that you seem very different now; not the man you presented yourself as in camp.'

He looked faintly amused. 'Ah, I had a role to play then. Bill Peters the engineer. Lower-class boy who had dragged himself up in society with his brain, then became possessed with a passion for travel. I think I played it rather well.'

'You fooled us for years.'

He cut a slice of his meat and lifted it, examining it in the low light. Amber almost expected him to summon the waiter and send his compliments to the chef.

'Yes, I did, didn't I?'

Amber managed a mouthful of the bean mash. She had been famished only minutes before, but eating in front of this man made the food taste like ashes. She forced herself to swallow.

'We met a man in Addis. He said you are not Bill Peters at all.' Then she looked up. 'Who are you?'

He looked taken aback for a moment at the force of her gaze.

'You are more beautiful even than my daughter was. Extraordinary.'

She looked back down at her plate. The scrape of cutlery on porcelain seemed to stretch her nerves to breaking point.

'You will not tell me your name then?'

'You may call me James.' Suddenly he reached forward and grabbed her wrist so tightly that she dropped her knife. He pulled her abruptly towards him.

'Remember where you are, Amber. On top of a mountain, the only path so steep in places hardly a mule can climb it. One wrong step and you'll plummet a hundred feet and your pretty face will be smashed to a pulp. You are surrounded by twenty of the best fighting men money can buy. Stop planning your escape, child. It is hopeless. Your fate is sealed, I'm afraid. And if you attempt to run before I am ready, I will give you to my men to use as their plaything.'

She stared straight at him. 'James, you're hurting me.'

He released her at once. 'My dear, I'm so sorry.' He cut another slice of his meat and ate it with obvious relish. 'Do remember what I have said, though.'

* * *

The trail had been interfered with, a careful confusion of hoof and footprints in the dust where the path divided into two. Each hillside would take at least an hour to climb, and a wrong decision now could cost them not just time but, if they were unlucky, the element of surprise also.

Penrod favoured the trail leading north-west. It was wider and shallower, at least at this point. If the *shifta* were regularly moving their spoils up the slope, they must choose that over the sudden, narrow climb of the route Ryder favoured. They were arguing in low tones when Ryder suddenly stiffened and held up his hand. The prickling sensation of being watched shivered over Penrod's scalp. He sensed a movement in the scrub to the south. Ryder slowly took his revolver from its holster and turned. On the edge of the copse behind them stood an elderly Abyssinian man. He was stooped and leaning on his heavy walking stick, his hair as white as the *shamma* slung around his shoulders. Once he saw they were looking at him, he clicked his tongue against his teeth. The scrub shivered and a dozen youths – some armed with ancient muzzle-loading rifles, others with lances – appeared out of cover.

Ryder said something to them in Amharic. Penrod had picked up enough of the language to guess he was telling them that they were English, not Italian, and although they were not enemies, they would not be taken without resistance.

The old man held up his hand and shook his head. Penrod could not make out the reply, but Ryder hissed a translation as the old man spoke.

'The old man's name is Gabre; these are his grandsons, who were too young to join the army. They say a holy man at their compound wishes to speak to us.'

'We have no time to consult with a holy man.'

'Wait. The man has asked for us by name. He says he has seen Amber.'

Penrod had returned his revolver to its holster and was striding across towards the old man before Ryder had finished speaking.

The compound was not far away, hidden in a shallow bowl of land. The fields around it looked well tended and, hidden from the main tracks, they seemed to have escaped the requisitioning of the army.

Penrod and Ryder were ushered past a group of staring women and small children into the central *tukul* in the compound. A woman was kneeling by the earth bed in the back of the hut, offering the man who lay on it *tulla* from a horn beaker. Ryder's eyes adjusted quickly to the gloom. As the woman moved away, the man on the bed drew himself up on to one elbow and spoke.

'Mr Courtney.'

'Dan,' Ryder said, his voice sharp and angry. 'So you are a holy man now, are you?'

Dan had aged a great deal since he had murdered Rusty and left the camp. His face was gaunt but deeply tanned, covered in a thick network of wrinkles. His chest was bare, hollow and pale. The muscles that he had earned digging for treasure on two continents had wasted away. His beard was heavy and as snow white as his hair. If he had not spoken, Ryder would not have recognised him. He had a bandage tied around his waist, stained with blood on the right side.

'You know each other?' Penrod asked, looking between the men.

'We do,' Dan said, his accent still discernible, but faint as a distant echo.

'You are American,' Penrod said.

Ryder could not look at him any longer; he could not even speak. He stared at the earthen floor, his rage at Rusty's death consuming him as if it had only happened that morning.

'I killed a good man at Courtney's camp,' Dan was saying. 'Miss Benbrook released me rather than see me hang. Told me to do penance for my sins, and I have done so. I do so now.'

Penrod did not need to hear the history. 'Miss Benbrook's been taken. What can you tell us?'

Dan shifted and gasped at the pain in his side, but he spoke quickly between gritted teeth. 'They took her up the second sister. I live up on the steep flanks of the first – it is higher, but the peak has only space for my hut. Men have been living on the second sister for some months now. They leave the local people in peace, but they are known as bandits. Their leader is white.'

'We know that,' Ryder said. 'It is Peters, the man we hired to replace you at Courtney Mine.'

'Did you see Amber?' Penrod asked. He itched with impatience to be gone.

'I did,' the wounded man answered. 'I had been to visit Ato Gabre, to fetch supplies and pray with the wives of his sons who have gone to fight. As I was walking back, I saw the raiding party return and that they were carrying a woman with them. At first I did not know it was her, then I saw her hair.'

'Was she injured?'

'Unconscious. I called out and ran towards them. It was stupid, I carry no weapons, but I did not think of such things. I saw her come awake and begin to struggle. She called out, but his men were upon me. One of the bandits struck me once with his spear. The white man, Peters, ordered them to leave me.'

'Why not kill you?' Ryder asked, his voice still leaden.

'Perhaps they thought they had done so. Perhaps they feared the local people would turn against them if they killed me.'

'Is there someone here who can show us the path up the second sister?' Penrod asked.

Dan nodded. 'The eldest boy here will show you the way. I shall pray for her protection, and your success.'

'I do not want your prayers,' Ryder said.

'Still you have them.' Dan drew in his breath painfully. 'I thought their leader must be the devil come back to haunt me once more. His name . . .' His voice was growing faint.

'What do you mean, Dan?' Ryder asked.

'I saw him only from a distance, back in Cairo, and he has changed. But then I heard his name. The name that the people here call him. Ras Shama.'

'What of it?'

Dan's voice was weak. 'Ras Shama.'

No one spoke for a long time.

'It cannot be . . . That man is dead. He blew his own head off,' Ryder said.

'What is it?' Penrod demanded.

Ryder passed his hand over his eyes. 'Ras Shama. It means Prince or Duke of the Candle.'

Penrod felt the tumblers of his mind turn. The body in Cairo with its face ruined by the shotgun blast; the ivory mask Penrod had left behind that was then missing from the safe. Penrod had been sure the duke was dead, but what if he had decided to escape, lie low and lick his wounds in one of the most remote corners of the globe? The duke had run mines and mining operations for years; he would be able to pass for an engineer.

'The Duke of Kendal,' Penrod said.

'Is this who he is?' Ryder spun around to stare at Penrod. 'Did he know you loved Amber? Did Kendal attack the camp and seize Amber to revenge himself on you?'

Penrod did not answer him. 'We go now,' he said, then approached the bed where Dan was lying and put out his hand. Dan took it. 'And even if Courtney will not accept your apologies and regrets, I shall. I give you my thanks in return.'

Dan lifted his hand in blessing, and Ryder and Penrod left him to his nurse.

Dinner progressed in silence. The only sound was of James's knife sawing through his meat. Outside Amber could hear the squeaks and whistles of the blue starlings foraging for their own supper. She sipped her wine. James looked across at her plate.

'Do try and eat a little more. It is your last meal after all.'

Amber pushed a little of the bean mash onto her fork and swallowed mechanically. He watched her and seemed to approve.

'I like your mask,' she said, nodding at the rosewood box on the table.

'I am glad,' he said. 'It is of Caesar, you know. A reminder of a former life, and of the fact great men can fall, and then rise again.' He picked up the case and slipped it into his pocket.

'How did you survive the flood?' she asked.

'I have developed a talent for resurrection,' he said and made no further comment.

Amber watched him from under her eyelashes. In the camp he had occasionally reminded her of a snake, a combination of the way he moved his head at times and the blankness of his dark eyes. But a snake is a creeping, malicious creature, and now in his kingdom James was happy to display his strength and command. A cobra, she thought. Rearing up over her with its hood expanded, its flickering tongue tasting the air.

'It is so long since I ate in this manner,' she tried again. 'Years and years. How did you manage to bring all these things here?'

'The caravans along the coast produce many treasures, such as the dress that you are wearing.'

Amber looked down at the froth of snowy lace around her throat and at her wrists. 'The colours are a little bold for me,' she said.

He pushed away his plate, then crossed his legs and picked up his wine glass. 'Not at all. My daughter Agatha had a taste for strong colour and was regarded as a leader of the fashionable set.'

A deep cold chilled Amber's heart. 'Lady Agatha?' she asked.

He looked at her with a thin, flickering smile, as if she were a pet who had just managed an endearing new trick.

'Well done, Miss Benbrook. I am waiting for news from the battle. When it is over I shall have a message conveyed to Penrod Ballantyne, telling him you are here and in my hands. He will rush to your rescue, and find you dead with that ivory mask beside you, and myself gone.'

'Was this always your plan, James?'

He chuckled softly. 'Oh no, my dear. I have had my eye on Courtney Mine for years. You know I had one of my men sabotage the steamer all those years ago, then blackmailed Dan to make sure the enterprise failed. I was simply going to buy it when Ryder had finished bankrupting himself. Then Penrod ruined me. Eventually I found my way here and my new plan was to use my bandit friends to take the mine when it suited me, ideally after that bull Courtney had returned to Cairo, but then –' he leaned forward, waving his steak knife like a wand – 'I learned Penrod Ballantyne was still alive, and taking my revenge on him became very, very important to me. Murdering the woman he loved while he was so close, but not close enough, seems an ideal way to do so. And just to tie things up neatly, between my highway robbery and a little extra sabotage before we fetched you, Ryder will certainly lose the mine now. I shall take it over when banditry begins to pall.'

'You have been very clever, James,' Amber said hollowly. Everything lost: Penrod, the mine, her own life.

'Yes, I'm quite pleased,' he said, swallowing his wine with pleasure.

'I would like to go outside.' She spoke without thinking, only knowing that to stay in this room a moment longer, in this treasure house of blood and perfidy, would drive her insane.

'I have spoken to you about any attempt to escape, my dear.'

She set down her knife and fork very carefully, willing herself to move slowly.

'You have said you are going to kill me anyway; why shouldn't I run?'

His smile was sympathetic. 'Dear Miss Benbrook, behave and I promise you a quick death. Run and you will suffer all the horrors of hell in your last hours.'

Amber flinched. She had to make him think she was afraid of him and too scared to run, but not overplay her hand. She blinked quickly and let a single tear run down her cheek.

'Let me feel the sun on my face one last time then, James. I will not run.'

He laughed and shook his head, the way men do at the whims of beautiful women. Then he stood and offered her his arm. Amber got up from her chair and placed her hand lightly on his forearm, and then as he turned towards the door, she reached behind his back to pick up his steak knife from the table and slipped the greasy blade into her sleeve.

• • •

Two other huts had already been built among the trees on the flat summit of the *amba*. Several tents had been set up and two of the slave girls tended a cooking fire. The mules were in a small enclosure set a little back from the human habitation.

Amber could see smoke in the distance, a heavy band of it like a fallen cloud.

'The Italians have been utterly defeated at Adowa,' the Duke of Kendal drawled.

'This pleases you?' Amber said, picking up on his satisfied tone.

'Oh yes,' he said, and patted her hand where it lay on his sleeve. She managed not to flinch away. 'Menelik will take his army home, and my friends and I will have greater freedom to act across Tigray. Your death will send Penrod back to the arms of opium, Ryder and Saffron will return to Cairo, shattered by your loss, and I shall take the mine in due course.'

Amber stared at the ground in front of her, unable to respond and thinking of Dan's murdered family, of Rusty, of all the stories of blackmail and corruption she had read in the newspaper. She was sickened with revulsion.

'Do you know, after my troubles in Cairo, I read your little book and I have concluded that I have much in common with Osman Atalan,' Kendal continued cheerfully. 'I can see us meeting as equals one day. It would be interesting. We have both, after all, stolen one of the beautiful Benbrook sisters from Major Penrod Ballantyne.'

Amber lifted her head. The evening was just coming on. Let him visit all the horrors of hell on her; she would not submit to this monster, no matter what it cost her. She carefully worked the steak knife out of her sleeve, feeling the warm steel, the edge serrated to tear apart animal flesh, ready to do what she needed to.

'You have something else in common with Osman Atalan.'

'Do I, my dear? What is that?' he said, bending towards her with an indulgent smile.

'Someday, Penrod Ballantyne will kill you both.'

She spun around and drove the steak knife upwards into his eye. He screamed and dropped to his knees, and Amber threw herself off the edge of the mountain.

• • •

Penrod and Ryder looked at each other as the cry of agony echoed down to them.

'Amber's work,' Penrod said with grim pride.

'Probably,' Ryder replied. 'But it has lost us the element of surprise.'

'Not at all,' Penrod said, removing his revolver from its holster and checking it. 'She'll run. They'll be chasing her. That means they'll scatter and be too occupied looking for her to realise we are picking them off one by one. It is the perfect diversion.'

'She'll not come down the main track,' Ryder grunted.

'No,' Penrod said, 'which means she could find herself at a dead end. I suggest we go through the camp and follow her trail. The aim is to follow her rather than waste time killing the bandits still in camp. So we move fast, add to the confusion and keep going until we reach her.'

'Agreed!' Ryder said, and they began to run up the steep incline.

• • •

To anyone other than Amber, it would have seemed like suicide. The *amba* seemed to drop away at murderous angles with the main track providing the only possible route to and from the summit, but Amber had been hunting and exploring the land around Courtney Camp for years. She had learned that the mountains of Tigray were more forgiving to those who knew them well: cliffs were secret stepladders, the worn stone had weathered into a thousand handholds, one could always find ledges overhung with vines and smooth, shallow angles where a person might rest as they climbed, or slow their descent. The important thing was to stay low, close to the hidden chances, trust yourself to find them, and never, never look down.

Amber slid and tumbled for over thirty feet down the incline before she could check her descent, then she began moving sideways as quickly as she could. She found fragments of an old path mostly eroded into almost nothingness, some ancient way carved by a forgotten hermit, but enough for her. She could hear Kendal's voice shouting orders above her, calling for ropes and his rifle. She hoped he was in a great deal of pain. It sounded as if he were. She continued her half-controlled descent, trying to ignore the sounds of pursuit behind her. The track disappeared entirely here and she was forced sideways again, across a rain-warped smoothness of stone. Her right foot found a crevice, but as she searched for another with her left, the toe of her slipper caught on a knot of rock and fell from her foot. Before she could stop herself, she turned her head to watch it fall. It disappeared downwards for a hundred feet, bouncing and spinning off the sheer walls till it was only a glimmer of red, then disappeared completely from view. She felt her heart beat faster, and her fingers began to sweat and cramp. She had to move, had to find the will from somewhere. She heard Kendal's voice again, shouting commands in his terrible Amharic. She breathed softly in and out, as if she were preparing to fire her rifle, then released the hold she had with her left hand, reaching up for a fresh grip. She found one, solid under her hand, and pulled herself up, then began moving across and upwards, slowly at first, then with increasing confidence and speed as the pain and panic faded, until she had crossed the glassy cliff face and fallen onto another remnant of the path. Now she could stand upright without clinging on to the wall. She paused for a moment, letting her heart slow. Above her she heard the quick popping concussions of gunshots, a ripple of them, but too distant to be fired at her.

●　●　●

Penrod and Ryder almost ran into three of the bandits who had been sent down the main track. The *shifta* were dressed in a mix of traditional clothing with military-issue jackets, rifles over their shoulders and large knives through their belts. They spent their last moment on earth staring, stupefied at these two white men charging up a path where they had no right to be. One was broad-shouldered as a young ox, the other with the lithe grace of a cheetah.

Ryder and Penrod both shot twice and all three *shifta* fell backwards in the dust, a neat hole in the centre of their fore-heads, their blood and brain matter spattering the track behind them. The man in the centre died with two bullets in his brain.

By the time they reached it, the camp was in chaos. A slave girl saw them and screamed. Penrod and Ryder raised their revolvers again and brought down the fighters on either side of her. Two others, shielded by the shadows cast by the huts and canvas tents, managed to get off a round each before plunging into cover. One shot went wide, and Ryder felt the second bullet graze his neck, a sharp nick, but he could tell that the shot had done no serious damage. He did not even put up a hand to touch the wound.

'Look!' Penrod shouted, pointing to the lip of the plateau, where stakes had been driven into the ground, with rope looped around them. He was already running across to them. Ryder holstered his revolver and followed him.

• • •

This half-eroded section of track led downwards from the ledge. Hope leaped in Amber's heart. She kicked off her remaining slipper. This time she did not wait to watch it fall but ran down the steeply sloping path. She heard a scream behind her, one of a *shifta* who had failed to find a way across that glassy section of the cliff. She hoped it was one of the men who had taunted her as she tried to escape the first time, and she glanced over her shoulder as she dashed forward. Her leading foot met not solid earth but air. Even as her momentum carried her forward, she twisted her upper body hard and grabbed for some hold, any hold. She grabbed on to the roots of a thorn bush and managed to haul herself backwards. She landed heavily and felt a sharp pain as her ankle gave way. Dazed, she clung to the solid ground for a moment, then raised her head and looked about her. She had ended up on a wide granite ledge, a freak of geology that extended some ten feet out from the side of the cliff. The stone she clung to was polished smooth. Above her she could see a deep and narrow cleft running from the top of the *amba*, and where her ledge and the cliff wall met, the side of the cliff had been worn into a shallow bowl. She realised that when the rains came the cleft must become a waterfall, and her perch had been left like an eagle's nest, high and isolated, as the softer rocks were worn away around it.

She pulled herself upright, and the pain in her ankle shot up her leg, making her gasp and grab for a hold on the wall of sandstone beside her. She looked over the edge. The mountain had decided to betray her after all. No hidden track led down at a manageable angle from here, only a sheer, uncompromising drop to the rock-broken valley floor far below, scattered with great blocks of stone worked free by the action of wind and water.

If she had time, or even the shortest length of rope, she might find a way downwards. She leaned out a little further in search of some possible hand- or foothold, and as she put weight on her ankle it threatened to give way beneath her. That told her all she needed to know. She had no chance of leaving this ledge, unless it was with Kendal, her captor, or by leaping to her death. She heard his footsteps coming closer down the last remaining stretch of forgotten track before it disappeared completely at this precipice. So be it, she thought, and with one hand on the cliff wall to save her ankle, but with nothing but the cool air of Tigray at her back, she waited for him to find her.

• • •

It was only a minute, but in that time she thought of Saffron, Ryder and the children, and sent them her love and hoped for their happiness. She did the same for Rebecca and her children by Osman Atalan. And then she thought of Penrod. She prayed he had survived the battle and would not grieve for her too long. For all the pain she had suffered, she would never regret for an instant loving him. She hoped Saffron would find some way to explain that to him. The thought of him brought tears to her eyes and she blinked them away, determined to see clearly in the last moments of her life. She thought of the book she had written, and what she had done for the camp and the refugees who found their way to her, starving, but left with new strength and hope. She thought of her orchards and how soon the rains would come and they would flower and her bees would get to work once more filling their hives. She thought of Hagos and wondered if the lioness was raising cubs of her own somewhere. Finally she thought of her mother, dead so long ago she was only a lost, vague memory, and of her father. She was ready to join them.

Kendal came slowly down the last few feet of the path. He was alone. His right eye was roughly bandaged and blood spattered his collar.

'Miss Benbrook,' he said, and bowed as if they were meeting at the home of some mutual friend to take tea.

'Your grace,' she said.

He stared at her for some time, his head slightly on one side. 'So you have chosen hell,' he said at last. 'Very well. Or perhaps I shall take you here and now. If you please me, I might let you live a few more hours. If you do not, then I shall throw you off the cliff myself and Penrod can find you there.'

She did not flinch, blush or turn away. 'Let me save you the trouble,' she said instead and took a step backwards.

'No!' Kendal hissed, holding out his hand, and Amber could see it was shaking. 'You will die by my hand! Mine! Kill your-self and I shall skin Ryder and Saffron's children in front of them!'

How strange, she thought. He does not like to have his toys taken away from him. It was some small recompense to see how much her suicide would anger him. She allowed herself the luxury of enjoying his desperation for a moment.

'I will pour molten silver down the throats of every woman in the camp and hunt your refugees for sport!' he hissed again.

He was getting too close. It was time for her to make the leap. His words meant little or nothing to her. Ryder would protect his family and their friends, and as soon as Penrod found out the duke was still alive, he would track this snake down and kill him. She was already slipping her foot backwards along the smooth stone, feeling for the edge of it under her toe. Then she looked over Kendal's shoulder and saw a figure . . . No! Two figures on the track, moving quickly and quietly towards them. She recognised Ryder's broad shoulders, then her lips parted in a soft gasp. The second man was Penrod.

She tore her blue eyes from the face of the man she loved and fixed them on the duke. 'Kendal, do you remember I told you that Penrod Ballantyne would kill you?'

He was still reaching for her; only inches remained between them now.

'Yes, and that is proof of what a little dreamer you are!'

'Well, he's going to kill you right now,' she said, and smiled sweetly.

Kendal's eyes went blank as he heard the sound of a revolver's hammer being cocked. He spun around and found Penrod behind him, with the Webley service revolver aimed at his chest, his finger resting on the trigger.

'No!' he hissed. 'It's impossible!'

'But here I am,' Penrod replied evenly.

'Not you! Not yet! Damn you, Ballantyne!' Kendal threw himself towards Penrod, his hands high, as if he could catch the bullet out of the air.

Penrod squeezed the trigger and the revolver leaped in his grip. A spurt of smoke and flame shot from the muzzle. The bullet smashed through the duke's splayed fingers and drove on into his chest. As he reeled backwards, trying to keep his footing, Amber stepped gracefully aside and he teetered on the brink of the abyss, windmilling his arms.

'Farewell, your grace,' Penrod said, before firing a second shot. It drove Kendal back into the void. All three of them froze in the silence that followed, and then breathed again at the sound of Kendal's body striking the rocks hundreds of feet below them.

Amber was suddenly very, very tired. Her legs buckled under her and she slumped to the ground. Ryder ran across the ledge towards her, dropping to his knees beside her and gathering her into a fierce bear hug.

'My God, Amber! Are you hurt? Tell me you are not hurt. If you are, my wife will never speak to me again.'

She gave a snuffling, tearful laugh and locked both arms around his neck.

'I am well, Ryder. Only I'm afraid I've made rather a mess of my ankle. Thank you for coming for me.'

He kissed the top of her head like an affectionate brother. 'You knew I would. And I had some help, of course.' They both turned their heads and looked at Penrod Ballantyne, who was still standing in the same place that he had fired the shots, with the smoking pistol in his right hand.

'Hello, Penrod,' Amber said.

Penrod would never forget that moment, seeing her face, not through his field glasses but with his own eyes for the first time in years, with the splendour of the Tigray landscape disappearing into the haze behind her.

'Amber,' he replied, and for a moment he could say no more.

'Can you stand?' Ryder said gruffly, clearly not wishing to be involved in a grand romantic reunion.

'Just, but I cannot walk. I am sorry to be so helpless. The path ends here, and I don't think I shall be able to climb back up the way we came even with your help.' She frowned, then brightened suddenly. 'Ryder, perhaps you might go back and fetch some rope, and you can haul me straight up to the summit from here. I am sure Penrod will look after me while you are gone.'

'What an excellent plan,' Penrod said, holstering his revolver.

'Excellent plan be damned,' Ryder said. 'Any number of your friend's bandits might still be about the place, not to mention that sideways climb a hundred yards back.' He looked down at Amber. 'How you managed to get across in that ridiculous skirt, I have no idea. You must be part monkey.'

She giggled. 'I rather like this skirt.'

'I'm sure a couple of bandits and that climb would give you no problems, Ryder,' Penrod said lightly.

'If you're so damn confident, go yourself.'

Amber sighed happily and settled herself more comfortably on the cool stone. They would work everything out now. She had done her part, and Penrod was here. She thought of herself as the queen of infinite worlds.

Ryder still had his hand on her shoulder. 'We've lost the mine, al-Zahra. Kendal destroyed the Lion Dam on the night he took you. We can't make up the shortfall of silver in a month and I don't think we'll be getting any more extensions from Menelik. I'm sorry.'

She smiled up at him. 'Can't you just give Menelik the silver Kendal stole, Ryder? It's all up there in the cabin. I suppose he couldn't sell it with the war going on.'

Ryder grabbed her by the shoulders, his eyes wide. 'What? It's there? It's all there?'

She grinned. 'Yes, I counted. I found it while I was looking for this stupid bodice.'

Ryder let out a whoop of joy, which echoed between the mountains with the music of Amber's sudden laughter.

'Hey, Mr Ryder! Miss Amber! Are you well?'

They looked up and high above them Amber saw a face peering down and a waving hand.

Ryder jumped to his feet. 'One of my men from the mine,' he said quickly to Penrod, then shouted up in Amharic. 'Geriel! Thanks be to God, I am well. What are you doing here? And watch your back – I don't think we dealt with all of the *shifta*.'

Geriel's rich laugh tumbled down towards them. 'Mrs Saffron persuaded Ras Alula to send you some help as soon as the battle was won. He sent myself and Maki and twenty others. No bandits left now, my promise to you.'

'Then you had better find some ropes, my friend.'

• • •

Neither Amber nor Penrod would leave until they had seen the dukes' body, so they spent the night in the bandits' camp. Ryder reclaimed his silver ingots, counting them more times than Penrod thought was strictly necessary, while the treasures the *shifta* had amassed in their months of looting were quietly requisitioned by Alula's men. Penrod and Ryder were offered the pick of the European luxuries the duke had accrued in his short career as a bandit, but they had as little use for them as the Abyssinians. Amber insisted on taking the jewellery with her in the hopes she could find its rightful owners in the fullness of time. After a small struggle with her conscience, she decided to keep the skirt and bodice and the jewelled combs for her hair.

The slave women and girls who had been serving the bandits offered their devotion and service at once to Geriel and Maki. Ryder was confident they would be well treated.

As dawn broke, the party made its careful way back down the track. Where Amber could not ride, Penrod carried her. Ryder suspected he did so more than was strictly necessary. At the foot of the path they circled the *amba* until they found the broken corpse of the Duke of Kendal. Ryder stayed with the men and the animals while Penrod and Amber approached more closely.

'Did you know he was still alive?' Amber asked as they looked down at the corpse, broken across the sandstone.

'I suspected it,' he said, 'when Sam Adams told me his secretary Carruthers could not be found and said the face of the corpse in the Cairo house had been completely obliterated. I could find no trace of him in Europe, however – nothing but a wisp of a rumour once in Bohemia, that was all. I suppose he sold the mask of Caesar in some flea market to fund his escape.'

Amber frowned. 'An ivory mask? A carving?'

'Yes.'

'He did not sell it. He showed it to me. He had it in his pocket.'

Penrod bent over the body and searched the jacket, then withdrew the rosewood box. He stepped back to Amber's side and opened it. The face of Caesar stared back up at them, undamaged. Amber reached out and brushed the ancient Roman's lips with her fingertip.

'I think he looks like you, Penrod. You should keep him.'

He closed the box. 'Thank you, al-Zahra, but I shall sell him. The King of Italy was keen to buy it at one stage.'

She put her arm through his. 'I am so sorry about your Italian friends, Penrod.'

'So am I. They were brave men.'

Ryder called out, blowing the heavy smoke of his cheroot into the damp morning air. 'Are we burying Kendal or leaving him for the hyenas?'

'Let them have him,' Penrod shouted back, then led Amber across the rough ground to where the others were waiting.

• • •

One more farewell remained. Once Amber had learned that Dan had survived and sent Ryder and Penrod to her rescue, she would not leave before seeing him. He was feverish, but he knew her and thanked God for her rescue. The old man and his daughter-in-law were hopeful that he would survive.

Amber removed the jewelled combs from her hair and, with only the smallest pang of regret, she handed them over to pay for Dan's care. They refused her at first, but she was gently insistent. Here was one family at least who would be able to buy seed and pay for oxen to help plough the fields when the rains came.

• • •

They reached the battlefield of Adowa late in the morning. Penrod had given them his own account of the battle the previous evening, but nothing could have prepared Amber for the horror that awaited them. At first, as they reached the crest of the hill, Amber thought of the London parks in late autumn. The plain was scattered with heaps of what looked like fallen leaves, raked into piles. Then, with a turn in her chest, she realised that these were piles of bodies. Thousands of Ethiopian and *askari* soldiers tumbled together in death. Among so many black bodies, the smaller groups of white infantry, or single Italian officers who led the native battalions, stood out. They had been stripped naked and left sprawled under the blank stare of the climbing sun.

Ethiopian burial parties were dotted across the plain, digging deep pits in the sandy soil, carrying their dead from the crush of corpses and laying them to rest. The *askari* and Italian bodies they searched for any remaining valuables, then pushed them aside.

As the party followed the twisting path into the valley, they were observed with quiet suspicion, but the presence of Alula's men meant they were not threatened or approached. Amber saw that some of the bodies had been mutilated. She turned away, her eyes glutted with death.

Ryder and Penrod offered no comment, and though it was clear the victory of Menelik's army had been overwhelming, Geriel and Maki did not boast or preen. Too many of their own men had died for that, throwing themselves forward against the Italian artillery.

As they picked their way through the horror, Geriel began to speak, and Amber translated quietly for Penrod's benefit.

'We were sent against Albertone's brigade,' he said. 'I and those who are best skilled with a rifle were sent up along the valley walls, and we watched as they fired bursting shells into the centre of our lines. We saw men disappear, blown apart and leaving only blood. It was a terrible time. Until I could reach a place close enough to fire at the gunners, all I could do was count those bursts of smoke and fire, then watch as they broke great holes in the ranks. I thought: the emperor cannot have more men; no matter how vast our army, he cannot have more men.

But still they came, knowing it was to their deaths. A white man was standing by the gun, directing the crew. Twenty times, as I crept forward, he pulled the lanyard to fire it, then ordered the reload and adjusted the aim. Twenty times that one gun turned our men into nothing but blood and bone before I was in range and killed him. One of his crew leaped into his place and managed to fire twice more before I killed him too.'

'I was taking messages between Alula and the emperor,' Maki said in the same soft, sad tone. 'I saw Taitu herself directing our guns against them. I saw her turn to Menelik, her whole person afire, and tell him to send in his own men after Alula's. They came fresh and fast, just as they were needed, and as they came the Oromo cavalry tore through the centre. I knew then the Italians were dead. They only had to choose how much we would pay for their corpses.'

'They asked a high price,' Amber said. Even as she spoke, she lifted her eyes and saw the body of an Italian officer. His naked body was maimed and torn, his legs a mess of bone and exposed muscle. Across his belly was a deep sword wound and his entrails showed purple and obscene. His face, though, was unmarked – a young, handsome boy, pale-skinned for an Italian. His eyes and lips were closed and his expression was peaceful, as if he were only sleeping under the African sun and dreaming of some sweetheart at home.

Geriel answered her. 'Indeed, Miss Amber. They asked a great price.'

'Were any prisoners taken?' Penrod asked, and Ryder translated the question.

'Many,' Geriel said. 'Most fought until they were killed, but some we surprised or surrounded. Menelik told us to allow surrender, to bring him living men and do no harm to those we could take alive. Not . . .' As he spoke he made a swift, short cutting motion in the air.

Amber knew about the tradition of castrating dead enemies and prisoners. It was proof a warrior had taken a man, and robbed him of his power to make another generation of fighting men. She was glad that Menelik had issued orders against the practice, though judging from the bodies she had already seen, it was not a command all of his men had followed.

At last they were free of it. The battlefield was behind them and they were moving into the camp of Menelik's army. The scale of it defied Amber's senses. It was an entire city reaching all the way back along the road to Adowa. Children dashed forward and back between the tents, keeping a watchful eye on small herds of thin-looking goats. Women sat in small groups grinding teff, or walking between the tents and campfires with woven baskets on their heads. Their costumes and faces came from all across Ethiopia, each tribe keeping loosely together, tailing out from the larger tents of their commanders and princes, which were in turn clustered around the huge tents of the emperor himself. Oromo cavalry led their sturdy horses, hung with silver ornaments, out to pasture; groups of priests sang their devotions in the open air; and the warriors watched the activity around them with grave and formal expressions. Some carried Italian revolvers on their hips or wore Sam Browne belts across their traditional clothing. From time to time one or another called out to Geriel: 'Who are your prisoners?'

'English guests,' Geriel answered each time, but Amber felt the looks that were cast towards them as hot and hostile.

They saw prisoners too – small groups of men in torn and dirty uniforms, herded together and guarded. The *askari* and the Italians had been separated, but their expressions were the same. They hunched together on the ground, hollow-eyed, too exhausted and afraid to even look up as their captors passed.

As they approached the great red tent of Menelik himself, Amber saw something like field hospitals had been set up. Men were lying in lines on the ground, but under canvas. Women moved back and forth among them.

From the shadows she heard a shriek of delight and suddenly Saffron was running towards them. Geriel helped Amber down from the mule so she was ready when her sister pounced on her.

'Saffy! Ow! No, it's only my ankle, but I'm quite well. Bill is dead. Oh, and we got the silver back!'

Saffron turned from her sister to her husband with a squeal of pleasure, then, when she was content they were both unharmed, she saw Penrod. She hesitated and glanced at Amber, who blushed slightly and nodded. Saffron at once bounced forward, put her hands on Penrod's shoulders and stood on her tiptoes to kiss his cheek.

'Penrod, I am glad you are alive. We heard you were with the Italians, and I was afraid . . .' She swept her arm behind her, at the prisoners and the wounded and beyond the battlefield.

'Mrs Courtney,' he said. 'I am glad to see you again.'

She wrinkled her nose at him. 'You haven't changed at all.' Then she put her head on one side. 'Perhaps a little. Your eyes are kinder, I think.'

Penrod smiled at her.

'What news, Saffy?' Ryder said.

She reached out and took his hand, becoming suddenly serious. 'Ras Alula would like to pursue the Italians and drive them into the sea, but I don't think Menelik is going to do it. Tigray has no more forage, and it could become a massacre. He knows the European newspapers want to call him a savage, and he wants to be a statesman.'

'What of the prisoners?' Penrod asked. 'What will happen to them? Was Baratieri taken?'

She shook her head. 'No, he escaped. Menelik will share the Italian prisoners among the chiefs, but hold them responsible for their safety. They are arguing about the *askari* now. Most of the princes say they are traitors.'

'That means they will have their right hand and left foot cut off,' Ryder said.

'I would like to speak on their behalf, if you can arrange for me to see Menelik,' Penrod said, but Saffron pursed her lips and shook her head.

'You mustn't say anything to him in front of his advisors,' she warned him. 'But Amber, he will want to see you. That might give you the chance, Penrod. He has had me sketching and painting, and Amber is to write an account of . . . well, everything, I think.'

'I wasn't even at the battle!' Amber said, but already she was wondering how to describe to an audience in England the camp and personalities of Menelik and Taitu.

'Then you'd better find some paper and start talking to the people who were,' Saffron said firmly. 'Your friend the scribe is in camp somewhere. He'll help.'

'I'll need a walking stick,' Amber said with a sigh.

'Tadesse will find you one. Good gracious, your outfit! It's rather magnificent, but perhaps something less showy would be better for camp?'

• • •

Ryder and Penrod left the women to their work. Ryder found Menelik's steward and presented him with the missing ingots. He seemed shocked to see them, but there was no doubting their number and each was stamped with the sign of Courtney Mine. Ryder was ushered into the audience chamber and Menelik placed the roll of vellum, dotted with seals and ribbons, which granted permanent title to the land, into Ryder's hands himself, in the presence of all his princes.

'I had these prepared some weeks ago,' the emperor said. 'I had faith in you, Mr Ryder.'

'As I had in you, sire,' Ryder replied and bowed.

'You did,' Menelik conceded, 'and your faith has been rewarded. When you read the documents you hold, you'll see the tax on the silver is reduced to fifteen per cent.'

Ryder made some quick and gratifying calculations in his head. Menelik raised his voice so the assembled elite of his warriors and princes could hear him.

'When I was a boy, I guarded my father's herd. When I was a youth, I ploughed the fields that feed my people. When I became a man, I fought to protect those lands and add to my patrimony. Now I thank my friend, Ryder Courtney, for proving that this new work, which will enrich my people still further, is as honourable as that of the farmer or the warrior. Let no man speak against this endeavour or shun any man who chooses to work with metal again in my lands.' Then Menelik bent forward and asked quietly, 'Who am I, Ryder Courtney?'

Ryder went down on one knee. 'You are His Imperial Majesty Menelik the Second, Conquering Lion of the Tribe of Judah, King of Zion, King of Kings of Ethiopia and Elect of God.'

Menelik smiled and got up from his throne. He put out his hand and Ryder clasped it warmly as he stood. 'I am indeed. Now go in peace, Mr Ryder.'

Penrod persuaded Geriel to act as his guide and went among the Italian prisoners, giving what comfort he could and filling his notebook with names so that their families might be informed of their survival and capture. It was sombre work. He heard tales of heroism and confusion on the battlefield. General Dabormida had failed to support Albertone, but instead led his men almost into the enemy camp on the northern flank. Some troops escaped in good fighting order from the encirclement that followed, but the young general himself, so eager to see his first combat, had died on the field. Most of the Italians seemed stunned, half dead with exhaustion and the crushing knowledge of their defeat. Penrod encouraged them to be hopeful.

The sky was already beginning to darken when he came across Albertone, the braid torn from his jacket and his face and hands still stained with dried blood. He looked at Penrod with an expression of deep loathing and would not speak to him.

At last a young Abyssinian found him and told Penrod in delicately accented English that he was expected at Menelik's tent. The youth introduced himself as Tadesse, and Penrod realised this was Amber's young friend.

Geriel went back to Alula's camp to find food and rest, and as they passed through the crowds, Penrod asked Tadesse if he planned to return to Courtney Camp.

'No, Mr Penrod,' he said. 'The emperor has invited me to Addis Ababa. I shall go. He has plans for a new hospital in the city. I might learn much, and serve him better.'

'Have you told Miss Amber?'

'I have. She offered to send me to England to learn medicine, but this is my home. I do not want to forget it and fill my head with your ways and customs. I have said the same to Mrs Saffron and Mr Ryder. They are my family, but it is time for our ways to part.'

They had reached one of the entrances to the red imperial tent. The guards nodded to Tadesse, and he pointed Penrod inside.

'Go in. You are waited for.' He hesitated. 'Mr Penrod, Miss Amber is my very great friend. You caused her much pain.'

'I understand, Tadesse. I will not do so again.'

The young man nodded, then stood aside.

Penrod passed into the main body of the tent, though it was more of a canvas palace, carpeted and hung with coloured silks. At the far end of the room Menelik sat on his throne. He was leaning sideways towards Amber. She stood beside him, supporting herself with a heavy walking stick and dressed in the simple white clothes of the Abyssinian women, a thin veil over her hair. She had asked the emperor something and was now taking notes of his reply. Penrod took the chance to study Menelik, this king the Italians had thought more a myth than a man. He was talking to Amber in a low, even voice, sketching patterns in the air. Even without knowing the language well, Penrod could tell he was describing the action of the battle, and he saw neither rage nor exultant pride, only the neutral narration of an experienced commander.

Menelik glanced sideways and saw Penrod waiting for him. He finished the point he was making to Amber, then looked at Penrod coldly and spoke. Amber translated.

'I am told you wished to have speech with me?'

'Yes, sir,' Penrod replied with a bow, neither servile nor insolent. 'I have learned to admire the troops of the Italian native battalions. I hope to persuade you they should not be maimed, but treated in the same way as your Italian prisoners.'

Menelik was silent for a moment, and when he replied his voice sounded dark and growling. Then Amber said the words in her own sweet, clear tones. It was, Penrod thought, like communicating with some ancient oracle through his virgin priestess.

'You have set yourself a hard task then, Major. You know, I think, the traditional form of punishment for traitors such as they are. Those that survive their punishment will be allowed to return to their Italian friends as they can; in Eritrea they will be no further threat or charge to me. The Italian government will pay to have their white soldiers returned to them, but you cannot think I am such a fool as to believe they would pay ransom for prisoners with black skins. Why should I keep them then?'

He might be right. It was impossible to tell what the Italian government would do when news of the defeat reached them.

'Sir, I do not deny what you say,' Penrod said. 'But I believe that even if they are unwilling, the government might be forced to recognise their responsibility for their men, whatever their colour. However, if you continue to allow this punishment, they will delight in branding you a savage.'

It was a risk, and Penrod saw Menelik's expression grow fiercer and darken as his words were hesitantly translated.

'Savage? Tell me, Major, what would you do with British traitors?'

'I would shoot them, sir. But I am a soldier. You must now be acknowledged emperor of a sovereign African state. You are a soldier too, but you must also become a statesman.'

This time the corner of Menelik's mouth twitched into a smile. He knew he was being flattered.

'I have heard you, and I will consider what you say.' His face grew serious again. 'Do you know what will happen after the rains, Major Penrod?'

'I do not.'

Menelik sat forward, resting his elbows on his knees. 'Then I shall tell you, and you shall understand the ways of savage warriors like myself. I will sit outside my palace, with my men around me. They will open the gates, and old men, women and children, who have walked many miles, will come in turn to stand in front of me. We will greet each other, I shall look into their eyes, they shall look into mine, and then they shall leave. Who are these people? They are the wives, the mothers, the fathers and children of the men who were killed yesterday. I will look at each of them, be seen by each of them. For as many days as is needed

I will sit on my throne through the hours of daylight and they shall see the man for whom their loved ones died. And I shall look into their eyes and know their son, their husband, their father is dead for me. I read the Europeans always speak of a reckoning after a battle, but they do not do this, I think? They do not look into the faces of the families of those killed.'

'No, sir, they do not.'

'Yet we are the savages.' Menelik sighed. 'Go, Major Penrod. You may speak to the prisoners as you wish and travel as you see fit on my word. I have no quarrel with the British. Tell your queen that.'

• • •

They stayed in the camp for two more days while Amber gathered accounts of the battle from the Ethiopian princes, the soldiers and the Italian prisoners, and while Saffron sketched furiously. Then, with the mineworkers now released from their service in Menelik's army, they made their way across the battlefield and west into the mountains towards Courtney Camp. They were greeted with rejoicing and grief. Not all the men had returned.

The following day everyone gathered outside the church to see Amber typing up the agreement transferring the management of Courtney Mine to Patch. The women carried her table and chair into the central square and bickered until they were sure that both were level.

Patch, Marta, Saffron and their children took their places in front of Amber while Ryder began to dictate. Amber's fingers danced over the keys and the women craned their necks to see the writing appear on the page, murmuring their congratulations.

It was a simple document. Courtney Mine was placed under the control of Patch and he now had an official share in the enterprise with Ryder. He would continue the agreement with Menelik, but from this date onwards was responsible for every decision in the running of the mine and camp and its supply. He would be advised by a group of six men drawn from the senior workers, but his decision would be final. He would split the profits of the mine with Ryder, with a sixty per cent share going to Ryder, and send those profits to his bankers in Cairo in a timely fashion.

Amber pulled the paper free from the carriage with a flourish and the two men signed it.

Marta organised a feast to celebrate the signing, and they were all glad of an excuse to raise their spirits.

As the Courtneys and Amber began to pack their belongings, they did so to the sounds of services given in the church in both thanksgiving and mourning. The families of those who had died bore themselves with an intense pride: their sons and husbands had sacrificed themselves to save and unite Ethiopia, and it was a victory they held close to them, a warming flame in the cold of their grief.

Ryder and Patch made arrangements for accrued wages and pensions to be paid to the families of the dead, and let them know that they were at liberty to continue living in the camp if they so wished it. Some did. Others returned to their former homes.

For Amber, even though she felt the pain of leaving the camp and the people she knew, every moment was lit up by the joy of Penrod's presence. She showed him her house and her gardens, her dams, orchards and beehives, and delighted in his praise and interest. He had changed. He was calmer, more ready to smile and more gentle in his language and his treatment of those around him. Little Leon worshipped him on sight, and when Penrod told him he would make a fine soldier, he almost went wild with excitement.

On the second afternoon of their stay, they found themselves alone, high on the southern flank of the hills above the camp. The place Amber had raised her lion cub and begun writing again. The air was dry and the whole of Tigray seemed to lie in front of them, a tumbled horizon of tawny mountains and deep shaded gorges.

'Amber,' Penrod said softly. 'I must speak to you.'

A sudden terror gripped Amber's heart. She did not want to think about the past, about what he had said or done to make her break off the engagement. She was terrified that they would argue again and he would disappear once more from her life. The thought was agony. She steadied herself, just as she had clambering across the glassy rocks of the *amba*. The danger had to be faced.

She took a deep breath. 'I am listening, Penrod.'

His voice sounded thick, as if he was forcing the words out with great difficulty. 'I seduced Rebecca out of vanity, and because I knew she was fond of Ryder. I wanted to beat him, prove myself the better man. That, and my pleasure, was all I thought of. I then spoke ill of her to Lady Agatha because it hurt my pride that Rebecca had turned to Ryder for comfort when I was gone.'

The names of his lovers felt to Amber like physical blows, but she refused to show it.

'My greatest sin, however, was that I did not tell you the truth,' he continued. 'I thought it was beneath me to explain myself to you. I let you believe a lie and for that I am sorry, most sincerely.' He took her hand. 'You know I have never stopped loving you. I will always be proud, but I have learned to control that pride. I will always be driven to serve my country, but I mean to do so honourably, and I promise you, if you will become my wife, I will never lie to you or keep you in ignorance again. Is that enough?'

She found she could not speak, but she managed to nod.

He dropped down to one knee and looked up at her. 'Amber Benbrook, my darling girl, will you marry me?'

How many times in these last years had she imagined just this moment? Penrod finding her, Penrod wiping away all the hurt she had ever felt, Penrod offering to love her forever. A thousand times, ten thousand, but the intensity of her joy and relief was still a revelation.

'Yes, yes, Penrod! I will marry you.'

He stood up and pulled her into his arms, and that first kiss after so long a separation made Amber bloom like a desert rose in the rain. She shivered in his embrace and while he held her, the earth stopped spinning and time waited for them.

At last he broke from her, unsure if he would be able to control himself any longer if he did not.

'I have no ring for you, my darling,' he said with a shaking laugh. 'I promise I shall buy you a diamond the size of your fist when we get back to Cairo.'

Amber blushed. 'You don't need to do that, Penny.' She reached up to a simple silver chain around her neck and drew it out. Threaded through it and sparkling in the afternoon light was the engagement ring he had given her at her sixteenth birthday party at the Shepheard's Hotel eight years ago. She had kept it through all her trials and loneliness, just as he had kept the watch she had given him. She fumbled with the catch and he stepped forward to help her. His fingers brushed her neck as he undid the clasp, and the flash of feeling that ran between them seemed a harbinger of the coming storms and lightning of the summer rains.

He unthreaded the ring and held it in his palm for a moment, before taking her left hand and slipping it on to her finger. They were still standing there, hand in hand, when Belito came upon them, a basket of cuttings for the orchard on her hip. She looked between them and laughed out loud, then, much to Penrod's surprise, said in Italian: '*Il matrimonio s'ha da fare!*'

Amber blushed and put her arm through Penrod's. 'Yes, Belito, this marriage will be performed.'

• • •

Back at the camp they received the congratulations of all their friends, and if Ryder was at all uncertain about having a military man in the family, he had the good sense to hide it. The farewell feast became a celebration of the engagement, and the singing and dancing lasted so long into the night they could see no point in sleeping.

As dawn broke, Saffron was checking one more time that her painting gear was securely packed and that the children had not managed to lose their favourite toys again. Ryder came to find her and for a moment they ignored their duties and looked at the thriving camp and the silver mine.

Saffron leaned into her husband's shoulder and he put his arm around her. 'You built something amazing, Ryder,' she said.

'We did, didn't we?'

Saffron, never sentimental for long, grinned up at him and her eyes sparkled. 'I forgot to ask: are we rich again now?'

'We are. Menelik will repay the loan we made to him, and the profits from the rest of the silver that has passed through Addis in the last five years are waiting for us in Cairo. We are, in fact, obscenely rich.'

'Good,' she said. 'I shall need a new dress for Amber's wedding.'

'You may have a room full of new dresses,' he said, and she kissed him before breaking away and putting a hand on her belly.

'I may not be able to fit into them for long. Leon and Penelope are going to have . . . a little brother this time, I think.'

Ryder lifted her high into the air and spun her around until she lost her breath with laughter.

• • •

Their caravan made steady progress towards the border with Eritrea, and as they travelled, they were joined by a dozen *askari* and Italian soldiers, who had been hiding in the hills since the battle. They offered their protection, food and drink to the starving and terrified survivors, and if Ras Alula or his men ever heard about this strange caravan passing through his territory, they made no attempt to stop them.

They had just crossed the Mareb River into Eritrea, and turned back for one last look at the place that had been their home for so long, when Amber gasped and pointed. On a low promontory on the other side of the river, they could make out the silhouette of a full-grown lioness showing herself against the skyline.

'Is it Hagos?' Saffron asked, in wonder and delight.

'Yes,' Amber said, shielding her eyes.

The lioness roared, surveyed her territory, then padded proudly away and out of sight.

Penrod's time with the Italian forces had come to an end with the Battle of Adowa, and he learned in a letter from Sam Adams that Kitchener was very pleased with his work. As they waited in Massowah for passage back to Cairo, Penrod was asked to visit the governor's mansion. News of the defeat at Adowa had caused consternation in Europe. Crispi's government fell, and Baratieri was awaiting court martial under house arrest in Asmara.

Penrod left Ryder sending telegrams to his bankers in Cairo, and Amber and Saffron hard at work on their writing and painting, and he went at once to answer the summons.

He found himself in the same high-ceilinged chamber with its view over the port where Baratieri had first greeted him on his arrival.

A man was sitting behind Baratieri's magnificent desk, but he had his feet resting on its marble top, crossed at the ankle, and his face was hidden by an Italian newspaper. The headline read: *Humiliation of Army. Disaster in Africa*.

The doors closed behind Penrod and the man flicked down the page.

'Lucio!' Penrod exclaimed.

His friend sprang up to greet him and they embraced.

'I should have known the king would send you,' Penrod said, holding his friend at arm's length. 'You look tired.'

'And you look very well indeed, Penrod. I understand you are to be congratulated?'

Penrod confirmed it and saw genuine delight in his friend's rather worn face.

'Now, Penrod, I need you. The reports I am receiving from the battle, and of Baratieri's action and strategies, are so confused, so packed with horror, it is impossible to make sense of. I need you to tell me what truly happened.'

'I shall and gladly,' Penrod said. 'Do you have maps of the area?'

Lucio pointed to a table set near the windows that opened out on to the balcony and Penrod saw the neat stacks of papers on them.

'Excellent, but first I have in my notebook a list of names: prisoners I spoke to in the aftermath. I promised I would try and get word to their families.'

'Thank you, my friend.'

Penrod saw his friend's eyes were filling with tears. Lucio turned away and clapped his hands. The servant who answered the summons was sent in search of a scribe and refreshments, and the two friends settled down to work.

Penrod left at midnight. He had given his honest opinion on the behaviour and actions of Baratieri and the men under his command. Lucio thought that Baratieri would be cleared of some charges against him, and that the conclusion would be that an excess of zeal in a dangerous country and the provocations of the disgraced prime minister had led to the disaster. Any suggestion that one of Baratieri's generals had disobeyed orders would be carefully suppressed.

• • •

Amber worked at lightning speed and by the time they reached Cairo, her manuscript was ready. She called it *African Dreams and Nightmares* and sent it off to their solicitor in London within hours of their arrival in the city. It became known as the definitive account of the Battle of Adowa, as well as a unique portrait of the rulers and people of the independent kingdom of Ethiopia.

Saffron's sketches and paintings were engraved for the newspapers and sold as a series of prints. The images were soon famous across Europe.

The ivory mask of Caesar was sold quietly to the King of Italy and its price allowed Penrod to buy a large villa by the River Nile in Cairo for himself and his wife-to-be. Ryder agreed to purchase another close by.

Penrod's sister-in-law, Jane, joined them in Cairo in time to see Penrod and Amber married in the cathedral, and she stayed with the sisters when Penrod joined the campaign to retake the Sudan from the Mahdist dervishes, seeing action at both Firket and Atbara.

Ryder found himself supplying Kitchener's army with American wheat to bake their bread and his fortune increased still further, but even he began and ended every day wondering if Penrod would encounter Osman Atalan in the Sudan, and what he might learn of the fate of Rebecca Benbrook. Saffron and Amber thought of little else.

On the evening of 2 October 1898, Penrod returned without ceremony to Cairo from the Sudan. Amber heard him calling for her and raced down the wide staircase of their home to meet him with the eagerness of a child. His kiss tasted of sand and heat.

She buried her face in his chest, her fingers gripping his strong shoulders and feeling his hands on the small of her back, pressing her to him. She felt his coming home again like a fresh miracle, as sweet and full as their wedding day.

'Oh darling, I'm so glad you are here.' She wanted to ask him about Rebecca at once, but the words stuck in her throat like thorns.

'Come sit with me on the veranda, Amber,' he said gently, and led her to the back of the house with its view over the lawns and the swift-flowing Nile. He sat her on one of the wicker armchairs and brought his own as close to her as he could, then took her hand.

'We have heard the news from Omdurman,' she said quickly, looking away from him. 'A great victory – the Sudan retaken. Everyone is saying we have avenged General Gordon finally and destroyed the Mahdi as a fighting force. Is it true, Penrod?'

'It is true, my darling.'

'I'm so glad. And Osman Atalan? And . . .' Her voice choked. 'Rebecca . . . Do you have news of Rebecca?' She was already breathing quickly, as if she could read the whole sorry story on his face.

He stroked the back of her hand with his thumb, felt the slight tremor of her fingers.

'I faced Osman at last, Amber.' She gripped his hand more tightly. 'Yakub and I tracked him after the battle to the oasis of Gedda and we met there.'

'You fought him alone?' she whispered.

He nodded. 'And he fought well.'

When he had ridden out with Kitchener to retake the Sudan, Penrod had known, somehow, that fate would arrange a final confrontation with the man who had tortured him all those years ago, and it would be a battle to the death. His wife did not need to know the details of each thrust parried, the glint of Osman's blade. His strongest memory was of the look of rage and hate in Osman's eyes as he died. That rage, that hate had driven Osman to make his one mistake in the fight between them. His eagerness to destroy Penrod made him, for one crucial second, predictable. Penrod had understood that hate, had been able to control his own anger and rage, and that had given him the edge he needed. Compassion and control, those were the tools given to him by his Sufi teacher Farouk as he recovered from his addiction to opium, and he had used them.

'And Rebecca?' she managed to say at last.

'I saw her, Amber. He had indeed married her, raised her above all his other women.' He struggled to find the words he needed to tell his wife what happened when her sister, that once beautiful girl, emerged from the shadows of the Gedda mosque and saw him standing over the body of her dead husband.

'She killed herself, didn't she?' Amber whispered, and she could see the answer in Penrod's eyes. A tear ran down her cheek and she wiped it away with the back of her free hand. 'It's all right, Penrod. I never thought I would see her again. Saffron was right: Rebecca belonged to the desert in the end.'

He put his hand to her face, remembering the first time he had seen her, a child in Khartoum, then a young girl ill at ease with her newfound fame at the Gheziera Club, and now his wife, a woman who had raised a lion and stood at the side of the King of Kings.

'Amber, Rebecca was not alone.'

At that moment a woman's voice called out from the echoing hallway. 'Al-Zhara! Come greet your old nurse.'

Amber squealed and leaped to her feet. 'Nazeera!' She flew back into the house and Penrod followed at a more measured pace, but he was still in time to see his wife throw her arms around the woman who had been almost a mother to her in her youth in Khartoum.

A boy and girl stood next to her: Rebecca's children by Osman Atalan, both olive-skinned with copper-coloured hair. And keeping a watchful eye from the open door was Yakub, Penrod's gear at his feet.

'What's all the fuss?'

Penrod turned to find Saffron coming in from the rear of the house. 'Oh, Penrod, you're home. I am so glad.' She stood on the tips of her toes to kiss his cheek, then noticed the group in the hall. 'Wait! Is that . . . Nazeera!' She dashed forward to join the embrace.

Penrod decided to leave the women to share their news, their laughter and tears, and he returned to the veranda, where he found Ryder smoking a cheroot and watching the river.

'Did you kill Osman?' Ryder asked.

'Yes.'

'Good.' Ryder flicked open his cigar case and offered it to Penrod. He took one, but didn't light it at once, his eyes fixed on the horizon and the shifting colours of the river.

'And Rebecca?' Ryder asked.

'Dead by her own hand and left her two children in our care. The eldest, a boy, I cannot like, but her little girl has all the beauty and spirit of the Benbrook women.'

Ryder blew out a stream of smoke. His own children were playing on the green lawns in front of their neighbouring villa under the watchful eye of his servants.

Penrod struck a match, and when he had the tobacco burning steadily, he flicked the match into the crystal ashtray on the table in front of him.

'Rebecca was a remarkable woman,' Ryder said.

'She was,' Penrod replied. 'So are her sisters.'

They watched the sunset in silence, listening to the voices of the women echoing in the house behind them.

The Courtneys and the Ballantynes meet for the first time in . . .

THE TRIUMPH OF THE SUN

Menace emanated from them as fiercely as the heat from the sun. Night and day, the drums never stopped, a constant reminder of the mortal threat that hung over them. She could hear them booming across the waters, like the heartbeat of the monster.

An unimaginable enemy will bring them together . . .

In the burning heat of the Sudanese sun, the city of Khartoum is under siege from the fearsome forces of the Mahdi, the charismatic leader of those who tire of the brutal Egyptian government. In Khartoum, along with thousands of innocent citizens, are trapped the fanatical General Charles Gordon, intrepid soldier Penrod Ballantyne of the 10th Hussars, English trader Ryder Courtney and the British consul and his three beautiful daughters.

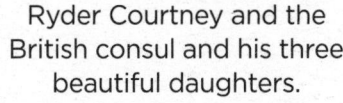

As rescue becomes increasingly unlikely, this group of Queen Victoria's loyal citizens must unite to prepare themselves against a nightmarish enemy, and for the savage battle to survive that must surely follow . . .

AVAILABLE NOW

Turn the page for an extract from . . .

GHOST FIRE

A brand new Courtney Series novel by bestselling author, Wilbur Smith.

1754. Inseparable since birth and growing up in India, Theo and Connie Courtney are torn apart by the tragic death of their parents.

Theo, wracked with guilt, seeks salvation in combat and conflict, joining the British in the war against the French and Indian army. Connie, believing herself abandoned by her brother, and abused and brutalized by a series of corrupt guardians, makes her way to France, where she is welcomed into high society. Here, she once again finds herself at the mercy of vicious men, whose appetite for war and glory lead her to the frontlines of the French battlefield in North America.

As the siblings find their destinies converging once more, they realise that the vengeance and redemption they both desperately seek could cost them their lives . . .

An epic story of tragedy, loss, betrayal and courage that brings the reader deep into the seething heart of the French and Indian War.

AVAILABLE NOW

'I'm bored,' Constance declared. 'Who could have imagined that war should be so tedious an affair?'

She lounged on a chaise in a white cotton sari, examining her reflection in a hand mirror. She was practising making faces, affecting different attitudes and studying their effects. Her hair hung in braids; her cheeks glistened with perspiration. Her French grammar book lay untouched on a side table.

She pouted at Theo. 'At least you could run away and join the army.'

Theo looked up from his book. 'Do not think I have not considered it. I am as bored as you are. But Father would find me soon enough. I cannot leave, any more than you can.'

They had been cooped up inside the fort for almost a month. The house they had taken belonged to a Company trader who was away in Bengal; his agent had been happy to let it to Mansur in consideration of a debt the trader owed.

For the first fortnight Theo and Constance had complained relentlessly about having to leave their home on nothing more than a rumour. Then the French had arrived. They had made camp near the great pagoda to the south, and erected gun batteries around the town. As Mansur had predicted, the Courtney family's drawing room now hosted two nine-pound field guns.

A dull boom echoed through the town. It had been going on for days now, though it still startled Theo each time. The French did not prosecute the siege with any great vigour: they rarely fired more than three shots an hour.

'I do not know how Mother can sleep through that,' said Theo. Verity was upstairs, having adopted the Indian fashion of napping after lunch.

'Perhaps growing up in so many sea battles she got used to it,' said Constance. 'At least she was allowed some excitement.'

'Father says we must carry on as if nothing was happening.' Theo turned to his book. It was *The Life, Adventures and Piracies of the Famous Captain Singleton* by Daniel Defoe. It was his favourite book. The tale of the pirates trekking into the undiscovered heart of Africa made him long for adventure, and to see those exotic landscapes for himself. His father had told him many stories of his escapades on that mysterious continent as a boy, which further ignited Theo's restless imagination. But it was hard to concentrate on fictitious pirates when real French gunners were trying to pound your home into rubble.

'I have always preferred *Moll Flanders*,' said Constance. 'Twelve years a whore, five times a wife, including once to her own brother, transported to America, yet she still grew rich and died comfortable. That is the sort of adventure I should like to have.'

'Mother says it is very unsuitable,' said Theo. He did not like hearing his sister use words like 'whore'.

Constance examined her face in the mirror again. 'Perhaps one day I will be a kept woman and marry for an obscene amount of money.'

'What a ridiculous notion. I want to marry a woman I love, like Mother and Father.'

Constance said nothing. Suddenly she put down her mirror and stood. 'Enough. Why should we speak of adventures in books when there are real adventures happening right on our doorstep? I want to go and see.'

Theo closed his book. 'Harjinder will never let us out.' Mansur had posted the guard at the mansion's door, with orders to allow none of the family to leave without his express permission.

'Surely you will not let that get in our way.'

Despite himself, Theo's eyes drifted to the window. Constance caught his gaze.

'What will Mother say if she wakes and finds us gone?' he said.

'We can be back before she wakes and she will be none the wiser. Or you can tell her yourself, if you are too afraid to come.'

'I'm not afraid.' He could not let her encounter danger alone. He put down his book and lifted the damp mat that had been hung over the window to cool the air. Constance swung her slim legs over the sill and dropped gracefully to the ground outside. Theo followed.

At that hour of the afternoon, the city was quiet. Most of the British inhabitants were asleep.

'Where shall we go?' asked Theo.

'Up to the walls. That will give us the best view.'

'But they will be guarded,' Theo objected.

She stuck out her tongue at him. 'I know a way.'

'How?'

'Follow me.'

She led him along the wide, sandy streets, keeping as much as possible to the backs of houses, and the alleys behind the Company warehouses. The buildings ended suddenly in a group of shacks and crumbling storerooms, crammed so close upon each other that it took Theo a moment to realise the brick wall behind was actually the outer wall of the fort.

'Lift me,' Constance ordered.

Theo cupped his hands and hoisted her onto the lowest roof, then hauled himself up behind her. The outbuildings made a giant staircase that they could scramble and clamber up until they pulled themselves, dusty and sweating, onto the rampart.

Theo ducked behind one of the battlements, but Constance stood fearless, leaning forward to peer out through the embrasure.

'Get down,' hissed Theo. 'What if someone sees you?'

'Who?' countered Constance. 'Father says the garrison is stretched so thin they can only man the main towers. And if some soldier comes by, I shall simper and smile and clutch his arm, and he will be convinced it is all a great misunderstanding.'

'The French?'

'I am sure they are too gallant to fire on a lady.'

At that moment, a puff of smoke and fire blossomed from the French lines. They heard the boom a moment later, felt it reverberating through the walls under their feet. A spray of sand fountained up from the plain below, as the cannonball fell harmlessly short.

'You see?' Constance exulted. 'There is nothing to worry about, little brother.'

'Don't call me that.'

Theo rose and peered out cautiously. Fort St George and the town of Madras had been built on a sandbar, a long finger of land crooked down the coast, separated from the mainland by a tidal lagoon. Across the strand, behind the lagoon, he could see the French encampments dotted among the palm trees around the great pagoda: rows of tents, baggage wagons, and stores. A makeshift parade ground had been cleared, where a company of fusiliers was being drilled. In front, native labourers had dug a row of entrenchments, where half a dozen guns sat mostly idle. Theo could see the gun crew lazily sponging out the gun that had just fired. The Company gunners in the fort showed no great desire to retaliate.

'If Father was commanding he would have fired four broadsides before the French had reloaded once,' said Theo, with a touch of family pride. Mansur had often told them how he had rescued their mother from her wicked father, how he had commanded his own sloop and engaged Guy Courtney's flagship, running right under her guns. Since Theo had first heard the story, sitting on Mansur's knee, he had longed for the thrill of battle. Yet now, confronted with the reality of guns aimed at him, it seemed more complex than Daniel Defoe made it sound.

'Keep down,' he told Constance. 'We should not expose ourselves to danger needlessly.'

'That last shot did not come within fifty yards of the walls,' said Constance. Her eyes were bright and wide, her face flushed. 'They are out of range.'

'You are enjoying this,' Theo said in wonder.

She turned to him, one hand resting on her chest. 'Of course. Isn't it thrilling?'

The cannon fired again.

. . .

The blast echoed through the fort. The crystal chandelier shivered and tinkled as Mansur entered the house. All the blinds were drawn, and the doors closed against the afternoon heat. Shafts of sunlight lanced through, showing eddies of dust in the air. However much the servants swept and cleaned, you could never escape it in this country.

'Verity?' he called. 'Constance? Theo?'

His anxiety increased as he climbed the stairs – though he told himself there was no reason for alarm. They would be sleeping, as they always did at this time of the day. And the house was well chosen – far back from the western walls and the French guns.

He opened the door to Constance's bedroom. It was empty, the bedsheets stretched tight and untouched. Uneasy, he tried Theo's room. The same. Perhaps they were with their mother.

Verity lay stretched out on her bed in a thin cotton shift, fast asleep. Even now, approaching forty, she was the most beautiful woman Mansur had ever seen. He thanked God every day for the chance that had brought them together.

But worries drove those thoughts from his mind.

'Where are Constance and Theo?' he asked, shaking her awake.

She rubbed her eyes. 'Are they not in their rooms?'

With greater urgency, they ran through the house, throwing open doors and calling for their children. It took them only minutes to realise that Theo and Constance were not at home.

'Where can they have gone?' wondered Verity. 'They knew they were forbidden to leave without permission.'

Another bang shook the house: louder, this time, as the English gunners decided to return fire. The vibration agitated the dust, spinning it into angry swirls in the sunbeams.

'The walls,' Mansur realised, with a jolt of horror. 'You know what Theo is like – always playing at soldiers. He will have gone to see the battle.'

'And Constance?'

'He must have taken her with him.' Mansur was already at the door.

Verity hurried after him. 'They will be exposed to the full force of the French artillery,' she fretted.

Mansur remembered the engineer's warning: 'They are in more danger from the walls they are standing on.'

He led her at a run across the parade ground in front of the governor's house, then past the church and the well. The scent of pepper, tea and spices surrounded the warehouses, but he did not notice. Cannon fired again, several shots so close they almost rolled together in a single noise. The French had increased the tempo of their attack, and the English responded in kind.

I pray we will not be too late, he thought.

They reached the bastion at the south-west corner. A sepoy sentry at the foot of the stairs made to stop them, then thought better of it. Mansur raced up the steps.

At the top, an English lieutenant blocked Mansur and Verity's way. The men at the guns, naked to the waist and dripping sweat, stared in surprise at the new arrivals.

'What the deuce are you doing?' shouted the lieutenant. 'This is no place for civilians. We are fighting a battle.' But looking along the walls, Mansur had seen what he was seeking. He pushed the lieutenant aside – harder than he intended. The officer stumbled, screaming as he fell against the scalding hot barrel of the cannon. By then, Mansur was beyond him, Verity too. Her skirts swished past the astonished gunners.

Mansur raced along the wall, his feet tripping on the uneven stones. 'Theo!' he shouted. 'Constance! Come down this instant. It is not safe.'

From the French lines, the cannon roared again.

• • •

At first Theo and Constance didn't hear their father's shouts. They were watching the French, and the sound of the guns had dulled their hearing. Then Theo noticed movement from the corner of his eye. The anxiety he had been feeling turned to horror.

He tugged on Constance's dress. 'They have spotted us. We will be in such trouble.'

Smoke from the bombardment drifted along the wall. The haze obscured the figures running towards them, but as they drew closer and clearer, Theo felt an ominous sense of familiarity.

'Father?' His gaze shifted to the figure behind. 'Mother?'

The rush of guilt was so great it drowned everything else. He turned and ran, no longer a young man but a boy who wanted to hide. He heard his father shouting at him to stop, screaming something about his safety, but he blocked it out. He didn't hear the cannon fire, or the louder sound that rose, like thunder, behind him.

His mother's scream cut through it all. Whether he heard it, or simply felt it ring in his bones, he paused. He turned.

The wall behind him had disappeared. The rampart he had been standing on seconds earlier was obliterated, collapsing on itself in an ever-widening hole. Bricks cascaded down, like water released from a dam, vanishing into the cloud of powdered mortar and dust that rose out of the rubble and engulfed it.

Theo ran back, holding his sleeve against his mouth. He paused at the edge of the hole. Loose bricks slithered and tumbled beneath him. How could one cannonball have wreaked so much damage?

'Go back.'

The voice was so faint, he hardly heard it above the settling stones. He didn't know where it had come from. He looked down.

His father was below him, clinging to a fragment of wall that had somehow remained upright. Further down, a bundle of limp white fabric lay at the bottom of the hole, pinned under the rubble, like a discarded rag. It was Verity.

'Get back,' Mansur hissed. Falling bricks had knocked out his teeth and left his mouth a bloody mess. His face was ghostly white with dust. 'Save yourself.'

'I can reach you,' said Theo, obstinately. He lay flat and stretched out his hand as far as he could. Mansur tried to reach back, but the pillar of bricks swayed at the least movement.

The gap was wider than it looked. Even at full stretch, Theo's fingertips came up short. He edged further out. Loose bricks fell from under him. He was inches from his father's hand. But he could feel the void opening beneath him. Another movement might bring the whole wall crashing down.

'Go back,' croaked Mansur. His precarious perch tottered on its foundations.

'I can save you,' Theo insisted. He reached further. His fingers brushed Mansur's but could not find a grip.

The rampart shivered. Theo, lying on his stomach, felt the vibrations in his skull, like a ringing bell. The French had not been idle. They had seen the damage they had caused and trained all their fire on it. Another cannonball slammed into the wall. More bricks shook loose and the shaky pinnacle Mansur had clung to gave way with a crack and started to collapse.

Forgetting all reason and safety, Theo lunged. Too late. Mansur was already falling away from him, slipping beyond his reach even as his hand stretched out. Mansur mouthed something that Theo could not understand. He wondered if it might have been 'Constance'.

Theo felt the slightest brush on his fingertips – then nothing. Mansur fell into the cloud of dust and smoke and disappeared.

There was nothing to stop Theo following him. The cannon fire had weakened the rampart he lay on, and his final lunge had taken him beyond safety. He didn't care. He had lost the two people he loved most in the world, and there was nothing left for him. Too late, he remembered the last word framed on his father's bloody lips. *Constance.* If he died now she would be left alone in the world. His father's dying wish, and Theo had failed it.

His thoughts flashed through his mind in an instant. As the full weight of guilt and failure hit him, he suddenly stopped falling. For a second, he seemed to hang in mid-air.

He looked around and saw a red-faced sergeant staring down at him, one hand locked on Theo's belt.

The sergeant hauled Theo back and laid him on the rampart. The ground felt heavy and solid beneath him. Before he could get up, Constance ran over and hurled herself onto him, cradling his head to her breast. 'I thought you were lost,' she said. 'I thought we were lost.'

More soldiers had arrived. The sergeant was shouting, telling them they must get away to safety. But Theo and Constance were unreachable, locked in a private world of grief. Theo was crying, adding shame to his misery: he should not be so womanly. But his parents had gone. He felt such despair that it was breaking his heart.

When he told Constance what had happened, she howled with anguish. She was inconsolable, and Theo held her tight, rocking her like a baby. Their world had exploded, shattered in an instant, hopes and dreams in fragments, loved ones pulverised. This was the bitter, brutal reality of war. Theo saw his fate anew through his tears, as the dust stung his eyes, and it was broken and twisted. How could he rebuild his life?

'This is my fault,' Constance whimpered. 'We should have been safe at home. If I had not led us here . . .'

Theo gripped her wrist too hard. 'Never say that again. We both came. We are both equally to blame. I will not let you take this on yourself.'

She brushed a lock of hair from his eyes and wiped the tears off his cheek. 'Thank you. We will have to look after each other now.' She started sobbing again.

There was a terrible void inside him, growing until he thought it would swallow him. 'Promise me, Connie. Promise me, whatever happens, you will never leave me.'

'I promise.'

'Never ever?'

'Never ever. I promise.'

Below, a party of sepoys began to pick through the rubble to recover the lifeless bodies of Mansur and Verity Courtney.

THE EPIC UNTOLD STORY

ON LEOPARD ROCK

A LIFE OF ADVENTURE

Wilbur Smith has lived an incredible life of adventure. Now, for the first time, he shares the extraordinary true stories that have inspired his fiction.

From his childhood in the wilds of Rhodesia, through to becoming a globally bestselling author, Wilbur Smith tells the intimate stories of his life that have been the raw material for his fiction.

Always candid, sometimes hilarious, and never less than thrillingly entertaining, *On Leopard Rock* is testament to a writer whose life is as rich and eventful as his novels are compellingly unputdownable.

AVAILABLE NOW

Want to read
NEW BOOKS
before anyone else?

Like getting
FREE BOOKS?

Enjoy sharing your
OPINIONS?

Discover

READERS FIRST

Read. Love. Share.

Sign up today to win your first free book:
readersfirst.co.uk